## SEASON'S GREETINGS

This holiday season is one that brings the spirit to life. This is the time when the blessings of faith and joy shine bright and hope rings through the hearts and souls. A time when love, in all its power, can truly make dreams come true . . .

# BOOK YOUR PLACE ON OUR WEBSITE AND MAKE THE ARABESQUE ROMANCE CONNECTION!

We've created a customized website just for our very special Arabesque readers, where you can get the inside scoop on everything that's going on with Arabesque romance novels.

When you come online, you'll have the exciting opportunity to:

- View covers of upcoming books
- Read sample chapters
- Learn about our future publishing schedule (listed by publication month *and author*)
- Find out when your favorite authors will be visiting a city near you
- Search for and order backlist books from our online catalog
- Check out author bios and background information
- Send e-mail to your favorite authors
- Meet the Kensington staff online
- Join us in weekly chats with authors, readers and other guests
- Get writing guidelines
- AND MUCH MORE!

Visit our website at
http://www.arabesquebooks.com

# SEASON'S GREETINGS

# Margie Walker
# Roberta Gayle
# Courtni Wright

**P**

Pinnacle Books
Kensington Publishing Corp.
http://www.arabesquebooks.com

PINNACLE BOOKS are published by

Kensington Publishing Corp.
850 Third Avenue
New York, NY 10022

Copyright © 1998 by Kensington Publishing Corp.

"Stone's Joy" © 1998 by Margie Walker
"Just in Time" © 1998 by Roberta Cohen
"New Year's Eve" © 1998 by Courtni Wright

All rights reserved. No part of this book may be reproduced in any form or by any means without the prior written consent of the Publisher, excepting brief quotes used in reviews.

If you purchased this book without a cover you should be aware that this book is stolen property. It was reported as "unsold and destroyed" to the Publisher and neither the Author nor the Publisher has received any payment for this "stripped book."

Pinnacle, the P logo and Arabesque, the Arabesque logo are Reg. U.S. Pat. & TM Off.

First Printing: December, 1998
10  9  8  7  6  5  4  3  2  1

Printed in the United States of America

# CONTENTS

STONE'S JOY by Margie Walker     7

JUST IN TIME by Roberta Gayle     115

NEW YEAR'S EVE by Courtni Wright     223

# STONE'S JOY

# Margie Walker

# Chapter 1

He looked back to make sure he was being followed.

Hope had her eyes on him. Faraha had refused to allow her to hold his hand, she recalled, granting his unvoiced request with a nod to go on. Her energetic, independent five-year-old then ducked into yet another store.

The second day after Thanksgiving and a Saturday, they had joined the throng of holiday shoppers at the Galleria Shopping Center. Every store window boasted some version of Santa's arrival. The decorations evoked such yuletide cheer, one could forget that the mild wind and drizzling rain outside were the closest Houston would get to a picture-postcard white Christmas. It seemed that more than a few had, as the mall was packed, all four city blocks long and three levels of it.

Hope felt as if Faraha had walked her over every inch of it, too. Having reached the third floor, she mused that if he didn't find what he was looking for, then they would go somewhere else ... another day. They had been in the Galleria since ten this morning, and it was now after four. It seemed the crowd had not waned, though her energy definitely had.

She yawned just as a snazzy version of "Winter Wonderland" replaced the previous Christmas song being piped throughout the plaza. Bumped by a passing shopper, she moved to stand next to one of the huge round posts in the corridor. She still had a clear view into the jewelry store, whose enticing displays of precious gems had caught Faraha's eyes.

She could insist that they leave, but she didn't have the heart to call a halt to his shopping. Faraha didn't know she knew that he was also looking for a gift for her. She'd overheard him talking to Monique Thomas, his godmother and her dear friend, one night. Monique told him to find what he wanted and she'd take him to the store to get it. Though she planned to dissuade them from buying her an expensive piece of jewelry, Hope felt she already had everything she wanted for Christmas right now.

Smiling secretively, her loving eyes on her son, she watched Faraha engage the salesman in a conversation. He looked so cute, with his gold turtleneck under his Osh-kosh overalls, the legs cuffed at the top of his soft leather, tan desert boots. His dark hair was cut close to his head with a thin ponytail hanging just past the nape of his neck.

He was smart, her son, and often quite precocious. Her father used to call him a "man-child," claiming that he was born grown, she recalled. Now no one could call him a little boy to his face. Sometimes he seemed so mature that on occasions she had to remind herself that he was not her little man.

He had taken his responsibility of buying presents for three children, ages seven, eight, and ten, seriously. She had the mother's gift in the shopping bag clutched close to her. All their gifts would be delivered by the community center from which she had drawn the Blake family's name. They would have no idea who their Santa was . . . only that Saint Nick had come to their home this year.

Hope was pleased by the innocent illusion, as she leaned comfortably against the post. Sharing her and Faraha's blessings made her feel proud of herself. Something she wasn't six years ago, she thought. Humiliated, brokenhearted, and pregnant, she'd returned home to her parents, who could have easily said, "I told you so."

Instead, they nurtured her beaten soul back to health, she

recalled, her eyes glazed with fondness. Women friends supplied the remaining means to getting back on her feet, helping her to recover her sense of self-worth.

A wave of shoppers crossed Hope's vision, and the lost view of Faraha snapped her from her mental wandering. Straining to see around them, she wondered how long he had been in that store. It seemed to her that it was quite a while. By the time the group of shoppers passed, she had moved for a better vantage point.

He wasn't immediately visible, and her heart skipped a beat even as common sense told her to check inside the store. She did, scanning the first area keenly before walking around the L-shaped counter to look on the other side.

"May I help you?" a salesman asked.

Jolted, Hope spun to see a short, rosy-faced man with thin speckles on his nose and thinning silver hair. He was standing between the cash register and a door leading to a back room from where he'd apparently come. She relaxed a little on spotting the door, for she knew her son: Fearless and sociable, he would have invited himself back there to satisfy his curiosity. Walking toward the salesman, she said, "I'm looking for my son. His name is Faraha. He's about"—holding her hand just above her waistline, in a gesture indicating three feet high—"this tall."

"Oh . . . he left." The salesman smiled. "Cute kid."

"Left?" Hope echoed. Panic kicked her in the gut. She almost couldn't speak, but managed to croak out, "Did you notice which direction he was headed?" Her feet were already moving to the door.

"Right," the salesman replied. "I think."

Hope was gone before he had the chance to change his mind.


Stone Henderson didn't have anybody to shop for. If it weren't for the fact that he needed new luggage, he would not have set foot in the Galleria—least of all on one of the busiest shopping days of the year.

It looked as if the city's entire population was here, he

thought, with loathing in his expression. He could have kicked himself for waiting until the last minute. And to make matters worse, he'd entered the Galleria from the wrong entrance and on the wrong floor. The store he'd come to patronize was at the opposite end of the shopping center and a floor up.

Deliberately ignoring the Christmas decorations and blocking out the carols piped from an unseen source, Stone resolved to make the best of it. His long-legged strides assured his stay in the Galleria would be a short one as he began his trek for the Trunk Factory, side-stepping and dodging shoppers.

He had never been big on Christmas. As a kid, Christmas had been a harried affair at his house, with his mother always scraping pennies together to buy them some crappy toy that lasted as long as the wrapping paper she bought at half price a day or two before December twenty-fifth.

When he became gainfully employed, he gave his family— mother, two younger brothers, and a sister—money to buy what they wanted. Upon marrying Arsha, she took care of getting gifts. Although she dragged him with her, the fun for him was simply being with her. She loved not just the shopping but the whole idea surrounding the season itself. She became the meaning of Christmas for him, but his joy for the holiday had long since ended.

He'd thrown away everything that reminded him of her, including the set of Louis Vuitton luggage they'd purchased for their honeymoon five years ago. Now that he was going to the Bahamas for the holidays, he at least needed a suitcase.

Still, he was about as excited over the trip as he was about getting pneumonia. Unable to escape Christmas altogether, as it was celebrated around the world, the Bahamas promised something different—Junkanoo. Though an obscure word, with several different meanings attached, he preferred to believe that it referred to John Canoe, an African tribal chief who demanded the right to celebrate with his people after being taken to the West Indies in slavery. That had meaning, one that was far from the commercialism done to Christmas in the States.

The last two years he worked through Christmas and New Year's, so it hadn't been an issue. This year he wasn't so lucky, as he was forced to take off the entire month to make up for previously unused vacation time. "Use it, or lose it," his supervisor had said, refusing to allow him to carry over his time off into the next year. He knew if he could just get through the holiday, he would be all right.

There was little debate at the elevator—Stone took the stairs with purpose. It was amazing that he reached the second-floor landing without knocking anyone down. On arrival, he saw the potential for a collision instantly . . . a little boy, either a tall four or an average six-year-old, looking up instead of where he was going.

Stone couldn't help himself. Curious, he, too, looked up to see what had captured the child's interest: a gang of red balloons with white Santa faces painted on them was floating along the ceiling.

He snorted, retrieved his purpose, and resumed his strides. Before the second one, he noticed his prediction about to come true. A big woman, frazzled-looking and laden with shopping bags, was fast moving in the path of the child still looking up, fascinated by those balloons.

As quickly as Stone moved to prevent the accident from happening, he was still too late.

"Oh, I'm so sorry, honey." The woman stopped, leaned over awkwardly, and apologized to the boy, then to Stone, who was kneeling in front of the child, who lay sprawled back on his haunches. "I'm sorry, sir. Is your little boy all right?"

Stone ignored the reference to his parental ownership and spoke to the boy. "Are you all right, son?" Hesitant to touch the child, his eyes examined him. He was a handsome young fellow, who would one day attract the attention of many females. He had a long, narrow, open face, with the delicate features of youth in a warm brown complexion. His eyes were olive and peered out from under long dark eyebrows and curling lashes. From what he knew of kids, if they weren't crying, that meant they were okay. He helped the boy sit upright.

"Is he all right?" the woman asked again anxiously.

Stone saw that they had caused a traffic jam: The shoppers

eager to move on tried to get past the curious onlookers who blocked the passageway.

"Are you all right, honey?"

"I think so," the little boy replied.

"Yeah, he looks okay," Stone said to the anxious shopper.

The woman's face twisted into another apologetic look, then she shifted the shopping bags in her grip and disappeared into the crowd.

Stone was equally eager to get on with his business but reluctant to leave the child unattended. "Who are you here with?" he asked.

"My mama."

"Well, where is she?" Stone asked somewhat forcefully. He would have expected the woman to have rushed out of the adjacent store or burst through the crowd to her son's rescue by now.

He looked around. The gawkers began to dissipate, finding nothing sensational had occurred. But there were still so many people walking to and fro on this pathway, it was apparent that the boy couldn't see anything. Just as Stone reached out to stand the youngster onto his feet for a better view, the boy blurted, "What's that around your neck?"

Curious, his small hands were already reaching for the necklace around Stone's neck, and Stone pulled away abruptly. The boy stared at him confused and a little frightened. Stone was embarrassed by his behavior, jumping away as if he were threatened by a little boy.

"It's a necklace," he replied plainly.

"Yeah, but what's that purple-looking diamond in the middle of it?"

"It's not a diamond," Stone said, holding the necklace out for display. The youngster took this as a sign of permission to touch and reached for the stone to examine it. "Those are diamonds around it, but that purplish stone in the middle is called tanzanite."

"I saw one like this in the store. It costs a lot of money," the boy said with awe.

Not like this one, Stone thought. *Mine is priceless.* But this was getting them nowhere: He had something else to do, he reminded himself.

"Where is your mama?" Stone asked. His tone came out gruff, and the boy reacted to it immediately. He ran a hand down his face in frustration.

"You're not a policeman," the boy said with challenge, stepping back.

Stone blinked surprised. "No, I'm not," he said, knowing that he was the cause of the child's sudden wariness.

"Then let me see some ID," the youngster commanded. "My mama told me I'm not supposed to talk to strangers."

*Right,* Stone thought sarcastically. *His mama equips him with survival knowledge, then promptly sends him out on the streets alone. Some mama.*

"Yes, and where is this mama of yours?" Stone asked, pulling his wallet from his hip pocket.

The little boy didn't answer or move. His eyes held Stone's steadily with brave fear. Stone handed his driver's license over, wondering if the kid was even old enough to read, then wondered why he was entertaining the kid's antics. He had something else to do, he reminded himself, his impatience mounting.

The child scrutinized the driver's license, matching the small picture to the man. "S . . . t . . . o . . . n . . . e," the boy spelled out, then phonetically said his name. "Stone. You got a funny name, just like my mama," the boy pronounced, chuckling.

"What's your name?" Stone asked, returning his license to its place.

"Faraha Ellison," the boy piped proudly.

"Nice to meet you, Faraha," Stone said, extending his hand to the little boy. The child shook his hand.

"What are you doing here at the Galleria?" Faraha asked. "My mama and I came to buy some gifts for this family that don't have any money for Christmas. She got the mama a gown, but she called it a pigwar or something. It's pink. She doesn't like that kind of stuff," he avowed, his face screwed up in distaste. "She likes to sleep in big T-shirts."

Stone wanted to be annoyed. Instead, his mouth twitched as he tried not to laugh. He doubted Faraha's mother wanted her sleeping apparel broadcast. "Do you have any idea where you mother is?"

Faraha Ellison looked around, over his shoulders, then up at Stone. There was a look of masculine frustration at the corners of his small mouth, his eyes narrowed. He sighed gustily, and his little shoulders moved with the intensity of the effort. "She must be lost."

Nerves at full stretch, Hope was utterly frantic—despite the security manager's attempt to allay her fears with promises of finding Faraha, which he couldn't guarantee. It had been almost two hours—the longest minutes of her life—since she'd last seen her son and reported him missing. She hoped he was just lost within the shopping center.

"Have you seen this little boy?" she asked the teenage-looking salesman at Radio Shack. He glanced at the color copy of Faraha, with the physical description written in caption-sized, hand-printed letters.

"No, ma'am," he replied with a quirky shrug, returning the flyer to her.

Hope noticed two other salespersons in the store and sought them out, repeating the routine she had begun only moments ago. In less than a minute, she was heading out for the adjacent store.

Even though it made more sense to remain waiting in one place, she told herself again, she couldn't sit idly by, waiting while others combed the center for her son was against her nature. She *had* to be out with the team of Security personnel looking for Faraha.

She concentrated her patrol on the third floor, repeating her inquiry in each store.

"Have you seen . . . ?"

"No, ma'am. Sorry."

Before alerting Security, she had double-checked the stores they had visited initially, she recalled. But after asking around in two or three, she had decided not to spend any more time looking on her own. She had asked the jewelry store salesman to contact Security. The Security manager had arrived right away. He patiently took her statement, then escorted her to the Security office, which, for the Galleria, was located in a separate building in front of the center.

There they had blown up her wallet snapshot of Faraha, printed a description of him, then made copies of their quick work. Houston Police Department was notified, and a team of Security personnel was dispatched to circulate the flyers from store to store.

At the next "No, ma'am," Hope struggled to suppress the nightmarish visions prancing around in her head. She was just too scared to think sugarplum thoughts, so she prayed: *Please, God, let him be all right.*

A chorus of "ahs" and "oohs" rushed up from below, and her heart leaped as she hurried toward the center of the plaza where crowds encircled the rail. Too short and too far away to see, she nudged her way through to get as close to the rail as possible.

A kindly man, standing behind his child with his hands on her shoulder, made room for Hope. A wisp of melancholy crossed her face, and silently she cursed herself. If only she had held on to Faraha like that, she thought. She gulped, remembered to mouth a "Thank you," then squeezed into the spot next to his daughter.

A lone male ice-skater performing to "The Little Drummer Boy" backed up by an ensemble of young percussionists had caused the sound of excitement from the crowd—not the dreaded scenario that had come to her mind. Though relieved that her son had not fallen over the rail onto the ice rink below, fear of not finding him alive and well kept her at the peak of intense feeling.

Just as she was about to shove her way from the rail and head to the next store, something . . . there below, on the second floor, directly across from her, snagged her gaze.

Her face scrunched up in a frown, her brows drew together as she stared unwaveringly at the young boy in a bright gold turtleneck.

Her mouth dropped open with incredulity—it seemed she

couldn't get enough oxygen into her lungs. That was her son, Faraha! But who was that holding him? she wondered, struggling to get control of her breathing.

Her eyes shot to the man. The stranger stood relaxed, his tall frame straight, even with the weight of Faraha on his hip. Her gaze raked all that she could see of the big, brown-skinned stranger. Her mouth seemed suddenly dry, her mind momentarily dull and witless of fear.

Her son said something to him, and in the next instant she could guess what it was. There was a hint of grace in the way he hoisted Faraha to sit straddling his broad shoulders. Her heart flip-flopped in her bosom.

The crowd cheered at another of the skater's stunts. It would have drowned out the scream to *stop that man,* clawing up her throat. With every nerve racing inside her, she fairly flew through the crowd to get to the second-floor. Bumping and shoving through the hordes of shoppers, it seemed she couldn't move fast enough.

By the time she reached the second-floor landing, the crowd was dispersing, and she realized the performance was over. Her heart thudded violently in protest. That man would be gone with her son, and she would never see Faraha again, she thought, hope threatening to abandon her.

Even if they got away, a description of the stranger was indelibly impressed on her mind, she somewhat consoled herself.

He was as tall as a spruce—otherwise, she wouldn't have spotted him. Just the way he stood spoke of power, with a face she'd never forget. As much of it that she could see from that distance anyway, she amended.

He had a medium brown complexion, with dark hair cut close to his square head. He was athletically built, but without the cumbersome bulk of weight-lifters. The way the winter green, tapered shirt clung to his body, molding the commanding breadth of his chest, was further testament to his strength. She shivered imperceptibly. Black pleated slacks belted at his waistline completed his ensemble. Except for her son wrapped around his neck.

She wished she had a better description, a closer view of his face. But what she had should be enough for the police, she told herself as she headed for the nearest store, which was Victoria's Secret.

Several feet from the store's entrance, she froze . . . for just on the other side of the window she saw her son. He was holding up a peignoir, just like the one she'd bought for Ms. Blake's Christmas present, showing it off to the stranger.

Hope's eyes slid up from Faraha to the stranger. Taut skin, the color of chocolate coffee pulled evenly over his clear-cut, forceful face. She watched mesmerized, her heart hammering in her bosom. His chin was strong, a perfect complement to his firm mouth. Who was this man who'd convinced her son to forget every lesson she'd taught him about talking to strangers?

She tilted her head from one side to the other, as if to get a better look at him. His eyebrows were heavy, with eyes that held a direct, piercing gaze. He looked nothing like the monstrous pedophile she had thought to imagine but couldn't picture in her mind. And no wonder, the man was walking testament to masculine virility in the flesh, she thought, a disruption in her midsection. But he still had her son.

With laughter on his wide mouth, he looked up directly into her eyes, and Hope felt a certain expectation. Then a look as hard as marble drained the amusement from his expression. Hope gulped. He said something to Faraha, then took one long-legged stride to the saleslady standing nearby.

As he spoke with her, he stood with his arms folded across his wide chest, and the shirt molded his rock-hard upper body. One long leg had edged slightly in front of the other, stretching his pants to outline a powerful thigh.

He had an air of entitlement about him, Hope thought, her gaze vigilant on him. She sensed once he staked his claim on something, he never let go. A barely perceptible, but nonetheless holiday tingle coursed down her spine.

# Chapter 2

Some people didn't deserve children, Stone was thinking as he watched Faraha, whose eyes were aglow with merriment. His mind inevitably reminded him of one woman who did. He deliberately suppressed the thought from growing as Faraha moved to another display of ladies' lingerie.

It was uncanny, but the youngster seemed attuned to his every mood. He'd never met such a sensitive child before, one who wasn't consumed by his own needs.

"These would cover my mama's whole body."

Faraha held up a pair of blue nylon panties that would fit Santa himself. His laughter was chalked with excitement and infectious. Stone covered his mouth, chuckling into his hand. He saw that several other customers in the store were similarly amused and trying not to show it.

His elfin new friend was entertaining himself rather nicely. It was apparent that somebody had been taking good care of Faraha Ellison. He was well dressed and well behaved. Although, he thought with a flicker of disapproval, he wouldn't have allowed his son to wear a ponytail on the back of his head. Still, he had nieces and nephews, all older than Faraha, but none of them possessed the composure of this five-year-old.

He was a gutsy little guy, Stone mused, recalling that Faraha hadn't whined or cried for his mama. He had given the boy his necklace to wear inside his turtleneck before he learned that the child was not going to erupt into a bawling fit when they went in search of Security.

Either Faraha was too young to realize the gravity of the situation, or he was simply an independent child. Maybe he was just confident that she would turn up, or he was used to it.

A scowl slipped into his expression. Stone didn't like that thought one bit. He wondered what kind of person his mother was. Probably an excitable neurotic who can't remember her name from one minute to the next, he humored himself, unamused. That was probably why Faraha was so calm. But the child was devoted to her.

The boy never said anything bad about his father, but then again, Stone recalled, the boy said nothing about him. He talked about his school, a private day care where he played on the chess team, coached by Dr. Hassani, who was also his foreign language teacher. That seemed to be his most influential male role model. His grandparents were dead, and he lived with his mother in their house.

His mother couldn't be all bad, Stone somewhat amended his impression—she was providing him a good education. But her other mothering skills were sadly lacking. He and Faraha had been together for two hours now. He wondered, disgruntled, what was taking Security so long to arrive. They'd been called a good ten minutes ago.

Stone sighed deeply with impatience. His gaze crossed that of a woman who was standing outside the store looking in, and a jingle surged along his pulse.

To "Deck The Hall" playing softly in the background, he noticed she was shorter than average with a petite frame. She had the look of a woman who inspired protectiveness in some men. He was not one of them, but there was a definite sense of softness about her. She'd been there an inordinate amount of time. Long enough to decide whether or not she wanted to shop in this store, he thought, feeling his whole being suddenly filled with waiting. Why didn't she just come in, make her purchase, and move along?

He couldn't take his eyes off her. In spite of his total captivation, he was conscious not to openly stare and content to chalk his behavior up to natural curiosity. It was something that had served him well professionally as a geologist who ferreted for oil and gas.

She was strikingly attractive, with golden brown skin spread evenly across her angelic-featured face. She had a small nose, with full cheeks, and a well-formed, generous mouth. Dainty gold bulblike earrings pierced her tiny ears. She wore a royal blue blazer with patches of kente at the pocket over matching pencil-slim trousers. The single-breasted jacket was open to reveal her fine neck in the gold ribbed pullover, with its bottom banded in kente just above her tiny waistline and flat stomach.

She was rather overdressed for shopping, he thought, then remembered, with an unconscious smile on his face, that his wife used to get all dressed up, too. He felt a lurch of excitement and quickly unsmiled, his mouth taking on an unpleasant twist.

From the look of indecision on her face, he'd bet that she didn't have a thought worth holding in her head. Such a pretty head, too. She had long brownish-red hair, with wisps of bangs dropping to just above her elegant eyebrows. They arched over large almond eyes, gentle and star bright. His heart shuddered unexpectedly.

Realizing that she had been standing still, staring as if starstruck and holding her breath, Hope breathed and rushed inside the store.

"Faraha, where have you been?" she demanded.

Faraha dropped the peignoir and faced her with an "uh-oh" look on his face, his mouth hanging open. Usually quick with an excuse, he stared at her wordlessly.

Hope knew she should be angry, but in truth she was so relieved he was all right that she could easily forgive and forget that he disobeyed her on more than one count. He was all she had in the world, and she hugged him to her dearly. "I've been looking all over this place for you," she whispered fiercely, residuals of the agony she'd gone through in her voice. Holding him away from her, she said with a scowling look, "There's a whole team of Security people looking for you, too."

"I assume you're the mother."

The words were chipped from an iceberg.

Hope's eyebrows flew up the instant she felt the shadow with a pure baritone voice looming over them. For a moment it was as if a thick liquid warmed her blood, then her eyes met his, hooded like those of a hawk and cold with a look of disdain. In that same instant she wondered how she could have forgotten the stranger standing nearby.

"Mama, let me tell you . . ." Faraha blurted excitedly, finally finding his voice.

She cut Faraha off without looking at him. "Don't even try that one, mister," she warned, her gaze scaling the immense height of the stranger. He stood at least ten inches taller than her own five feet three inches. She was as intimidated as she was intrigued by the reproach in his alluring eyes—a deep and penetrating dark brown under long, thick lashes—as she stood. She struggled to stand firm her ground and control the medley of emotions coursing through her as she drank in the sensuality of his physique. "You scared me to death," she scolded Faraha. "I've told you—"

The male mumble of exasperation over her head cut her off, and the words that followed contained a strong suggestion of censure.

"Don't fuss at him. It's your fault. You should have taken better care of him. With all these people in the Galleria, anybody could have gotten lost."

Hope couldn't help thinking that his voice and eyes were intimate twins. She didn't think to wonder why he seemed so angry as she breathed a shallow breath, then licked her dry lips. "They wouldn't have gotten lost, if they'd kept their promise not to go off without telling anybody."

A probing query came into his eyes, with disbelief parked

in the frown lines stretched across his forehead. "You can't expect that kind of behavior from a child," he said with disapproval in his rich-toned voice, as if what she suggested was ludicrous.

Feeling the heat of his nearness as surely as she smelled the woodsy fragrance of his cologne, Hope sputtered as she stared up at him. "You stay out of this, whoever you are."

"Mama . . . Mama," Faraha said, tugging on her jacket.

"Not now, Faraha," She shooed him.

"It's too late for that. I'm already involved," he retorted. "I've contacted Security to report *your* lost child. And where were you anyway, that you could have misplaced your own child?" Outraged, he demanded to know, "What kind of mother are you?"

His contemptuous tone sparked Hope's anger. She'd had enough of this stranger's interference. "What do you know about children?" she fired back at him. "Do you have any children?" A glimmer of emotion flashed in his eyes, but she could have mistaken it, for a warning cloud was there now. She had the wherewithal to step back fractionally, and though she forbade herself to tremble, such a sensation whirled inside her nevertheless—it wasn't fear, but commingled with confusion.

"Excuse me." The saleslady who'd been standing nearby broached them cautiously. "But could you take this in the back?" She pointed toward an unseen back room. "I'll double-check with Security to see what's taking them so long."

Hope heard the saleslady but couldn't respond. She felt ensnared in an odd tension that was alive and interesting and alien, all emanating from the stranger. She realized she was enjoying the verbal spar.

"But, Mama, Stone rescued me from this fat lady," Faraha said insistently.

Hope frowned, puzzled, looking down at Faraha, then up at . . . Stone, her son called him as she put the pieces together. Now she had to be beholden to this scrooge, she thought, noting a hint of arrogance on his reserved face. With a humbled expression on her face, she extended her hand.

"I'm sorry, Stone," she said contritely, extending her hand. "I'm Hope Ellison, Faraha's mother." For a second she thought he wouldn't accept her apology, or her hand.

Finally, he offered her a reluctant smile that didn't reach his eyes as he took her hand. "Stone Henderson," he introduced himself.

Her hand disappeared in his, but only for a second, as he made quick work of the handshake. Hope felt bereaved of the warmth of his touch, and she shivered as if suddenly chilled. She didn't know what else to say as she stared into his deep soulful eyes. Her insides seemed to sing the refrain of "Jingle Bells" playing over the speaker.

"Stone," she said inanely, a contemplative quality to her tone, as if testing the strength of his name on her tongue.

At that moment the Security chief raced in. He looked around, then spotting Hope, hurried toward them. "Ms. Ellison, we've been looking all over the place for you," he chastised politely.

The room was as dark and silent as a tomb. The blinds were drawn and curtains closed tight over the lone picture window that split the fourth wall. A shaded lamp on the end table adjacent to the couch provided the only light in the room. It was sparsely decorated, barely functional for its purpose, the living room, a social area. Stone hardly ever used it, and never for anything social, since he'd bought the condo a little over a year ago.

He also never drank any more than half a can of beer in public, as not to endure quips of being *stone drunk* . . . a state he was deliberately trying to achieve now.

He'd left the Galleria without the luggage he'd gone to buy. After the ordeal of his detainment, he just wanted to get out of that place.

He wondered if his plane ticket was refundable. He seemed to have lost what little desire he had about leaving during the holidays altogether. He wanted to refute that the Ellisons had any bearing on his decision or the present confusion and loneliness he felt. But approaching thirty-eight, he was past lying to himself. He was hoping the liquor would help him forget.

He cursed himself again for going to the Galleria ... for believing that he was strong enough to withstand the emotions the season wrought in him. Even now, with the one source that should have brought him comfort, solace escaped him.

He drank a sip from his brandy glass of dark liquor, his other hand clutching a silver-framed, color picture of a pregnant woman. Arsha had been six months into her term—their child was due in the early part of March 1996. The kind of person who couldn't wait to open her presents, she had known the baby's sex. He hadn't wanted to know, and now that he did ... Stone drank the rest of the thought, sipping half a jigger's worth of his drink.

He'd felt something today in the company of Faraha Ellison. He didn't know what it was, and that was as far as he wanted to take the memory of that feeling now.

The heart could hold only so much emotion, he mused, with his thoughts digressing as they sometimes did. He'd believed all of his feelings died with Arsha. It was disturbing to realize that that wasn't true.

Unable to remember what she looked like, or imagine what their child would have looked like, had sent him in a wild panic. He came home and tore up the place looking for a reminder, something that would help erase this horrible sense of emptiness that had assailed him.

The pain was not as unbearable as it used to be, he thought, glancing at the picture. He didn't even wish that he could have altered the past anymore, as he remembered the message given to him by the emergency room attendant. The man, he recalled, even had tears in his eyes when he repeated Arsha's words: *"Tell my husband ... that I love him dearly. Don't grieve too long. Get on with his life. Our daughter and I will be waiting in heaven for him and his new family."*

Unfortunately he'd been unable to obey her edict. He'd tried a couple of times, albeit halfheartedly. But he was convinced that there wasn't another woman alive in the world for him. Until now, a silent voice taunted him.

Stone tossed back a swallow of liquor.

Soon the dark brown eyes in the heart-shaped face in the photo changed colors, brightened in intensity. The round shape narrowed to delicate almonds, with calm in their olive depths, in a perfectly oval face.

A shudder coursed through Stone. He drained the contents of the glass, then got up to pour himself another drink.

Yeah, he intended to get stoned.

Piqued by the power of his memory, his imagination roamed freely. He pictured Hope Ellison, refined and poised, in his house, wandering from room to room, like an angel . . . standing at his bedroom door.

> *Her lyrical, docile voice calls out his name . . . "Stone . . ." and he answers, "In here." She appears at his bedroom door, a lively ethereal vision. No longer afraid of him, she floats into his arms, wanting his embrace. How nicely she fits in his arms. Her slender body presses in close contact with his. He can taste his own excitement as he peels the clothes from her body. Beautiful and naked, she comes to him . . .*
> *Faraha pokes his head into the room.*

The image jolted Stone. He snapped to attention abruptly, spilling liquor over his hand and the edge of the couch. He looked around as if he didn't know where he was, couldn't remember sitting after he'd gotten that last drink. With a growl in his throat, he stormed across the dark room to the bar and poured himself another one.

He could explain his lustful mental wandering, the hot bothered rise in his body, he rationalized. But he still felt guilty for betraying Arsha's memory with wanton desires for another woman.

Stone lifted the glass to his lips . . .

Hope accepted that it was only natural when she dreamed of Stone Henderson Saturday night. She even considered the idiotic notions of sleeping with him on Sunday. But when Monday rolled around and he was still in her thoughts, she was thoroughly annoyed with herself.

The pharmacy was as busy as the rest of the store, and the flow of customers seemed unending. She had filled roughly one hundred fifty prescriptions during her shift. With less than an hour to go before quitting time, she was still replaying the weekend fiasco at the Galleria in her mind.

Security arrived with two uniformed police officers in tow, she recalled, while scanning the shelves for the five-milligram box of Enalapril. There had been questions to answer, interviews with the three of them, a lecture about safety and precaution for her and Faraha, and forms to be signed, releasing the Galleria from responsibility for what happened.

Stone was hailed a hero, "the kind of citizen that makes Houston a great place to live" by the Security manager. Her son seconded the opinion.

She muttered a sound of disgust under her breath as she moved to the counter where her counting tray was already set up. She began counting out a hundred tablets in multiples of five, remembering from that point on, she had had to endure Faraha's constant chatter about Stone Henderson the rest of the weekend.

"Stone is a geologist. Stone uses computers at work. Stone doesn't have any children. Stone said I was a big boy . . ."

That last "Stone" revelation had gotten to her. Even now her hands shook slightly as she poured the tablets into the brown plastic vial and sealed it with a childproof top. Faraha never let her call him a big boy, she thought, setting three prescriptions for Freeda Henderson on the counter for Brenda, the pharmacy's technician, to file until the customer arrived.

How could that man have made such an immense impression on her son in such a short time? Or for that fact, on her? she wondered, recalling his majestic size and attitude. She shivered as if cold and shook the image of him from her head.

Moving to fill the next prescription, her thoughts returned to Faraha's unusual behavior. She had believed that she satisfied all of his needs as a parent. He hadn't asked about his father in over a year, which became noticeable after Tyrone broke several promises consecutively, either to send for Faraha or visit. He never called and had returned his calls reluctantly and infrequently, always claiming to be busy. She suspected Tyrone was afraid that she'd demand child support. He didn't know she knew he had another woman ... one different from the one he was seeing while she had been carrying their child.

Brenda, a young woman of twenty-two, and in her fourth year of pharmacy school, would have called Tyrone a gigo-whore, the black male version of gigolo, she thought, amused. Unless he'd changed, he didn't know the meaning of commitment to one woman, she thought with a mocking snort. And subsequently, without active prodding, she wondered if Stone Henderson was any different ... whether he could sustain warm emotions for one woman longer than it took to satisfy a body's physical needs. Hers certainly seemed in need of something, betraying her with erotic sensations at the mere thought of him. It had just been a long time, she reasoned to herself.

"Girl, what are you mumbling about over there?" Brenda asked.

Hope smiled, embarrassed. "Sorry." She hadn't realized that she'd muttered a sound of her wishful thinking. Whatever Stone Henderson was like didn't matter, for she would never see him again. If Faraha understood him correctly, he was going to spend Christmas in the Bahamas. "I was just thinking about my son."

"Uh-huh," Brenda replied suspiciously, filing prescriptions.

"I was." Despite the tone of protest in her voice, Hope felt a guilty twinge. No, the real substance of her thoughts was not five years old and three feet tall, but probably in his mid-thirties, and more than double that height." As my mama would have said, he's just getting too big for his britches," she said, carrying on the lie, with a quiver in her bosom, unable to forget the way Stone's slacks had fit his fine body.

Brenda's next statement indicated she wasn't buying it. "I sure would like to meet that brother."

"Oh, you're talking about Stone," Hope exclaimed innocently. She had relayed her weekend experience to Brenda this morning, and they had a good laugh about it then. Though she hadn't let on, it had ceased to be funny, she thought, bemused by her inability to forget Stone Henderson. Still she snorted peevishly in response to Brenda while examining two different boxes of eyedrops. She chose one and returned the other to the shelf. "He's a Scrooge," she declared vehemently, pulling a label off the computer printer to slap on the box.

"Well, if he is such a Scrooge," Brenda said with a laugh of lusty innuendo, "he must be a good-looking one. Maybe you ought to let him slide down your chimney. Who knows, you may find out that he's Santa instead."

"We don't have a—" Hope clamped her mouth shut, realizing that Brenda wasn't referring to a fireplace. A customer appeared at the window, taking the technician away before she could think of a suitable comeback.

Which was just as well, for she couldn't think of anything except that maybe Brenda was closer to right than she knew.

# Chapter 3

Stone didn't want to be out in this dreary weather, but he'd been such a grouch all day that his mother sent him on an errand just to get him out of her house. The skies were thick with gray clouds, the temperature was dropping. The added combination of brisk wind and mild rain contributed to the major chain drugstore's business. He was driving around the crowded parking lot, looking for a place to park.

He recalled that as he had been about to leave, his brother suggested that what he needed was to get laid. Not that he needed to be told, for the thought had been on his mind ever since he met Faraha's mother. But thoughts of Arsha, whose ghost had been intruding on him more and more these past three days, kept him from using the phone number that had literally been burning a hole in his pocket.

Faraha had given it to him, he recalled, rationalizing then that a call to the five-year-old wouldn't be too farfetched, except it wasn't the child he wanted to talk to.

He did have one excuse. Faraha still had his tanzanite and diamond necklace. But the youngster might feel betrayed if he used that as a guise to call, he thought.

Maybe he *should* have gotten drunk last night. As it turned out, he didn't—Arsha would have been disappointed. Besides, alcohol prohibited sound reasoning. But the cool logic he sought only dredged up more questions, mainly one: How could he be attracted to Hope Ellison?

He'd managed to live unencumbered by visceral emotions for three years. He felt he had more than made up for them during the past three days.

Stone spotted a customer racing from the store to his car. As soon as the man backed his car out, he eased his truck into the spot. He hurried into the store and was instantly greeted by traditional Christmas music performed by a black choir that played subtly throughout.

There was just no escaping it, he mused, resigned, unzipping his leather jacket. He pulled a shopping cart from the stack and a slip of paper from his pocket. His mother had also given him a list of other things to buy. Wrapping paper was supposed to be on sale, and she also wanted a box of those cane-candy sticks for her Christmas tree.

He decided to start at the front and work his way to the back of the store where the pharmacy was. He'd never shopped at this particular Walgreens, but it was the nearest to her Third Ward home, and it kept her medicines for glaucoma and blood pressure on file.

As he made his way up an aisle, Stone heard, "Mama, can I have this?" join the cacophony of shopping noise. He ignored it as he avoided a collision with another shopper. He sighed on low volume, thinking he should have tried to get out of this chore.

He'd originally gone to his mother's house to do some repairs to keep it from falling in on her head, he recalled, eyeing the various wrapping papers. Unconsciously he tossed a six-roll pack, a four-roll pack, and a three-roll pack into the cart, then strolled off to the next item. The house had been a gift from him six years ago. His brother, who lived there, was supposed to have helped with the monthly mortgage note and upkeep, but he always had an excuse for escaping his responsibility.

Dennis was six-five, two hundred ten pounds, and twenty-four. The baby of the family, he was eight, twelve, and fourteen years, respectively, younger than older siblings Kevin, Rose, and Stone. A former guard in college, too many knee operations had killed his professional basketball career. Dennis had been sulking the last four years, as far as he was concerned, Stone thought. He rasped under his breath, throwing in two boxes of plastic tape with four rolls in each. He didn't know why their mother continued to put up with him. He guessed he'd never understand a mother's love for her youngest son.

The quandary led his thoughts to the Ellisons as he faced the shelf of Christmas candies. In hindsight he knew Faraha was wrong for walking off the way he did. If Hope had been his mother, and he'd done something like that, she would have beat him shamelessly right there in the store. But of course, those days were over, he chuckled with a silent "Thank God" on his lips. Into the basket went the peppermint, apple, cherry, and grape candy canes.

Besides, Hope Ellison, already a wisp of a woman, didn't look as if she would step on a roach, so disciplining her child with anything harsher than a scolding look was out of the question. She didn't even raise her voice, he remembered. With the tone she'd used on Faraha, she could fuss at him any day. He chuckled, adding bags of bows to the cart.

That's how Arsha used to be ... what attracted him to her in the first place: her gentleness. She was no pushover, he recalled, smiling unconsciously before the stocking display. But she always tried to treat people fairly and with respect.

But that's where the similarities ended between Arsha and Hope. And he wasn't all that sure that it was so. He'd only sensed Hope's gentle nature, and maybe that was nothing more than myopic thinking on his part. For all he knew, her sweet manner was reserved for her son.

He threw five stockings into the shopping cart as if disgusted. He wasn't making any sense, he chided himself, looking at his cart. It was full of Christmas paraphernalia. "Junk," he muttered bitterly to himself, stuff that wouldn't last long. He knew he wasn't referring to the items in his cart.

He'd better get back to the pharmacy before he bought out the entire store, he decided, suddenly displeased with himself.

Hope was nothing like Arsha, he told himself, pushing the cart up the aisle. He liked women with meat on their bones, not some anemic-looking china doll. He liked women with character not angelic faces. How could he be attracted to this woman? He realized that it always came back to that. He wondered what Arsha would think of her. Or him, for even thinking about another woman.

The bench for customers waiting to get their prescriptions was filled. He knew that some of them would inevitably—if they hadn't already—buy something else as he had.

He didn't really need this stuff in the cart. He really didn't need anything. He set the shopping cart aside and stepped up to the pick-up window in the pharmacy. "Excuse me," he said loud enough for the woman in the white jacket to hear." Do you have a prescription ready for Freeda Henderson?"

Hope's head snapped as she looked across the glass enclosure surrounding the pharmacy to the customer pick-up opening. She still couldn't see over the counter, but she'd recognize that sumptuous baritone—the one that set her heart to beating absurdly—anywhere.

She was in the pharmacy, bundling up to face the weather. It was four-thirty, and her shift was over. The evening pharmacist, Mark Harper, had arrived on time for a change.

What was Stone Henderson doing here?

She hadn't told him where she worked, she thought, her mind rummaging back to the events this past Saturday at the Galleria. Unless he'd queried the Security manager in private, he wouldn't have known that she was a pharmacist, or that she worked at this store. So how did he find her? she wondered, excitement mounting inside her.

"Her doctor prescribed Vasotec, not this. I don't know what this is," he was saying argumentatively to Brenda.

"Sir, this is only a generic brand," Brenda replied, "and it does the same thing. Unless her doctor specifically requested Vasotec, then we automatically switch to a generic brand.

Which is a lot less expensive," she tagged, trying to reason with him.

Yeah, that was her Scrooge, Hope thought, somewhat disappointed. She almost yelled out to Brenda to save her breath. She should have known that he wasn't the type who'd go on a search for anybody. With a sigh of regret, she shook her head. Well, Mark could handle it. She was going home.

"I don't know," he wavered. "Let me speak to the pharmacist," he insisted.

Hope grabbed her shopping bag, filled with wrapping paper and other assortment of Christmas tree decorations that were on sale, and was about to head out when—

"Hope, would you please come speak to Mr. Henderson?" Brenda called out to her with polite pleading.

Hope shook her head vehemently and pointed to the pharmacist, who was talking on the phone, trying to tell her to pass the problem on to Mark. Brenda frowned, confused by her signals.

Finally, "That's him," Hope mouthed to the technician, pointing toward Stone, whom she still couldn't see.

Brenda's frown turned into a look of understanding. She flashed Hope a conspiratorial smile, then faced the customer. "I'll get Ms. Ellison to explain it to you, sir," she said sweetly. "Hold on a moment."

Brenda loped toward her gleefully, a bounce in her step, undaunted by the look of murderous intent on her face. Mark was still on the phone. He didn't have a clue and didn't care, assured that Hope would pitch in where needed—even though she'd put in her eight hours today!

"I'm going to kill you," she promised Brenda softly between gritted teeth.

"Come on, girlfriend, this is your chance to find out if he's Scrooge or Santa," Brenda whispered encouragingly.

"I don't want to find out," Hope protested, her loud whisper earning Mark's attention. He merely looked at them a second, then gave his complete attention back to his caller.

Brenda got behind Hope and literally pushed her across the area to the window while pulling her coat off at the sleeves.

\* \* \*

Stone's heart was pumping furiously in his chest—he feared it would jump out. He cautioned himself not to get excited, for it was impossible to believe the pharmacist could be *his* Hope Ellison.

But the notion wouldn't go away. Was it possible that the woman who'd misplaced her child was the same one who'd haunted his thoughts like Dickens's ghost of the future? It was impossible, he rejected again, with a sharp shake of his head as if to toss the idea out of his mind.

It just couldn't be the same person, he told himself fervidly, but waiting for her to arrive was unbearable. And then he saw the top of a head, the thick mane of chestnut-colored hair, with a fan of bangs pushed away from almond, olive eyes, and golden brown skin caressing an oval face.

The beat of his pulse became a vibration that hummed through his body. Then she appeared before him at the window, and his heart slammed into his ribs. The white lab jacket she wore over street clothes was an incidental observation, for his eyes were riveted on her face, her eyes, her mouth, small succulent lips, as she spoke.

"Yes, may I help you?"

Though he heard the sound of her voice, his brain scrambled her words as he stared tongue-tied, stomped by the assault of sensual sensations coursing through him. He couldn't remember any other reason for being here except to savor his very real and remarkable apparition.

He felt like a geomancer, one who foretells the future by studying the composition of randomly thrown earth. His eyes surveyed her with the concentration of his trade as if examining the layers of her presence for any sign that would distort his memory of her. Instead he realized that his mind had played tricks on him, for she was even more enchanting than he remembered. A temperate sun had stroked her flesh, painting her glowing brown skin the color of honey. And he felt certain she was exactly what he'd first perceived: nature's sweetness.

"Is there something I can help you with, Mr. Henderson?" she asked.

A dash of some indefinable look flickered in the depths of her bright-colored doe eyes, but Stone found it gratifying. "Stone," he replied, barely recognizing his own voice. "Do you remember me?"

"Yes, I remember you, Mr. Henderson."

There was a breathless quality to her tone, but her voice was that same dulcet instrument as when she'd scolded Faraha.

"Brenda said you had a question about the prescription for your . . . ?" The sentence incomplete, she arched a fine brow in question.

What he was supposed to ask her? Stone frowned, preoccupied. He was remembering the pink of her tongue as it slipped back into her kissable mouth after wetting her full lips. "Right"—he recovered suddenly—"my mother. It's for my mother. Freeda Henderson. I was wondering why it was changed."

"It wasn't. We merely used a generic brand. It's standard procedure," she said. "However, if you want the more expensive name brand, we'll oblige your request. Have a seat, and we'll get right on it."

"No, no," he said hastily. "I don't want you to go through any trouble." At least, not for that, he thought.

"No trouble, Mr. Henderson," she said, extending her hand to take the prescription.

Stone clasped the bag of prescriptions close to his chest where his heart was beating anxiously with a message he couldn't seem to decipher. "Never mind," he said, stepping away from the window. "I'll just take this."

"All right," she said.

Did he detect a note of disappointment in her voice? he wondered. "Well," he said, with a knuckle-wrap on the counter as he stepped away from it. "You have a good evening."

"You, too, Mr. Henderson."

*Stupid! Stupid! Stupid! You let a perfect opportunity slip right through your big hands!*

Stone blasted himself all the way from the pharmacy in back

of the store to the front, while he stood in the checkout line. Too bad he didn't think like his smooth-talking, glib-tongued baby brother, he thought, paying the cashier. He could have invited her out for coffee or something. *Maybe even to see your gemstone collection,* he told himself mockingly.

His purchases bagged and paid for, Stone snatched his package and readied to face the weather when he saw her, his Hope Ellison, again. She was leaving the store.

A trembling thrill raced against the anxious beat of his heart as he hurried to catch up. Having just passed through the automatic opening doors, she was standing under the building's cover, looking out across the parking lot. It was raining harder than before. The temperature had dropped another five degrees. She pulled her coat closer around her, preparing to walk off.

"Ms. Ellison . . ."

Startled, she jumped, then faced him warily. The cautious look was replaced by relief with her recognition.

"I'm sorry, I didn't mean to scare you," he said. *This is your last chance, don't blow it,* the voice in his head encouraged him. "Uh, can we go someplace and talk? I mean, you know I'm not a killer or anything." *Great line, stupid!*

The question froze in the air between them, invigorating, intoxicating. Stone held his breath in the cold, tensed moment, waiting for her response and warmed by a reckless passion.

"I . . . I really must go," she stammered in reply.

"I won't keep you long," he replied on a long drawn-out breath. He felt a sense of desperation to secure her consent that didn't have a thing to do with wanting to get out of this horrible weather. Strangely, he didn't feel the cold.

"Faraha needs to be picked up."

"He has chess practice today and won't be done until six-thirty." He looked at his watch. "It's only four forty-five. Let's go to RJ's for coffee or something—it's in the area."

"How did you know that?"

Stone knew instantly to what she referred and placed meaning in his ability to read her mind. He smiled down at her with a quiet sheepish look. "Faraha told me."

"Why? You can't possibly want to be in the company of a woman who doesn't know how to take care of her child."

Stone felt pinned by the intense look in her eyes. Though she was apparently still smarting from something he'd said three days ago, her voice was without the weight of anger.

"You said some pretty harsh things yourself," he said, with a somewhat wry expression on his face. He reached out to graze the side of her cheek. Her cold skin was soft as velvet. He saw the movement in her lovely neck, a swallow, but couldn't find the command to remove his hand from her flesh.

"I don't see the point in it."

Though a look akin to acquiescence lurked in the depths of her big bright eyes, her words were clear and decisive. His hand back at his side, Stone knew he had better do something, and fast. "We can clear the air between us."

Her bottom lip folded into her mouth, and she glanced out onto the lot again, then up at him. Stone couldn't tell whether he was going to be successful or not. The wait was daunting.

"I want to see you again," he said plainly, remembering that honesty usually worked. And it was more true than anything else he could ever say.

"What else did my son tell you about us?"

Stone breathed a sigh of relief as glimmering hope streamed through him. "I'll tell you over coffee."


"You let this man engage you in a thirty-minute . . ."

Hope could hardly believe it herself . . . standing out in the cold, having a "summer conversation," she thought, squeezing past her pregnant friend, Monique, in the hallway with an armload of clothes. But Monique didn't need any more encouragement. "No longer than ten," she corrected.

"Never mind that," Monique replied, trailing after her. "You were still standing outside in the freezing rain—"

"Not freezing," Hope interrupted, continuing to the master bedroom where she dumped the clothes on the high, four-poster king-size bed.

This used to be her parents' room, and though both were

deceased, she kept her old bedroom down the hall. She'd taken to using this room to fold clothes, which she began doing. Monique leaned against the old dresser to stare at her with disbelief and continue arguing her case for Stone Henderson.

"In the cold rain then!" Monique said exasperated, folding her arms across her protruding tummy. "You still turned him down."

Hope sighed her regret inwardly as she snapped a towel to fold. After leaving Stone outside the store—at the time, it seemed as hard as giving birth—she'd come home to finish some of the chores that had gone undone yesterday. Monique had dropped by with her stepdaughter, Ariana, who'd then raced right back out to pick up Faraha. Even though he had a ride home, she couldn't pass up the opportunity to drive her stepmother's Porsche.

"I know single black women who would die for a chance to meet a single, employed anywhere, black man," Monique declared.

"He's a geologist, and I'm a picky black woman," Hope said. Though only a few years older, Monique was one of those women with seemingly endless energy, she mused admiringly. Once she set her sights on something—caution be damned—she went after it with a vengeance. Her husband, Solomon Thomas, learned that before they married, she mused, recalling the story of their breathless courtship. Yes, that drive had served Monique well, as she also owned T's Place, one of the more popular nightspots in Houston.

"So are the Marines," Monique quipped. "But they apparently can teach you a lesson or two about the recruiting process."

"Recruiting is easy. It's the retention that's the problem."

"First you have to get the problem," Monique reminded her dryly.

"You just want me to have a date for your Mistletoe Jam," Hope replied with teasing. That had been the purpose for Monique's visit, to drop off a pair of tickets for the all-night, pre—Christmas Eve concert at T's Place on December twenty-third.

Monique uttered a sound of disgust, then announced with

displeasure, "Gotta go again." She disappeared into the adjacent bathroom.

She and Monique had known each other before Hope left town and Monique married Solomon, who now managed the club. She had been Hope's lifesaver when she returned to Houston from California, where she worked for a medical supply company as a sales representative. Monique had refused to let her wallow in despair by constantly checking on her, getting her involved in community activities, and even helping her secure a scholarship to return to college and complete her pharmacy program.

Monique returned from the bathroom to warn, "Don't pick yourself right out of the market."

The taunt had a bleak ring to it, and Hope felt dissatisfied with herself. She grabbed another towel to fold and remembered another feeling, a speck of heat on her cold skin that had fired up her senses. Every feeling in her had clamored to go with Stone, she recalled, with that familiar warmth swelling inside her anew. Then the feeling fled at the vulnerable look that came to his eyes. But most telling and frightening of all was the oddly gentle tone of his voice, the sincerity of his words. That combination scared her witless, afraid of where they would lead her, and all she could think was to escape.

"I don't want to rush into anything . . . again," Hope said with musing in her tone, another memory crashing into her thoughts.

"Rush?" Monique said, flabbergasted. "Girlfriend, let me remind you that Faraha is five years old now."

Though she appreciated Monique's concern, she was beginning to wish that she hadn't told her about Stone Henderson. "I'm satisfied with our lives, okay?" Hope said, feeling the onslaught of melancholy.

"I give up!" Monique threw up her hands.

"Thank you." Hope chuckled. "Gather up Faraha's dirty clothes for me," she called after Monique, who was departing from the room. Monique just wanted her to be as happy as she was, she mused, thinking that the Thomases had a great life.

But things weren't always what they seemed, she reminded

herself with a wistful sigh. Thinking of Tyrone, her mind picked up the strings of time.

Her parents couldn't afford to keep her in college, so after two years, she dropped out to work full-time for the company as a secretary. Within a year she was promoted, trained, and sent to the company's Oakland office. It was while there that she met Tyrone Herrington.

Tall, suave, and handsome, he was a man destined for success. That he'd come from a background similar to hers meant more to her than it should have, she realized now. A newspaper reporter aspiring to become a TV news producer, with a knack for being in the right place at the right time, he advanced rapidly.

That should have been a warning to her. Instead he became her purpose, the reason for her existence . . . so even when he started keeping strange hours and flirting with other women in front of her, she excused his behavior.

Following a party at some star's home—she couldn't even remember who—Tyrone was unusually amorous. In such a hurry to get her into bed, the protective measures they'd been keen to obey before were forsaken. Four months later she discovered she was pregnant. It prompted Tyrone's exodus. He didn't even have the guts to accept the role he played. Instead he claimed she got pregnant to tie him down. She came back home to have her child.

With time she had gotten over Tyrone and hadn't let the experience tarnish her like of men. But Stone Henderson aroused some of the same old fears and uncertainties in her, as certainly as he incited other feelings of want in her.

"What's this?"

She heard Monique before she appeared in the doorway. She had Faraha's clothes tucked under one arm, while holding a shiny item in her open palm. "You need to take better care of heirlooms this expensive," she said.

Hope frowned, then got up to take the item from Monique's hand. She saw it was a thick, gold rope necklace, but her eyes widened and her heart thumped at the stone clasped to it. A heart-shaped gemstone, bluish-purple in color and about the size of a quarter and half an inch thick was encircled by diamonds. The whistle on her lips died in her throat as she remembered Faraha's excursion in the Galleria jewelry store. Shaking her head, she discounted that he could have stolen this expensive piece of jewelry in her hand.

"I've never seen this before," she said, puzzled. "Where did you get this from?"

"Your son's pocket," Monique replied, holding up a pair of overalls. She searched the pockets to pull out a white business card, and a secretive smile spread across her face.

"What?" Hope asked suspiciously.

"Guess whose number this is?" Monique replied.

Hope's eyes narrowed in a frown. "Tell me," she said in an I-don't-want-to-know tone of voice.

"Go home, Stoney."

Stone looked up from where he was sitting at his mother's kitchen table with disbelief dripping from his expression. His brother, Dennis, who was sitting across from him, stuffing his face in a big ole' bowl of gumbo, snickered.

"I'll—" Stone started threatening.

"You'll go home is what you're going to do," Freeda Henderson cut in sassily. She was piddling between the stove and the cabinets overhead, obviously looking for something that didn't want to be found. Boasting all the modern conveniences, with a farmer motif in yellows and brown against white appliances, the kitchen had been enlarged out of necessity. One had but to look at any of the Henderson clan to know why. Their father had been a lumberjack of a man, and their mother was no slip of a woman, standing five foot nine—it was she who'd taught Dennis to play basketball.

Stoney was his nickname, and his mother used it only when she was denying him something. It was as affectionate as she ever was with him, Stone thought, completely accepting of the fact.

"Yeah, Stoney, go home," Dennis chimed in tauntingly.

Dennis was their parents' last-ditch effort to make a go of

their off-and-on-again marriage. It lasted three years before their father was killed in a car accident. Dennis had been mama's baby ever since.

"I can't believe you're kicking me out like this," Stone said to his mom, who was holding a big scooping spoon in her hand. At fifty-six, she carried her age and size far better than her health had been the last couple of years, he thought. But that was because his sister, a nutritionist, nagged her into good eating habits and exercise.

"You've been bitching and moaning and groaning about something ever since you got here, and I'm sick and tired of it," she said. "Now I appreciate everything you've done, but it's time for you to go home," she said, her back to them.

Stone wanted to scream that he paid the notes on this house, and she couldn't kick him out. But each of them, Dennis included, knew he wouldn't. He saw Dennis open his mouth with some smart-aleck remark, and his eyes narrowed into slits of angry warning. But he need not have bothered expressing it.

"All right, Dennis," Freeda warned.

Neither brother spoke. But the looks on their faces showed that they still wondered how their mother did that. Stone cut a smirking look at Dennis, who stuck out his tongue at him.

He'd returned from the drugstore in a worse mood than before he'd left, Stone mused. He had no one to blame but Stone. He'd made a fool of himself with Hope Ellison. For all he knew, she already had a man . . . that Dr. Hassani, Faraha's chess coach. And to think that he stood outside in the cold rain, practically begging that woman to talk to him; it was more than his pride could take. He shook his head, confused and disgusted.

"I haven't eaten all day," Stone said. "The least you could do is offer me dinner before the human garbage disposal over here consumes it all."

"No need to call nobody no names," his mother said. "I'm fixing you a bowl to go."

Dennis chortled in his hand, his cheeks bloating with suppressed laughter.

The doorbell rang, and Freeda stopped what she was doing to answer it before either of her sons could move. Stone guessed it was the widower Taylor—Mr. J.T., the neighborhood residents called him. He didn't want to think about what those two fifty-something-year-old seniors did away from prying eyes.

In spite of his foul attitude, he felt at home in the warm kitchen, and he didn't just mean the temperature as opposed to the cold outside. His mother still turned on the stove to heat the house, even though he'd had central heat and air installed years ago.

Still, he had to admit, it was cozy here, far better than what he faced at his home. Sometimes, he sighed inwardly, loneliness was just too hard on a man.

"Couldn't get none, huh?"

Stone stared annoyed at Dennis, who'd broken into his thoughts. His brother didn't know how close to the truth he was, but he'd never tell him that.

"Well, that's not surprising," Dennis continued with a rasp of disgust in his tone. "Look at yourself—you're a zombie. You've been moping for the past three years. I can't blame a woman for not wanting somebody only pretending to be alive."

The truth of his brother's jibe hurt, and Stone retaliated. "Please tell me why I would listen to somebody who can't keep his zipper up?" he retorted rhetorically.

A suggestive grin spread slowly across Dennis's face. "And you wish you were just like me," he chortled mockingly.

"At least I'm not a grown man, still living at home with my mama," Stone tossed back.

"But *still living*," Dennis pointed out victoriously.

"Stone . . . telephone."

"Telephone?" Stone echoed, puzzled, to his mother's voice calling him from the other room. "Who would be calling me here?" he wondered aloud, getting to his feet.

"Probably your boss calling you to work, 'cause we know it ain't no woman," Dennis said loudly and amusedly after him.

# Chapter Four

Hope was darting about her bedroom like a chicken with its head cut off. Her thoughts reflected a similar state.

She was doing nothing productive in the way of readying for Stone's arrival, although she had been sent by Monique to change clothes. Instead, she was tidying up the room. Freshly cleaned and folded clothes were making their way to the respective dresser drawers.

With Faraha due home in a few minutes, she wondered when Stone would arrive. He'd said he would be right over, and she knew that his mother lived nearby. She hoped he'd hurry, then be gone before Ariana returned with Faraha.

Then another thought occurred to her. If he was still here when Faraha showed up, she'd have a problem on her hands. She couldn't afford to risk her son getting the wrong impression. She would have to make sure later that Faraha understood that this was a one-time, special situation and that he was not to expect Stone to become a frequent visitor to their home.

Since her parents died, she never invited men to her home socially, unless a crowd was present, so as not to get Faraha's hopes up by some interest she may have had. That hadn't been an issue to date, she mused flippantly while retucking the white cotton sheets tightly at the mattress corners, for she hadn't met any man who either wanted or interested her beyond a third date. And even then she always met her dates someplace else.

But if Stone was gone, and Monique blurted out that he'd been here—she gasped wide-eyed—then Faraha would accuse her of going behind his back to invite Stone over when she knew how much he would have liked to talk to him. She snapped the comforter to spread evenly atop the bed, recalling that Faraha had not told her he had Stone's phone number. Which could only mean that he'd forgotten all about it, and it was her, not Faraha, who had made a big deal about Stone's impression on him.

Why did she let Monique talk her into calling Stone in the first place? she bemoaned, hanging a white lab jacket in the tiny closet. She could have waited for another time to call him, she chided herself, wondering whether she had done the right thing. She didn't want him to think she was chasing him, or that she had been playing some stupid female game earlier by refusing to see him when she really did want to see him again.

Maybe she just jumped the gun, she considered, stacking her shoes on the rack behind the door. Maybe the necklace wasn't as expensive as Monique claimed. Neither one of them was a jewelry expert. There was probably no need to have called Stone at all, she reasoned this time. Certainly he knew Faraha had his necklace. So that meant he must have given it to him and, like Faraha, had forgotten all about it.

Hope shook her head. She was driving herself crazy, she thought. Blowing the air from her cheeks, she stopped moving about to check her efforts. She looked at the room as if trying to see it through another pair of eyes, a man's eyes ... soul deep and dark brown.

Crimson and gold shakers hung on either side of her high school graduation cap on the pink walls. Stuffed animals lined the headboard of her regular bed. Except for the cherry, waist-high bookshelf containing pharmacy magazines and books, the furnishings were white lacquer. Geometric print curtains covered the twin windows facing the backyard. White floorboards with gray carpet completed the room's look.

"Hope . . . I think that's him driving up," Monique called from another room in the house. "Are you ready?"

No she wasn't ready, Hope thought, with a barely perceptible shiver coursing through her. She wasn't planning to entertain company back here, she chided herself. And thank goodness for that. Though clean and tidy, the room represented the years of her youth, but it lacked the character of the woman she had become. She wondered for the first time why she hadn't redecorated.

The painted, curbside letters of the street address had faded out, but Stone had no problems finding Hope's house. Nestled between two others in the middle of the cul de sac, it was a cute little blue and white house made of brick and wood. A swing attached to a decrepit-looking old tree in the small front yard swayed gently in the wintry night air.

Stone parked his truck on the street and sat there a moment with the engine running. With his heart beating like an electric-driven sleigh, he felt as if he needed to slow down and examine his motives. But he was simply here to pick up his necklace.

*Oh, the priceless one you entrusted to a five-year-old?* a cynical voice inquired.

*You're stalling, Stone,* he told himself. Showered, fresh-shaven, and pressed, he was as ready as he was going to get. Dennis's taller height but slimmer body build made his clothes a perfect fit, although they were flashier than he normally wore. But it was either raid Dennis's closet, or show up carrying the odor of his day's work. His brother's sweet-smelling cologne, however, lost to the scent of Irish Spring soap.

He just didn't want to be a fool and rush into anything, Stone explained his sudden hesitation. But at the thought of going home, he decided that maybe he just needed a friend . . . of the female persuasion. He'd never been much on male buddies. Although he had palled around with his mostly male coworkers occasionally, that was more for professional reasons than social.

Unable to stand this useless introspection any longer, Stone cut off the truck's motor and got out. The rain was little more than a drizzle, the temperature colder. If this weather continued, he thought, pulling the borrowed knee-length wool coat tighter around him, they just might get a slushy Christmas in Houston this year.

He strolled up the sidewalk that split the small front yard in half. His pulse clanged like cymbals in a momentous buildup with every step.

*Admit it,* his conscience demanded.

"Yes," he whispered fiercely to the silent voice in his head—he was attracted to her. From the very first he laid eyes on her, he liked her looks. But now, realizing he'd taken another step in the liking department, he was just a little bit afraid.

The door opened from the inside, warmth rushed out to greet Stone, and his heart somersaulted. The "Hi," on his lips died unvoiced in the peeved set of his mouth. This woman wasn't Hope! his brain screamed, thinking of the precious time he was losing, not that he could have possibly come to the wrong house.

"Hi, I'm Hope's friend, Monique. You must be Stone. Won't you come in?"

She'd dated since Faraha was born but hadn't been intimate practically since his conception, Hope recalled. She didn't know if she remembered how, though her festive reactions to Stone Henderson would suggest otherwise.

By the time she emerged from hiding in her bedroom, Monique had let him in. With majesty in his beautifully proportioned body, he stood before the mantelpiece in the family room, looking at the gang of gold-framed family photographs. She was acutely aware of his effect on the size of the room—the ceiling seemed to have lowered and the walls compressed.

As quiet as a mouse, Hope admired the view from the doorway, marveling at the breadth of his back, his powerful shoulders, his tight round bottom. She shook her head before the delicious sound in her throat gave her away. Still a licentious tremor twirled its way up from her toes. Well, not exactly her toes, she rectified, clearing her throat softly as she advanced into the room.

Stone turned and smiled at her with his brilliant brown eyes. The magnitude of his silent greeting pervaded her senses, and Hope gulped, as tremors of rapture caught in her throat.

"Hi," he said, almost shyly.

"Hi," she replied in a similarly shy tone around her thick tongue. Her gaze fastened into his. She felt embraced by the strange, faintly eager look in his dark eyes.

"It's good seeing you again," he said.

With a dazed smile implanted on her face, Hope sensed Stone wanted to say more. She couldn't think of a thing. The room seemed to dazzle in his presence, and she sensed a tad of difference in him. Or maybe it was simply her heightened awareness of him. He was ultracomposed, confident, as if justifiably assured of his place in her home. The aura enhanced everything about him—his skin tone smooth like rich mocha; his teeth strikingly white in his wide, firm mouth; and his eyes, with soul appeal, just striking. She shuddered imperceptibly as a string of desire looped through her.

The time passing seemed excessive though only seconds ticked off before her fascination passed and she found her voice.

"After I didn't get an answer at your home . . . I found your phone number on the card you'd given Faraha . . . I called the pharmacy and got your mother's number. I remembered you picked up her prescriptions." Hope knew she was babbling but couldn't help herself.

"I'm glad you did."

"Did you have any problems finding the house?" she asked, recognizing that he'd changed clothes since she last saw him. In comparison she felt downright dowdy. He was now spiffily dressed in a gold blazer over a teal blue shirt and cobalt blue slacks, with black tasseled loafers on his feet. She almost looked down at her feet, her toes wiggling in the Mickey Mouse head of her fluffy red and white house slippers.

"No, not at all," he replied. "My mother doesn't live far

at all. In fact, she's about four blocks on the other side of Texas Southern University.''

From somewhere in her head filled with cacophonous thoughts and appetence, Hope heard Monique telling her to offer the man a seat. "Please have a seat," she invited, gesturing toward the couch against the wall in the middle of the room.

"Thank you."

Hope took her father's old recliner and instantly regretted her decision, as her feet dangled over the edge. She heard for certain the Christmas music playing subtly and thought to wonder where Monique had slipped off to. Though glad not to be spied on, she could have used a buffer, although she wasn't sure that Monique could help her explain her healthy appetite of sexual wants that defied explanation.

"Is it still raining outside?" she asked.

"Just enough to make a mess of the streets and cause a couple of accidents," he replied.

Trying to still her fidgety insides, Hope picked up the tune playing. A saxophonist was covering "Pure Imagination," something she could definitely identify with as she gazed at Stone. She liked the curve of his mouth, the gentleness in his eyes, the way he was looking at her. With her insides jangling and her pulse beating a waltzy rhythm, she wanted to bask in the engaging tension. Hearing the words in her head: *"If you want to see paradise, all you have to do is . . . see this gorgeous man."*

"I need to get your necklace," she announced suddenly, remembering why he'd come.

"No hurry."

His reply halted her clumsy climb from the chair. Gratefully, if not with the ease of grace she wished, Hope resettled herself, this time tucking her feet under her.

"I gave it to Faraha that day in the Galleria," Stone was saying. "After he told me you were lost, I—"

"I was lost?" she repeated, amazed and amused.

"Yeah." Stone chuckled with merry musing. "He's such a big boy, you know. Anyway, when I suggested that we'd better contact Security to find you, I thought he was going to start crying, so I gave it to him. I don't know if it was the diamonds or the tanzanite stone itself that attracted him, but he seemed to like it."

Hope tried to look at Stone squarely in the face as he gave a detailed account of her son's antics that memorable Saturday in the shopping center. She noted he spoke with his hands, long-fingered and strong—they flicked and twisted, aiding him to make a point. But soon she found herself staring mesmerized by the brown in his eyes, the chiseled shape of his mouth. Inevitably she was merely listening to the sound of his smooth, deep voice, her gaze riveted on his firm mouth.

He got to the part about lingerie. By then she realized she couldn't have repeated what he'd said if offered a million dollars. A second of silence lingered, and his eyes darkened with a haunting, hungry look. Unconsciously she licked her lips and gave her head an imperceptible shake.

"I'm sorry," she said hastily, snapping to attention. She needed desperately to withdraw and regroup from the dynamic force of his presence. "Can I get you something"—unfolding herself from the chair—" ... water, coffee, a beer?"

"The chili will be ready in a few minutes," Monique called out from the kitchen.

"Oh, I'm not ..." Stone started, but a loud growl erupted from his stomach, and he clamped his mouth shut. He looked at Hope with a sheepish grin on his face.

Hope burst out with laughter—she couldn't help herself. "I'm sorry," she said, feeling released from the strain of anxiety she'd brought on herself. The light laughter in her voice was met by an amused chuckle from his big-chested, deep voice.

"I really haven't eaten all day," Stone said.

"You're more than welcome to join us," Monique piped up when Hope didn't.

Hope didn't because she suddenly remembered that there was only enough chili and rice for two people the size of her and Faraha. As big a man as Stone was—although she was not complaining—well, he could eat the entire fixings alone and still not get full.

"Please join us." Hope heard herself mimicking Monique's invitation.

For a moment, not long, Hope thought he would refuse. He was staring at her from a place which she couldn't see into, but his eyes held her in a look that was deeper than mere masculine awareness. She felt a snap, a tangible breakage, inside her body, as if to release something but more to receive.

"Well, if you're sure it's all right," he said at last.

Hope realized she had been holding her breath and praying he would accept. When he did, a rainbow of joy erupted inside her.

"How about that drink first?"

He hadn't felt this excited since his first helicopter ride to reach an oil rig site in the Gulf, Stone thought, staring after Hope as she disappeared into the kitchen. It was a good thing he was sitting down. He was like a seismograph going off on picking up the movements in the earth's crust.

"I sent you to your room to change clothes," Monique whispered in peeved disbelief. "Look at you, you look like a ragamuffin."

"Shhh."

Stone smiled to himself. He couldn't make out all the words, but he understood the tone of harsh admonishment and that it had something to do with clothes. Hope looked fine to him, Mickey Mouse slippers and all, he mused, feeling acclimated to the shafts of delicious sensations she stirred in him. He was glad she hadn't gone through the hassle of dressing for his benefit. If she'd been decked to the nines when he arrived, he probably would have turned tail and run.

It seemed she liked big shirts for more than sleeping in, he mused, feeling a grin in his chest as big as a lollipop. Her honeyed complexion was striking against the burgundy shirt that picked up the reddish hue of her dark hair resting about her delicate shoulders that were practically lost in the shirt.

With its long tails hanging in front, he'd gotten a glimpse of firm thighs in the faded blue jeans that hugged her slender form. Remembering everything Faraha had told him about the two of them, and seeing an older man in one of the mantelpiece pictures, a look of pleasure shone in his eyes. He was glad the shirt must have been her father's, and not that Dr. Hassani's, he thought.

With his pulse subsiding, Stone settled comfortably on the couch, his arms splayed across the back and legs crossed at the knee. He imbibed the smells of spicy chili coming from the kitchen and the holiday's scent of pine in the air. Swayed by the music flaunting chestnuts and open fires, unconsciously, he pictured a cold night with Hope in his shirt. His imagination could put her in nothing else but his arms, and his pulse took off again in a clamorous flame of arousal.

"You did what?"

Hope's surprised raised voice from the kitchen broke into his fantasy, and he sat up with a jerk on the couch. He wiped the non-existing perspiration from his forehead and sighed, relieved that he hadn't been caught daydreaming with lascivious thoughts cast on his face. Exhaling sharply, he had to force his attention elsewhere. The room was a good place to start, as he'd hardly noticed it, his mind preoccupied with seeing her again when he first arrived.

And now that he did, although it didn't negate the yearning that had been deposited in him, he liked it. It had a loving feeling, marvelously comfortable, unlike his own, he thought. Arsha would be appalled by his neglect.

The thought unnerved him, and his face clouded with his sudden uneasiness. He felt an impulsive urge to flee. But he was stuck now, he told himself, looking at the big green leather recliner where Hope had sat moments ago. It looked out of place, which was how he was beginning to feel.

There were African wood carvings and oil-based paintings that hung on the salmon-colored walls. The couch was covered by a multicolored fabric in shades of beige, brown, and orange with a design which looked African, or at least ethnic, that drew in all the other colors. Both the coffee and dining table were teakwood, as was the lounge and ottoman covered in an accenting gold fabric to his left. Behind it, a floor-to-ceiling ladderlike panel served as a divider, separating the rooms.

Under the mantelpiece was an imitation fireplace. Instead of housing wood, a bookshelf containing children's books filled the nook. To the right of it must have been Faraha's place. Wondering for the first time since arriving where his elfin friend was, he rose to saunter to where two child-size wooden chairs winged a matching table. Green marble chess pieces were set up, ready for a game.

A family lived comfortably here, he thought, his gaze moving over the room. Hope had created a cozy little universe, and there was no place for him in it. He had his own life, he asserted stubbornly to the envy tugging at him. And if it were solitary and routine, with no surprises, it was just the way he preferred it.

Hearing Hope and her friend piddling about in the kitchen, he thought about making excuses for his departure—and just as quickly discarded the idea. He inhaled deeply and resolved to make the best of it.

"Sorry it took so long," Hope said, sauntering into the room.

Look at her, he thought. And in so doing, his stomach clenched, noting her genial mouth and sparkling eyes. There was a zeal for life about her, and she transmitted that feeling to him without even trying.

"I hope this is okay," she said, holding out a tall glass of beer to him. "I ran out of real beer. This is the nonalcoholic kind."

"Perfect," Stone said. Accepting the glass from her hand, their skin touched, and an electrical current shot through him. Yeah, he thought, at the first opportunity he was heading home where he belonged. "I'm not much for alcoholic beverages anyway. You're not drinking?" he asked, noticing her empty hand.

"I'm not serving. You're going to have to come get your own plates," Monique called from the kitchen.

He didn't know what all he had expected, Stone thought, as he set his glass on the table. But it wasn't the breath of heaven he felt. It was going to be a long evening . . . particularly with the regret nipping away at him.

# Chapter Five

"I knew it was you! I knew it was you!" Faraha exclaimed. He literally flew across the room to Stone, who was sitting at the dining table, and jumped onto his lap.

It had been ages since she'd had a real conversation with a man. The time had passed with such relative ease that Hope forgot all about her son until he and Ariana walked in, and she looked up at the clock to see that it was nearly nine. She didn't get the chance to ask them where they'd been all this time, when Faraha spotted Stone.

"Oh yeah?" Stone pretended skepticism, his mouth curled in a smile. "How did you know it was me?" he asked, his expression fond, with a hint of teasing.

"Because you told me you had a green, extended cabin Chevrolet truck with a gold pinstripe, and I remembered," Faraha replied in his typical five-year-old decibel: loud.

Hope was standing between Monique and her eighteen-year-old stepdaughter, Ariana, who was taller than both of them. From the center of the family room, they watched Faraha seize Stone's full attention. A sidelong glance at Ariana, a lovely brown-skinned young woman with braids and a firm, curvy figure, showed that Faraha hadn't claimed all of the attention. She was almost drooling at the mouth.

Smiling to herself, Hope concurred with the sentiment. Stone had removed his gold blazer, so every time he moved, the muscles rippled under his shirt and quickened her pulse.

"Can we take a hayride in the back of your truck? My teacher said—"

"Faraha . . ." Hope said with scolding in her tone. Though Stone looked intrigued by the idea, she was embarrassed by her son's audacity. She clapped her hands with the command, "Come on, let Stone finish his dinner."

"Ariana took me to Pizza Hut!" Faraha exclaimed.

As Hope mused that's why there was enough dinner for the three of them, Faraha took the opportunity to impress Stone with his wit. "Stone, I bet everybody in my school can fit on the back of your truck."

Stone laughed, which Hope knew was only further encouragement for her son. With her hands on her hips and her voice lowered, she said in final warning, "Faraha."

"Okay," Faraha relented in a small voice. With a pouty, crestfallen expression, he added, "But my teacher, Mama Rowe, said she went on hayrides when she was a little girl, and they used to be fun."

"Oh, I'm stuffed," Stone said, patting his stomach. "I can't eat another bite. It was fantastic," he added, tipping his head in appreciation to Monique.

Monique truly deserved their gratitude, Hope thought, for she had performed a miracle in the kitchen. She cooked more rice and added microwave-thawed ground meat to the chili. Finely cut vegetables helped thicken it, and a tossed salad and crackers contributed to the savory meal.

"The chef thanks you," Monique responded with a slight curtsy. "Stone, I want you to meet my daughter, Ariana. Ariana, this is Stone Henderson."

Stone rose with Faraha on his hip, extending a hand. "It's a pleasure to meet you, Ariana. Your mother's told me how proud she is of you."

Hope noticed that Monique literally beamed as if she had

given birth to Ariana. Nevertheless, the two of them were great friends. She wished the same were possible for her and Faraha.

"How do you do, Mr. Henderson?" Ariana said, shaking his hand.

"Well, we're going to get out of here," Monique said. "Stone, it was a pleasure meeting you."

"The same here," Stone replied.

"I hope you'll be able to make it to the Mistletoe Jam at the club," Monique added. "A very talented local band, called Collector's Item, will open the show for Kevin Mahogany."

Hope's mouth dropped open spontaneously as she glared at her friend. She knew she was being set up, didn't want him to feel put upon—yet she couldn't help hoping it worked. "Stone's not going to be in town," she said, more as a reminder to herself.

"We'll see," he said noncommittally.

"Faraha, it's past your bedtime," Hope said. She chided her disappointment at his reply, even though she knew it was best this way. "Say good night to Monique and Ariana."

"Good night, Nanny, Ariana," Faraha obeyed.

Hope noticed that her son waved to them, but didn't relinquish his place in Stone's arms. She was almost jealous.

There was "G'night, sweet," from Monique. Ariana added affectionately, "Bye, knucklehead."

Hope walked them to the door. In the small entryway, Monique was slipping into her long winter coat. "Girlfriend, it's time to put picky away."

"Yeah, Aunt Hope," Ariana chimed. "He is fine," she added, accentuating each word, shimmering visibly.

Hope laughed at her reaction, though it was very similar to the sensation that rippled through her. She knew the feeling was motivated by lust, but felt good nevertheless.

"See, even young girls still wet behind the ears can spot a good catch," Monique said.

"Wet behind the ears?" Ariana puffed as if offended, her hands on her hips.

"You're taller but not wiser," Monique told her.

After Monique and Ariana departed, Hope leaned against

the door with her arms folded across her chest, concern etched on her face and butterflies in her stomach. Part of her hated her reaction to Stone. It brought back memories of a stupid passion that wreaked havoc on her life.

But she was no longer a twenty-year-old, fresh out of her parents' home, on her own for the first time. She was a woman now, older, she hoped wiser, and more responsible. Nothing had to happen with Stone that she didn't want to happen.

"Come on, let me show you my room, Stone."

Hearing Faraha's voice, she tensed, mindful that it was not just herself that she had to think about. Her son could suffer even more than she by a wrong decision on her part.

"Quite frankly, I knew the necklace was in good hands with Faraha. But I appreciate the trouble you went through to reach me."

A short time later Hope was once again in the tight entryway. Stone's presence filled the space, as well as her senses. She could feel the intensity of his gaze and see under his thick black lashes the dark brown rings circling the light brown ones of his irises. Shivering inwardly, she wondered what reaction his touch would bring if he could elicit excitement from her with just a look.

"It was no trouble," she replied. He wouldn't even have to fully extend his arm, she thought with a strange and imperceptible tremor coursing through her at the mere idea of his touch. "The necklace looked so expensive, I could only think to get it back to you right away." All she had to do was lean forward and she'd be in his arms.

"Yes. It means a great deal to me."

Straining to hear him, for his voice had dropped to a near whisper, Hope caught herself before moving, or she would have missed the silent sadness that flashed across his face.

"Thanks for inviting me over," he said politely.

A subtle change occurred between them. It was as if the light in the entry had gone out, and she lost all hint as to what he was thinking. Still she sensed a vulnerability in him.

"It's been quite some time since I've had a home-cooked meal," he said. "It was truly wonderful. You be sure to tell Monique again how much I appreciated it."

She stared, entranced. "I will," she replied, wondering if she had mistaken his fleeting somber look.

"I'll hold you to that."

She waited, but he didn't follow up with a request to see her again. She flirted with the idea of extending him another invitation. Instead she put his necklace in his hand, bid him good night, and went to bed with regret as her sleeping companion.


"This is not the time to have nothing to wear, girlfriend," Hope told herself while rummaging through her closet. It had to be warm, bright, and cheerful, and definitely pleasing to the male eye.

For practically every hour that had gone by since Stone's visit, she had alternately wondered if he would ask her out and fretted that he wouldn't. That day finally arrived, December seventh—she mentally marked it as one to remember.

Of course, she was running late. If she'd come home instead of going shopping for bedroom furniture after work, she wouldn't be in such a rush now. Still her mood was buoyant. Stone would be here at six-thirty.

Oh, she knew she shouldn't let herself get carried away—after all, she didn't know how he felt about her. Still, just thinking about him brought the woman inside her to life.

Making her selection, Hope laid her clothes across the bed. A velvet vest in emerald green, silk opal shirt, gray wool slacks with matching blazer, and black leather boot-shoes. Not exactly the sexy look she wanted, but at least she wouldn't freeze in the thirty-two degree temperature outside, she assuaged herself.

"Faraha, how are you coming?" she called out from her bedroom door toward his down the hallway. She had already pulled out his clothes. Knowing Stone was coming was enough inducement to prompt his independence of dressing himself.

"I'm putting on my shoes," he yelled back.

Hope returned to getting herself ready. With hurry in her

actions and Stone in her thoughts, she pulled matching underwear from the dresser drawers and tossed it onto the bed next to her clothes.

It was thanks to Monique that she knew just about everything she needed to know about Stone. Or rather, Dr. Stone Henderson, she corrected, smiling with remembered pleasure as she shrugged out of her robe. One of the few African-American geologists in the country, he'd been to Tanzania, Australia, and Alaska, where he was also a member of the team of experts who assessed the damage of the oil spill a number of years ago.

Sitting on the side of the bed, she generously applied a scented lotion to her body, recalling that Stone had been married before. His wife was dead, but he clammed up on that subject, refusing to divulge the details surrounding her death.

She had her secrets and their reasons, too, Hope mused, slipping into her lingerie.

If he were the kind of man who wasn't interested in a woman with a child, he certainly hadn't shown it. Rather, he'd been wonderfully patient with her chatterbox son. So what if it took him several days before inviting them out? He was merely being cautious, and she should take a cue, she told herself.

He was unpretentious and not a man to reveal his emotions easily. The strong, silent type. Her insides quivered uneasily with that bit of knowledge. *Her* man would have to be a little more giving than that, she thought resolutely.

Her man? Where had that thought come from? Stone hadn't even kissed her!

Hope muttered a mild expletive. She couldn't believe what she was thinking—bedding a man she hardly knew and contemplating permanence, as if the two were mutually exclusive. Her heart thumped madly, her mind a crazy mixture of hope and fear.

She chided herself for the latter, and forgave herself the former. A holiday affair was not a commitment, she told herself rationally. Stone Henderson could be a pleasant diversion. She wasn't ready for anything else, wouldn't let herself hope for anything beyond that.

It was apparent Stone felt the same way, she thought, proud of her insight. Besides, she reminded herself, if it hadn't been for Faraha, they probably wouldn't be going out tonight.

The doorbell rang.

Hope deserved more than his lust, and Stone had feared that was all he had to give. It was what had kept him away. Each day of his absence, he just sank deeper and deeper into despair over his quandary. He convinced himself that what we wanted went against the grain of common decency. His body was willing to pursue Hope, but his mind wasn't willing to proceed in that manner.

And Faraha had been most persistent throughout his emotional ordeal. The five-year-old made him feel guilty for making up claims of busy work.

*"You're just like my daddy—you're always too busy."*

Stone could have kicked himself when he heard that, he recalled. So he had screwed up his courage and vowed to make a move. Now that he had, he realized what a fool he'd been for waiting so long. He blamed it on cold feet.

"Do you have a preference?" the salesman asked Hope. "We have these Noble firs right here. They just came in today."

Stone brought up the rear, following Hope, Faraha, and the salesman up one of the many aisles of Christmas trees. After spending what really was the most enjoyable evening he could ever recall, he was almost embarrassed to admit that it had taken the impetus of a five-year-old to exact another opportunity to be with the Ellisons. In fact, more than one, for Faraha came up with all kinds of things for them to do—he even made a list, and topping it was tree shopping.

Stone was more than happy for the suggestions. He had been living on his memory of Hope, which had been miserly, he mused, feasting his gaze on her as she stopped to inspect a tree. He was astonished by the sense of fulfillment he felt in her presence, though he stood nearby, utterly useless in their ritual.

Hope stopped in front of a tree whose sticker identified it as a Douglas fir. "I think I like this one better," she said to no one in particular.

"I thought we were going to get the other kind," Faraha said. He was walking alongside his mother, mimicking her perusal.

The tree was at least five feet, eight inches tall. A calculating intensity shone in their expressions. The look was cute on Faraha, but seeing it on Hope made him wonder whether she did everything with such single-minded focus. He placed himself at the center of that focus, feeling a tingle in the pit of his stomach.

He lost sight of Hope when she strolled behind the tree and felt a void, an instant's panic. His heart was thudding like a kettle drum in his chest, and a vague memory caused a sudden sadness to edge his senses like a shadow. Hope came back into view, and the veil of his thoughts receded a little. He drew in a deep, restorative breath.

He could no longer blame Arsha's ghost, Stone told himself. She had ceased to haunt his sleep. Hope had become the main feature of his dreams—and practically every waking hour as well.

"Grandpa said that Noble was the best," Faraha reminded her pointedly.

"Normally I would agree," Hope said. The expression on her face showed she was speaking her thoughts out loud. As if second-guessing herself, she gazed around the enclosed area off the shopping center's parking lot that was filled with trees. There were rows and rows of them, with as many people searching for the right tree. "But the ones on this lot are too dry. Their leaves are shedding."

"We can go somewhere else," Stone offered. If that was what it took to stretch out his time in her company, he didn't mind at all. He was compelled to explore his feelings, disconcerting though they'd been at times.

"No way," Hope declared. "It's too cold out here to keep this up." She shivered as if to punctuate her words.

Now was not one of those times, Stone thought, clear about what he was feeling. Even though Hope was bundled up under layers of clothes, sparks of excitement shot through him.

"I'll take this one." She finally decided with a firm nod of her head.

"You heard the lady," Stone said to the salesman, who had remained nearby unobtrusively.

"Where are your poinsettias?" Hope asked the man.

He pointed toward the opposite end of the enclosed area. "All the way to the end, then make a right," he said.

"Okay, I'll be right back," she said.

Stone stared after her, with a sigh swelling in his chest. It was one of those crazy feelings, he thought, like his recent interest in his house. With Dennis's help, he'd begun dressing it up to resemble a home. It was how he'd spent his days, trying to reconcile body and mind.

"Hold up," Stone told the salesman, who'd begun removing the tree from the water-filled base. "I want to get another one."

He hadn't bought a tree in years, Stone mused, as he sauntered several rows of trees away. He steeled himself, as if expecting the memory to hurt. Surprisingly it didn't. Stopping before one as tall as himself, he imitated the inspection Hope had conducted. If it hadn't been for her, he probably would have picked up the first one in his path. But of course, he reminded himself, if it hadn't been for her, he wouldn't be buying a tree at all.

"Do you like my mama, Stone?" Faraha asked.

Stone had a feeling he was about to be set up. He'd had the experience with Faraha in a chess game as recently as a couple of hours ago, while Hope finished dressing. Underestimating his youthful opponent, he had been beaten by Faraha in three moves their first game. "Yes," he said warily.

"You like me, too?"

Stone felt foolish for being suspicious. Faraha was merely indulging his nature as a curious five-year-old—he had no ulterior motive. "Of course I like you, Faraha."

"Then why are you buying two trees?" Faraha asked.

Stone was momentarily stumped. "For my house," he replied at last, mirth in his expression.

"You can have Christmas with us at our house, then you won't have to buy another tree," Faraha said, his hands splayed as if his suggestion made more sense.

Faraha had pulled off another "gotcha" on him, Stone mused, chuckling. "I think you better clear that with your mama first," he said.

Still he didn't mean to force a decision right now. His hand raised in a halting gesture as Faraha dashed away in search of Hope. Staring after the youngster, he mulled the idea. He was not displeased by it, probably more delighted than he should be, he told himself. But he still had a plane ticket to the Bahamas.

If Santa knew what she was thinking, he'd declare her a naughty girl. The expression on her face, Hope was certain, mimicked her usual calm smile, but inside her, unseen, a feeling that was elemental and older than Christmas was making merry havoc.

Stone had become a daily presence in their lives, and for a couple of hours tonight, Faraha's baby-sitter while she attended choir practice. She didn't know what they had done, but when she returned home, Stone was putting an exhausted Faraha to bed.

He joined her at the dining-room table, where she was wrapping the Blake family gifts. Wrapping paraphernalia littered the table, as well as boxes whose sides revealed a chemistry lab, race car set, a doll with a set of dishes. She was wrapping the mother's gift.

"I warn you, I'm not good at this," Stone said uneasily, when she placed a roll of wrapping paper and a box in front of him.

"Do the best you can. I promise you the kids will hardly notice," she joked with laughter.

Stone began wrapping awkwardly. He was standing a good arm's length away, but her awareness of him was as sharp as ever. He wore his customary casual outfit, plaid flannel shirt, starched jeans and lace-up soft leather boots. And his favorite scent was a faint citrus aftershave. He could have been naked, by her reaction to him.

"What's your trick?" she asked.

"Huh?"

She started to explain that after his visits, Faraha was so excited he couldn't get to sleep. It reminded her of her own sleeping habits, in which explicit scenes of her and Stone dominated her dreams. Usually she was wrapped in his big strong arms and held next to his majestic chest as if she were as precious as a gift, she recalled, with a toasty heat sizzling inside her.

"Oh, you mean Faraha," he said, catching on. "He just had a hard day at school, that's all."

"Uh-huh," she replied suspiciously, smiling comfortably to herself. Despite the fact that his big hands were mauling the wrapping paper, she felt sure they were better at other things. At least he was engrossed in the task, and the gift was getting wrapped.

"He showed me his Christmas list. I got exhausted just reading it," he said laughingly.

The warmth of his laugh sent shivers down her spine. "Oh, yes—he honored me, too. It's as long the pharmacy's inventory at the store," she added, then fell silent, a look of concern on her face. She didn't want him to get the impression that she was looking for a father for her son. Before he popped into their lives, she wasn't looking for anyone.

"Stone, don't let Faraha fool you into thinking that he needs any of those things. He's good at manipulation and will use every trick in his little arsenal, from trying to make you feel guilty to harassment, to get what he wants. Don't fall for it. He really doesn't need anything."

"Oh, I know," Stone said. "He knows, too," he added. His deep mellow voice contained a cryptic tone.

Hope looked up from wrapping to stare into his face. His soulful eyes held her still with a look that was more than sensual. Caring glinted in their soft, dark depths, and she felt herself going hot all over. Again.

"He's a great kid," Stone continued. "But that's to be expected—he has a great mother."

Hope was thrown off by the voiced compliment from a man who kept his thoughts close to his chest. She relished it so much she feared it would go right to her head, already dizzy with a carnal wish. "Thank you," she replied softly. "Sometimes, I wish his father would have taken an interest in him, but—" She broke off and shook her head sharply, not wanting to ruin the pleasant mood.

"He told me his father was a TV producer in California," Stone picked up conversationally.

"Yeah," Hope replied reluctantly.

"I gather he doesn't stay in contact much."

Hope snorted. She fiercely pulled a strip of tape off the roll and it twisted, sticking to itself. "I can count the times on one hand," she said, balling up the ruined piece to toss aside and start over. "Tyrone saw Faraha only once, and that was when he was nine months old. His mother insisted on seeing her grandson, and he was forced to bring her to town."

"Hmm," Stone muttered thoughtfully.

"She died last year, and that was the end of that," Hope said, her tone chilly. "I gave up on Tyrone a long time ago." She mumbled, "Not soon enough, but—" then clamped her mouth shut, realizing her feelings were showing.

"But what?"

"Let's say Faraha is the best thing that came out of that relationship," she said.

"You must have loved him at some point," Stone pointed out, almost questioningly.

"I'm afraid I wasn't too bright as far as Tyrone Herrington was concerned," she admitted, the memory of her behavior embarrassing. "I let myself be used, so I guess I deserved what I got," she said with a self-derisive chuckle.

"You were young and naive, that's all," Stone said kindly. "And, as you said, you got Faraha out the deal."

He offered her a forgiving smile that completely replaced the serious, reserved look she'd come to expect from him. It softened the features of his face beautifully. In that moment, that look, she felt a deep, inexplicable feeling, different from lust. She could trust this man, she thought, startled and unsettled.

"Well, what do you think?" he asked.

Hope struggled to pull her thoughts together, accepting that she could do nothing about the longing. On noticing the wrapped gift he held up for her inspection, she faced another struggle to contain her laughter. She swallowed before she spoke. "You did the best you could"—her voice trembling with mirth.

"I always do," he replied.

Stone placed the angel securely on the top protruding branch of his tree, then descended the stepladder to look at the one who was assessing his work. Approval beamed in Hope's expression, which had the effect of giving him immense pleasure.

"You've done a pretty good job for someone who claims to be out of practice by more than twenty years," she said.

"You should give Faraha most of the credit," he replied humbly.

"And where is your little helper now?"

Stone chuckled at her dubious expression, eyebrow cocked and her cute little mouth pursed in jest. Though he'd picked up Faraha from school earlier, she had to work overtime and had not long arrived at his place. They were in his recently redecorated living room, where he'd set up his Christmas tree in front of the picture window.

"He and Dennis are upstairs playing video games," he replied. "But he did make a contribution. Come see," he said, taking her hand.

The effects of the contact unfurled streamers of sensations in him, and every last one of them was hot, stimulating. Stone released her hand, while reminding himself to breathe, plucked an ornament from the tree, and placed it in her hand.

"He gave you this?" she asked, amazed.

"He insisted," Stone replied, his gaze roaming over her as she studied the ornament. There was a glint of wonder in her sparkling eyes, as if seeing it for the first time, turning it over in her hands. It was a homemade ornament, made of a Styrofoam ball and decorated with patches of different fabrics. The final touch was a small picture of Faraha, dressed only in a diaper when he was six months old. "I told him he'd better get your permission first. I know your mother made it for him, and it's part of a set.''

Hope looked up at him mystically, and he had to remind himself to breathe. He wondered what she was thinking as he simply basked in her nearness, trying hard to keep his aggression under control.

"He had it planned all along," she said.

Stone noticed the hint of pride in her expression, and something else he couldn't discern, but he didn't understand what she meant. "He had what planned?"

"To give this to you," she replied. "Remember when we were decorating our tree?"

He nodded, recalling the marathon of hanging lights outside her home, then hurrying inside from the cold to spruce up their tree.

"Mother made six, but I could find only five. Faraha claimed he didn't know where the last one was . . . this one," she said, holding it up in emphasis.

"Uh-oh," Stone said, feeling like a snitch. "I see I'm going to have to have a talk with him," he added in a firm voice, though he didn't feel stern at all about it. Elation curled right up next to the desire swooping through him.

"Only about the lying part, not wanting to give," she said gently. She returned the ornament to his hand.

"Are you sure?"

"It was Faraha's gift to give."

The beautiful candor of the smile she gave him was echoed in her voice. He wondered if he was deserving of how she made him feel. *Blessed* was the only way he could describe it, a quiet, warm experience like reverence.

"Now I'd like the grand tour," she said, gesturing toward the rest of the condo.

Dennis managed to finish only the first level, he explained, beginning the tour. In the living room the gentle golden tone of colonial maple furniture was surrounded by a color scheme of alabaster white and a deep winter green. It gave the room an understated elegance. The pictures interspersed on the walls were few but large, and all bore the telltale thematic symbols of black culture in Houston by the artist, John Biggers.

He'd been surprised by just how talented his brother, Dennis, was, he admitted, continuing to the bar area. He had a keen eye for designs and was a more than able carpenter. Though they had broached the subject, he was hoping to talk Dennis into going back to school, he told her as they reached the dining room.

There was a picture on the wall in this small, intimately enclosed area that he hadn't intended to be hung. In fact, he'd forgotten all about it, hadn't seen it in a long time. He guessed Dennis must have dug it out from some hiding place—he knew only he wasn't pleased by its presence. He tried not to show it.

"Who's this?" Hope asked.

"Arsha," Stone said more sharply than he intended. "This kitchen is . . ." he said hastily, trying to lead her away from the charcoal sketch. But Hope wasn't following.

"How did she die, Stone?"

Stone was looking at the floor. They'd decided on an off-white cement tile, with solid gold ones interspersed. It was Dennis's idea, and he had to admit, it truly complemented the cherry dining set. "Stone?"

"I can't talk about it now, Hope." He was looking her squarely in the eyes and saw the moment that disappointment flashed across her face. The doorbell rang. Seconds later the sounds of footsteps bounding down the stairs could be heard. "That must be the pizza they ordered," he said as if happy to announce it. "I hope you're hungry." He was far from pleased with himself.


After a long and troubled night wrestling with her feelings, Hope awakened even more baffled than before. She wished the problem were as simple as what to wear to his company's Christmas party. Instead at the center of her quandary was a truth she could no longer evade: She was in love with Stone Henderson.

They got through the remainder of the evening without further incident, she recalled, but she didn't know how much longer the relationship could last as she dressed in preparation of Stone's arrival.

She had pondered his refusal to talk about his late wife's death all day—until she was nearly sick with the struggle within her. She was no closer to understanding why and what it meant twenty-four hours later.

She knew how painful it was to discuss the unpleasant aspects of one's life. Sometimes only distance and time could heal the pain. In her case it had been the humiliation as well.

Maybe she was making it a bigger deal than it actually was. Stone possessed so many other wonderful qualities that *one* shortcoming could be forgiven.

But one had a tendency to add up, until eventually; the bad overshadowed the good, she reminded herself. She was referring to Tyrone, who was so different from Stone that she felt foolish for thinking it.

When she first learned of Arsha's death, she'd gotten the impression that Stone loved her dearly. She could even admire the devotion she sensed he had for his late wife. But if he was still pining for her, she thought, uneasiness adding to her turmoil, then he wasn't ready for a relationship with her or any other woman.

With rising dismay, she knew that was what she'd been trying to deny.

But Stone had made no commitment to her and requested none in exchange, she thought, breathing hard as if she couldn't get enough oxygen into her lungs. That simple fact had been so easy to forget, considering her feelings, the tenderness that melted her heart whenever he was near.

The reminder was like an awakening experience that left her reeling. An even more terrifying shocker came on its heels: She was already more than a little in love with Stone. She wondered if it was too late to put a halt to her emotions. It hurt just thinking it was possible.

The doorbell rang, signaling Stone's arrival. Hope had to

drag herself into action, for she still had to finish dressing. Jeans, a bulky sweater, and boots lay within easy reach.

"I'll get it," Faraha cried out excitedly.

Hope heard his exuberant race to the door. "Wait a minute," she called out cautiously from her bedroom.

She knew her command was fruitless, so she'd better hurry. The much awaited hayride was on for this evening. Faraha had secured the interest of his school friends, who elicited their parents' agreement to participate. Stone coordinated everything, from planning the route to buying enough hay for three trucks. They would meet up at the school, and the trip would culminate at City Hall for the tree-lighting ceremony. After making sure the kids were returned, the three of them were going out for a late dinner as school was out for the holidays. Faraha had been on a cloud, and she'd been right there with him—though the silver lining was a dull gray around hers now.

Shoeless, she was presentable, if not completely ready for Stone's arrival by the time she reached the front door. Faraha had already opened it. He was standing there frozen stiff, staring at the person who stood inches across the threshold.

Recognition jolted Hope. She stared speechless at the tall, bronze, brown-skinned man. She couldn't help notice that he was still good-looking—even more so with age that gave character to his narrow face. And he still had the most devastating smile she'd ever seen. She also remembered the lies that came from his pretty mouth.

"Tyrone, what are you doing here?" she asked, peeved.

"And merry Christmas to you, too," he replied, flashing pearly white teeth that he paid a fortune to maintain.

"Christmas is a week away," she replied, unimpressed.

"Mama, who is that?" Faraha asked. He had already backed away from the door and was hugging her side.

Tyrone kneeled. "Hey, little man, you don't recognize me? I'm your daddy."

# Chapter Six

Even though Hope let him in, Stone knew Faraha wasn't far away. He would have thought it odd, if not for the fact he needed to speak to her in private. A sense of urgency had hit him like a bucket of ice-cold water, waking him from a toss-and-turn sleep, he recalled. He knew exactly why.

"I know Faraha had his heart set on eating at Planet Hollywood—"Stone began.

"That's his new favorite place," Hope cut in.

"I know," Stone replied. They were standing in the small confines of her entryway. So close, the clean, fresh scent of her femininity was turning his body into a hard gem of need. Desire and disgust made for a raging battle within him.

"Mickey Dee's is still number one though," she said.

"I hate to have to disappoint him," he said. His nerves shook and trembled. His mind was clear on what he had to do. The words, however, were a little obscure, with the prohibition of touching her looming on the edge of his thoughts. "But it will be so crowded."

"I'm sure it would be hours before we got seated," she interjected.

"For sure," he replied, recalling that he'd been bowled

over so quickly by warm emotions for her and Faraha that it frightened him, and he'd backed off—careful to keep incidental touches to a minimum, not even a handshake or chaste kiss good night at the door. For usually a decisive man, floundering as he had was extremely unsettling. "I'm afraid it would be late by the time we'd be served," he said, knowing a great part of his behavior had to do with Arsha.

"I don't know if he could hold out that long," she said, chuckling lightly.

He joined her in laughter. "I don't know if I could hold out that long." Withholding details about Arsha from her had been his way of maintaining some semblance of control over himself, his emotions. He'd only managed to disappoint Arsha's memory, by defaming the very thing he had loved about her—her integrity.

He noticed Hope had gone quiet and sensed a peculiar eagerness in her deceptively calm demeanor as she couldn't keep her hands still. Hope didn't speak with her hands, but she had been—now she was squeezing them together. He was certain it was his fault, his wrong to right.

"Stone, there's—"

"I'm not in love with Arsha's ghost," he blurted. "But I can't forget her."

"Of course," Hope cried, her hands instantly flying to his face, cradling it between her hands. "I wouldn't want you to forget her. She's a big part of you."

"She had sickle cell anemia," he replied. "Sometimes the pain got so bad; nobody would believe how excruciating the pain could be. And she hated her dependency on the painkillers, the blood transfusions, the experimental treatments." He held on to Hope's wrists, restraining her hands on his face. "None of the promising new treatments helped," he rasped with embittered sarcasm. "The last time it got real bad," he said, feeling a vague sense of unreality as he clasped her wrists. "I had been called away to a drill site. The communications equipment malfunctioned, and the drillers needed the new set of surveys." His breathing labored in his chest, beads of perspiration dotted his forehead. "When I got back into town, she was in the hospital''—his eyes absent, glazed. "She didn't know I was there. I begged her not to give up, to fight a little longer." He swallowed the lump in his throat, his head lowered and eyes closed briefly. "She never woke up."

"Stone," Hope called him softly. "Stone." Slowly he focused his eyes on her. "It wasn't your fault. It wasn't anybody's fault."

How long had he waited for absolution? Coming from Hope, it seemed to free him from his terrible, irrational guilt. His eyes focused, and he stared into her exquisite face, her olive eyes, radiant and warm with welcome in their almond shape. "Thank you," he said.

"She must have been some lady," Hope whispered with admiration in her voice, smiling up at him.

"What makes you say that? I've given you only a piece of her life," Stone replied.

"She was loved by you," Hope replied, "and that alone is enough to make her special."

Stone trembled visibly, affected by another calling, a sweet solemn, ancient feeling coursing through his blood. He noted surprise flash across her face when his arms snaked around her waist, pulling her close to him. Then a mirror of his aroused state brightened her expression, and he lowered his head to touch her lips with his.

It began as a light, questing kiss that quickly evolved, deepening, when her lips parted in a tantalizing invitation for more. Her gentle hands entwined and stroking the back of his neck, his senses throbbed with the soft feel and sweet scent of her, lighting a fire through every nerve in his body.

When he lifted his head, at last, reluctantly, he still felt the breathless wonder of a first kiss. She looked up at him with a luscious glaze coating her eyes.

"You better stop that right now, or we'll never get out of here," he threatened, his deep voice husky and sensual.

Within the blink of an eye, her expression changed. Every trace of the previous delight drained from her face. She lifted her forehead from his chest and looked up at him, a vulnerable sheen in her eyes. She opened her mouth to speak, then swallowed, but couldn't get the words out.

"What is it?" Stone demanded, his brow arched in a frown. "Did I do something wrong?" he asked anxiously. That Faraha hadn't appeared increased his uneasiness. "Where's Faraha?" He didn't give Hope a chance to answer. He walked around her, bolting into the family room.

Faraha was sitting gentlemanly in the recliner, still as a statue, hands folded in his lap, quiet and solemn like the introvert he wasn't. Even though he could discern no immediate danger, Stone knew something was dreadfully wrong.

"You can't smoke in here," Faraha shouted belligerently. "My mama don't let nobody smoke in our house."

Puzzled, Stone frowned as he advanced into the room to see whom Faraha was talking to. It was then that he spotted the strange man emerging from the kitchen, stepping into the dining area. It was also when Faraha noticed him.

"Stone!" Faraha scooted out of the recliner and raced to be scooped up into his arms. "What took you so long?" he demanded, squeezing his neck with a tight embrace.

"I'm sorry," Stone apologized, kissing the side of Faraha's face.

There was a sense of routine in the gesture, but Stone never once lost visual contact with the stranger. They eyed each other like wary combatants. The man stood a little taller than six feet, with a model-pretty face and slim, muscular build. He was fashionably dressed. Stone didn't know designer names, but expensive flashed like a neon sign from his tailor-cut, wool, sooty-gray suit.

"No wonder my son doesn't know who I am. You got another nig—" The man cut himself off, pocketing his gold lighter.

So this was Tyrone Herrington, Stone mused with prejudice. It was evident Hope was not going to perform the honor of an introduction. A quick glance over his shoulder showed she was hugging the door frame, her expression painfully neutral. He introduced himself. "Stone Henderson."

Tyrone stared fractionally at him before he replied. "I'm ha's father. Tyrone Herrington," he said with importance.

"What brings you to Houston, Tyrone?" Stone asked.

"I came to see my son," Tyrone replied, as if his presence was evident.

After a five-year absence? Stone wanted to ask, but didn't for Faraha's sake. Likewise, he was concerned about Hope's behavior. He didn't want to speculate on what she was feeling or thinking, but he was upset that she hadn't thrown Herrington out before now. The man had no legal rights whatsoever, regardless of his reason for dropping in unexpectedly. Certainly she knew that.

"We're on our way out," Stone said firm, inarguably. Fatherly visit or not, Tyrone was not going to disrupt their plans this evening, or any other. "Perhaps you'd like to come back another time."

"Didn't you hear what I said?" Tyrone demanded.

Stone knew something else about Tyrone not evident in his appearance, but rather in his attitude. In addition to being a deadbeat father, he was spoiled and used to having his way, as if the world owed him something. He set Faraha on the floor.

"Go get your coat." He shooed the boy off in the direction of his room. "Hope, are you about ready yet?"

"Just give me a few more minutes," she replied in a barely audible voice.

Before she could move, Tyrone did. He advanced menacingly, ranting, "I came all the way from California to see my son, and you're not going to stop me."

Stone stood straight, yet relaxed and casual looking, his capacity to inflict pain contained within him. He could feel his sinews rumble in the blood flowing through his veins like the rapids. Though he doubted violence would be necessary, he would relish the opportunity to serve justice up to Faraha and Hope.

Tyrone had the wherewithal to stop several feet away. He turned his glowering, fiendish look on Hope, who'd moved to stand inches from Stone's left shoulder.

"Call first next time," Stone said.

The veins twitched angrily in Tyrone's face. Wordless, he

spun from them, snatched a long camel coat from the couch, and draped it across his arm.

"I want my son, Hope," he said harshly, shaking a finger in her face. Then he bolted from the room.

Seconds later Stone heard the front door slam shut. He was alone in the room, for Hope, too, had walked out. He blew the air from his ballooned cheeks. He felt as if he'd had a victory nullified.

It was a beautiful, clear, cold night. Stars twinkled in the blue-black skies; Christmas carols filled the air. City Hall was surrounded by thousands who'd come out for the annual tree-lighting ceremony. But Hope couldn't enjoy the warmth of the occasion.

With so many people around, she kept keen, vigilant eyes on Faraha. He was sitting with his friends in a section that had been roped off near the reflection pool. Stone had arranged it, though she didn't know how.

Attempts to warm up by blowing into her gloved hands and patting her shoulders were futile. Tyrone had put a decided chill in her bones. His unexpected appearance reeked of an implied threat. She couldn't shake the sense of foreboding that he was serious about taking Faraha from her.

A choir from one of the local churches was onstage singing "Silent Night." Her thoughts of danger couldn't be stilled, and she couldn't count on Stone for protection against the cold. He was one of the chaperones for this excursion, but she'd lost sight of him in the crowd.

She took her eyes off Faraha for only a second to scan the crowd, as if expecting Tyrone to pop out from one of the pockets of people who gathered close to keep warm from the cold. But faces were mostly outlines in the dark.

She returned her attention to Faraha. If she didn't get control over her thoughts, she would be a basket case before night's end, she warned herself. And it was still early.

"Hmm . . . you're wearing peaches tonight. I like this better the sesame."

Hope jumped instinctively. Her nerves took off in flight. But the cocoon of a hard, familiar body and strong arms enveloping her like a magnificent quilt quickly soothed her startled senses. Her pulse eased into a familiar rhythm, and she relaxed into the pillar of warmth at her back, reveling in the sense of protection she felt.

"I didn't think you noticed," she said softly, a smile in her voice.

"Hope, there's very little about you that escapes my notice," Stone replied with a chuckle.

His deep rumbling voice and the whisper of his breath on her cheek released a cascade of sensuous sensations in her. "Ditto," she said, with a shudder of delight.

"Oh, yeah?" he replied, his arms tightening gently around her. "What have you noticed about me?"

"You seem to have changed," she said shyly. She recalled the unexpected kiss that had awakened and set her dormant sexuality on fire. In spite of all that had happened, desire continued to simmer in her blood. "You're more talkative than usual. There's flattery on your tongue."

"That's because I've made a decision," he said.

"Oh?" she said, angling her head to look into his face. She felt eager tremors of delight as she studied the look of warm regard in his expression. "What decision would that be?"

"About what I want." His voice was calm, his gaze steady.

"And that is?" she asked in a broken whisper.

"You," he said with quiet emphasis.

The underlying sensuality of his reply sent Hope's spirits soaring. Her common sense skittered into the shadows.

The crowd erupted into applause, the choir began to leave the stage, and Santa announced the guests of honor. The mayor and his wife, waiting in the wings, promptly appeared onstage.

Hope neither heard nor saw any of the program's goings-on, for she was living out her fantasy, wrapped in Stone's stone arms, cradled next to him in a tempered bear hug. His heartbeat thudded against her bosom, a sound as sweet as song, as she familiarized herself with the dark velvet recesses of his mouth.

The skies suddenly erupted in a fit of sights and sounds. The night lit up under a colorful bevy of lights as gunpowder from firecrackers perfumed the air. Jolted into dismay, Hope sprang back from Stone, her gaze anxiously seeking out Faraha.

"I have my eyes on him. He's okay," Stone said soothingly over the loud noises, stroking her back.

Hope couldn't believe she'd gotten so carried away that she turned her back on her child. It wouldn't happen again, she vowed.

"Don't worry about Tyrone," Stone was saying. "I'm not going to let him take Faraha . . ."

The trees surrounding City Hall lit up, and the crowd responded jubilantly, blocking out Stone's voice. Hope thought he'd tacked on "from us," but the words were lost, the mood shattered.

Thoughts of what Tyrone was up to accompanied them to the restaurant. Faraha was beside himself with delight on learning they were going to sit in a section that boasted a huge stone fireplace. Stone was not pleased by her behavior, she knew, but with Tyrone on the loose, a jolly mood was not on her agenda.

As the waiter was seating them, Faraha noticed a couple sitting four tables away. "Mama, there's Nanny and Uncle Solomon," he said, not waiting for permission to dash off.

She and Stone followed. He stood by silently as hugs and kisses were performed, then Monique did the introductions.

"Stone, this is my husband, Solomon Thomas. Honey, this is Stone Henderson."

The introduction complete, Monique orchestrated the seating arrangements. They were to share her and Solomon's table. Though not as close to the fireplace as Faraha would have liked, the camaraderie of male company won out. After their orders were placed, Hope excused herself to go to the ladies' room. Monique waddled along.

"Okay, I can see Faraha's happy, but you and Stone look a little pink around the edges," Monique said, after checking the stalls to assure they were alone. She leaned against a face bowl. "What gives?"

"Tyrone," Hope replied. She stood before another face bowl and turned on the faucet. She screeched when the cold water hit her hands.

"Tyrone?" Monique echoed, bemused. "What does he have to do with you and Stone?"

"He's in town," Hope explained. The water now warm, she began to wash her hands. "He came by the house tonight."

"For what?"

"Faraha."

"What does he want?" Monique asked insistently.

"Faraha," Hope snapped. She took out her anger on the faucet as she turned off the water. Her hands dripping, she walked to the towel rack on the wall to dry them. "He claims he wants his son," she added in a teeth-gnashing tone.

Monique rolled her eyes. "Oh, pooh," she declared, flicking her hand in a dissuasive gesture.

She agreed with Monique about one thing, she thought. Tyrone's sudden streak of paternalism stank. After five years of absence, it seemed highly unlikely that he wanted Faraha.

"Girl, please. I can't believe you're getting all worked up over nothing," Monique continued. "Even if that's what he wants, it won't happen. He abandoned you and Faraha, paid no child support, and visited him only one time when he was a baby."

True, Hope thought, one wouldn't think Tyrone had a legal leg to stand on, that no self-respecting judge would grant him custody, or even visitation rights. But stranger things had happened in today's courtrooms. Still she knew something else about Tyrone that she'd made the mistake of overlooking before.

"Monique, you're not paying attention," Hope said, her expression pained, frustration in her voice. "Tyrone just doesn't do things impulsively. That is not his way," she said. Even though things may seem that way initially, she mused with certainty.

"Okay, calm down. What did he say exactly?" Monique asked patiently.

"He's thinking about taking a job in Houston and wants to get acquainted with Faraha," Hope replied.

"The first I can buy, but the second, no way," Monique quipped. "He may want a job, but after five years, he does not want a kid," she said emphatically.

"The first one I definitely will not buy," Hope retorted vehemently. "As for the second, I only know he's up to something. Houston is not the big television market Tyrone aspires to work in. Atlanta, maybe; New York, definitely. But not Houston," she said, shaking her head.

Monique drew a deep breath. "Okay," she said pensively, biting down on her bottom lip. "I can see telling you not to worry won't work. So, tomorrow morning, first thing, we're going to see an attorney."

Hope expelled a harsh sound of disbelief. "What attorney works on a Saturday morning?"

"Mine will, if I call him," Monique replied confidently. "Then we'll go pick up your dress for tomorrow night."

Hope frowned. "Tomorrow night?"

"Hel-lo," Monique said rhythmically, snapping her fingers in Hope's face. "Stone's company Christmas party."

"Oh, man, I had forgotten," Hope exclaimed, rubbing her forehead.

"Girl, don't let Tyrone back in your life under any circumstances. He's not worth the worry you're doing, and he's certainly not important enough to push Stone aside for," Monique warned, concern etched in the frown lines on her face.

Hope felt Monique's gaze and even suspected what her friend was thinking. But her brain was close to short-circuiting already. Between Tyrone's sudden appearance, Stone's implied commitment out of the blue, and feelings she could no longer deny, her head was spinning. She needed time and space to sort these things out, but first and foremost was making sure she didn't lose her child.

# Chapter Seven

Who knew what was in a man's mind?

Stone pondered the answer for himself, as well as Herrington. He was standing before the well-dressed tree in Hope's small living room. Tiny bulbs winked in the dark: red, gold, blue, and white lights reflected in his eyes.

To say he resented Faraha's biological father was an understatement. He wondered why a man would come back for the child he abandoned. A sudden bout of conscience? After five years, not likely, he thought, snorting disbelief. Maybe Herrington needed Faraha for health reasons. But why not say that?

Stone passed a frustrated hand across his face. He recalled that Hope had been uncharacteristically skittish and distracted ever since Herrington showed up. He, too, was frightened by his sudden appearance, concerned about the effect of his presence on him and Hope.

She was a loving, attractive, and intelligent woman, and he more than wanted her each time he saw her. He knew she was attracted to him. He'd even go so far as to say that she liked him more than a little bit.

He also knew she was scared of losing her child. There were no limits to what she would do to keep Faraha. Going back to

Herrington was not an option he could overlook, for he had done nothing to assure it wouldn't happen, he mused.

His action, or lack thereof in that regard, brought him full circle to the question, his own doubts and insecurities. A wounded expression on his face, his mind twisted. He felt as if he were trying to free himself from a tangle of angel hair.

He'd known Hope for only a little over two weeks. Despite the qualities that attracted him to her in the first place, he felt another set of feelings for her that he hadn't for Arsha. He knew he had loved Arsha, but with Hope, he aspired to be perfect.

Was he being sensible, or a coward? he wondered, blowing the air from his cheeks.

Regardless how irrational his feelings were, he wanted to be the one thing she could count on, like the sun rising and setting every day. He wanted to be the one that put the sparkle in her eyes, to be her first thought in the morning and her last at night. He wanted to be all things perfect for her that were not in the realm of human possibility.

"A penny for your thoughts."

The frown on Stone's face fell. A smile turned up the corners of his mouth as he turned to see Hope standing in the doorway. She took one step into the living room toward him, and electrical sparks pricked his flesh.

He couldn't believe his luck in finding her after all his years of a lonely existence. He wondered if Arsha's ghost hadn't brought her to him.

He could almost feel her femininity responding to him when she stood an arm's length away. Her eyes glowed as bright and beautiful as the lights on the tree. Here, with a thread of mellow tension between them, under the sweet melody of silence, he felt compelled to finish the story of him and Arsha.

"We met at an environmental convention in D.C., in 1991, and dated for two years off and on before we got married," he began. "She was as cautious as I was, if not more so." He chuckled lightly. "Every time the question of marriage came up, we imposed distance with excuses or sometimes physical separation."

It had taken time to get to know one another. Though both were often called on to make presentations in their work—she was an environmental lawyer with the EPA—they became "uncannily word-shy around each other," he admitted sheepishly.

But they came around eventually. "She confessed her fear of dying on a loved one because of her disease." His parents' marriage had made him leery, but he wanted her despite the disease's clock. "New discoveries were being made every day. There was the possibility of robbing old man death." He chortled with a hint of self-derision in his expression.

They married on Valentine's Day, February 14, 1993. "The disease won in October 1995," he finished solemnly.

Her face was wet when he focused his gaze on her. He dried her eyes, one at a time, using a finger in a featherlike touch. They were sitting on the floor, with their backs against the couch, facing the tree.

"Don't cry for Arsha," he said, feeling a sense of tremendous relief. "She's not in pain anymore." He took Hope's soft hand in his. "I want to be able to celebrate her life now." *And cheer her for bringing you to me.* "Did Faraha wake up as you suspected?" he asked, changing the subject. She had left him to put Faraha, who'd fallen asleep on the ride home, to bed on their return from dinner.

"Barely a peep," she replied, soft mirth in her tone. "Did I remember to say thank you?"

He turned to face her fully. Her vulnerability showed. His desires increased and coalesced into a frightening mixture of tenderness and sexual need. He swallowed tightly before he asked, "For what?"

"A number of things. Being there, being patient," she added with a slightly mocking chuckle. "I let Tyrone get the best of me, I'm afraid, and I'm sorry."

"You don't have to apologize," he replied. "You were worried about your son. That's understandable. But I meant what I said." *He just didn't know how he meant it yet.*

Stone didn't know who moved first, but the contact of Hope pressed against his body set off explosive charges in him. She sighed, surrendering in his arms. He had no intention of quitting, or losing her to Herrington, he thought—common sense be damned. He smothered her mouth with his, kissed her like a man who'd gone without sustenance for days on end.

No, she wasn't his yet. But Arsha had done her part. The rest was up to him. Her hands began to explore him—his clothes became offensive to him. Fueled by her tiny sighs signaling her want, he wanted to feel her touch on his flesh, as surely as he felt her in his senses.

Somehow. Forever and always.

Saturday arrived with a cheerful fervor. Hope felt a sweet awaiting in the air. It could have been Christmas Day, except it had been hard leaving her bed this morning—as difficult as letting Stone go last night. Under his persuasive mouth, she had felt like a dangling string of desire. One good yank, or "yes" from his lips, and they would have tested the new queen-size bed she'd bought. Had it not been for his strong sense of propriety, all her pent-up prurient interests would have spilled out in that bed.

With her hands sticking out from long billowing sleeves of a shiny white, caftan-like gown, Hope blushed just thinking of Faraha walking in on them. She appreciated Stone's circumspection, for her son usually awakened early on Saturday mornings. This one had been no different. He'd come to her room bright and early.

"Mama, do you wish Stone was my daddy?"

The question was still with her, hours after her meeting with Aurelius Redmon, the attorney recommended to her by Monique. She was breathing a little easier now, while Badu, the Ghanaian dressmaker, put the finishing touches on her gown for tonight. Monique was browsing somewhere within the African dress shop.

"Turn to your left a little," Badu instructed. He was kneeling at her feet, tacking the hem with pins.

She had lied to Faraha, she recalled, pivoting as if on a motorized pedal. But it was only half a lie, she rationalized.

"No, then I wouldn't have had a sweet little boy like you," she had replied. Faraha had been pleased by her response and paid no attention to the slip of her tongue when she called him a "little boy."

His father was not what he expected. Tyrone had managed to frighten him as surely as he'd put terror into her. She felt badly for her son, but not for his father's loss.

The attorney confirmed what she suspected but feared believing. She felt fairly confident now that Tyrone wouldn't have the patience to withstand the legal procedures necessary to get custody of Faraha. There were petitions to file, paternity to establish, blood tests to arrange, and more court dates to file more petitions.

It was no overnight process. The red tape would tie him up endlessly. She would ensure that he went through every step of inconvenience there was associated with giving up her child—*if* he truly wanted Faraha.

She didn't want to think about what she would do if he proved sincere in his desires to take Faraha from her, she thought with a shudder. An errant pin stuck her flesh, and she cried out.

"Sorry," Badu said. "Okay, what do you think?" he asked, sitting back to observe her in his creation.

Hope faced her reflection in the long mirror, looking at herself from one side, then the other. The gown was gorgeous. Silky to the touch, it had a low, slightly rounded neckline. Gold and turquoise embroidery in a design of myriad ankhs pressed against the bodice and cinched at her waistline, flowing with bold, graceful pleats that fell to the floor. A matching cape with lining in white, boasting the same embroidered pattern at the collar that clasped at the neck, hung on a mannequin near the small fitting room.

"I like it," she said, wondering about Stone's reaction. Recalling the look in his eyes last night, he'd want her if she wore a croaker sack. She shivered imperceptibly. He'd be pleased nonetheless.

"Then let me have it."

Hope walked into the adjacent room to change, pulling the

curtain closed behind her. She began removing the gown to change into her street clothes.

"Do you have shoes to go with the gown?" Monique asked from the other side of the curtain.

"Black will do," she replied, still dressing. The most important matters had been taken care of, she mused. Ariana was going to baby-sit; Stone would give her his pager number in case of an emergency, and they'd take his portable phone to the party.

"That's what I thought," Monique replied with a tsk. "We need to find you an appropriate pair of shoes and a few other accessories."

"I'd rather be with Faraha and Ariana," she said, emerging from the room fully dressed, with the gown across her arm. They'd gone to the community center to deliver the Blake family gifts and frolic in the snow that was to have been brought in for the children.

"I'm sure you would," Monique replied cheekily. "But you'll thank me later after Stone gets a look at you tonight."

"It's going to take me only a few minutes to do this," Badu said. Having taken the gown from Hope, he was adjusting it in line with the needle on his sewing machine.

Hope exchanged a look with Monique that said they both knew a few minutes meant a few hours. Badu's clock was different.

Anticipation was his middle name now. His body had been rock hard ever since he tore himself away from Hope last night. Stone felt the tension even now, standing in the dressing room with only his underwear on and risque thoughts dashing through his mind. He'd come to have the final touches to his black tux for tonight—there'd been a problem with the crotch.

He opened the dressing room door following a knock. The tailor, a sword-thin Vietnamese, stood there, holding out black tuxedo pants, a tape measure wrapped around his thin shoulders.

"You try now," he instructed, handing over the pants to Stone.

Dennis appeared in the mirror behind Stone as he pulled up his pants. His brother towered over the tailor.

"Dennis, camp out at one of your lady friend's tonight," Stone said, zipping up his pants. Ever since Dennis started remodeling his home, he slept over nights in his guest room.

"Why?"

Stone angled from the mirror to look Dennis squarely in the face. "You really need me to answer that?" Turning back to the mirror, he buttoned the pants. He and Dennis had become quite chummy the past couple of weeks, more than in all the years of their youth.

"Stoney man, don't be so cheap," Dennis chided him. "Get a room at a swanky hotel. Isn't the party going to be at the Four Seasons? Do it up right."

Had Dennis changed, or were the changes all from him? Stone wondered, inspecting the pants fit. His fleeting curiosity led his thoughts to Tyrone Herrington. A leopard does not change spots, he decided, fully intending to thwart whatever the man was up to. Letting those thoughts go for now, he began to carefully consider Dennis's suggestion.

"She might be too embarrassed to stay at the same hotel," he considered aloud.

"Make reservations at another one. Or," he added grudgingly, "put a bottle of champagne on ice at the condo just in case." He was clearly not pleased by that idea. "Now a friend of mine owns a fleet of limousines," he continued, not giving Stone a chance to change his mind. "I hooked you up for one tonight."

"A limousine?" Stone echoed, then quickly held up his hand like a traffic cop to stop the complaint forthcoming from Dennis. "All right, all right," he acquiesced. Hope deserved every amenity he could provide. Maybe the Christmas season was just mellowing him out.

The rest of the day passed like a wonderland fairy tale to Hope, with no end in sight. The approval in Stone's eyes when he picked her up heightened her enthusiasm even more. The way he looked in his black tux fueled the tremors of anticipation she felt for the evening. Their carriage, a white limousine with driver, carted them off to the Christmas Party at the Four Seasons Hotel, where excellent food, live entertainment, and fun awaited them.

If Stone knew her childhood fantasy, he didn't say. He just gave it to her. Hope felt like Cinderella at the ball. Only there was no chance of her becoming anything else at midnight but Stone's lover.

They left the party then: It was a foregone conclusion that she wasn't going back home tonight. Offered a choice between a luxurious suite at the hotel, or his home for a nightcap, she chose his bed.

The rest of the night began with a scorching kiss at the front door. It had begun on the dance floor for Hope. The firmness of his body pressed against hers, swaying with the flow of his movements, stoked the fire that was burning inside her. She had wanted then the way it was between them now.

His black tux and her white gown led the parade of clothes left behind on an intimate route that started at the bottom landing and ended up in his bedroom. There the fairy tale continued, pushing back reality. The shadows of the night held no thoughts of Faraha or Tyrone. Here only the sounds and sensations of passion and pleasure reigned.

There was tender, and then there was tender. Having waited, lived so long for this moment, Hope and Stone fell into bed like sex-starved mendicants. There weren't any secret spots to uncover, for every nerve ending was primed for the promise of satisfaction they gave each other.

She felt his heat, his strength, and his tenderness. He was extraordinarily sensual, and she couldn't get enough of him. Possessed. That's what she was. Driven to touch him, to taste him, to consume his essence until she was filled to overflowing.

He touched her hair lightly. Traced the features of her face down to her bosom, lightly. He stole her breath away with his kiss, light as a feather, more potent than fire. Her heart pounded harder, and her blood rushed faster under the mastery of his soul-searching kisses and hot, passionate caresses.

He put on a condom, then straddled her to began the sweet torture all over again. He suckled at her breasts, teasing her nipples with his tongue. He stroked her flesh—down between her breasts, over her belly, along her thighs—exploring, memorizing her with his hands, pressing onward to torment the throbbing between her legs. More than once, her breath caught in her throat. He treasured her there until she was thrashing wildly on the big bed, and whimpers of pure need were siphoned from the depths of her. Then he was inside her, and she cried out at his possession—a slow, methodical penetration that reached clear to her soul.

She thought she knew of the passions within her. But nothing like this—sensations so filling, so hot, so euphoric. She felt them all for the first time. Senseless and all-feeling, she arched passionately to meet him, trembling with each stroke of his possession. Moments before ecstasy exploded all around her, she wished the rapture would never end. Her cries of joy enjoined with the guttural sound from him. She lay stunned and paralyzed beneath Stone, whose harsh breathing matched her own.

Stone hugged her endearingly, savoring the last of his pleasure. He was in a kind of dazed shock. Nothing in his life had prepared him for the wondrous feelings he was having now.

He rolled to her, pulled the covers over them, and tucked her into his side. He waited for his breathing to return to normal before he spoke. "What are you thinking?" His voice held a breathless wonder. He'd begun to wonder what he had done to deserve this . . . this indescribable but utterly fulfilling moment.

Hope squeezed him tightly with her gentle touch before she spoke. "That you are absolutely wonderful," she replied, her voice soft with awe and a smile in the dark.

"Is that a specific performance rating or in general?" he asked laughingly.

Laughter preceded her reply. "Begging for compliments?"

"No, I just want to be sure you're all right," he said. He'd realized the moment he entered her that she hadn't been with a man for quite some time. He shivered just thinking about her warm, tight treasure that had awaited him. In answer, she rose slightly to kiss him tenderly on the mouth.

"I'll be sore tomorrow, however," she added with jest in her voice as she resettled next to him.

A pregnant pause lingered in the air between them, a comfortable silence that would hold spoken thoughts.

"I never dreamed big," Stone said with amazement in his voice, feeling his way around words. "You know, like some kids wanted a million dollars, or like my brother who wanted to become a superstar athlete."

"I don't believe you," she said with disbelief.

"Huh?"

"A black man with a Ph.D. in a field African Americans hardly ever go into, and you're not a big dreamer," she said, mocking disbelief in her voice. "Give me a break."

"I never thought of it like a big dream," he replied pensively. "I mean, that was a survival thing. Like getting the equipment you need to have in order to do a good job."

"You are too humble for your own good," she said with admiration in her voice. "If the right people knew of your existence, you'd be paraded around like a poster boy during Black History Month, a role model for black youth. I know some people who wouldn't pass up such an opportunity to have accolades heaped on their head."

He squeezed her affectionately. "I don't need accolades, I have what I want right here. You're all I dreamed of, and then some," he added, his voice deepening with thought. As if talking to himself, he admitted aloud, "I never realized it until now." He knew he'd been given something truly wonderful, and he never wanted to lose it. "I want you and Faraha in my life. I want to take care of you."

"Oh, Stone, that's so sweet of you," she said, cuddling closer to him.

"You don't understand, and I see I'm not making a good case for myself. I want you to move in." He felt her stiffen next to him and misinterpreted her sudden stillness. "Faraha, too, of course. I want to be a father to him. " He felt her fidgeting about. "What are you doing?"

"I'm looking for the light," she replied.

Stone reached over his head in the center of the bed, and a soft white light in the headboard lit the bed. Hope had moved away from him, the covers bunched up to her neck. She was staring intensely at him.

"Now let me see if I understand this," she said, wetting her lips as if nervous. "You want us to move into your place? Here?"—pointing toward the bed with emphasis.

"Yes, you saw the rest of the condo," he replied. "It's more than big enough for the three of us."

"You're serious, aren't you?" she asked, then answered herself from what she saw in his expression. "You are serious."

Stone sat up, placing a pillow at his back. "I am very serious."

"Stone, that's . . ." she stammered. "I don't know what to say. I never expected this."

"You can't tell me you don't have any feelings for me," he said with eminent reasonableness. "You don't sleep around casually, for one."

"And two?"

She was looking at him from down her slender nose, so he knew right away that he'd offended her even though it was the truth. He also suspected that his suggestion was too soon for her. It was a little soon for him, too, but time was not on his side. "I want to take care of you and Faraha."

"I don't need you to take care of me and my son," she retorted. "We've been doing quite well, thank you," she added sarcastically.

"Of course you have," he said, placating her. Perplexed by her behavior, he knew only that this wasn't going the way he intended. Though it appeared to be a spur of the moment decision, he realized it was where he'd been headed all along, even when he attempted to run away from it. "I already know you can. That's not the issue." He'd never felt more right about anything in his life. "I want to take care of you. I want us to be a family."

She just sat there, staring at him as if he'd suddenly grown horns, or something. He didn't understand her objection to marrying him, and his temper flared.

"It's him, isn't it?"

"Him?" she asked, puzzled.

"Herrington," he said in a growl, ignoring the silent taunt that her ex-lover had spurred his offer. "You want him back, don't you?"

"What?" she yelled. "I don't know how you came up with that. I can't believe it. You may be a good geologist, but you can't add."

"It's fairly easy to figure," he snapped. "Why haven't you been to bed with a man in all this time?"

"You've got all the answers, you tell me."

But she wasn't waiting for his answer. She struggled out of bed, the comforter twisted around her body. "What are you doing now?" he demanded, when she dropped to the floor, disappearing from sight.

"Looking for my clothes," she replied sharply. She stood with one hand clutching the comforter around her, and her panties and bra in the other. "Where's the bathroom?"

"Hope?" he said imploringly.

"I'll be dressed in a minute, then you can take me home," she said, walking out of the room without waiting for directions, leaving Stone alone with a familiar wretchedness.

# Chapter Eight

"I'm sorry. I know that's not good enough to make up for my behavior. But . . . it's all I know to say."

He was the picture of contrition. If he'd been on the silver screen, making this apology, the actress would have fallen all over herself accepting it. But this wasn't the silver screen, and the apology was just an act. He was right about one thing—there was nothing he could ever say to make up for the way he'd treated her and Faraha.

"I want you out of my house, Tyrone," Hope said. Her voice was flat. She looked vacant, spent, all emotions gone like broken Christmas toys. The door was open, her hand was on the knob. She had been about to run out to buy some eggnog. She didn't normally consume hard liquor, but intended to indulge her misery in the bottle of Remy Martin Monique had given her.

She had been staying with the Thomases since that horrible breakup with Stone, needing them as a buffer. She didn't want Faraha to see her as she really felt—fooling him would have been out of the question. They had helped keep him so occupied that he didn't have time to notice or ask why her eyes were so red and puffy. It hadn't, however, stopped him from asking about Stone. They all had a time of it, keeping him from calling Stone.

"Please, Hope, I really need to talk to you."

"Faraha is not here."

But she couldn't stay away from home forever. Faraha was staying with them a few more days, until Christmas Eve. She'd promised Monique she'd be better by then—all cried out for sure. She'd give herself twenty-four hours to expunge her anguish and get on with her life.

"I know," Tyrone replied somberly. "It's you I need to speak to."

Hope led the way to the family room. She dropped onto the couch lethargically. She hadn't been home long enough to warm up the house, so it was cold, adding to her inner loneliness.

"What do you want to say to me, Tyrone? You can't take Faraha from me." There was no pleading in her tone, a confident dare in the look she shot him from her sidelong glance.

He assessed her quietly, then sadness singed his expression. He removed his coat and tossed it onto the recliner before he spoke.

"I know I acted a plum fool the other day," he began, his tone and demeanor rueful. He sat on the edge of the recliner, uncaring about wrinkling his coat. "It's just that, well ... I got this letter, and it got to me, you know. My wife read it, too." He chortled with self-derision. "She stopped talking to me, after she called me a sorry you-know-what. But I didn't need her to tell me that. Damn, Hope!" He sprang up to walk across the room to look out the sliding glass doors to the backyard. "It's just that when I showed up the other day, and he didn't even recognize my face, and then your boyfriend showed up and he jumped in his arms like that," he said with a snap of his fingers, spinning to face her with a wounded expression. "I know that's no excuse," he said tiredly, passing a hand across his head. "I'm not even going there, especially with you. I messed up with Faraha real bad. I didn't mean to scare him like that." He turned, facing her, pulling an envelope from his Italian suit coat pocket. "I didn't mean to scare you, either." He sighed deeply, withdrew a letter, and passed it to her. "Read it."

Wondering what Tyrone was up to this time, Hope simply stared at him.

"I'm not going to try and take Faraha from you," he said as if to encourage her to accept the letter.

She accepted the letter this time, unfolded it slowly. Surprise flashed across her face the instant she saw the handwriting. It was Faraha's youthful script, with big letters that almost fell within the wide spaces of a sheet of writing paper. It was properly headed with their address and dated the first of December. Some of the words were misspelled, but the meaning was clear.

It began, *"Dear Daddy"* Hope corrected the misspelled words as she read: *"My teacher said we had to write a letter to somebody. I see Mama all the time. I'm suppose to tell you something important, but I don't have anything important to say to you. But I have to write this letter and mail it, or my teacher will tell Mama, and I'll get in trouble. I know why you hate me, cause you hate yourself. This is all I have to write. I know you're not going to answer. But that's okay, cause I'm not your son anymore"*

It was simply signed, *"Faraha Ellison."*

Hope didn't realize she was crying until her tears fell onto the well-read page. She cried for her son, her little boy, her "man-child." She had no idea just how deep his suffering over his father's rejection, and to realize he'd no longer have Stone . . . She pressed a hand to her mouth, her clamped lips imprisoning a sob. As she returned the letter to Tyrone's outstretched hand, she noticed him wipe his face.

"I know now is not a good time, after the way I acted," he said, his voice quivering. He cleared his throat. "But I do want to see him sometimes in the near future."


"I'm afraid this ticket is nonrefundable, Mr. Henderson. Now, if you'd like . . ."

Before the airline clerk could enumerate the conditions under which to make use of the round-trip ticket to the Bahamas, Stone walked off. He adjusted the small suitcase in his grip and followed the arrows to exit the Mickey Leland Terminal for international flights at Houston Intercontinental Airport.

He'd had enough rejection for a lifetime. This one was just another in a long line of troubles he'd brought on himself, he thought.

He realized now that the remark about Herrington had been a stupid thing to say. But he couldn't take it back. Hope wouldn't even give him a chance to.

He'd tried reaching her, to no avail. Her answering machine picked up every time he had called. None of his messages were returned. He'd gone to the drugstore only to be told that she was on vacation until the fifth of the new year. He'd tracked her friend, Monique Thomas, who promised to tell her to call him. She hadn't. As a last-ditch attempt, he drove by her house. Her car wasn't out in the driveway, and if she was home, she didn't answer the door. He'd blown it.

Hopeless, both of them, he mused. He didn't know what to do with himself. Getting angry hadn't helped. It only caused him a wasted trip to the airport. He had fully intended getting on that plane when he arrived. But he couldn't do it. His heart wasn't in it. He'd lost his heart.


Tyrone left, and Hope was alone again, warming that same spot on the couch. The room was beginning to thaw, but her insides were colder than ever. She didn't have the heart to move, bearing the cold silence like penitence.

In her hand was an envelope which contained a cashier's check worth five years of child support. Tyrone insisted she keep it to use any way she wanted. He'd also left a gift for Faraha and a stack of calling cards for his son to call him. He promised to be acessible this time. Then he left, but not before he begged her forgiveness, an apology just to her.

She was surprised by how easily she forgave Tyrone. It could be that easy with Stone, even more so, she told herself—even though he misjudged her so badly and hurt her even more than Tyrone had.

She had been merely charmed and fascinated by Tyrone. She knew that now, since with Stone she had learned what love really was. How many times had she run to the phone to call him, to accept him on whatever level he was willing to give, ready to forsake her hard-won independence. It meant nothing now that she didn't have Stone.

*That's what love is,* Hope thought, as she rose from the couch. Her feet moved her to the kitchen, and the phone, there on the wall. *Love knew no compromise, had no bounds or limits.* She stared at the phone, then closed her eyes with a painful realization.

Today was the twenty-third—the day of Stone's departure for the Bahamas. She didn't know what time his flight was scheduled to leave, but she figured he was already at the airport.

Woodenly she walked to her bedroom. Recently decorated, it reflected a woman's taste, calm in character with flashes of fun in the accessories. The new furniture held its just-off-the-showroom-floor scent. But the room was freezing—it felt as empty as she did.

What a hell of a Christmas present she'd gotten, she thought, as she fell across the bed and cried on her new silk sheets.


It was the morning of December twenty-fourth. With a picture of his bleak future engraved on his mind, Stone found himself wandering around the Galleria Shopping Center. Unconsciously he was hoping to find Hope here.

But he'd never find her here, he thought morosely. The center was packed with last-minute shoppers. Oblivious to the bumping and shoving he endured in their rush, he knew only that he had to think of a way to reclaim his heart, the joy Hope gave him.

There had been no woman of significance before her, he thought, looking at his past habits, hoping to find a clue there. No one would believe he'd been largely celibate by single men's standards for most of the three years since Arsha's death.

A well-paid woman here and there when he was out of the country was the extent of his sexual exploits.

On the rare occasion, when he did meet a woman with whom he could conceivably have a relationship, he inevitably found her lacking, unable to stand up against the goodness of Arsha.

With Hope, he realized woefully, he'd simply fallen back into his all too familiar pattern of pushing women away. He'd done it again, with the most important woman in his life. Now he had nothing to look forward to but years of emptiness. A zombie. That's what Dennis had called him. A man pretending to be alive.

He didn't know what to do with himself, how he was going to return to his former lonely existence before he'd been rolled over like an insignificant thing in the path of a mud slide. Nowhere to hide or run, but straight to Hope.

Didn't she know that? Couldn't she fathom what it had cost him to admit to those kinds of feelings? Didn't she know he wanted her in his life forever? Didn't she know those things?

*No, because you never told her.*

Stone swallowed his unwieldy despair. Maybe he should ask Dennis for advice, somebody with a more modern outlook about women, he chortled. But before he could completely cast aside the thought, his eyes glazed with the quick calculation going on in his mind.

Stone stopped in the middle of the passageway and looked around as if noting where he was for the first time. He was bumped by a harried shopper, whose "Excuse me," came after he'd been passed.

Stone hardly felt the jolt. He needed somebody younger all right, but it wasn't Dennis, he thought, spurred by the jockey of memory.

He could barely contain himself as he searched for the first exit. He hopped on the nearest elevator, nearly skipping up its steps, singing along with the song being piped throughout the center.

"Santa Claus is coming to town . . ."

\* \* \*

Christmas Eve was ending the way it started for Hope—with her heart open to an infinite sorrow and tears in her eyes. It had been four days, but who was counting, since ending her affair with Stone. She started to think romance, but it wasn't that, either.

Oh, Stone had courted her all right, unlocked door after door inside her until she let him in. But he wanted a possession, not a woman, a lover, a friend. Those were the things she wanted in a relationship, someone who would be an equal partner. The word *love* was never once mentioned. She had been reminding herself of these things like an epitaph. But she knew the refrain was but an excuse to ease her hurting.

"You missed a fantastic show last night," Monique said, trying to coax life from Hope.

She was unable to muster enthusiasm for even her basic need. She doubted she would have enjoyed herself at the Mistletoe Jam.

"I wish you and Faraha would come stay with us," Monique said, her tone a blend of pleading and exasperation.

Faraha had been returned by Monique as promised, only her promise hadn't been fulfilled, Hope mused morosely. Still weepy with grief, she added embarrassment and guilt. She couldn't take any more advantage of her friend's hospitality. She and Monique were standing in the entryway.

"I'm afraid to leave you alone."

Hope tried to laugh, but it was a pitiful sound. "Don't worry. I'm not going to do anything foolish," she said. "It's just going to take a little time, but I'm going to get over him." It would probably take a lifetime.

"Calling him is what you should do," Monique said. "You have to remember the man's been out of practice when it comes to women."

"He was married, remember," she quipped.

"Yeah, to a woman who knew him. She had him long enough to be able to read his thoughts and know what he was feeling without him having to say a word. You need time all right, but to think about how he made you feel. *If* you really love this man."

There were no ifs, ands, or buts about what she felt for Stone, Hope thought, as she waved good-bye to Monique from the door.

After locking up, she saw Faraha eyeing the Christmas tree speculatively. He must have stolen into the living room from the kitchen. She wondered if he had overheard their conversation, watching him count his presents. There were two exceptionally big gift-wrapped boxes with his name on them. One was from his father, the other from Stone. On top of the big one from Stone was a smaller one. All from him had been special-delivered earlier today.

"Mama, when did these come?"

Hope didn't pretend to misunderstand him. She knew he was referring to the gifts from Stone. "Today," she replied.

"I thought you said Stone went to the Bahamas."

In one of his calls home, under the guise of checking on her, he'd asked if Stone had called for him. She'd told him that Stone had left town as planned. "You knew he was leaving, Faraha," she said with reprimand in her tone.

"Well, if he went to the Bahamas, how could he bring these over today?"

She felt the sting of tears and knew she had to get away quickly, or she'd start bawling in front of her son. "A special mailman brought them, Faraha," she replied, her feet planning her escape. "Why don't you pour yourself a glass of eggnog. I'll be right back," she said, halfway down the hall.

"Okay," Faraha said absently. His gaze was on the small package from Stone. It was wrapped in shiny green paper with a red bow. Ideas were taking form in his mind. His eyes slid to the opening, his mouth pursed in deep thought. Keeping his eye on that opening, he slid one foot, then the other in the opposite direction, toward the kitchen. The phone was on the wall.

Faraha was sneaky quiet with his resolve. He climbed on the counter and dialed the number by rote.

\* \* \*

The night before Christmas, Hope's mind was heavy with memories of Stone. Sleep was long in coming, but when it claimed her, sweet and tender visions danced in her head.

Stone was everywhere her dreaming took her, and happiness stole into her subconscious. With warm fuzzy feelings guiding her dreams, all her friends joined the picture. In a setting of peaceful reverence, they were standing around the Christmas tree in a moment of prayer, so full of holiday cheer, she felt she'd burst with it.

Hope sighed, nestled deeper into her warm bed, listening to Faraha offer his thanks to God and Santa for his Christmas bounty.

Inexplicably she squirmed in her sleep. Something felt askew about the dream because she cracked open an eye, straining to hear.

She heard something all right, but it wasn't Faraha in prayer. And it couldn't be Santa, for she didn't put her present for Faraha under the tree until after she was sure he'd fallen asleep.

Slowly she sat up. The noise continued. It sounded like mice scampering around in the attic. The cold weather must have forced them to the shelter of her warm home, she thought groggily.

Then a giggle.

That was no mouse. Reluctantly she swung her feet to the floor. Glancing to look at the clock on the bedside table, she saw it was eleven-thirty, still a half hour before it was officially Christmas Day. She should have let Faraha open one of his gifts last night, she chided herself as she slipped her robe over her gown. She'd given up big T-shirts—and this black, see-through negligee, she'd intended to wear a week ago. Conscious of the dismal truth, she shook the reminder from her mind.

She tiptoed briskly to the hallway that opened into the living room and leaned just enough to peek in and catch her little "mouse" in the act.

When she did, intense astonishment touched her face, and a blissful thrill shivered through her senses.

There were two mice, freeing a box of its bicycle parts—it was the gift from Tyrone. With the lights from the tree and the kitchen as a backdrop, Stone was helping Faraha put it together.

With warm approval beaming out from her like the midnight star, she watched them for several moments in full, satisfying silence. Her eyes moved over Stone covetously as he worked with the efficiency and grace of one in total control. Her son imitated his confident manner. During that time, words lost their importance to her. She'd had flowery words from Tyrone once, but they had been meaningless.

"What are you two up to?" she asked. She felt lighthearted, pressed by delight as she strolled into the room.

Two heads turned simultaneously; twin "uh-oh" expressions faced her. Stone dropped the tools in his hands and crossed the distance to her instantly. For one anxious second his dark, soulful eyes searched her face. Finding welcome there, tenderly, his eyes melted into hers.

"I love you, Hope."

Hope cried out softly, a feeling of glorious joy sprang to her heart. Before she could speak, Stone clasped her hands together and held them against his chest.

"I haven't been good about saying the words, but the feelings are here," he said, pressing her hands against his chest with emphasis. "I've loved you, probably from that very first moment. I don't know. You've brought me so much joy."

The beat of his thudding heart shot up her arms and vibrated through her. He spoke urgently, as if fearing he'd forget what he wanted to say. Hope couldn't speak around the lump in her throat, or the tears of joy streaming down her face. But she had to shut Stone up for a moment.

"I can't go back to the way I lived before. We'll do it on your terms, any way you want, as long as you let me share your life," he said, beseeching her with his gaze, his voice.

Staring at him with love through her tearful gaze, she pressed her fingers against his lips. He stopped only to kiss her fingers.

"I should have told you then, instead of assuming you already knew how I felt, that you could read my intentions. I'm certain that I want you and Faraha in my life," he declared fervidly, looking at her as if in pain.

"I should have known," she said, her voice trembling. She caressed his jaw with her hands, her eyes moving tenderly across his face. "Everything you've done, the way you've been. The words were always there in the strength of your actions, and I should have known." She wrapped her arms around his waist, and he held her even closer to him.

"Hope . . . ?" He called her name in a fierce whisper, his intensely sweet gaze pleading.

"I love you, Stone Henderson," she said, her lips moving against his mouth. Her arms slid around his waist, pressing him to her tightly. As if in one movement, he embraced her as his lips seized hers in a deep emotional commitment. Languidly his tongue entwined with hers in silent melody, then the pressure of his lips increased. She trembled against his warm, virile nearness, a joyful carol singing in her heart. Before the flames of their passion erupted out of control, their lips parted slowly.

Both aware of Faraha's presence, their heads turned to look at him. Her son had covered his face with his hands, for sure, but his fingers were splayed wide open, through which to peek.

"Go to bed, Faraha," he growled playfully.

"All right." Faraha acquiesced surprisingly quickly. "But don't y'all mess with the cookies and milk I left for Santa— he may want to bring me some more presents."

"Good night, son," Hope said. Santa was hers for the night.

Faraha started off, then stopped and faced them. "Are you going to be here when I get up, Stone?" he asked anxiously.

Stone looked at Hope hopefully.

"Don't worry," she replied, a sidelong sexual glance up at him. "He'll be here."

Merry Christmas!

# ABOUT THE AUTHOR

Margie Rose Walker is a multi-published author of African American romance and romantic suspense novels which have garnered rave reviews, awards and devoted fans. She lives in Houston, TX with her family. Look for her next romantic suspense, REMEMBER ME, September, 1999.

# JUST IN TIME

# Roberta Gayle

# Chapter One

When Geri walked in, the house was quiet. The Tambray-Smith residence was never silent like this. With her seven uncles all living under the same roof, the walls rang with the sounds of laughter, heated arguments and occasional wrestling bouts. Uncle Terry liked to play his music loud. Deafeningly loud. Uncle Bruce, who refused to admit his hearing was going, watched C-SPAN all day and all night at decibel levels that kept the neighbors awake.

There were four cars, besides her own, parked outside. So there had to be a contingent of her army of uncles at home. After a quick check of the kitchen and living room, Geri headed for the basement, affectionately nicknamed the playroom when she'd moved into it on her arrival in New York. When she'd moved from the basement up into the renovated attic, her old bedroom had gone through a gradual, but complete, transformation.

Gone were her posters, books, and computer, and in their place a pool table had been installed, salvaged from a neighborhood bar that went out of business. A large-screen television dominated the entertainment center that took the place of prominence against the far wall of the room. A full bar had been built by Uncle Bert, although luckily neither her mother's brothers, nor her father's, were big drinkers. The guys used the wooden cabinets only to store their beer and forbidden snacks.

Four of her seven roommates were retired or semiretired, and generally one or two would be found down here, but when she opened the door, Geri didn't hear the quiet thwack of wooden cues hitting pool balls, nor the thrumming of the stereo or the blare of the television. As she went down the first few steps, the reason for this unprecedented quiet was made clear. Her uncles—all seven of the dwarfs—were engrossed in conversation.

"So we're agreed." Uncle Bruce's voice rang out over the others. "We each get to choose one guest, one night."

As she was about to make her presence known, Uncle Bert spoke. "If we had two a night, Geri would have a greater variety to choose from." Hearing her name, Geri stopped in her tracks.

"The more the better," Uncle John agreed.

"But she wouldn't be able to get to know them," Uncle Terry said. "Each guy's got only the one night to make an impression. Let's give them a fair shot."

Geri leaned back against the wall for support as the full impact of her uncles' words struck home. All seven men had been nagging Geri about her love life for years, but they'd gone too far this time. Now they were actually hatching some kind of matchmaking campaign against her.

"There are seven nights of Kwanzaa. That's seven men. One each. She's got to like one of them," Uncle Bert, the mediator, soothed the warring factions.

"Maybe more than one," Uncle Hal said, chortling.

"That's fine, just fine," Uncle Bruce chimed in. "Just so long as she ends up dating somebody decent. That last fella Geri brought home looked like a convict."

The others erupted. "She wasn't on a date, he was just a friend," Gene protested.

"That's the way boys dress these days," said sweet Uncle John.

"He was too young for her anyway," Steve sneered.

"Did you see that thing on his head?" Uncle Bruce continued, as if he hadn't heard a word they said, which he probably hadn't.

"Look, it doesn't matter whether *you* all like the guy," Uncle Steve pointed out, surprising Geri with his insight. "Geri has every right to date whomever, or whatever, she chooses. But if we want some nieces and nephews, she's got to settle down. We've got to get her hooked up. Soon." The grim, relentless determination that made Steve such a wonderful police officer was not such an attractive quality in an uncle.

Murmurs of agreement took the place of the excited voices of a moment ago. Geri started to back slowly and quietly up the stairs.

"There are plenty of good men out there, whatever she may say. We need only one," Uncle Bert said.

"It took God only seven days to create the world. We should be able to find our Geri a sweetheart. She'll be home for dinner every night during the holiday," Uncle Terry added in his usual calm tones.

"I know who I'm going to invite," Steve said.

"We all know who you're going to invite," Uncle Hal and Uncle John chorused. "Ben Johnson."

"I hope we're doing the right thing." Uncle Gene finally spoke. He was the second youngest, and closest to her age after Steven. He was her ally. If anyone was going to stand up for her, it would be him. "I don't think Geri's going to appreciate this. If she wanted to date Ben Johnson, she'd have done it by now. Steve's been pushing the sergeant on her for a couple of years now." Geri paused as she reached the door, waiting to see what effect his argument would have on the others.

The argument came from an unexpected source. "This way she doesn't have to put herself on the line," Uncle John said. Although she hadn't expected the meek and mild-mannered Jonathon Tambray to endorse a plan as underhanded and devious as this one, his reasoning was exactly what she would have expected. "It'll be real easy for her, whether she likes the dates we pick out or not. If she does—"

"She will," Steve insisted.

"If she does," John repeated, "she can just go with the flow." On second thought, John's defense of the plan shouldn't have surprised her. Her mother's oldest brother was nothing if not a follower. He would never have come up with a plot like this, but once one of the others had suggested it, it made perfect sense that he went along with them. "If she doesn't like the dates we choose for her, she can just ignore them. At the end of the night, we can send them on their way." Uncle John's docile passive nature was demonstrated even in his defense of the plan.

"But—" Gene started to argue.

"Eugene Smith, you cannot have any objection to Geri finding a man of her own." Uncle Hal stopped him. "That girl needs a little romance in her life. She's too independent to do any serious shopping around, but that doesn't mean she'll be happy if she ends up single like us. Maybe we're the reason she is single. We haven't exactly set a good example for her."

"She's a grown woman," Steve said. "Not a child. She can make up her own mind."

"But a little push in the right direction couldn't hoit," Uncle Hal said in his "enforcer" voice. She could picture his silly smile as he made the lame joke. "We're the only ones who care enough about her to do something about the situation," he concluded.

Geri had to consciously release the tight grip she held on the banister.

"The right man is out there somewhere," Bert added.

This was just what she needed, seven black middle-aged yentas trying to fix her up.

Uncle Gene was silent, and the others started to debate who was going to invite whom and on which night, and Geri silently slipped out the door. She had a couple of phone calls to make, a counter-offensive of her own to launch, and she knew the value of surprise as well as her uncles did. They couldn't know she was home until after she had set her plan in motion.

Geri fished from her handbag the slip of paper on which she'd written Professor Wilton Greer's phone number. She had intended to call him even before she overheard her uncles' harebrained scheme. Greer had sent out an interoffice memo looking for black veterans who'd gone into combat to interview for his research—and all of her uncles had served their country. She'd put off making this call as long as she could, but the irritating professor would be the perfect decoy. Pompous and arrogant as he was, she needed him.

Geri dialed the phone. She took several deep calming breaths as she prepared to launch her own offensive to combat her uncles' sneak attack. Wilton Greer might seem an unlikely ally, but she had something he wanted, and that would serve as a bargaining chip. She was sure he'd jump at the chance to include her small army of uncles in his paper on African-American soldiers. She could only hope he needed her uncles' cooperation enough to help her. For her purposes any warm male body would do.

His answering machine clicked on after the fourth ring of the telephone. "Wilson Greer, here. You know what to do," his recorded voice entoned.

"Professor Greer? This is Geraldine Tambray-Smith calling. I've got a proposition for you, concerning your latest research paper. I got your number from the memo you sent out. Please call me as soon as possible." She left her cellular phone number in order to make sure he didn't call and leave a message that might attract the attention of her roommates at home or her staff at the office. "It is important," she stressed, before she hung up the telephone.

Next she called Candy Watkins to update her best friend on the latest developments on the home front, and her plans for a counterattack.

"You're going to date Professor Sneer?" Candy exclaimed, disbelieving.

"I won't really be dating him," Geri tried to explain. "He'll interview my uncles about their experiences in the army, and I'll just make them think we're involved, that's all."

"I bet you won't make it through one dinner with that windbag without giving yourself away, let alone seven nights."

"Don't be so negative. I can do this, Candy. Be a little supportive."

"Okay, okay." Geri could picture her friend's wry expression. "If you say you can do it, all I can do is back you up. Okay?"

"Great. Thanks. Now the big problem is getting Greer to agree."

"He'll jump at the chance, and you know it. Uncle Bruce can tell him about World War Two, and Steve just flew a chopper all over the desert during the Gulf War. Four of your uncles came home from the war in Korea and Vietnam virtually unscathed. If he's not salivating like Pavlov's dog after your proposal, you'll have only yourself to blame," Candy said in her blunt way.

"And what do I tell him about the other?"

"Just tell him you need him to be your date for Kwanzaa. Get him to agree first, then give him the details."

"I couldn't," Geri said, but even to her own ears her voice lacked conviction.

"It's for a good cause," Candy pointed out. "You'll be heading your uncles off at the pass, and helping Greer out in the bargain."

"I'll try it," Geri reluctantly agreed. She prided herself on her honesty and integrity, but for once she could drop her usual code of ethics. This was, after all, an extraordinary situation.

She had moved into her uncles' duplex in Queens at eighteen, when she'd matriculated as an undergrad at Columbia University. Geri and her mother hadn't known how they would afford to send her to Columbia despite the full scholarship she'd received, which covered her tuition. The cost of living in New York City was so high—the rent for a small apartment was twice as expensive as the mortgage on her mother's house in Ohio. Geri had been grateful for her uncles' offer to make space for her in their already crowded home. At the time it had been expected that the arrangement was only temporary, but by the time Geri earned her bachelor's degree, she couldn't imagine living anywhere else.

Seven ex-army men, of varying ages and temperaments, might have seemed strange roommates for a naive teenager from Ohio, but she enjoyed being introduced to the city by her new roommates, whose appreciation of the metropolis included not only the theater, arts, and music, but the sporting events, and even local bazaars and festivals. They took her under their collective wing, watching out for her, waiting up for her, and generally trying to take the place of her absent parents.

Six years later circumstances had changed. It was Geri who took care of them, as much or more, than they did her. She made sure the bills were paid, the refrigerator stocked, cars serviced, and clothes laundered. She organized the household, and the men's schedules, and made sure everyone attended their medical exams, as well as their meals. She was the unofficial umpire (and catcher) at impromptu family baseball games, and the official referee for family quarrels.

The celebration of Kwanzaa had been introduced only a few years earlier, but as housemother, it had been Geri's influence that had made the new holiday as much a part of the season as Christmas and New Year's Eve. She had no desire to play the dating game on top of taking care of everything else.

As exasperated as she was by their maneuvering, Geri didn't want to hurt any of these men, who only tormented her because they loved her. She didn't want to fight them on this. She just wanted to ... neutralize them. If she had to spend a week pretending she was in love with Greer the Sneer, it was a small price to pay for continued harmony in the family. And it was a better than even trade-off against having seven bachelors foisted on her by her well-meaning but hopelessly old-fashioned housemates.

# Chapter Two

As he walked through the crowd of beautiful young men and women thronging the Bar None, Wilton Greer couldn't help feeling that someone had pulled off a fantastic hoax. In all the years he'd spent on college campuses, all the hours he'd spent in the classroom, he'd never before really seen these kids. Tonight the earnest young people whom he passed every day in the halls had been magically transformed into glittering young hedonists like the flappers of the roaring twenties, or the courtiers of the Sun King's court.

He had always enjoyed watching his students dashing about, from class to class, friend to friend, love to love, and had talked with them, counseled them, and taught them, without ever seeing their true natures. Suddenly it was clear to him, as he watched them dance and drink with abandon, how different they were from himself . . . how young and alive they were. And Ms. Geraldine Tambray-Smith—ridiculous name!—looked as wild as any of them. Her hair was braided close to her head and worn in a crown of red and black. Two ebony plumes of hair bracketed her forehead, the tips resting against her high cheekbones.

It was a very contemporary look, but he had never been able

to understand the allure of appearing in public in ripped or ill-fitting garments, underwear worn as outerwear, or any other badge of freedom or unconventionality that went no deeper than the skin. Clothing, to his mind, was just clothing, no matter how it clung to, exposed, the body. The woman he had come to meet clearly didn't share his views on the subject. She fit right in the with rest of the students. Her diaphanous blouse was decorated with bright beads that caught the light as she moved, drawing attention to the lithe curves visible through the black chiffon.

She was seated at a table in the middle of the room, surrounded by a group he assumed were students. They crowded around, standing behind her, sitting across from her, one young man was leaning down over her, whispering, or perhaps shouting, in her ear.

Geri Smith was only a few years out of grad school herself, he remembered. And her work in the office of the Dean of Students did put her in constant contact with them. He supposed it made sense that they considered her one of them. She spotted him and stood. He stopped dead in his tracks as she wended her way through the crowd toward him. Her thigh-length blouse was longer than the short black spandex miniskirt and, as she drew nearer, he could see the black lace top beneath her blouse quite clearly.

Her appearance should not have made him so uncomfortable, but coupled as it was with this strange new world he'd entered, he felt completely off balance. He glanced around again as she advanced on him. The bar did not have a dance floor, but that hadn't stopped couples from throwing their arms around each other and moving to the seductive beat of the music. A promising student from his own department—a girl that he was mentoring himself—was dancing with two men by the jukebox. Sandwiched between the two, she swayed forward and back, her hips undulating in a slow sensual circle.

" 'Professor Greer, let's go to the bar,'' Geri suggested when she'd arrived within earshot, which was only a few inches away. He followed her to the end of the bar, a less crowded corner of the room. Removed slightly from the chattering patrons crowded in the middle of the establishment, the deafening roar that had overwhelmed him faded to a constant, cacophonous hum, punctuated by bursts of laughter.

"Thank you for meeting me. May I buy you a drink?" she asked.

"I don't think so," he demurred. "What are we doing here?" he asked, as curious about her choice of the Bar None for their meeting place as by her surprising request to meet with him about his research project.

"Here, here? Or here, together?" she asked perceptively.

"Both," he answered.

"Here, here because this is where I usually meet people from work. It's the closest to the campus. I forgot about the basketball game though. It isn't usually this crowded on a weeknight," she apologized. "When you said you'd be working late tonight, this was the first place I thought of." She examined him curiously. "You've never been here before?"

He almost didn't respond, as the answer to her question was self-evident. But she looked genuinely intrigued.

"I wasn't even aware this place existed," he said wryly.

"But—" she started to say, then seemed to catch herself and didn't finish. A twinkle entered her eye. "I should have known."

Wilton agreed. The Bar None was clearly not his cup of tea. Usually when he socialized with his colleagues, he met them for tea at an establishment called the Coffee Pot, which was located a few doors down the street from the Bar None. But since Geri had invited him to the Bar None, he supposed she didn't know that much about him. Therefore her response made him curious.

"Why should you have known?" he asked.

"Oh, you're just . . . let's just say that a college bar doesn't exactly seem your style," she said. Her eyes were still smiling, as if at a secret joke, and Wilton couldn't resist questioning her further.

"My style? You mean my clothing?" he prompted.

"Among other things. I bet you didn't go to places like this even when you were in school."

"No, Ms. Smith," he said definitely. "I didn't." He had always had what his mother called an old soul, even as a child and an adolescent. In college, rather than carouse with his classmates, Wilton had spent his evenings working and studying. His few friends had teased him about it, but that had stopped when they found out about his affair with his psychology professor. That had raised his status from that of a hopeless drudge to one of a successful Don Juan.

He hadn't appreciated their approval of his clandestine activities, any more than he'd cared about their teasing, but he had learned a valuable lesson from the events of his first year as an undergraduate student. He could be as demanding and downright obnoxious as he wanted as long as he had a beautiful woman on his arm. His contemporaries then, and his colleagues now, all respected a man who could attract an alluring woman to his bed.

"Call me Geri," she said, recalling him to the present. He could imagine what his friends would say if they could see him with this . . . temptress.

"All right, Geri," he agreed reluctantly.

"I know you're curious about why I asked you here," she began.

"We've established that," he pointed out.

"It's sort of hard to explain," she said, and drained her glass.

"You said you wanted to talk to me about interviewing your uncles for my research project. There are seven of them?"

"Yes."

"All ex-army."

"Yes." She reached for her glass again, then drew her hand back when she realized it was empty.

"That sounds fine," he said happily. Perhaps this meeting had been worthwhile after all.

"There's just one thing," Geri said, then she paused.

"Yes?" he prompted her.

"Well, my uncles are a little unusual."

"Unusual how?" he asked.

"All different ways," she said. "You might even call a couple of them eccentric."

"Do you think they'll be interested in being subjects?"

"Some of them might," Geri said slowly. "But all of them would if they thought you ... if they thought I ... if they thought we ... were dating." She looked down at her empty glass again.

"Dating?"

"You see, Uncle Bruce and a couple of the others are a little, umm, wary about being research subjects. The Tuskegee study, you know. You should have heard them when I wanted to be a paid subject for an experiment the Psychology Department was conducting."

"You and I?" Wilton couldn't believe she'd suggest a date with him.

"It wouldn't be a big deal. The holidays are coming up, and Kwanzaa is kind of a family tradition. Well, we've been celebrating it for the last few years anyway, so if I asked you to dinner each night, that's seven nights. You could interview one of them each evening."

"Why can't I just interview the ones who aren't so ... eccentric," he suggested.

"I don't know how many would do it—if any. Bruce is the oldest, and he's pretty opposed. But if you were my ..."

"What?" Wilton tried to sound encouraging rather than impatient, but he couldn't help feeling that the seven candidates she'd offered were slipping through his fingers.

"My boyfriend," Geri said, so softly he almost didn't hear her.

"This is ridiculous," he said. "How old are you, Ms. Smith?"

"Geri," she corrected him automatically. "I'm going to be thirty in a few weeks, and that's why they want to find me a nice steady guy to date."

"So ..." he said, his mind working on the problem already. "That's why you want to do this?"

"It's not a matter of wanting to do it. But if I bring you home, my uncles will be satisfied, for a while anyway. And maybe they'll stop fixing me up. They're the sweetest men, but you can't imagine how embarrassing it is to have the seven dwarfs offer you to every able-bodied man they meet."

"It can't be that bad," he soothed.

"They really don't want to see me turn thirty alone."

"Uh-huh," he murmured in agreement, although he was trying desperately to think of another solution to their respective dilemmas, especially his own. Unfortunately he couldn't think of any other solution to their two problems with the information she'd given him thus far. "And just what would I have to do?"

She still wasn't looking at him. "Celebrate Kwanzaa with my family. I'll be visiting my mother in Ohio over the weekend through Christmas. I'll fly back early the next day, and they could meet you that night."

"Won't they think it's odd—me just showing up with my research to do?"

"I can take care of that," she said, unconcerned. Geri looked up hopefully. The glimmer had returned to her big brown eyes. He felt a slight answering smile tug at the corners of his own lips. This was madness. But he couldn't help thinking it just might work.

"They wouldn't be surprised at all if I suddenly appeared with *you*," she clarified. Wilton would have asked what she meant by that, but she went on too quickly. "I'll tell them we've been seeing each other since the term began, but I didn't want to tell them. I don't tell them much about my love life, for reasons which you can probably guess, Professor, given my current situation. If we do this right, though, I should have them off my back for months."

"Good," he said, uncertain what kind of response was appropriate.

"Don't get me wrong," she said. "I love my uncles, and I know they only love me. But this time they've gone too far."

"What?" he asked. His mind had wandered back to the short dress she was wearing, the length of leg it exposed, and his colleagues' probable reactions on seeing him here, with her, dressed like that. Her declared devotion to her family had barely registered.

"Never mind." She dismissed it. "Do you really think you could do it? They're going to expect us to act like we're in loooove." She drew the word out, rolling her eyes and leaving him in little doubt of her opinion on the sentiment. "Do you think you could manage it?"

His ego pricked, Wilton said sarcastically, "I don't think it will be all that difficult."

"You're not gay or anything, are you?" she asked.

"I'm engaged," he spluttered, taken aback by her directness.

"I know." Her expression didn't change.

"No, I'm not gay," he stated firmly.

"Good. Let me buy you that drink, and we can start discussing the details," Geri offered.

"Fine," Wilton agreed, but something told him he had just embarked on a dangerous adventure, with this insouciant little devil as his partner.

# Chapter Three

Geri thought the first phase of her plan had gone quite well—better than expected, in fact. Professor Greer, Wilton, she hastily corrected herself, had not been nearly as difficult as she'd expected. Once or twice she thought she'd even seen a gleam of laughter in his eyes.

It would be nice to discover he had a sense of humor. She'd never thought of him as having such a normal, even desirable, character trait. In her previous encounters with him, she'd thought he'd had ice water in his veins.

But it didn't help to think of him like that. She was going to have to sell him to her uncles as the newfound love of her life. That wasn't going to be easy. She hoped her uncles believed in the old adage, "Opposites attract." Otherwise she didn't have a chance of convincing them that the professor was her soul mate.

Despite her reservations, she was really looking forward to phase two. The morning after her meeting with Wilton Greer, she sat down to breakfast with Uncle Bruce, Steve, and Gene and announced, "I've got a friend I'd like you all to meet. I was think of inviting him here to celebrate Kwanzaa with us."

"Him?" Uncle Bruce echoed, clearly amazed.

"Wilton Greer. Professor Wilton Greer," Geri said, trying to look coy, without actually batting her eyelashes.

Steve hastily gulped down his mouthful of scrambled eggs and washed it down with a quick swig of coffee. "Kwanzaa?"

"Yes." She buried her face in her mug of tea so they wouldn't see her triumphant smile.

"Why?" Uncle Bruce asked, still looking shell-shocked.

"It's a good time to meet the family. Everyone will definitely be here."

"Who is he?" asked Uncle Gene. There wasn't a hint of suspicion in his voice. He knew her better than all the rest of her mother's and father's brothers combined. If she could convince him, she was home free.

"Yeah, who is this guy?" Uncle Steve chimed in. She'd expected an interrogation from him. He was a cop, after all. And Geri figured he'd be the most disappointed of the seven sneaky matchmakers, since he'd been trying to get her together with his partner, Ben Johnson, for some time. Still he had no right to talk to her as if he were interrogating a suspect.

She was careful to keep the resentment out of her tone as she answered. "A man I've been seeing." Their reactions were everything Geri would have hoped. Their astonishment was complete. She had considered waiting to drop her bombshell on them when all seven of her uncles were together so she could really watch the fur fly, but she was satisfied with the response she was receiving from these three.

"Since when?" Gene looked a little hurt. Geri supposed it was because she didn't usually keep secrets from him. For a moment she wished she could have told at least him the truth, but her resolve returned as she reminded herself that he had betrayed her when he'd joined the others in the insane plot to pair her off during the upcoming holidays.

"Since the beginning of this term, almost. He's the head of the Anthropology Department," she elaborated. "You'll like him, I'm pretty sure."

Uncle Steve wasn't buying a word of it. "To what do we owe the honor of this belated introduction?"

"I've been thinking about it for a while," she said wryly.

"But I didn't want to get your hopes up. Especially yours, Uncle Bruce. I know how strongly you feel about my finding a boyfriend. Besides, you guys get so emotional about my dates, it can be rather embarrassing, especially when things don't work out. But Wilton is special."

"Wilton?" Uncle Bruce spoke up. "What kind of name is that?"

"I like it," Geri said calmly. "And no one asked you for your opinion."

"Let's not get off track here," Uncle Steve said.

" 'Train's leaving the station," Geri said, finishing off her muffin. "You can give me the third degree later. For now I'm outta here." She placed her dish and mug in the dishwasher and walked to the door, ignoring Steve's startled cry,

"Wait!

And Gene's "But—!"

"Humph," Bruce said behind her. "Sounds like some kind of a joke to me."

"It's for real, so you can call off the Kwanzaa parade," Geri said, sticking her head back in the doorway. "I am off the market." She saluted them. "Tell all your friends." She had no doubt they'd pass along this information to the others.

Gene's jaw dropped, she was pleased to note when she stuck her head back into the kitchen one last time. "Uncle Bruce, don't forget you have an appointment with your internist today. Uncle John will drive you."

She left them gaping after her and nearly skipped to her car. She'd been right about this plan. It would work.

"What do we do now?" she asked the living-room furniture.

She would have loved to have seen the others' expressions when they heard the news. Uncle Terry would come down from his room in a little while, spruce and neat, having worked on his latest never-to-be-seen novel since sunrise. Uncle Bert would come down midmorning in his sweats, a look he'd enjoyed since his retirement.

Her father's four brothers were as different as her mother's three brothers were similar. Bruce, nearing eighty, had grown into his crotchety disposition and refused to put himself out for anyone. Hal, only a few years younger, was always smiling, and ready with a joke. Terry's passion was books. He was semiretired and spent half his time reading to the blind and elderly and every spare moment writing novels which he was too shy to show to anyone. He was constantly revising them, he was a perfectionist about his fiction. He had written and published numerous articles and occasionally read them bits and pieces of his work, both fiction and nonfiction. Her uncle Bert was the mediator, not only for his brothers but also for his brothers-in-law.

John, the doormat, agreed with everyone and everything rather than risk any kind of confrontation. Gene, a lawyer, and the strong, silent rock whom everyone else turned to for advice and support, was her mother's second eldest brother. Steve, the youngest—and most assertive—of them all, didn't at first seem to be cut from the same cloth as his two older brothers, but despite his stubborn determination, he wasn't any more contentious than they were, and he was just as much a problem solver, if not as gentle a one.

Each would react differently when they learned she'd messed up their little matchmaking scheme—just as Bruce had been skeptical, Steve suspicious and Gene hurt—they'd all be upset, if for different reasons. And they would be waiting to question her further when she came home that evening, so instead of returning to the duplex after work, she went out to dinner with Candy.

"So far, so good," she reported when Candy asked how things were going with the good professor. "Greer, I mean Wilton, agreed." This time she actually did bat her eyelashes as she spoke his name in dulcet tones.

"Really?"

"Piece of cake," she confirmed. "I broke it to the guys this morning at breakfast."

"Did they plotz?" Candy asked.

"They weren't happy. Bruce and Steve nearly had a fit."

"Grumpy and Sneezy?" Candy had given each of the uncles a nickname from the Disney movie *Snow White and the Seven Dwarfs*. "Why am I not surprised?"

"Gene wasn't thrilled, either."

"Gene? Oh, no. Don't tell me he was in on it, too?"

"Yup. They all were. And they all deserve to think Wilton Greer is going to be their nephew-in-law."

Candy wrinkled her nose. "It's harsh, but maybe it will teach them a lesson. Better no nephew than a dead nephew."

"Actually, he was pretty cool about the arrangement. I expected him to . . . I don't know, call me crazy I guess. But he was pretty sympathetic."

"He must really want black vets for his study."

"I'm sure. I think he was very happy to get seven at once. But . . . it wasn't just that. You should have seen the way he looked in the Bar None. He was wearing a suede blazer over a flannel shirt, I swear." Geri smiled at the memory, but Candy was shaking her head.

"How old is he anyway? her friend asked.

"I forgot to ask. I'll find out before the first big date. I'm meeting him for drinks next week, before I leave for Ohio, and I'm going to get more info and give him a cheat sheet on the guys and on me."

"I still can't believe you're actually going to do this."

"I can't believe I have to."

"It's so hard to imagine the two of you together," Candy said.

"Well, get used to it. I want you there the first night, for moral support. You can help smooth over any rough edges. If you act like you've known Wilton all along, Uncle Gene will think it's all true."

"Okay," Candy quickly agreed, then grinned sheepishly at Geri's look of surprise. "I can't wait to see this," she admitted. "You want me to go with you to the briefing?"

"The briefing? That makes it sound like a military campaign."

"Your drinks date, then?"

"That's even worse. It's not date. I think I can handle it alone."

But she was surprisingly nervous when the day dawned for her second meeting with the professor. She'd spent the preceding week doing all of the various chores necessitated by the season. Christmas and Kwanzaa shopping had to be done at the same time that the end of term activites at school kept her busier than ever. And there was her large and rather demanding family to take care of, as well as last-minute arrangements for her trip to her childhood home in Ohio.

Geri had taken her mother into her confidence about Wilton Greer, after explaining her uncles' nefarious plot, and Mary Tambray-Smith had been amused and eager to help.

"There's not much you can do, Mom, but wish me luck," Geri told her, but she was heartened by the enthusiastic response.

"Luck, darling? You don't sound like you need it. Guts, you may need, if this guy is the pill you say he is. And any acting ability you have will come in handy. But you've got that. Your father was a heck of an actor."

Geri didn't exactly tune out her mother's reminiscences about meeting Benjamin Smith in college, but she'd heard the story so many times before that she listened with only half an ear while she thought about her mother's earlier comment. It was true she had her work cut out for her if she hoped to pull off this act—convincing her uncles she was in love with the Professor was not going to be a simple task—but she was highly motivated. That would get her through this. She wasn't afraid of the arrogant Wilton Greer anymore, even though he was a bit stiff and unbending. She'd butted heads with him a couple of times, professionally, and emerged frustrated but otherwise unscathed.

He was conservative, even old school. He maintained a high standard for his pupils, especially minority students. Anthropology was a field of study that was losing money all over the country, being combined with the English Departments in many major universities. As funding grew short, higher demands were put on the students to weed out those on whom tight budgets were being wasted.

Geri stood firmly on the side of the debate that insisted that African-American, female, and other minority students be provided with any or all of the few remaining positions if they were qualified. The field had been dominated by white men—like most in the world of academe.

Professor Greer did not make allowances for his minority students—and in fact he admitted to being harder on them than the others because, as he said, they needed to learn that this was a world where privilege and connections counted for a lot. Minorities had to be better than their more well-connected counterparts, because that was the only way they could succeed.

As assistant to the Dean of Students, Geri had defended more than one student from Greer the Sneer and his subtle, if well-intentioned, discrimination. When he refused to give a top student an extension on her paper, when she went into labor a month prematurely, Geri won that battle hands down. However, in the case in which she'd argued that a young black man on athletic scholarship deserved extra time to study for tests, because his schedule with the basketball team took him out of town almost every weekend, the professor refused to bend. Greer insisted the student would have an unfair advantage over the rest of the class, and the administration agreed. Eventually the basketball star did drop the class because of the pressure, just as Greer said he would.

Geri thought she was right then, and she thought it still. Greer, she was sure, was equally convinced that his position was the right one. She knew she and Wilton Greer had a lot of dissembling to do over the next few weeks, but at least, in this case, they were on the same side. No, it wasn't Professor Wilton Greer that scared her when she considered the charade she was about to embark on. She might lack the bravery to confront her uncles head on, and forbid them from interfering in the most intimate aspects of her life, but Greer she could handle.

"I wish you really had fallen in love," her mother was saying. "Then you would know what I'm talking about." She gave a heartfelt sigh.

"I haven't given up hope, Mom. I just don't think it's something you can force. If it happens, it happens."

"You're right. And your uncles are old enough to know better," her mother agreed. "I can't help feeling a little bit sorry for them though." Geri had no sympathy to spare for the meddling old fools. She had right on her side. She had the right to choose whom she would date, and when and for how long, and even if she wanted to date at all.

"If you're going to feel sorry for someone, let it be me," she ended the conversation. "I'm the one who has to spend seven nights making goo-goo eyes at the world's oldest geek."

"You have to admit, it's ironic," she told Candy as she prepared for her appointment with Wilton. "I'm dating someone I don't like much and with whom I have no interest in developing a relationship so that I can avoid dating men I don't like much and with whom I have no interest in developing a relationship."

"Go get him, girlfriend," Candy said.

# Chapter Four

Wilton chose a coffee shop for their second meeting, but not his usual spot, the Coffee Pot. Given the purpose of their rendezvous, he felt more comfortable choosing a place where he didn't think his colleagues or friends would chance to meet them.

Geri walked in the door, dressed in shredded jeans that revealed as much of her long brown legs as they covered. He admired them as she stood, hands on hips, just inside the door. She glanced around the room and saw him. He stood as she approached the table. Geri raised her eyebrows but nodded approvingly. "My uncles love that kind of old-world courtesy."

"Habit," he explained. "My father said a gentleman should always stand for a lady."

"Thank you," she murmured. "That should help them understand why . . ." She paused, drawing out the statement and shooting a mischievous grin at him before finishing her sentence. ". . . I love you."

Wilton barely stopped himself from shushing her. He did glance about, checking to make sure no one had seen or heard her.

"Do you really think that kind of talk is necessary?"

"Absolutely," Geri said with conviction. "We've got to make this believable, and my uncles know me very well. They will expect some public display of affection. It might make it easier for you, though, if you think of the whole thing as . . . well, a practical joke. You can tease me as much as you want. I can take it. And I can dish it out. The point is, we do a lot of that in my house. They'll *believe* you're just joking."

"Even if I am."

"Especially if you are. I always have liked men with a good sense of humor."

"I'm not the first one you've taken home, then?"

"I've been living with these guys since I was eighteen years old. They've met a number of the men I've dated. I just haven't had anyone I wanted to take home in a few years. That's why they've gotten so pushy, I guess."

"We shouldn't take the joke thing too far, then. Or they'll never believe we're really serious."

"I wouldn't worry about that," she reassured him.

"But what if I laugh at the wrong time?"

"There's never a wrong time, not in our house. Now"— she became suddenly very brisk and businesslike—"here's a brief history on me, and a little story we can tell about how we got together. Did you bring your stuff?"

Reluctantly he gave her the single sheet of paper on which he'd typed the facts about himself that he thought she ought to know, for their masquerade.

"Family, ex-girlfriends, resume . . . This is pretty thorough, Willie."

"Wilton, please," he requested.

"See, that's the kind of thing I need. Nicknames—"

"None," he interrupted.

"Okay." She nodded. "Favorite color? What kind of music you like, etc.?"

"I see what you mean," he said, glancing inside the folder of information she'd given him. "Favorite movie: *Charade*, 1963, starring Audrey Hepburn and Cary Grant. Is that really your favorite movie?" He hadn't expected her to be so sentimental.

"Yeah, but it's not what you're thinking. *Charade* is a murder mystery. It's nothing like this."

"Like what?" Wilton asked.

Geri looked a little flustered, finally. "You and me. Our charade."

"Oh, sure, I know," he told her.

"So why did you ask?" she asked, exasperated.

"I just thought you'd have chosen a different genre. Something new, today, sexy." He looked at her provocative attire. "Like . . . ahem, that outfit you're almost wearing."

"Oh?" she said, stiffening. "Didn't think I'd go for the classics, huh?" She sounded miffed. He imagined it would really bother her to know he could read everything she felt on her expressive face. Much as she might have wanted to remain unaffected by him, she couldn't help being a little annoyed.

He smiled, he couldn't help it. "Sorry. No," he said honestly.

"That's fine," Geri said, to herself as much as to him, he thought. She tried to smile. It didn't reach her eyes, which had darkened at the perceived insult. Her tone was aggressive as she asked him, "What about you?"

"*Boyz 'N the Hood*," he answered. "Do you know it?"

"Doesn't everyone?" She shrugged, and with that gesture some of the tension seemed to flow out of her. "It was a good flick," she said with grudging approval for his choice. This time her smile was a real one. "What else?" she asked. "I'm going to need more personal information." She tapped the slim file folder sitting on the table in front of her, and waited.

He looked down at the list she'd given him, planning to follow the same format as he fulfilled her request. "My parents live in L.A. My relationship with them is good." She had written that her father died in Vietnam before she was born, but she loved him to bits. Her relationship with her mother was "close and cuddly." He might have admired her openness if she had expressed herself less playfully. But this syrupy outpouring made him feel slightly uncomfortable. "I call them every couple of weeks."

"Mom's going to back us up, by the way. If asked, she'll

say she's spoken with you on the phone. She's sort of stuck in the sixties."

"So we do have something in common," Wilton offered. "My parents are both social workers, still organizing rallies and protests on their days off."

"Really?" She looked surprised. "My mom isn't real political or anything. She's just still sort of waiting for my dad to come back. I mean, she doesn't wear miniskirts or listen to Jimi Hendrix. She's got a regular civil service job and lives in a little white house in a nice middle-class neighborhood. After my dad died, she had a slight breakdown and lived here with my uncles for a few years. That's when they all chipped in and bought the house together. But we moved to Canton when I was four, because it had a good school district and she had an aunt there who could get her a job with the company where she worked."

"Oh," Wilton said. He couldn't imagine this live wire of a woman growing up behind a white picket fence.

She was observing him with equal curiosity. "So your parents are radicals?"

"Activists," he corrected automatically.

Geri was shaking her head. "I never would have guessed."

"Well." Wilton cleared his throat. "That was the purpose of this meeting, wasn't it? To find out about each other."

"Yeah. Sure." She looked down at his bio again. "Any more surprises in here?"

"I think most of it is pretty straightforward," he said gruffly. Unlike hers, he noted, as he continued to read her file. Most Embarrassing Moment, First Love, and Friends and Enemies were all covered in her précis. She'd written almost a full page about her best friend, Candy. Under the heading of Achievements, which were divided into the categories Personal, Professional, and Other, she'd included keeping a goldfish alive and well for four years. Its name was Lucinda.

"I have a feeling it would take a lot more time than we've got to pry the details out of you," she said. "I guess I'll just say you're not much of a talker." She pursed her lips and shook her head. "I am going to need something, just to give our audience an idea of what we do talk about." She thought for a second. "I know. What are you proudest of?"

"Well, uh," he stammered. He thought about the accomplishments he'd listed on his resume. "My first book, I guess," he answered finally.

"Oh. Okay." She sounded vaguely disappointed.

"None of my fish made it," he joked, feeling awkward. She didn't have to look so hopeless. Her uncles would probably be quite impressed when she brought home the head of the Anthropology Department at a major university. If nothing else, he'd probably provide a good contrast to the other jokers she'd dated. He could just imagine the types she usually dated ... clad in ripped jeans even tighter than hers, no doubt.

"Have you ever celebrated Kwanzaa?" She abruptly changed the subject.

"No. I live alone, and I never really understood the appeal. There are plenty of real holidays, in every culture, celebrating this season. African Americans didn't need to create one for themselves. It seems unnecessary."

"My uncles loved the idea the first time they heard about it. We've been celebrating it for a few years now. Do you think you could try to keep an open mind about it, until you've actually seen how it works?"

"I'm an anthropologist," Wilton answered.

"Is that a yes or a no?" Geri asked.

"It's my job to keep an open mind."

"Good." She held out her hand. He looked at it dubiously. "Shake on it," she said.

He took her hand in his. "This isn't necessary," he protested lamely. He released his grasp on her small, fine-boned fingers, but she didn't do the same.

"If we're going to pull this off, you're going to have to touch me," she warned.

"Of course," he said. When she looked at him warily, he assured her, "It will not be a problem."

She let his hand go, reluctantly it seemed to him. "What are you going to tell your fiancée?"

"You know about her?"

"It's a small campus, Professor."

"Amanda will be in Colorado, with her family. They go there every year. Her grandmother is selling the house, so this may be their last year skiing all together."

"Sounds like a real old-fashioned holiday," Geri commented, with a grimace of distaste.

"It's actually very pleasant. I accompanied her last year. Do you ski?"

"It's right there, under Hobbies. Yes, I do. But not very well. I just started a few years ago. It's fun though."

"Luckily I learned to ski when I was quite young. Even though I had given up the sport when I moved here, I enjoy it. It's one of Amanda's passions. I prefer skiing out west. Less ice."

"I'll have to go out there some time and try it."

"But you've been all over the country," he said, referring to the Travel section of her biography.

"Not to ski," Geri explained. "It's an expensive hobby."

"I know, that's another reason I didn't do it for a while, until I met Amanda. But you seem to have a lot of unusual hobbies for a school administrator: travel, photography, theater, horseback riding, scuba diving, and let's see . . . what else have we got here . . . ?"

"I've tried a little bit of everything, but I haven't really had the time or the money to become expert at any one thing," she admitted sheepishly.

"Why do I get the feeling that it's not as much a question of money as of inclination?"

Geri looked embarrassed. "You're right. I love to try new things, but once I've done something, I generally mark it off the list and go for something new and novel."

Wilton couldn't imagine Amanda admitting to such impulsive behavior. When they had gone on their first vacation to the Caribbean, she had signed up for three months of scuba lessons at the YWCA. Geraldine definitely suffered in any comparison to Amanda, but her attitude was refreshing. He had always admired Amanda's perfectionism, but now that he thought about it, he supposed it did demonstrate a rather competitive nature.

"And you?"

"Me?" He had lost the thread of the conversation.

"Any burning ambitions you haven't fulfilled yet?"

"I'd like to write a second book. This research project may win me a grant. And, of course, tenure."

"You're working on that. Probably smart, keeping your nose to the grindstone, but what about personal goals, outside your profession?"

"I suppose I'd like a family."

"Kids, huh?" She looked at him measuringly. "I can see you as a father," Geri pronounced. Wilton felt absurdly flattered.

"Thank you."

"You're welcome," she said sincerely.

"I'd better get home to study this," he said.

"All right. I guess we've pretty much finished here. I wrote my schedule, phone numbers, address, etc. So I guess we're all set."

"We won't see each other again before I meet your family?"

"That's right. I leave for Ohio in a couple of days, and my schedule is pretty full until then. Call me if you have any questions. I'll be running around getting candles, tree, decorations, presents, and, of course, food. I'll be back on the morning after Christmas—the first day of Kwanzaa. I'll be preparing for the evening's fesitivities for most of the day, probably. It would have been nice if we'd had more time to prepare, but if you memorize that material, we should be okay."

"I'll study it faithfully," Wilson agreed with only the slightest tinge of sarcasm.

"Great. I think I remembered everything. My uncles will never believe that I've suddenly turned into the strong silent type, so you would probably know most of that if we'd been dating since September."

"I'm sure we'll muddle through," Wilton said. "I'll see you one week from today. Seven o'clock sharp. Your place."

"Here's to us," Geri said, lifting up her coffee cup and smiling delightedly.

"Us," Wilton echoed weakly, trying to match her high spirits. He'd been lulled for a moment into thinking of their next meeting as almost a normal date, albeit one with subtle undercurrents, but her toast reminded him that he had committed himself to a much bigger endeavor—pretending to be in love with this irrepressible woman. Before more niggling doubts could surface, he gestured to the waiter to bring him their bill. He had a lot of homework to do.

# Chapter Five

Geri threw the door wide open when Wilton knocked. "Habari gani!" she greeted him. "Now kiss me." She wrapped her arms around his neck and pulled his head down to hers. "Say umoja," she commanded.

"Umoja," he obediently responded.

"It means 'Unity' in Swahili," she told him, right before she kissed him.

The speech Wilton had been rehearsing all day to use at this moment was forgotten as her full lips covered his. The chill air he'd brought in with him, on his coat, his hands, his face, couldn't compete with the heat of her body, which mingled with the warmth behind her coming from within the house. His arms went around her, to pull her as close as she had him.

"Kujichagulia is tomorrow's response to the greeting," she murmured against his lips. She pushed away from him. Raising her voice, she said. "Whoa, there, big boy. I guess I don't need to ask if you missed me as much as I missed you." She winked. Her conspiratorial smile acted like a bucket of cold water on his libido, dousing the quick flame that had sprung from nowhere at her sudden, unexpected action.

She stepped back into the house and took his coat, while he

glanced about. Four men sat on a couch facing the door, three stood around the room. The kiss had apparently surprised her uncles as much as it had him. They stared, open-mouthed, regarding the two of them with expressions ranging from a highly suspicious glare on the face of the youngest, whom he guessed to be Steve, to pleased approval in the happy smile of one of the elderly gentleman seated on the couch.

"Hello," he offered with a nod.

"Let me introduce you to everyone," Geri said, holding his arm possessively. "Wilton Greer, I'd like you to meet my family. This is Steve."

He'd been right in his guess, Steve was the sullen young man standing a couple of feet behind his niece. "Hi," Wilton said, offering his hand. Steve reluctantly shook it.

"Bruce, Hal, Terry and Bert," Geri introduced the men on the couch, from left to right.

Bruce spoke first. "So you are Wilton Greer?" Bruce Smith was the oldest of her father's brothers. Wilton thought this uncle was the only one who looked his age, but that might have been because of the sour expression on his wrinkled face as he peered at Wilton through thick eyeglasses.

"Yes, sir," he answered.

Hal, Terry, and Bert sat in a row next to the old man. Wilton rapidly cataloged what he remembered about each man. Hal was the jokester, if he remembered correctly. Terry was the semi-retired professor, and the one who had smiled so widely when Geri kissed him. Bert was the carpenter with the bulldog jowels and the impassive face. They, and Bruce, were her father's four brothers. If they hadn't been sitting in a row on the couch, he wouldn't have ever put them together. They didn't look at all alike. From her description, they were just as dissimilar in personality.

"John is setting the table, and Uncle Gene is standing by at the kitchen door." Geri finished the introductions.

Unlike the other four men, Gene, John, and Steve, her mother's brothers, could have been triplets, except for the difference in their ages. All three were big, round-faced men, who stood in the same position, and looked at him with identical round black eyes. Only their expressions differed: Steve was suspicious, Gene assessed him with an open, friendly mien, and John's wide trusting smile was like a banner.

"Would you like a drink?" John asked. He was the oldest, after Bruce, but he was a Tambray, related to Geri on her mother's side. He looked a good bit younger than Bruce, though Wilton knew the difference he perceived might have been due more to their different responses to him. John smiled widely, well pleased to meet him, even though Wilton had barely uttered a word. By all outward appearances, Uncle John was exactly as Geri had described him—a big pushover.

"You finish that," Gene told his older brother, who was busy arranging some kind of centerpiece on the table with fruit, ears of corn, and a candelabra with black, red, and green candles. "What would you like?" he asked Wilton, going to the bar on the far wall. "Beer? Wine? Something stronger?"

"A glass of red wine, if you have it," Wilton answered.

The bar seemed to be fully stocked, but then that was no surprise, as this room seemed to be designed for comfort. The sofa on which her uncles sat was large and plush, positioned in front of the three large windows that looked out over the front yard. The heavy dull gold curtains were pulled open and hooked inside two large brass brackets, which matched the brass light fixtures placed high up on the walls. The couch, matching easy chair, and the fixtures were oldfashioned, and slightly worn, as was the blue and gold Persian rug on the floor and the large wooden coffee table which sat on it.

The accoutrements were very masculine in look and feel, but the African prints and masks that hung on the clean, white walls made the livingroom a backdrop that seemed to suit Geri just as well as it did her male relatives. The other half of the room was filled with a large dining room table surrounded by wooden chairs, where her uncle John appeared to be finishing up with his arrangement of fruit, vegetables, baskets and candles.

"If we have it?" Hal chortled. "She stocked up on everything." He nodded toward Geri. "Vodka, rum, tequila, whiskey. You're not some kind of alcoholic or somethin', are you?"

He shoved his elbow into Terry's ribs, inviting his sober older brother to share the joke.

"It is almost as if she didn't know what you'd like," Terry commented thoughtfully. Clearly the idea had just occurred to him. Wilton understood immediately. Hal was the observant brother, Terry the analytical one. Together, they might have figured out exactly what it was that Geri was up to. He hoped they wouldn't think to discuss their observations with each other.

"I bought the drinks for everyone," Geri protested.

"Oh? I sort of liked the idea of your shopping for all my favorites," he teased her. Hal and Terry both smiled.

"Honey," Geri responded playfully. "You know how I like to take care of my man." She leaned up to kiss his cheek.

"Geri isn't usually this domesticated. It's just for the holidays," Steve inserted.

"I've always found her to be very ... accommodating," Wilton said.

"Accommodating?" he repeated doubtfully. "Geri?"

"Careful, buster," she warned. "If you want to eat—"

"Okay, okay. No need to get so touchy," Hal interjected with a chuckle. Wilton understood what Geri had meant when she'd described him as the world's worst comedian. Virtually every word out of him was spoken in jest. And none of it was particularly humorous.

Wilton summoned up a weak smile for Hal, then addressed Steve. "I don't think you and I could possibly see this woman in the same way. She's your little niece. You've known Geri all her life. You expect certain things from her. I don't have the right to expect anything from her. I'm just her ..." He couldn't bring himself to say the word *boyfriend*. "I'm just glad she invited me into your home." He wanted to establish some kind of bond with this man, who was close to his own age, and would probably be less resistant to the research he wanted to do.

Geri shot him a warning look, which he easily interpreted to mean: *Don't forget the reason you're here.* He looked down at her, still clinging like a limpet to his arm and said, "I hope you'll tell me all about her. Got any baby photos?"

That won him a smile from her. Steve didn't respond to his overture, and Wilton sat uncomfortably on a chair at the end of the sofa. Four faces turned to him expectantly.

"So, Professor, Geri mentioned something about a research project you are working on which we might be able to help you with," Terry said.

This wasn't the moment he would have chosen to bring up this controversial subject, but a glance at Geri elicited only a shrug. "Yes, I'm interviewing African-American soldiers and veterans."

"That sounds interesting." Terry nodded, encouraging him go on.

"I have a thesis I'm trying to prove about the assimilation of the African-American male into mainstream American culture through the government's use of our minds, bodies, and spirits in warfare."

Bert looked a bit nervous. "We served our country, but I think the fact that we did serve proves that we were already assimilated."

"Maybe," Wilton cautiously agreed. "But given the statistics I've been able to acquire from Department of Defense studies done since World War Two, blacks were encouraged to enlist only as infantrymen and for other high-risk assignments. When they had, or received, training for higher rank or positions that might lead to advancement in the ranks, I found that the armed forces were a lot less eager to allow or encourage their placement. It's very well documented."

"I can't agree with you," Bert said. "I was there and whatever those crackers might have thought, when we were covering their asses, they figured out pretty fast who could do what!"

"Course not," Bruce shouted. "He knows what he's talking about. You got it, boy. We were cannon fodder then, and whenever they can get away with it, we're cannon fodder now."

"That is the traditional role of the poor," Terry tried to clarify. "I don't know how much it has to do with being black, at least not in today's army."

"Were you aware that the servicemen who served in the Gulf were forty-six percent African American. And the ninety percent of the American public who supported that conflict were white; less than forty percent of the African Americans polled thought we should have sent in the troops."

"All right, all right," John said. He appeared to have finished whatever it was he was doing at the table.

"Are we ready to begin?" Geri asked.

Bert answered her instead of his brother-in-law. "Dinner, yes. Kwanzaa? There doesn't seem to be any big hurry. We're rather interested in this project of your professor's." Geri shot a triumphant glance at Wilton, but he couldn't decide whether it was because Bert had called him "hers" or because her uncles seemed so eager to discuss his project. Either way, he decided, their unholy alliance seemed to be working to the advantage of both of them. Her scheme was actually working.

He, Bert, and Terry discussed his anthropological research, while he watched Geri take care of her elderly uncle Bruce. She talked to him in matter-of-fact tones as she arranged him comfortably in a chair at the head of the table. She was incredibly patient and gentle with the querulous old man, and Wilton found himself wondering again at the many incompatible aspects of her character. A couple of weeks ago, he'd have described her as a ditz, but clearly there were facets to this woman's personality that were at odds with her open face and forthright manner. From the look of her, he defied anyone to guess Geri could be so devious as to orchestrate this Machiavellian plot.

Hal was teasing Steve about some team he followed that wasn't doing well, much to the younger man's annoyance. But Steve actually took his brother-in-law's teasing in stride, with more grace than Wilton would have expected, given Steve's surliness when he had arrived. Apparently Uncle Steve took his duties as family protector seriously. John's role in the family, too, was quite clear. He scurried between the kitchen and the dining area, putting the finishing touches on the table, filling the ice bucket on the sideboard, and setting out butter, condiments, serving implements, etc.

Gene was watching them all, inserting a question or comment in Wilton's conversation with Bert and Terry, while laying a hand on Hal's shoulder, which seemed to calm him.

"It's time," Geri called. "Or dinner will grow cold."

She came and took Wilton by the hand and led him to his seat. The others were all in their places in moments, and silence reigned for a second.

"Habari gani," Bruce addressed them all from the head of the table.

"It's the greeting we use throughout the holiday, or you can say Harambee instead, which means 'Let's Pull Together' in Swahili," Geri explained in an undertone.

"Umoja," seven voices replied. Wilton echoed them.

"The concept of Umoja, unity, is celebrated on the first day of Kwanzaa," she continued her running commentary. "That's how we respond to the greeting on the first day of the holiday."

"I see."

"Do you know the origins of Kwanzaa?" she asked.

"It was created by a militant in the sixties, wasn't it? Karenga, right? He wanted to create an African-American holiday to celebrate our unique struggle in this country, I believe."

"So you do know a little about this..."

"Will there be a quiz later?" he asked, teasing her.

"No quiz."

"I've read about it, but I'm not familiar with all these rituals," Wilton confessed.

"They're not too strange, are they?" she asked, perhaps in response to his skeptical tone. "I think it's an interesting way to celebrate our heritage."

"In Swahili?" he questioned. "Isn't French more widely spoken in Africa?"

"Swahili is a nontribal language, and I think it's pretty," Geri defended. "For example, the straw mat in the center of the table is called a mkeka. It's a symbol of past traditions. The candelabra is called a kinara, the bowl of fruit it the mazao, and the ears of corn are mehindi, and they symbolize the harvest. Everything has more than one meaning. I can lend you a short book on the subject, and there's a discussion after the libation,'' Geri said.

She lit a black candle in the center of seven in a candelabra, saying, "This first candle is lit in the name of unity—Umoja."

A small clay pitcher was being passed around the table, and a little liquid was poured into a round cup in front of each family member's place setting. "That is the kikome cha umoja, the unity cup." Wilton mimicked the others, and passed the libation water along. "We'll all drink together," she said.

John stood and read, and the others repeated, "For Africa. For our ancestors and their indomitable spirit. For our elders from whom we learn much." At the end of each sentence, a bit of the libation was sipped by each of them.

"For our youth, who represent the promise of tomorrow. For our struggle, and in remembrance of those who have struggled on our behalf." Wilton didn't drink but rather concentrated on listening to the words John was intoning.

"For unity—the ability to understand each other, and the will to love and be loved." This holiday had never made much sense to Wilton, but watching the Tambrays and the Smiths simply being together and speaking words that could have been written expressly for them, he thought he understood its allure.

"On the first day, we discuss the idea of unity. Umoja," Gene said, when the chanting was done. "Does anyone have anything to say on this topic?"

Terry fished a small notepad out of his suit jacket pocket. "I wrote down a quote that I found, but before I read it, perhaps we should ask our guest if he has any questions?"

"Who wrote that prayer?" Wilton obligingly asked.

"It's not a prayer," Geri said. "Kwanzaa is not a religious holiday. We based our libation statement on a text we found in a book on how to celebrate Kwanzaa, and each of us added a little bit to it."

Hal objected. "It feels religious to me." Everyone turned to look at him but, for once it seemed there was no punch line. He was serious.

"It has a feeling of spirituality about it," Bert agreed.

Steve smiled. "Here we go," he said, sitting back in his seat.

As if on cue, a heated debate began about the definition of religion as it pertained to Kwanzaa. The many strains of the conversation were too much for Wilton to decipher, and he let it wash over him, watching Geri as she argued passionately with Bruce, who sat on her left.

After a few minutes, when it became clear that this was an old, and probably a never-ending, argument, Wilton picked Geri's hand up from the table and brought it to his lips. He didn't know why he did it exactly, but it certainly achieved an effect.

Geri stopped arguing with her uncle and stared at him as if he had gone crazy, and it was only when a lull occurred in the other conversations going on around the table that she remembered her role, with a start.

"Wilton, are you hungry?" she asked sweetly.

"Starved," he answered. "How did you know?" He sucked the tip of her index finger into his mouth.

"I just had a feeling," she said with a gulp. Her family by now had stopped talking among themselves and were watching her and Wilton avidly.

"If you'll return my hand, I'll get dinner," Geri offered.

"Thanks," he said, relinquishing her hand.

"My pleasure," she replied, her eyes glittering in the candlelight.

Wilton thought he might have gone too far this time. But after she stood, Geri reached out her hand to grasp his chin lightly. Turning his face, she planted a big, wet, loud kiss on his mouth. Before he could react, she was gone.

# Chapter Six

On the second day of Kwanzaa, Geri suggested Wilton conduct his first interview. Gene volunteered to be the subject. It didn't take long for Wilton to figure out that Geri's favorite uncle had an ulterior motive to his eager participation. He was pumped, hard, for information about their relationship. Though he managed to steer the conversation back to his own questions about Gene's service in the army, the interrogation was only delayed. When they returned upstairs to the others, the subtle questioning began again.

Geri was busy cooking dinner, and she and John were in and out of the room, but Wilton was Gene's captive, and the rest were on hand to throw in their collective two cents as well.

"Geri really hasn't told us anything about you," Bert said apologetically, as he handed Wilton a second glass of wine.

"Of course, we're very curious about the man who has finally captured our little niece's heart," Hal said in his usual joking manner.

"Of course," Wilton agreed as he sipped his drink.

"It's not like her," Bruce barked, staring at Wilton accusingly.

"Geri's always been very outspoken," Wilton said amenably. "I've never known her to be secretive about anything."

"She is honest to a fault," Terry said tolerantly.

"A rare quality in a woman." Hal guffawed at his own joke, but none of the others joined him.

"That's one of the things I admire about her," Wilton responded to the sexist comment. "You always know where you are with Geri."

Gene and the others nodded in agreement. "She usually tells us about the men she's dating before she brings them to meet us."

"If she brings them to meet us," Steve amended.

"I think she mentioned you once," Gene went on, ignoring his brother's inflammatory remark. "But you two were on opposite sides of some kind of . . . debate?"

"Hmmm," Wilton said, noncommittally.

"When was that?" Bert asked.

Gene looked at Wilton, a question in his eyes.

"I think that would have been at the beginning of October," Wilton offered reluctantly.

"Before you starting seeing each other," Bert suggested, ever the diplomat.

"Hmmm," Wilton murmured again.

Gene, deprived of a definitive answer to his provocative line of questioning, pressed futher, "Geri's boyfriends have always before been somewhat . . ." He hestitated to continue, then rushed on. ". . . they've been what you might call 'easily led'."

Wilton believed it. What he didn't know was whether her uncles approved of the jokers she usually dated.

It wouldn't surprise him at all to learn that Geri had berated him thoroughly in front of her uncles while they were involved in that confrontation in October, and then promptly forgot that she'd mentioned him in her tirade when she chose him to play the part of her devoted boyfriend. Her family would remember, though. And while they might have thought it perfectly natural that Geri would argue with her lover, they seemed to think he might not be as easily overpowered by their strongwilled niece as her former boyfriends had been. He was flattered by their assessment of his character, but Wilton recognized the danger. They didn't think he was Geri's 'type'.

So he only volunteered the comment, "Geri is definitely her own woman.' "

"That she is. And as for her ... ahem ... men, well, she likes 'em sort of ... ahem ... she likes them to share her opinions on things," Bert said, still trying to be diplomatic.

Terry interjected. "Geri holds very strong views on certain subjects."

"I've noticed," Wilton said feelingly—perhaps too feelingly since Gene sat forward in his seat, clearly preparing to ask another question.

Bruce beat him to the punch. "You don't seem like the type to let himself be led around by the nose," the old man said bluntly.

"I don't think I am," Wilton said.

"It's a woman's prerogative to change her mind," was Hal's oblique response.

"Why do you suppose she was attracted to you?" Terry asked.

"I couldn't say," Wilton answered. "Pheromones?"

"This is really none of our business," Bert suddenly said.

"We're just concerned about our niece," Gene offered in explanation. "I'm sorry if that make us seem ..."

"Nosy?" Wilton supplied.

"Overprotective," Gene finished.

"Maybe she's tired of dating idiots," Bruce suggested.

"I didn't think they were idiots," Terry protested. "Not really."

"I suppose I should be flattered," Wilton said. "Since I gather what you're all trying to say is that you don't think I'm like the idiots Geri's brought home in the past."

Nods of acknowledgment, accompanied by some uneasy shifting in their seats, told him he'd suceeded in wresting control of the Q and A session from his inquisitors.

"Might I suggest these questions could be better answered by Geri, herself," he said, just as Geri opened the kitchen door.

"Dinner's almost ready," she announced. Then she noticed

the stares of the six men whose eyes had turned to her when she entered. "What?" she asked, hands on hips.

Wilton couldn't resist. "Your uncles have a question for you," he announced.

She stood waiting expectantly. "Well, what is it?" she asked finally.

"Nothing, nothing," Terry answered.

Geri regarded them all with a jaundiced eye, then headed back into the kitchen.

"That wasn't very nice," Hal told Wilton.

"But we deserved it," Gene said.

"Yes, I think you did," Wilton said amiably. Then he went into the kitchen and recounted to Geri exactly what had been said.

She laughed and gave him an exuberant hug. "We've really got them going," she said, pleased.

Apparently determined to keep the men off balance, she spent the rest of the evening touching his hand, kissing his cheek, and brushing against him—until Wilton started to feel as uncomfortable as her uncles clearly felt.

During the candle lighting ceremony, and the libation, she wouldn't even release his hand. But he did receive a reprieve from her attention during the discussion of self-determination which translated into an unpronounceable word in Swahili—Kujichagulia. The meaning of the candles, the mishumaa saba—had been explained to him: the three red candles represented purpose, creativity, and faith, and the three green were for self-determination, collective work and responsibility, and cooperative economics. Each day of Kwanzaa one of the Nguzo Saba (as the seven concepts were collectively called) was discussed during a session called kuchunguza tena kutoa na ahadi tena—as the concept of unity had been on the previous day. The principle of self-determination engendered a debate even more heated than the definition of religion had inspired the night before. The booklet on Kwanzaa from which John read defined self-determination: to make up our minds to accomplish the goals we have set for ourselves.

Wilton asked the table at large, "Why not use the philosophical definition of self-determination: the ability to determine our own fate rather than being controlled by some external force, such as destiny?"

Geri turned to him. "That's just one definition and is not, I think, the most common."

"It's the one I was taught in junior high school," he answered. "What about you?"

"Me, too," Terry chimed in.

"I think my first lecture on free will was directed by Mrs. Brown, in eighth grade," Gene said, "But we defined self-determination in different ways."

"Don't you think that's something each of us should decide for ourselves?" Bert asked.

"I like the book's definition," John said.

"So do I," Gene agreed.

"I didn't mean to imply there was something wrong with it," Wilton explained. "I just wondered, so I asked."

"That's why we discuss these principles," Bert said. "This is supposed to be an open forum."

"You didn't have to ask like that," Geri muttered.

"So do you think there was a specific reason that they redefined the phrase?" Terry asked the table at large.

"It wasn't redefined," Geri said. "The professor's definition isn't necessarily the only one."

"It's what the term connotes that's in question," Terry said.

"Well, to me it connotes making up our minds to achieve certain goals," Geri said, glaring at Wilton.

"That isn't what comes immediately to my mind," he said.

"We know, you think of it as the opposite of destiny," Geri said sarcastically.

"So you don't believe in destiny?" Hal asked Wilton.

"Yes," John called out.

"No," Geri said definitely.

"Yes and no," Gene and Bert both said at once.

The discussion became a free-for-all, and Wilton tried to listen to all seven voices at once. He was unsuccessful.

"Destiny, definitely," Bruce's voice rang out. "For example, how else do you explain these two getting together just in time."

All conversation halted as suddenly as it had sprung up.

Geri's eyes narrowed. "Just in time for what?" she asked.

Bruce didn't answer. Instead he turned to Wilton and smiled. "No other explanation for love," the old man said with complete conviction. "Don't you agree?"

All eyes were turned to Wilton, as seven men and one woman waited for his answer with bated breath. "I guess destiny is as good an explanation as any," he said.

# Chapter Seven

Geri was pleased with Wilton's performance as her lover. It had been three days, and her uncles were totaly convinced, and charmed as well—so much so that all seven dwarfs had agreed to be interviewed. Greer had appointments with them for the rest of the week, and although that meant he would be spending most of the day at her house for the rest of the week, Geri was pleased she'd been able to fulfill her half of their bargain, since Wilton was keeping his part of the deal with such ease.

He was interviewing Bert now. The uncle whom Candy had so aptly dubbed "Sleepy" was the only one of the group who still had reservations about the project. Slightly nervous about how the interview might be going, despite Bert's laconic disposition, Geri brought the two men a pitcher of iced tea.

Wilton barely acknowledged her presence. "I hope this paper will prove that African-American soldiers are more malleable, more programmable if you will, than Caucasians, because the army is the only real point of entry to acceptance by mainstream America and the powers that be."

"There are boys who become very gung ho when they're given the uniform and the gun and the power they bestow, but it's as true of white boys as blacks," Bert argued.

"But I suspect it's more prevalent among African-American men," Wilton persisted.

"I think you've got the wrong end of the stick there," Bert said. "Especially these days. Maybe when I was in the service, almost forty years ago, bigotry would have worked against me more. I know it was true in Vietnam. Before the civil rights movement was so successful, it was easier to be treated unequally, and for us to accept it. But Steve can work his way as far up the ladder as he likes as a policeman, or he could have accepted the offer he received in college to go into the pros. Nowadays our kids can aim as high as they like, whether it's in the private sector or the service."

"Maybe, but not without facing obstacles that they're aware of from the time they first go to school, or watch television. There's an underlying bigotry still, perhaps inherent in being part of a minority. It exists in this country. There's no denying it. The army, on the other hand, once they're satisfied that a soldier is completely indoctrinated—through methods that have been perfected since the dawn of time—welcomes us eagerly. We barely are a minority in that milieu."

"I'm not saying that there isn't racism in the armed forces," Bert said. "I'm just saying that it's a completely different ballgame now than when I enlisted."

Fed up, Geri left. She knew her frustration with Wilton Greer wasn't logical, but she couldn't like the professor using her uncles to prove his theory that black men were so easily manipulated by the system. It made her angrier still that, somewhere deep down inside, she agreed with a small portion of what he said.

She was a pacifist. She had never understood the allure of serving her country. She saw most of the propaganda generated by the government as racist, and felt it took advantage of a demographic which too often left young black men and women with little opportunity for education or advancement. She'd lost a father to one war, and had argued with her uncles throughout her adult life over their dedication to a country that had used them as cannon fodder. She had never understood how they could stand, hands over their hearts, as "The Star-Spangled

Banner" played before a sporting event, and she'd refused to join them. She'd accused them many times of being brainwashed.

But that was her prerogative. They were her family. Wilton had no right to say those things to, or about, them. Or worse, to blame it on the color of their skin. Who did he think he was?

Geri didn't feel she really knew Wilton any better than she had when this all began. He was a very self-contained man, and one, moreover, of whom she didn't completely approve. Sometimes she thought that he looked at her uncles as lab rats and herself as their keeper. There was an invisible line between him and her family, including herself, over which he never stepped. She guessed that he wanted to keep some distance between himself and his subjects, so that he could evaluate his research more objectively, but that clinical approach did not stop him from appreciating her uncles' distinct and individual personalities. She'd seen him repress a smile at one of Hal's terrible jokes, seen him jolly Uncle Bruce out of one of his black moods, discuss writing with Terry, help John clear the table, and toss an orange around with Steve.

He had unbent around the guys, to the extent that Candy had been amazed when she had arrived earlier that afternoon. A stomach virus had kept her from attending on the first night, as planned, but two days later she'd recovered and though Geri had tried to dissuade her from coming at all, Candy insisted. Geri hadn't felt the need for her support, but her friend was adamant. She wanted to see Geri and Wilton Greer together with her own eyes.

Which was why she was waiting in the kitchen when Geri came stomping back upstairs from the basement. "Trouble in paradise?" she asked.

"He doesn't even approve of Kwanzaa!" Geri fumed unreasonably.

"The nerve of some people," Candy said, shaking her head.

"He's got them all wrapped around his little finger, and he's scoffing at us."

"Scoffing at you?" Candy said in an exaggerated British accent. "That cad!"

"He thinks the mishumaa saba should stand for peace and harmony and all that stuff, rather than bloodshed and our struggle. He says half the concepts celebrated during this holiday are antithetical to the other half."

"Sounds like you've got him half convinced," Candy pointed out reasonably enough.

"I don't *care* if he's convinced or not. It makes no difference to me, but . . . but . . ." she spluttered.

"But what? Spit it out, girl. Go on! Vent," Candy urged.

"So it's a little counterproductive to preach peace while remembering the many battles we've fought to get where we are, but that doesn't make it an outdated, militant holiday. Karenga might have been a little radical, but Kwanzaa is based on some pretty sound principles."

"I agree with you," Candy said in soothing tones.

"Don't try to pacify me," Geri warned her.

"I'm just trying to be helpful," her friend defended herself.

"Don't help."

"Fine," Candy said, miffed. She sat in silence while Geri banged pots and pans onto the stove and started removing the greens from the refrigerator.

"You want to do the string beans for me?" she asked.

"I wouldn't want to step on your toes by helping or anything," Candy replied sarcastically.

"I'm sorry," Geri offered.

"Okay." Candy took the colander full of green beans and started snipping off the ends. She let a full minute pass before commenting, "You are a bundle of nerves tonight."

"I know, I know. That man is driving me up the wall." At her friend's baleful look, Geri added quickly, "And don't you dare say I told you so."

"Well, if you want to hear my opinion . . ."

When Candy paused, Geri said, "I'm not sure I do." But then she nodded.

"It's working out a lot better than I expected. He's loosened up a lot. And you two do look good together. If I didn't know better, I'd buy the act."

"Really?" Geri felt a tremendous surge of relief. She hadn't realized how much she needed outside assurance that this convoluted scheme was actually working. So many things seemed to have gone wrong.

"Really," Candy confirmed. "That kiss you gave him ... that was hot!"

"Yeah, well." Geri cleared her throat. That was the main problem. "I've got to give him some of the credit for that."

"I wouldn't have guessed he had it in him," Candy said.

Other than that first night, when Wilton had nibbled on her finger so unexpectedly, Geri had initiated the intimacies between them. But even though he was a cold duck, the professor was a great kisser. And those full lips were absolutely delicious. When that rare smile appeared, it had an unexpected effect on her. He had good hands, too. She'd never have expected the staid, sedate man to move her so with his touch, but the lightest contact between them made her blood race through her veins. Geri had no intention of telling Candy all that though. She couldn't quite believe it herself.

She had actually considered the prospect of an affair with him. The physical intimacies between them had left her shaken and off balance more than once. Despite his cool, reserved manner, she couldn't believe that he was unmoved by the interplay between them. Not when his kisses made her feel so ... excited.

As for his fiancée, he never mentioned her, but from the little she had found out before they started this hoax, she didn't think the woman was right for him. And Geri felt certain, she wouldn't react so violently to Wilton if he didn't feel something for her, too. Would she?

That night when Candy pointed out that Wilton Greer seemed to have discovered some merit to the holiday, she drew some small comfort from the fact. She listened as he argued with the family about the symbols, the meaning, and importance of the rituals they were celebrating, and she thought her friend was right—he did appear to have embraced some of the aspects of

Kwanzaa. The concepts of unity, purpose, and faith appealed to him—that much was clear.

Ujima—collective work and responsibility—was the subject of the nightly debate, and with three of her uncles completely convinced that communism was a dangerous system, the argument grew quite heated. Wilton, however, was obviously on the side of the younger contingent, comprised of Gene and Steve, who were much more open-minded about political systems that countered capitalism.

The lawyer and the police officer clearly appreciated the help of the college professor against Bruce, John, and Hal. Terry and Bert were noncommital. Terry had researched cases on both sides, ad infinitum, and had yet to draw a conclusion. Bert, the mediator, was too tolerant of both arguments to side completely with one group or the other. Bruce, John, and Hal had all fought the Red Menace in their youth, and were convinced communism could be implemented only by a fascist, corrupt government.

Geri admired Wilton's calm manner and grace under fire, and she and Candy threw in a word here or there to keep the conversation going. Of course, there could be no winner. The family might disagree, but there was an underlying respect for each member, no matter how fiercely they argued. These were old arguments, and there had been little change over the years in anyone's viewpoint but her own. When she was young, any or all of her uncles could convince her of anything. But as she grew older, Geri had formed firm opinions on the issues and ideas which were discussed at this dining-room table. She was often claimed, by one uncle or another, as his ally in a debate, whether she voiced agreement with him or not. She accepted that role, as she did the role of their child when that was called for; their nurse, when they needed care; and their housekeeper over the past few years.

Wilton actually said many of the same things she would have, as she and Candy discussed when they went into the bedroom to get her friend's coat. After Candy left, Geri realized that Wilton's attitude toward her had undergone a subtle change since he'd seen her in this setting. He was less arrogant and more respectful than he had been before—which didn't stop him from teasing and tormenting her along with the others.

In some ways he was more like them than she was. He was a man, after all. She couldn't believe she'd once suspected him of being gay. She realized she'd made fun of it because it had seemed to bring him down a peg or two. His conceit had rankled when she'd known him only as Geer the Sneer, the unbending head of the Anthropology Department. Now that she'd seen him clown around with her uncles, she realized it was a thin veneer, which he used to hide his vulnerability.

She wanted to crack that hard surface and get inside. Affair or no affair, Geri was determined that by the week's end she would understand what made this man tick.

Geri was glad in the end that her friend had been there to divert her uncles' attention away from Wilton and herself. She had needed a respite from the constant scrutiny of her family. For two nights it had incited her to carry the masquerade to extremes, and the sexual tension had grown so much that she felt the strain deep in her bones. That night she kissed Greer on the cheek and sent him home and didn't even watch as he walked away. For the first time in three days she slept peacefully, content and unworried about what the next day might bring.

# Chapter Eight

They kissed passionately under the watchful eyes of her uncles. After three nights of this ritual, Wilton's self-control was wearing thin. They danced the usual dance. He had his eyes closed but was very conscious of the eyes staring at the back of his head. She offered her lips to him again and again but never seemed to lose herself in their kisses, as he was so tempted to do. Her expression stayed guarded. He remembered when he had thought Geri so easy to read. All that was different now. She was not the woman he had thought.

He forced himself to try and think of something else ... anything else, but he couldn't get his mind off the woman in his arms. As he prayed for her to end this display, her arms went around his middle. He'd gained three pounds in the last three days, and he wondered if she felt it. The thought of the weight he'd gained helped him control his body's response to Geri's nearness, so he consciously thought about food. Kwanzaa might not be a legitimate holiday, but the African recipes and the African-American dishes Geri served in honor of the celebration were fantastic.

Even so, he found they couldn't compare with the taste, the texture, the tenderness of Geri's mouth. He hadn't had homemade fried chicken, collards, and sweet potatoes that good since the last time he'd been home, and it had satisfied appetites he hadn't even known he'd had, but he would never get enough of *her*. Not at this rate anyway.

Luckily they were never alone. Well, perhaps they were for a few minutes here and there, but their rare moments away from her family were spent talking about her family. Her uncles were always gathered around her, moving toward her, as if she were the center of gravity and they were objects pulled into her sphere. She handled them with amazing skill and sensitivity. It was not at all what Wilton had expected of her. If anything, he'd assumed she'd be more scatterbrained at home than in the office.

Geri had a way of controlling them all without needing to announce, or even acknowledge, her mastery of them. He was reminded of the stories he'd heard of southern nannies, who ran the houses of their so-called masters with a fist of iron. Her men were fed and cared for and kept amused—and she arranged everything so smoothly that everyone in the circle of her protection felt as thought they actually made the many decisions affecting their daily lives. In fact, she ran their lives smoothly, seamlessly, and without appearing to expend any effort on the making of order out of chaos. And each man felt that they were critical to her happiness and comfort, as she was to theirs.

He had to admire that. Even as Wilton tried desperately to find fault with her managerial skills, and to avoid being managed himself, he couldn't in good conscience accuse her of being manipulative when she was just trying to take care of them. Was it bossy of her to stand over Uncle Bruce until he took his pills? Was this whole hoax really just a passive-aggressive strategy she'd come up with in order to get her own way? Geri seemed to care for nothing more than her uncles' welfare. Her devotion to her family was evident in everything she did—from the moment she awoke to shepherd them through the day.

The welcoming kiss had become enough of a ritual that the others took it in stride. If they guessed how hard it was for him to greet them and converse normally afterward, they gave no sign. Of course, if he really were Geri's lover, it was to be expected that he'd need a moment to recover from these passionate encounters. It was Geri's behavior that was bewildering. He watched her walk away as if nothing had happened between them and shook his head in wonder.

For the rest of the night, he concentrated his attention on her uncles. Every once in a while, she stroked his back or touched his hand, but whenever he looked around, surprised that she'd chosen that moment for the public display, he'd find one or the other of her male relatives was watching them. As the evening came to a close, Geri came to sit beside him on the arm of the couch. Bruce had already disappeared up into his room, as had Terry, who always retired early. Hal and Steve were watching college basketball down in the basement, while Bert puttered at his workbench at the back end of the long playroom. Wilton had left them and come upstairs to talk with Gene about his latest case, which had come up at dinner and started a heated family argument.

"It's not uncommon for these girls not to realize they're pregnant until it's too late for them to obtain a legal abortion," Gene was saying when Geri joined them.

"I cannot believe you are going to try to justify that girl's use of crack during her pregnancy," John said angrily, in one of his rare displays of passion.

"They resumed the discussion while they cleared the table," Geri explained, sotto voce, her mouth so close to his ear that he felt her breath against his neck. "I still don't understand what the hospital did wrong," Geri said to Gene. "They had to report the abuse, right?"

"It's not a typical case of abuse. The girl is only four months' pregnant. She didn't even know."

"Ignorance of the law is no defense," John stated.

"This wasn't ignorance of the law, this was ignorance of a pregnancy," Gene averred. "Technically the fetus isn't even a person. The girl, who is nineteen years old, is definitely a person, and her civil rights should be protected, which means the hospital had no right to test her for both drugs and pregnancy. And when they did, they certainly were not required to tell the police and have them arrest her—even if she did refuse to enter the detox program. Reports of child abuse are required, but what they did, they did at their own discretion. This could be a real test case."

"But what would happen if they didn't test for pregnancy and the child was born deformed or incapacitated or dead? Or what if the girl died of complications during labor? Couldn't the hospital be sued for negligence then?" Geri asked.

"Look," Gene said patiently. "This isn't a simple matter of figuring out who was wrong and who was right. Everyone involved has a point of view and a right to protect themselves. My client is a teenager with a nasty habit and is in jail for a crime which doesn't even exist—at least not yet. The doctors want to cure the girl and, if possible, the baby. They can't force her into rehab, but they see a possibility of putting her in jail, maybe getting her some help. Whether it helps her or not, it makes it harder for her to get the drugs which will probably kill her baby. The hospital's lawyers are trying to help the doctors and, more importantly, cover their client's butt against any punitive action I may take.

"And the police are just trying to do their job, which is not at all clear in this case. Maybe they're even hoping to 'do the right thing.' Who knows? But when it comes down to this homeless, impoverished drug addict, one thing they're not worried about is being sued for false arrest. And they should be. Because the most dangerous element in this case is not the sad plight of a nineteen-year-old girl, the rights of her unborn child, or the doctors' needs to fulfill their oath, but the actions of an overzealous, unrestrained police force, who are making decisions based on the status of the citizens they encounter. They cannot abrogate the rights of one of the citizens they are sworn to protect with impunity. They must be held accountable."

"Hear! Hear!" Geri cried.

"Nonsense," proclaimed John. "This is not a good test case. What about the young black boys they hold without cause for hours, even days at a time, just so they'll have bodies for their line-ups? What about the rights of the women—the fine upstanding black women—whom they harass and even arrest because they're pissed off by the sisters' attitude? Why aren't you fighting one of those false arrests?"

"Because I can't win," Gene said sincerely.

"And you think you can win this one?" Wilton couldn't help asking, shocked.

"Probably not, but at least I can help this girl. Those kids they pull in for line-ups and those women they arrest for not responding to their catcalls and such are usually out of there in a couple of hours, perhaps a day. Much as I abhor the practice, I don't think taking one of those cases will change anything, or help anyone. Those things are better off, if not forgotten, at least not allowed to become nuisance cases. This girl could be railroaded into a halfway house or even jail. I'd like to get her out of jail."

"For what?" John asked, disgusted.

"Because she shouldn't be in there," Geri said, aligning herself firmly with Gene.

John shot a look at them that pleaded for patience and turned to Wilton. "You know how it's going to be, don't you? My blockhead of a brother is going to pound his head against a brick wall for nothing; no fee, no justice, no way to win. Whatever the outcome of the hearing, he'll still be the loser."

"I hear you," Wilton said, looking forward to recounting this whole scene to his parents during their regular weekly call. They'd love Gene, he was sure. Geri, too, he believed. She was their kind of women. They barely tolerated his fiancée, Amanda.

He realized it was the first time he'd thought of Amanda in the last forty-eight hours. He felt Geri, perched on the arm of the couch, leaning companionably against his shoulder. Wilton closed his eyes to offer up a quick, silent prayer: *Let me get through this without making a fool of myself, and I'll never even think about so much as looking at another woman again,* he vowed. He'd never been tempted by any other woman since he'd been with Amanda.

Right on cue, Geri suggested, "Why don't we go up to my room, Wilton." It was a test. It had to be.

Geri's room, in that male bastion, was the only one he hadn't been in. The house was small, but they'd arranged it comfortably, two men to each of three bedrooms, and one in a reconstructed walk in closet each with barely more than could be comfortably stored in a footlocker, except in Terry's case. Piles of books under and by his bed testified to his passion in life. And his desk and files overflowed into John's section of their shared bedroom. John's bed and bureau were as neat and clear as the man was himself, barely taking up any space at all.

In Steve and Gene's room, police manuals and lawbooks and their wardrobes dominated, giving the room a bit of a split personality: law and order on one side, civil disobedience on the other. Each man had a clothing rack in the room. Gene's was filled with expensive suits, presumably too numerous to fit in the one small closet. Steve's neatly ironed uniforms didn't take up nearly as much of the bar as his brother's, but his jeans and polo shirts and other casual wear hung beside his uniforms, equally well pressed.

In Hal and Bruce's room, Bruce's pills and other items for his care took over the dresser and tabletops. Hal spent his days at the post office, where he worked, and his evenings and weekends in the basement, with his music and videos. Bert was another retiree. His room still looked almost like the closet, it had been, and his clothes, mainly sweat suits, were piled on shelves he'd built into the walls above his bed.

Wilton couldn't help being curious about the sanctum sanctorum and glanced eagerly around Geri's bedroom as he followed her in. It was surprisingly feminine. Surprising not because she wasn't feminine, but because she seemed so comfortable in this house dominated by men and decorated to suit their taste.

He'd played pool with Geri in the basement playroom, and watched football with her on the thirteen-inch television in the kitchen while ostensibly helping her to prepare dinner. That time, too, they'd been behind closed doors together, but it had been different. Her uncles hadn't intruded on them, but they might have decided to come into the room anytime. He was sure none of the seven men would dream of disturbing them here.

Geri's domain wasn't at all what he expected, and yet it

should have been. Within this male bastion, her room was a pale pink color. The curtains on her windows were not the monochrome of all the others, but were paisley—red and deep purple and lavender. Her bed was brass, but not the dull antiqued brass of the fixtures that had been built into the house, but gleaming gold.

The bedspread was a rich red, and mounds of throw pillows of purple and light blue lay at both the head and foot of the bed. Her large desk was dominated by her computer and its cardboard frame, which was covered with the exploits of Warner Brothers cartoon characters. In contrast, an old hardwood rocking chair sat under the window, next to the radiator. A white lace shawl had been draped over its curving back.

And there were bookshelves against all the walls, almost up to the ceiling. They were filled with books, small knick knacks, and photo after photo. The decor was feminine, and busy, and a little silly, and, like so much else about her, it surprised him.

"Are you finished?" Geri asked, when he had thoroughly inspected the room.

"You can't blame me for being curious," Wilton said. Various uncles had given him tours of the house, but they'd skipped Geri's quarters—primarily, Wilton guessed, from habit. It was her domain, and they'd been well trained concerning her right to privacy within her own room. *If only they'd accorded her the same privilege in regard to her love life, I wouldn't be in this mess now*, he thought.

"I would think you'd know more about me by now than you ever could have wished," Geri said, smiling.

"I think I have begun to understand you, but I am a little confused about why you asked me up here. Obviously you want your uncles to think we're . . ." Wilton searched for the right words.

"Doing the nasty?" she said bluntly.

"Ummm, yes, well, but why now?" he asked.

"They know you well enough to approve," she said with a casual shrug of her shoulders. "And I thought, maybe we could skip the good night kiss. It's getting to be a real production.

If we stayed up here for a while, they would assume we'd said our good-byes in private tonight." She sat on the bed.

"Huh?" Wilton responded, shocked at this sudden display of modesty on her part.

"They might be suspicious if I give you another quick kiss on the cheek, after the way we've been saying goodnight all along, don't you think?"

"Sure," he said. "I understood you the first time. I was just surprised. I thought you ... um ... enjoyed those little performances." He took a seat at her desk, swiveling the chair around to face her.

"I did in the beginning," Geri said sheepishly. "But it's getting a little old."

He didn't think of himself as conceited, but Wilton found the distaste she expressed for their kisses a little bit insulting. He must have looked somewhat taken aback by her answer, because she hastened to add, "They're completely convinced, so it's not as much fun anymore. I feel a bit guilty."

"Now you get a conscience?" he said, smiling.

She stuck her tongue out at him. "I should think you'd be glad to take a break."

He shrugged. He was relieved, but he wasn't about to tell her that. "It doesn't make any difference to me one way or the other."

"Liar," she said.

Wilton stared at her in disbelief. "What did you call me?"

"You are so full of it," she declared.

"What exactly are you accusing me of?"

"You like kissing me. Admit it," she taunted him.

"I will not." He might concede to himself that this woman was getting to him, but he would never admit it to her.

"Right," Geri said. The single word dripped with sarcasm.

"What do I have to say to convince you?" Wilton asked.

"Hmmm." She considered it for a moment. "Look me right in the eye and tell me you don't feel anything for me when we're in one of those liplocks you lay on me every night."

He rose and stood before her. "I do not feel anything." He

had always been a convincing liar, so he didn't feel any qualms about lying to her.

She smiled at him saucily. "You paused."

"I do need to breathe," he pointed out reasonably.

"Funny, I haven't noticed any problem with breath control when you're kissing me," she teased.

"Oh, forget it," he said and started to turn away.

"Don't feel bad. I feel the same way," she said, offhand.

"How's that?" he asked, grasping at this chance to regain some control of a situation that was rapidly disintegrating.

"All this kissing and touching and everything. It's having an effect on me, too."

"Oh?" Now this was interesting.

"It would probably be the same with anyone. Don't flatter yourself," she said.

He probably should just have agreed with her and changed the subject, but after her needling, he couldn't resist baiting her a little. "Sure it would," he said with a smirk.

"Let's just drop it, shall we?" Geri suggested.

"Fine with me," he agreed.

# Chapter Nine

They had both settled in her room, each reading a book from Geri's shelves, when there was a knock at the door.

"Hello?" Hal called from outside. "I hate to interrupt you two, but I brought you a little dessert."

Geri was already up, off the bed, and she pulled Wilton out of the rocking chair. "One minute, Uncle Hal," she yelled. "Take off your shoes," she said to Wilton. "And give me your jacket, tie, and shirt." She stepped out of her shoes as she spoke and skimmed her skirt down over her thighs. She was thankful she'd worn her silky pink shorts and the matching pink camisole as she unbuttoned her blouse.

"Move!" she whispered urgently, when Wilton just stood gaping at her. Quickly he stripped down to his white undershirt, while she rolled around on the bed. "Coming, Uncle Hal," she called out as he handed her the items she'd requested. Not satisfied with the effect of her roll on the neat bedclothes, she pulled at the quilt until it dangled precariously off the side of the bed. Geri threw the jacket and tie on her desk and then she put his shirt on as she started for the door. "Lie down," she hissed.

She waited for him to lie on his side on the rumpled bed,

his head propped on his hand, then she opened the door. "This couldn't wait?" she asked her uncle in a long-suffering voice.

"My special rum balls," he said. "I know you like them warm." Hal craned his head to get a look over her shoulder. She pretended to try and block his view but actually made sure he got a good look at her provocative outfit and her coconspirator.

"Thanks," she said gruffly, taking the dish from his hand and closing the door on his smirk.

Wilton was already scooting off the bed by the time she'd turned around. "Do you think that was really necessary?" he asked. His pompous, overbearing attitude was so irritating, she barely managed to keep her temper under control.

"Don't you?" she snapped. She thrust toward him the plate she held in her hands, covered with golden rum balls glistening with honey. "In this family, Hal's rum balls are considered the ultimate aphrodisiac."

"An aphrodisiac, huh? So what do you think this means?"

"It means you're an idiot," she mumbled.

"Hey, I'm just wondering whether they're completely convinced. Otherwise, why offer us these?"

After his earlier comments about how unaffected he was by the physical contact between them, it had been hard enough to keep a civil tongue in her head, but for Geri this was the last straw.

"Because they're not as uptight as you are," she said, disgusted. "What does it take to get through to you, Professor. Do you need a brick to fall on your head? They like you. They approve." She sighed, exasperated. "How can a man with so many degrees be such a numskull?"

"Why are you getting so testy?" he asked, bending over to put his shoes back on. Geri almost dropped the plate of rum balls on his head, but she managed with considerable difficulty, to get a grip on herself.

Speaking slowly and clearly, she spelled out for him their newest dilemma. "You and I are supposed to be lovers. We have been secretly courting for the last three months. I bring you home to meet the family. This is a big deal to my uncles.

These men consider themselves like fathers to me. They want us to know we have their blessing. Their blessing, Wilton. Get it? What is so hard to understand about that?''

"So they send Hal up here with a batch of rum balls?" Wilton looked at her quizzically.

Standing in his shirt and her underwear, in her bedroom, feeling an inexplicable attraction to the last man on earth she would have ever considered she could be attracted to, Geri lost the last vestiges of control. "Try one. These things are like one hundred proof. Maybe two hundred." She picked up a rum ball and held it up to his lips until he ate it. Then she fed him another.

He chewed, swallowed, and smiled. "These are good!"

"I know," she said through her teeth. "They're foolproof. Though you may be the fool who disproves it."

"What are you getting so mad at me for?" Wilton asked innocently.

The anger drained out of her slowly. "Did you ever think that maybe this thing has gone a little too far?" Geri said wearily.

"I thought this was what you wanted," he said, taking another rum ball and popping it in his mouth.

"I think they're expecting a proposal," Geri announced.

"I had the impression that nothing would please you more." He licked his fingers and went back for more. "I believe your exact words were, 'If they thought you were marriage material, it might keep them off my back for months.' "

Watching him eat the delectable dessert whet Geri's appetite. She took one of the warm, soft dough balls, dripping in honey, and ate it slowly as she explained. "I know. But I didn't know I'd feel so . . . conflicted about it." Completely aside from her own burgeoning feelings for the impossible Wilton Greer, which were surprisingly strong, Geri had begun to worry about how her uncles would feel when she told them the affair was over. They would be so disappointed. She felt even guiltier when she imagined how they'd feel if they knew the whole romance was a hoax. They had deserved to be hornswoggled— one good trick deserved another—but she hadn't meant to break any hearts. And she was afraid that was just what she was going to do.

"So? What? Do you want to end it now?" Wilton asked.

Geri was pleased to note that he looked a little disappointed. Little as she enjoyed the effect he had on her senses, her ego had been stung when he insisted their kisses did nothing to him. Even though she knew it was a lie.

She sat down next to him on the bed. "No. I've gone this far, I might as well get something out of it." She sighed.

"I'm glad you said that," he said. "I've got two more interviews still to do."

"Don't you ever think of anything beside your work?" Geri asked, as she chose the largest of the remaining rum balls to nibble on.

"Sure," Wilton said expansively. Their argument seemed to have diffused some of the tension between them. She had never seen him look this at ease. Even half naked, lying on her bed and trying to look lascivious, there had been an air of reserve about him. But he'd finally lost it.

"Work is deeply satisfying. It's so nice and simple. You do it, you write it up, you get the publishing credit and the kudos from your colleagues. It's all very ... straightforward," he mused. "And the admiration and respect it earns you is an added bonus."

"There are more pleasant ways to get admiration," Geri pointed out, "without working yourself to the bone."

"Like wearing short skirts?" he prompted. "My legs aren't as nice as yours."

"No." Geri was too drained to be indignant. "I meant caring for people. I admire all of my uncles, and between them, they have only three bachelor's and one law degree between them, and less publishing credits. No one ever sees Terry's novels, but he tries. You've got to respect that."

"True," Wilton agreed. "I admire your family immensely. You've got something very special here."

Geri looked at him, astonished, and realized he had eaten nearly the entire plate of rum balls. The two or three she had eaten had helped her to mellow considerably. The other nine or ten had had a strong effect on him. "You're drunk!" she blurted.

"I don't think so," he said.

"Close your eyes," Geri commanded. "Arms straight out to the sides." He obeyed. "Touch you nose with your index fingers, right then left."

"I think I'm supposed to stand up to take this test." He stood, closed his eyes, tilted his head back, and nearly fell on top of her.

"Ooops," he said.

Geri started to laugh. "I wish I had a camcorder handy. No one will ever believe me if I tell them you said oops."

"Good thing you don't have one then," he said, laying back.

"Why? It wouldn't hurt if people saw you as a human being for once. You're just a man," Geri said, leaning over him.

"I didn't mean me, I meant you." He looked down at her and she followed his gaze. His shirt had fallen open, and her flimsy camisole did not leave much to the imagination.

"Sorry," she said, sitting up quickly.

"You've got a great body," Wilton said, his eyes sliding closed.

"If you've got it, flaunt it," Geri joked, embarrassed.

Her back to him, she took off his shirt and threw it behind her, aiming at his head. Then she stood and retrieved her own skirt and blouse, in a pile on the floor. When she looked back at him, he'd raised a corner of the cotton shirt off his face and was watching her.

"A gentleman wouldn't peek," she chided, buttoning her blouse.

"Who said I was a gentleman," he retorted, grinning wickedly.

"Show's over," Geri declared.

She slid her skirt on over her hips.

"What a shame." He sounded truly regretful, but he ruined the effect when he dropped the edge of the shirt he held so it covered his face again.

When her shoes were back on, Geri checked the clock. They'd been closeted up here long enough to satisfy the seven nosy dwarfs. Her uncles were in all likelihood in their beds by now. "Wilton, it's time to go." She grabbed his jacket and stuffed the tie in the pocket. "Wilton?" He didn't stir.

Slowly she slid his cotton oxford shirt off his face. His closed eyelids did not even flicker.

"You can't sleep here," Geri hissed. The only extra bed in the house was the foldaway in the basement, and she couldn't risk his discovery down there. "Please wake up," she pleaded.

He mumbled something unintelligible and tried to turn over, but with his legs draped over the edge of the bed, and his feet on the floor, he stayed in the same awkward position, despite his attempt to roll over.

Geri knelt over him and patted his cheeks. "Wilton!" His breathing remained deep and regular. "You don't drink much, do you?" The question was completely rhetorical. Clearly he wasn't going to answer her. "Great. Where am I supposed to sleep?" Geri asked the walls.

# Chapter Ten

Wilton found Geri curled up like a cat at the end of the bed when he woke up. She didn't awaken when he lifted her and placed her head on the pillows and covered her with the comforter she'd thrown across him the night before.

He snuck out of the Smith-Tambray residence just as the sky began to grow light. When he looked up at the house as he walked to his car, he noticed that two of the upstairs lights were on. Probably Terry, working on his latest opus, and perhaps Steve and Gene, whom he knew to rise early to commute into their respective offices in the city. So the family would know he'd spent the night, he guessed.

He'd made as little noise as possible when he left, but there was the telltale sound of water running in the bathroom, and the tread of his leather-soled shoes on the creaky wooden staircase. He didn't suppose Steve's trained ears would miss those.

He wondered how Geri would feel about that. She'd been upset enough the night before when those rum balls had arrived. He was still amazed at how Hal's simple offering had set her off. After the convoluted twists and turns of the plot they were involved in, it had been the offer of a harmless little dessert that had unnerved her.

"Harmless!" A bark of laughter escaped him. "Lethal!" he said aloud. They had destroyed him. All his pretensions, the illusion he'd held on to that Geri Tambray-Smith was just some scatter-brained female, the delusion that he was in complete control of the situation, and that his world hadn't been knocked upside down and sideways—all of it was destroyed. He had a lot to do. He had an engagement to break. He had short-term and long-term career goals to reassess. The offer he'd hoped for from Cornell University was no longer one he could or would accept. Geri would never move so far away from her family. Even assuming she gave him a chance to plead his case, he had his work cut out for him where Geri was concerned. She'd never agree to date him now. Her plan was effective only if he stopped seeing her when Kwanzaa was over. Time was running out. He had only three days left of the holiday to convince her to start fresh. And he had a nagging suspicion that she didn't like him much.

She'd been pretty open about her opinion of him. Geri thought he was a stuffed shirt, pompous and arrogant. She was polite about it, but he knew that that was how she perceived him. She hadn't tried to hide it much. He guessed that it was one of the reasons she'd chosen him for this experiment.

The problem was, how did he convince her she had him all wrong when, if he were completely honest with himself, he'd have to admit she'd summed up his personality quite accurately?

He decided on the spot that he couldn't afford to think that way. As Geri would say, he'd never get anywhere with such a defeatist attitude. He had to go for it—to use another of her aphorisms and just hope for the best.

That evening at dinner, he began his campaign with a subtle assault on her senses. He fed her her dessert, then licked whipped cream from the corner of her mouth. Her eyes widened in surprise, and only his hand at the back of her neck kept her from pulling away.

"What are you doing?" she whispered in his ear a few seconds later.

"Tasting you," he answered shamelessly, when she offered him her ear for his response. He nipped it. It was the one advantage he had, given to him by Geri herself, in her naivete. She'd admitted that his touch affected her. He felt no compunction in putting that information to good use.

A speaking glance from her big brown eyes promised retribution, but in the presence of their audience, she could do nothing but laugh and submit to his ministrations.

As usual, during the kuchunguza tena na kutoa ahadi tena, the time to recommit themselves to the Nguzo Saba, the seven principles of Kwanzaa, Wilton couldn't wait to argue semantics. The concept to be discussed on the fifth day of Kwanzaa was Nia, purpose, which was defined in the booklet as having a plan for the future and a willingness to help others to succeed as well.

"I think it's clear in this instance that the definition of purpose does not match that in *Webster's Dictionary*," Terry said, before Wilton could say anything. "But the intent of the authors is clear. To have purpose in one's life and to foster that sense of purpose in others is of inestimable value to our community. Wouldn't you agree?" He addressed the question to Wilton, but some of the others at the table were eager to respond.

Gene jumped right in. "I don't object to the definition—"

"For the record, neither do I," Wilton interjected.

"But it doesn't go far enough," Gene added. "It was written in the sixties, and things have changed. If Karenga were writing a guide to Kwanzaa today, he'd have to be more specific about what kind of plan we were talking about. Would it include other minorities? Would we support Hispanics and Asians? Would he call on whites to celebrate the contributions made to this society by African Americans in the same way?"

"I think this holiday is for us. That's why we celebrate our ancestry and traditions as well as trying to live up to these principles," John said.

"I enlisted in the army to get an education, but I don't think the concept of Nia was defined by Karenga as achieving our goals at any cost. Did my stint in Vietnam fulfill any of the principles that this holiday celebrates? Ever since that interview with Wilton, I've been questioning whether I should have 'gone along' with the family's tradition of military service. I have achieved much of what I set out to do, but I had to give up a lot to do it. I still do."

"You can accomplish a lot working within the system," Bert said.

"A racist, sexist system, that tries to exploit its weakest members? I don't think anyone could have predicted that we would come so far in thirty-some years and still face so many of the same problems," Steve said. "They might have predicted the Watts riot in 1968, but do you think they ever imagined that we'd have another one in the nineties?"

Wilton finally spoke up. "I think they would have predicted that the riots in the sixties would have caused a much greater change than they actually did. As you all know, I don't think Karenga and the militants of his time thought that fostering black pride and empowerment would lead to peace, or that peaceful protest would be effective against the white establishment. So they couldn't predict that racism could remain so prevalent, even in a society which prides itself on its emphasis on civil liberties."

"Would Karenga have supported Clarence Thomas's nomination to the Supreme Court?" Geri asked. "Would he have chosen a black man who, as the head of the Equal Opportunity Commission, had more discrimination complaints pressed against him than anyone in the history of the position? Would success for the race have meant more than living up to the principles celebrated during this holiday?"

"No," Gene said. "I don't think so."

"I find it hard to believe," John started to say, but he was drowned out by Terry and Bert, who both said, "But—" at the same time.

"It is important to have black representation on the highest court in the country," Bert said. "And Thomas, unpopular as he may be, is qualified."

"Perhaps he's not the most qualified," Terry went on. "Not even among the African-American judiciary, but that position is also a political one. Blacks have the right to be as conservative as whites."

Uncle Bruce started coughing, a deep, hacking, painful sound which brought the conversation to a halt. When he caught his breath, he had everyone's concerned attention. He took advantage of it to say, "We're not going to settle this here tonight or any other night. Maybe that's why the definition is so short. So that it might be left open to interpretation."

"I hadn't thought of that," Wilton said. The group broke into small side discussions of the topic, and he looked at Geri. "So do you want to fight about this?"

"Would you like to help me in the kitchen?" Geri asked, as she started to clear the table.

"Of course," Wilton agreed. He would not have minded being alone with her, despite the fact that she was going to punish him for his behavior at the first opportunity, but her uncles didn't afford them any privacy. John came in and out of the small kitchen, helping to clear the table. Bert and Hal offered their assistance as well. Geri was able to shoo those two away, but she couldn't get rid of John, who always jumped to help with the household chores. She had little more hope with Gene, who had been watching them curiously all through the meal, and wandered in and out of the room to check on them. Finally, however, her uncles left them alone to watch the playoffs in the playroom.

Mindful that Gene or any of the others could walk in on her and Wilton at any time, Geri waited until the last plate had been loaded into the dishwasher, and the only sound in the room was its soft steady hum, before she asked, "What did you think you were doing in there?"

"What? When?" Wilton asked, all innocence.

"You know exactly what I'm talking about," Geri said, just managing, with a visible effort, to keep her voice down. "That little display at dinner."

"You didn't like it?" He tried to sound disappointed.

"Didn't you think it was a bit over the top?" she asked. "Up until now I wouldn't accuse you of overacting, but tonight you went a little too far."

"For whom?" Wilton challenged her. "After last night, I don't think your uncles have any illusions left about their niece's ... discretion."

She seemed taken aback by his response. Wilton hadn't intended to sound so peevish.

"How can you talk about discretion after that performance? Do you think your fiancée would call that discreet?"

"You are worried about my fiancée?" he asked in patent disbelief.

"No, but you should be," Geri said. Wilton didn't think this was the time to tell her he planned to end his engagement. He had only two nights left of Kwanzaa to change her opinion of him, and he didn't think that would be the best place to start. If he sensed the slightest softening in Geri's attitude toward him, he'd tell her, but for the moment he was more interested in getting to know her better and letting her know him.

He changed the subject. "If you lived alone, you wouldn't have to worry about your uncles' shenanigans."

"Shenanigans? No wonder you get along with them so well. You're about as old fashioned as they are."

"Maybe, in some ways. Being an anthropologist, and classically trained, I tend to appreciate certain customs, even outdated ones. I would have thought that would appeal to you, now that I've seen the men in your life."

"I appreciate a lot of different kinds of men," Geri said. He recognized her attempt to scandalize him—it was her usual defense mechanism. Now that he had seen her in her natural setting, he thought he understood why she wore big African jewelry and short tight skirts, and perched on the edge of desks while speaking to faculty and students alike, in order to appear much less conventional than she actually was. It was not that she didn't want to be taken seriously, but rather that she wanted respect on her own terms or not at all.

It had been that other Geri Smith he'd expected to see when he'd first walked through the doors of this house. It was that provocative young woman he'd been afraid to tell his colleagues he was dating. But he'd discovered that the inner Geri Tambray-Smith was not nearly as outrageous as her clothes and hair and demeanor would suggest.

"Why do you do that?" he asked. She looked at him quizzically. "Why do you pretend not to care about your uncles' opinions? I know that you do. Otherwise I wouldn't be here."

"Of course I care. I just don't want them to try to run my life. It's mine. I love them, but I'm my own person, and they'll just have to accept that."

"Good thing you stood right up to them then," he teased.

"They won't listen," she excused herself.

"They listen to you. I don't know if you realize it, but you're the one running this house."

"Good," Geri said, pleased.

"So that's what you want? That's why you live here?" he pressed.

"Am I your latest research project?" Geri asked impishly.

"No, I'm just trying to understand why a young, beautiful woman chooses to live with seven substitute fathers and then pretend she doesn't."

"I do not pretend—" Geri started to protest. The door began to swing open, and Wilton pulled her to him and kissed her deeply.

"Don't let me bother you," one of her uncles said. Vaguely, Geri recognized John's voice, but for once she forgot about their audience and concentrated on the sensation Wilton aroused in her. At first, Geri stood immobile, but when his hands roamed over her back, her arms slid over his shoulders. John had quickly retrieved something from the refrigerator and left, but that fact had barely registered on her when their lips shifted and locked.

She had never imagined a simple kiss could be this dangerous. Before it had been she who'd been kissing him. Not that Wilton hadn't kissed her back, but he had let her lead the way, while he followed and held himself back. This time he didn't just passively allow her to take control, he took all she offered.

He deepened the kiss and it changed. Finally they were both giving all they had, and her entire body was seared by the heat. She gave in to the sensation of being surrounded by him, his strong arms a cage of muscle around her, his thighs pressed against hers. Her hand dipped down his back. He shuddered.

Abruptly she broke away. "We can't do this," she said.

"I'm not interested in a casual affair," he said.

"It would be easy to get carried away," Geri agreed. "All this forced intimacy—"

"It's not that," Wilton said. "Last night I realized something about us."

"Us?" she echoed, with a sardonic smile. "Was that before or after you ate that pound of rum balls?"

"Before . . . and after I woke up this morning," he persisted. "I felt it before, when we talked. As different as we are, I'm comfortable with you in a way I never have been with any other woman."

"What about what's-her-name, Amanda?" Geri reminded him.

"I never felt this way with her."

*Whew!* Geri thought. *Trouble coming.*

Before she could stop him, he said, "I know this is new to you—it certainly is for me—but I think we've got something special. From what your uncles say, I don't think you've ever let a man get close enough to you to see what I do."

"Oh, my, don't tell me . . . you've joined the ranks," Geri said, horrified. "You're supposed to be on my side."

"I am. I promise. But I have to say this—"

Geri interrupted. "Don't say anything. This will all be over in a couple of days, and then we'll go back to the way things were before. Wait. You'll see. You'll be wondering what you ever saw in me."

"That will never happen. I know myself. And I know you."

"You don't know anything about me," Geri said. "If you did, we wouldn't be making love. You'd be as frustrated and confused as I am about being attracted to someone whose beliefs are so completely at odds with your own."

"I think you're just so used to letting your radical views defend against anyone getting close to you, that you can't see the truth when it's right in front of your face. But I know you and I share similar views on a lot of subjects. Your uncles told me that talking to me about their military service is a lot like talking to you about it. And I know it's just stubbornness that keeps you from agreeing with me half the time. But that's beside the point. We don't have to agree. That makes no difference. My father and mother have had a happy marriage for forty years, and they disagree about politics, religion, all the sacred cows."

"You are not your father. Didn't you say he was an activist?"

"So what?"

"That's exactly what I'm talking about. I am attracted to activists. I've even dated a radical or two. No way would I ever date a conservative."

"You're being ridiculous. Those are just labels."

"Some labels mean something. They're descriptive. I am black. I am female. That makes me a woman and a minority. But where do I fit in when people talk about women and minorities? Nowhere. Because I am both. That makes me invisible."

"Maybe you fit in both places?"

"Of course I do," Geri said condescendingly. "But I belong to a third group: women who are also minorities. Our needs are not met when the needs of women or minorities are the issue. Our struggle is addressed only when the rights, or lack thereof, of minority women are debated."

"Okay, okay," Wilton conceded. "This is a very interesting debate, and I'd love to continue it, but we're getting away from the point."

"Wilton," Geri said through clenched teeth. "That is my point. You don't know what you're talking about, that's my point."

"You're just hiding behind this rhetoric, so you won't have to face the real problem here, which is that you and I do feel something special for each other," he claimed.

"It's something we shouldn't feel," Geri said. "And it will go away. When we're not in such close proximity all day every day, it will disappear."

That was exactly what Wilton was afraid of. He had no intention of letting her forget about him. And he wasn't going to give her the chance to try. She had to agree to keep seeing him after the new year began.

# Chapter Eleven

Geri couldn't believe she had kissed Wilton like that. One minute they'd been arguing about her choice of life-style, and the next ... the next she'd been exploring the warm, dark recesses of his mouth. This was Greer the Sneer she was falling in lust with. It was unbelievable.

He thought he knew everything, like her uncle Bruce. At least Bruce had a good excuse, he was almost eighty years old. And he suffered from arthritis. His inflexibility was at least partially the fault of his physical suffering, and even he didn't have the gall to tell her that she didn't know who she was. Geri knew exactly who she was. She knew she was a mass of contradictions, and she liked herself that way. Yes, she was a true woman of the nineties in her dress, her attitudes, and her ambitions. And at the same time, she did appreciate her uncles' old-world values and manners, and her family understood, for the most part. Bruce and Terry might think she should dress a tad more conservatively, and John and Hal might wish she had a bit less of a mouth on her, and Steve and Bert might disapprove of her choice of dates, but all of them loved her—warts and all, as Gene would have said.

If only Wilton were more like her favorite uncle. The two

men had a lot in common. They were both brilliant, dedicated to their professions and ambitions, but Gene didn't have an uptight bone in his body. And he certainly didn't share Wilton's attitude toward African-American soldiers. In fact, philosophically, they were polar opposites. Gene was caring, compassionate, and nurturing in his work and at home. Wilton Greer was demanding, an exacting taskmaster whose private life was just an extension of his profession. That fiancée of his sounded like some treat.

*So his girlfriend is a cold fish,* Geri thought, *it makes sense.* She was perfect for him. Geri would have been willing to bet that the perfectly coiffed, perfectly manicured, perfect Amanda would have died of shock if Wilton attempted to seduce her on the kitchen floor.

When she called Candy to pour out her troubles in a sympathetic ear, her best friend agreed with her assessment. "It sounds like you may have loosened him up a little too much."

"Oh, you know how it is." Geri tried to make a joke of the disturbing news. "I'm just too tempting to resist."

"Hey, I don't suppose Greer can afford to be too picky. He's lucky to be getting any," Candy said.

"He's not bad looking," Geri commented. She could have slapped herself, when Candy answered,

"What's this, girl—you starting to like him now?"

"I just meant he wasn't a complete toad. He could get a girl. You know there are a lot of women out there who will overlook almost anything for a man with a decent body and a good job."

"You got that right. Too many!" Candy exclaimed. That doesn't mean you have to make exceptions for that stuck-up, self-centered egotist."

"He's not that bad. He's all right," Geri defended him.

"All right? I don't know, babe. I still think he's doing better than he deserves pretending to date you."

"I'm no prize," Geri answered self-deprecatingly. "Ask the last ten or twelve guys I dated."

"I don't need to ask anyone anything. Geri, you're worth ten of him."

Geri realized she must be sounding somewhat pathetic if Candy was feeding her lines. Usually her good friend was also her most honest critic. She hadn't called her friend because she was feeling sorry for herself. She called because she wanted to be told she was right to send Wilton on his merry way.

It was time to lighten up. "If I do say it myself, though, I do look good. It's not hard to figure out why the professor lost his head."

"You had me worried for a second there, but I guess I don't have to be concerned about you, girlfriend. Kwanzaa ends tonight, and then he'll be gone—back to the Anthropology Department with all the other dusty antiques."

"I was thinking of asking him to your New Year's party. Just to celebrate the success of my little plan," Geri said hesitantly.

"Really?" Candy was surprised. "It's up to you, of course. You know my New Year's bash is always open to everyone. But you could do better, Geri," she said again. "A whole lot better," she asserted.

"Maybe," Geri agreed, but inwardly she was really looking forward to that last kiss. It seemed somehow fitting that on the stroke of midnight, during the first second of her thirtieth year, she'd be kissing Wilton Greer good-bye. Geri knew she could never explain what she was feeling to Candy though, so she didn't even try.

"We'd better get cooking, if we're going to give the guys the meal we promised them."

She had two more family dinners to get through before she was going to get rid of him, so Geri turned her restless energy to preparing special meals for both nights. Kuumba, creativity, was the concept celebrated on the sixth night of the holiday. That was her inspiration for cooking a traditional African dish as the centerpiece of her dinner. But before she had a chance to present her masterpiece, the discussion at the dinner table took an unexpected turn.

When John finished reading the libation statement, Wilton stood instead of Terry, who usually made the opening statement, the kukaribisha.

"I was thinking about reading this tomorrow night, but I

can't wait," he said. He pulled an index card from his suit jacket pocket and turned to her. 'And now abideth faith, hope, and charity, these three; but the greatest of these is charity.' "

Geri was too amazed to move as he leaned over to kiss her cheek. Then she smiled beyond him, at the others who were watching the two of them, entranced.

"Honey," she declared. "That was just . . ." She searched her befuddled brain for the right words. "A load of sentimental claptrap" was the phrase that came immediately to mind, but it was discarded just as quickly. ". . . just beautiful," she finished lamely. "But charity is not one of the seven concepts we celebrate during this holiday," she chided him gently.

"It's certainly implied," Gene said. "Don't you think so?" He polled the table. The other men all immediately murmured their assent.

"We're, ahem, supposed to be discussing creativity," Geri reminded them.

"Leaving out charity was a major oversight on Karenga's part," Wilton insisted. "I could use a night devoted to charity right about now. Specifically, a favor. From you."

"I cooked dinner," Geri said, deadpan.

"Just what is it you want from her?" Bert prodded gently.

"I want her . . ." Wilton said, gazing into her eyes. "To say . . ." He hesitated while everyone, Geri included, held their breath. "Yes."

"Yes to what?" Geri asked, disbelieving.

"What do you think?" Steve retorted, sarcastically dripping from every word.

"You're kidding," she said, averting her eyes so that no one would see her stunned expression.

Wilton sat next to her and leaned close. In a soft voice that only she could hear, he said sincerely, "No, I'm serious. I called off my engagement to Amanda. I think you and I should continue seeing each other. For real."

"You and I?" she echoed, still flabbergasted at this unexpected revelation.

"Yes," he whispered. "Don't you?"

Geri recovered her wits sufficiently to say, "We should discuss this later, Wilton."

"It's a simple question," he pressed, the urgency of his request not muted by his lowered voice. "Do you want to go out with me—yes or no?"

Geri didn't know where this was coming from. True, she found him attractive—even desirable at times—like when he ate too many rum balls and passed out on her bed, but that didn't alter the fact that she and he were like oil and water. She had had her office door taken off its hinges and installed easy chairs, while Wilton buried himself so deeply in those musty old tomes in his office that students could barely find a spot to stand if they visited his office during the few hours he was available to them. He didn't even believe in affirmative action, for chrissake! Where did he ever get the idea that they could spend time together without killing each other?

Sadly, Geri realized that Candy's party was out of the question now.

"No," she said. "I really don't think so." She must have spoken more loudly than she intended, because at least two of her uncles groaned.

"Excuse us," Wilton said politely to the table at large. None of her male relatives made any move to stop him as he nearly lifted her out of her seat by her arm and steered her into the kitchen, where he stood with his back against the door. With the only entrance to the room barred, no one could get in, but neither could Geri escape.

"No?" he asked in mild tones.

"I said no and I meant it," Geri said firmly.

"Why not?" he asked. "They'll think we're engaged, which should keep them out of your business, and we'll get a chance to see where this relationship could go."

"I can't believe you asked me that." Geri made a quick circuit of the small room. "We have nothing in common. We're miles apart in our attitudes and beliefs and goals. You have made it clear from the beginning that you don't even respect my opinion. You think I'm some kind of ditz . . . or a freak who has no idea who I am and am wrong in virtually everything I do."

"I never said anything like that," he started to protest.

"Let me finish," Geri snapped. "I thought I had made it quite clear last night that I don't think you're any kind of prize, either. You're conceited, arrogant, bullheaded, and uptight. And you drive me nuts."

"I thought we had come to respect each other," he said gently. He did not appear to be at all offended by her blunt appraisal of their relationship.

"You don't even like me," she said.

"I admit, when I met you, I thought you were a little bit strange ... all right, I thought you were totally bizarre. But after we worked together I admired your mind. I still thought you were a bit unfocused, but now all that has changed. Seeing you here, with your uncles, I've gotten to know you a little bit.

"You don't like pompous jerks like me and the administration belittling your extraordinary intelligence, so you hide it behind miniskirts and big earrings. You won't want to risk losing the approval of the seven men you love, so you hide the hard work you do running this house behind a flip attitude and pretend to flaunt convention. I see the incredible care you take of these men, and I recognize the amazing brain you try to hide under those dreadlocks, and I admire them both immensely."

"If there was ever a backhanded compliment contest, you'd take first place, no problem," Geri joked to cover her surprise. "And they're braids, not dreds."

"So I don't know what they're called. I still like them."

"You do?" she said stupidly.

"I like the way you dress, too. It's you."

She examined his face, but he wasn't lying or patronizing her. That convinced her, it wasn't just physical attraction. He did like her, and you could have knocked her over with a feather. Even her mother hated her braids.

"So now that that's established, can we get back to the real question here?" he asked.

"What's that?" Geri asked, bemused.

"Do you like me? I know I annoy you and otherwise get under your skin, but is that all there is to it?"

"I misjudged you," she apologized after a moment.

"So?" he prompted.

"I still don't think we should see each other again," Geri said.

"Why not? I like you. You like me—even if you won't admit it. We are certainly attracted to each other." He started to close the distance between them, but she held out her arm to ward him off, and he stopped.

"Yes, okay. I like you. But we are still too different. I don't just mean because I like being wild and crazy and you are the most buttoned-down man I know. We disagree on some basic levels."

"We're back where we started. Just because we don't always see eye to eye doesn't mean we can't date," Wilton said.

"Yes, it does! Your thesis for this research paper is a case in point. You think black men can be more easily manipulated than whites. I can't understand how you, especially, can believe that. And if you do, what does that say about you? About me?"

"In this society I think it's a reality," he said haltingly.

"You think black students should do twice the work their white counterparts do, just to come out even," she accused.

"Look, I don't want to get into a philosophical debate with you right now."

Geri jumped on that statement. "I agree. Let's go back to the table." He allowed her to shoulder past him and followed her into the dining room.

"So?" Uncle Bruce asked.

"So what?" Geri replied.

"We want to see you married before we die." Uncle Hal said. Geri assumed he was joking, as usual, but Bruce was completely serious when he said, "You may be the only woman living in this house, but you're not the only one with a clock ticking away."

"You guys are worse than women," Geri complained bitterly. "You're a bunch of mother hens. You want to set my wedding date for me, too?"

"If you want . . ." Steve let his voice trail off, but the threat was unmistakeable.

"I can't believe you," Geri said, disgusted. "Haven't you figured out yet that I'm not ready for that kind of commitment? Why do you think Wilton's here?"

"Honey," he said warningly, but she was too incensed to stop.

"I overheard you telling about your battle plan to set me up—"

"We thought as much," Terry said.

"I think that's enough," Wilton said firmly. Geri wanted to tell them the rest, but he shook his head at her and she managed to rein in her anger.

"I'm sorry," Gene said.

"They're not." She glared at the rest of her family.

"We didn't know about Wilton," John excused himself.

"That's not the point," Geri said. "You should have respected my right to choose for myself. I'm a full-grown woman. I have the right to make my own decisions!"

"We just wanted to help things along a bit," John said. At a look from Geri, he sat back, cowed.

"You'll be thirty in two days," Steve pointed out.

"I didn't notice that was my time limit."

"I thought we were pretty clear on that," Hal said with a smirk.

"Oh, shut up, Uncle Hal," Geri lashed out, frustrated. He looked hurt, but she was too incensed to feel more than a momentary pang of guilt.

"There's no need to bite his head off," Bert said.

"So what do I have to do, leave? I don't know how I could be any clearer. I don't appreciate your interference," Geri bit out. No matter how well intentioned their matchmaking, it still felt like a betrayal. Bert looked away. They were going down like flies. Terry appeared to be lost in thought, and Gene couldn't meet her gaze. Only Bruce and Steve were still prepared to do battle.

"Geri, you're acting like some shrew," Uncle Bruce said gruffly.

"I'm sorry, I guess I don't have your sunny disposition," Geri said unapologetically. "Grumpy," she added under her breath. Apparently he heard that. He started muttering to himself.

"That's it," Steve shouted. "I've had enough of this."

"No, I've had enough," Geri said, raising her voice as well. "You're not going to bully me into doing something I don't want to do, and you"—she turned to face John—"are not going to guilt me into it, and Gene isn't going to talk me into it. When I want your advice, I'll ask for it."

She stormed away from the table and headed for her room. Wilton came after her, catching her at the stairs.

"Listen, Geri—"

"Leave me be!" she demanded.

"They just want you to be happy."

"Then they should just leave me alone," she told him.

"They can't, any more than I can," he said. "We love you."

"I love them, too. That's why I don't try to change them."

"They don't want to change you," he insisted. "They want more for you."

"I've already got more than I can handle," Geri replied.

# Chapter Twelve

Candy usually attended the Karamu, the feast on the last night of Kwanzaa, but this year she had to prepare for her party instead. So Wilton was Geri's only guest at the crowded table that night. She'd hidden in the kitchen for hours preparing a traditional African meal of Gambian Fish Caldou, while Wilton did the last of his interviews down in the basement with Uncle Bruce.

Although a number of the guys had invited guests, Geri was the only single woman at the table as usual. Since Wilton still had the interview with Bruce to do, Geri had not turned him away when he'd shown up. She hadn't talked to him beyond saying "Hello" when he greeted her, since she had no intention of continuing the pointless discussion of the night before. However, he was still presented as her date for the evening. Despite the tension between them, it was a nice change to have a man of her own this year. For once no one razzed her about being single, and no one had to defend her from her uncle's annual birthday teasing about being another year closer to spinsterhood. Even better, the marrieds didn't feel the need to "comfort" her. Best of all, she really enjoyed it when all eyes turned to Steve when the subject of marriage came up. Apparently the guests had all been coached about the sensitivity of that particular issue.

"Faith is the subject of our last night of celebration," Terry intoned, when the time came to open the evening's discussion. "And I didn't bring any clippings or quotes on the subject tonight, because I just wanted to say that my faith is embodied in all my friends and family gathered at this table tonight." He cleared his throat and looked from his brothers to his brothers-in-law and included his niece as he continued. "We are complete, and I believe that makes us victorious in our struggle to survive and thrive in this world."

Geri's eyes misted up and she reached blindly for her napkin. Wilton captured her hand and held it for a moment. Geri gently disengaged herself. It was sweet of Wilton to let her know he'd forgiven her, but she still had an apology to make to the others. By tacit agreement, they'd all gone on as though nothing had happened. She had felt on coming into a room occupied by two or more of her uncles, that they had ceased talking, or changed the subject, on her entrance, but no one broached the subject of the ugly scene which had taken place the night before. For the most part Geri confined herself to her room and the kitchen, while the men spent a good part of the day in the basement.

"Umm, I'd like to say something as well," she said. "I feel just as Terry does and, more than that, I want you all to know how lucky I feel to be a part of this family. You are my strength, and I count on you to forgive my weaknesses, to bolster my confidence, and to support me in each of my endeavors. You have never let me down. I appreciate your faith in me. And I love you guys." There was a murmur of appreciation from their guests, and the sound of more than one throat being cleared signaled her uncles' emotional reaction to her words.

No one said anything for a moment after she sat down, then John said, "Let's eat."

After dinner everyone sat around the table talking and relaxing as coffee was served. Soon the guests would be leaving. Geri both anticipated and dreaded saying good night to Wilton. She assumed this would be the last time she would see him outside of the office, and she hated to leave things on this note. It was impossible to speak to him about what had happened between them in front of her uncles, and equally impossible even to imagine talking with him privately. She seized eagerly on the opportunity to run to the basement for Bruce, who had let it slip that he'd left his blood pressure medication down there. He was supposed to take his pills with every meal.

It was nice to have a few minutes of privacy to pull herself together. The whole plot had ended in disaster. Geri consoled herself with the reflection that her family would think twice before meddling in her love life again. As she searched everywhere for the small brown bottle, she concentrated on the one bright spot in this fiasco.

"Geri?" Wilton's voice brought her spinning around to find him standing at the bottom of the stairs, looking at her quizzically.

"Wilton, what are you doing here?"

"Hal said you wanted to talk to me."

"What?" she said, uncomprehending.

"I'm sorry. It must have been one of his stupid jokes." Wilton looked embarrassed.

"As long as you're here," she said as he turned to go. He stopped and faced her again.

"I did want to say thank you. Even though it didn't work out quite like I planned. And I'm sorry about your engagement."

"Oh, that. Don't worry about it. You probably saved me from making a big mistake. I know now that I wasn't in love with Amanda."

"I can understand how you could make that mistake. She's beautiful."

"And intelligent and ambitious," he added. "And competitive and—"

"Don't forget rich," she reminded him. Geri tried to laugh, but it stuck in her throat.

"And far too perfect," he added, that little smile lifting the corners of his mouth.

"Too perfect? Is there such a thing?" Geri answered flippantly.

"Sure. I've discovered I feel an affinity for women with a little baggage. Amanda rarely even speaks to her family, except to update them on her achievements. She'd never dream of blaming them for her problems."

"Is that a shot at me?" Geri asked suspiciously.

"No, it's not. Honest. In fact, I find it a little strange that she is on such good terms with every member of her rich, beautiful, cultured family. There was never a voice raised in that house."

"Yeah, you wouldn't want to get involved with folks like that," Geri agreed.

"This family, now . . . It's something else."

"I like it."

"And you don't want to share?" He was serious all of a sudden.

Geri was taken aback by his question. A number of answers occurred to her: "Yes." "No." "Take them, they're yours." Instead she said honestly, "I don't know what you mean."

"Is that it? Is that why this whole matchmaking thing upset you so much? You don't want to upset the applecart."

"I don't . . ." she started to protest, but as his eyes bored into hers, she couldn't finish.

"I guess I can understand it. Sort of. They adore you, your uncles. And you've got everything arranged pretty comfortably here. It's like a safe little cocoon. But are you sure it's enough?"

She was starting to get angry again. "I told you last night, it's more than enough. I've got seven men to take care of who depend on me for every little thing. I don't need any more family, whatever they may think."

"Maybe they just want you to have a family of your own. A husband. Kids. Is that such a terrible thing to wish on someone you love? You're a strong, capable, giving woman. No one knows that better than them. Maybe they don't want you to waste your life on them."

"I don't consider it a waste."

He changed tactics. "Why do you suppose they do?"

"They never said that," she said, defensive.

"So what you really think is they're doing all this to get rid of you."

Geri felt like he'd just given her a shot in the solar plexus. She realized, somewhere deep inside, that was her fear. Hearing Wilton say it aloud, gave it substance. They really might not want her, might be tired of her. It was hard to catch her breath. But she managed to shoot back at him, "You think you'd be better for me?"

"As a matter of fact, I do." Wilton said, surprising her once again. "See, I happen to be in love with you. I love that wild hair of yours, and the outrageous clothes, and that iron will you use to manage this crazy household, and the way you bully Bruce into taking his medicine, and—"

"Bruce's medicine!" His reminder served to bring her back to reality with a start. "I came down here to look for it, but I can't find it anywhere."

"The pills he always takes at dinner?" Wilton asked.

"Yes," Geri answered, trying to focus on the problem at hand rather than the wonderful things he'd been saying about her.

"I just saw him take one," he announced.

Geri felt a sinking sensation in the pit of her stomach. "Oh, no. Not again," she said. She walked past him and up the stairs to the basement door, ranting, "If they think they're going to do this to me again, I'll strangle them." She turned the doorknob, and it came off in her hand. "What the—" she exclaimed.

"What?" Wilton asked, looking mildly amused.

"They rigged the doorknob."

He laughed.

"This isn't funny." She gave the door a whack, then shook her tingling hand. "What are you grinning at?"

"It's creative, you've got to give them that." When she stared at him as if he'd lost his mind, he elaborated. "Creativity. The guiding principle of the sixth day of Kwanzaa. Guess what your uncles were up to last night?"

"Ha-ha." Geri wasn't amused. "Hey!" she shouted at the door. "Get us out of here!"

"Let's see, they've certainly got the unity thing down pat,

then there's self-determination in deciding to accomplish goals we've set for ourselves and collective work and responsibility and purpose and creativity . . ."

"You already mentioned that." This time she hit the door with the side of her hand. It didn't hurt nearly as much.

"That just leaves faith."

"They're out of their cotton-picking minds."

"They're military men. Men of action. And this was one heck of a campaign. Bruce, Hal, Bert—"

"Bert?" She decided to humor him. That was what she'd heard you were supposed to do with crazy people.

"He had to do the door thing. And Terry's little speech. What a dreamer!" He chuckled.

"I'm glad *you* think this is funny. We could be in here all night," Geri said, coming back down the stairs.

"I can think of worse things."

That stopped her in her tracks. She didn't look at him. She didn't dare. She just made her way sedately to the couch.

"No need to get panicky about this. They'll have to let us out eventually," Geri said, more to herself than to him.

"I wonder what Gene and Steve and John were supposed to do?" Wilton mused.

She tried to remember the subject of conversation she'd overheard earlier that day between Gene and Steve. It had been something about handcuffs, she remembered. Thank God they thought better of that.

"Probably backups in case Bruce and Hal couldn't get us down here," Wilton guessed. She didn't bother to enlighten him. In his current mood she shuddered to think what lengths he'd go to to collaborate with the enemy. As it was, she was in serious need of a tactical diversion.

"Did you ever figure our who the dwarfs are? Bruce is Grumpy, Hal is Happy, Terry is Bashful."

"What are you doing, Geri?" Wilton asked, coming toward the couch where she now sat.

Geri hastily stood and turned her back on him. "Just trying to make conversation. Bert is Sleepy because he rarely sleeps, John is Dopey, which is mean, but Gene had to be Doc, so . . ."

A quick look from under her eyelashes told her that Wilton had taken her place on the couch and was watching her.

"You want to play pool?" That seemed like a good diversion.

"Okay," he assented.

She went ahead of him, very conscious of his eyes on her as she placed the balls in the rack. "You want to break?"

"Sure."

They played for a few minutes, the silence stretching between them until she couldn't stand it anymore.

Her mouth was dry. She walked over to the bar to get a soda, but when she opened the refrigerator door, she couldn't believe her eyes. She didn't know how long she stood there staring before Wilton came up behind her.

"John," he said, as he surveyed the chilled glasses, champagne and crystal tray of fruit and cheese.

Everyone was against her. It was the last straw. She escaped back to the pool table. Predictably she missed her shot.

"One of the nice things about pool," he said, stretching across the table and giving her a glimpse of his taut backside, "is that you can play and talk."

"Uh, just concentrate on the game," Geri said, and sank the eight ball. "We weren't playing eight ball, were we?"

"Points," Wilton lied, knowing as well as she that he'd been stripes and she'd been solids. "I'm up one," he claimed.

He had much more of a lead than that. He wasn't touching her, barely even looked at her, but she knew he was as acutely conscious of her as she was of him. She missed her shot, and he took the cue from her nerveless fingers and chalked it. He lined up his shot. "You seem to have missed the point. Their point. My point." He sank his ball. "And you're bright. Really bright, I just don't understand it." He missed. "Oh, well, I guess everyone has their blind spots," he mused. I still think you're one of the most intelligent women I've ever met." He smiled.

He gave her back the cue. "I gather from something your uncles said when they met me that you prefer your men on the stupid side." Geri missed the cue ball altogether. She really sent the stick flying. "Whoops," he said.

"You did that on purpose," she accused.

"It was a cheap crack." He had the good grace to look somewhat abashed, but that didn't stop him from starting right in again as he took the cue back from her.

"Smart women turn me"—he paused, sighting down the stick—"on," he said with a grunt as he sent the ten ball rocketing into the corner pocket. He ran the table, and she realized he'd just been toying with her. "Care for another game?"

She ignored the double entendre and asked, "Where did you learn to play like that?"

"Well, as you yourself said, I wasn't the type to go to bars or frat parties when I was in school, and I needed something to do besides studying." He met her look of disbelief with a challenging look of his own. "To release the tension. I was an extremely conscientious student, but even I couldn't just work twenty-four hours a day, so I took up pool."

"And I'm sure you were just as driven to succeed at the game as you were in everything else."

"I like to win." He shruggged. "Who doesn't?"

"Do you know what my thesis was?"

"Your thesis?" he asked, confused.

"I have two master's degrees, and I tried to get funding to get my doctorate, but the university wouldn't approve my research. Do you want to know what it was?" Geri challenged.

"Sure."

"Basically I was attempting to analyze the role of black women in European literature of the seventeenth century."

"But . . ." he started to say, then appeared to think better of it.

"But there weren't many black characters in literature of that period, let alone females. And not many authors, either. Isn't that what you were going to say?"

"Uh-huh," he conceded.

"My argument was that even if there weren't, that too played a role in the literature, don't you think?"

"It could be."

"I had studied my subject. My first master's was in literature, on black women writers of the twentieth century. Second was in history. I researched extensively the role of black women in seventeenth-century Europe. I think I had the background to start my work on a dissertation. But I wasn't ever given the chance to try."

"Perhaps I could help—" he started to say.

This time Geri cut him off. "I don't want your help," she said. "I just don't think we'll ever see eye to eye on some of these issues. And they are important to me."

He made one last-ditch effort. "Your uncles aren't exactly the most enlightened bunch I've ever met, but that doesn't stop you from loving them. All I'm asking is that you give me a chance."

"I love my family but I didn't choose them. We're stuck with each other. We'll fight, and we'll make up, and we'll get along or we won't, but nothing will change the fact that we're blood. I couldn't possibly do that with anyone who wasn't family. I just know I couldn't."

"Why not?"

"Oh, you're impossible," Geri said, frustrated. "We're too different." She promised herself it was the last time she'd say it.

"Didn't you ever hear the saying, 'Opposites attract'?"

"That doesn't necessarily mean they should be together," she argued.

"They who? I'm talking about us. You attract me. You've changed me. I think I've had an effect on you, too." He had an effect on her all right. He infuriated her. "We complement each other. We'd be good for each other."

"What makes you so sure?" Geri asked, feeling herself weaken.

"Our strengths, our weaknesses, they are what attract us to each other."

They could be down here all night. She didn't really want to spend the time arguing, but she couldn't just surrender. "How do you know they'll complement each other, rather than just canceling out?"

"I don't, but I have faith," he said. "Ujima. Isn't that what we're supposed to say on the seventh night?" His words were so heartfelt, she felt herself swaying toward him.

She caught herself up. "I'm not sure I have enough."

"All I need is a little bit," he said. "Just believe in me a little, in us a little."

"You want me to trust you," Geri said.

"Because you love me," Wilton said arrogantly.

"There. You see." She was disgusted with him—with herself for wanting to believe him. "That drives me crazy. You haven't changed at all. You're still an arrogant, conceited, pompous—" she sputtered.

"But you love me. Admit it. You'll feel a whole lot better," he promised.

"Why should I trust you?" she asked.

"It's the last day of Kwanzaa," he said. "You've got to have faith."

# Epilogue

"What kind of anthropologist doesn't believe in ancestor worship?" Geri asked, kissing Wilton's neck.

"Look, I just don't feel comfortable talking about my mother and father and grandparents in bed," he said.

"Prude," Geri teased, stroking his chest with the back of her hand. "You promised you'd check out this African religion with me. I'm doing my best to make this a fun new experience for you. You're not even trying."

He rolled over on top of her, capturing her hands and holding them on the pillow beside her head. "There are certain times when a man doesn't want to think about his mother. Ask anyone. And most wives don't care to hear their in-laws' names cried out in the heat of passion."

"I'm not most wives," Geri said, trying unsuccessfully to wriggle out of his grasp.

"I'm quite aware of that," he said, then grunted as her hip bone collided with a rather sensitive part of his anatomy.

"In a movie I saw, they said there are never only two people in a bed. That's what gave me the idea to do this ancestor worship thing tonight. Here. Like this."

"Okay, Ms. Yum-Yum, but—"

"I told you not to call me that." She bit his chin.

"Hey!" he protested. "You're the one who made me listen to that rap music." He'd discovered quite a bit of interesting new slang, most of which he used in the privacy of their bedroom.

"I went to that stupid faculty dinner in that stupid black sequin dress, didn't I?" she said, aggrieved.

"You held up your end of the bargain," he conceded. "And very nicely, too." His eyes glinted in the moonlight. "But is everything we ever do going to come down to a bargain between us?"

"I've got another deal for you," Geri said, licking her lips. "You let me go and I'll—"

"Nuh-uh," he said. "I'm setting the terms this time."

As always, Geri took up the challenge. "What's it gonna be?" she asked.

"I'll give this new religion a shot, but you go first."

Her eyes sparkled. "And just what will you be doing?"

"You'll see," he said, lowering his head to cover her full lips with his own. Their tongues met, and dueled, and when he lifted his mouth, they were both panting.

"Sweetheart," he murmured against the column of her throat.

"Yes?" Geri asked, arching her back as his lips traveled downward on her heated flesh.

"I'm waiting." He raised his mouth from her breast.

"Dopey," she said. He lowered his lips to the firm mound eagerly awaiting his touch and drew the soft flesh into his mouth. "Happy," Geri sighed. He transferred both her wrists to his right hand and held her arms above her head as his left hand closed over her other breast. His long fingers covered one tight bud as he teased the other with his lips and tongue.

"Kiss me," Geri demanded. He claimed her lips again and released her hands, which went immediately around his shoulders, then down his back and lower still.

"Doc," she said breathlessly. "I wonder if it was like this for Snow White?"

"I don't know, but you've got to feel for the prince," Wilton said against her breast.

"You were right, I feel stupid talking about Sleepy and Grumpy and Sneezy." He settled himself between her thighs.

"Wait," she said, holding on to his hips. "I can't remember the last one." She laughed.

"Bashful?" he asked.

"Oh yeah, Uncle Terry."

"Oh, no," he said. "We're not talking about your uncles now."

"You said—"

"I know what I said. I didn't think you'd be able to do it. *I* certainly can't handle having the image of your uncles in my head while we do this."

"Me, neither. I was picturing those cute little dwarfs."

# NEW YEAR'S EVE
# Courtni Wright

# Chapter One

"I don't know why I let you convince me to come on this cruise. I should have stayed at home where I belonged. I would have been just as happy seeing in the New Year with a cup of tea while wearing my fuzzy slippers," Pat moaned as she unpacked her bag. All around her the piles of luggage awaited her attention.

"No one stays alone during the holidays. At least not anyone I know. I had no intention of letting you sit around moping in that lonely house of yours," Bea responded as she gently shook the wrinkles from her blue beaded evening gown.

"I wouldn't have been alone. I have term papers to grade and report cards to write. I had plenty to do to keep me busy," Pat replied as she stuffed her black two-piece bathing suit into the bottom drawer.

"You would have worked the entire holiday without seeing anyone if I hadn't rescued you. You would have put on that tired old blue robe and those ratty fuzzy slippers and padded around all week looking like something the cat dragged in. I can see you now with a cup of coffee in one hand and a red pencil in the other. You would have made one horrible sight," Bea retorted, growing tired of Pat's whining. Her lamentations had begun as soon as they arrived at the airport in Washington and had continued during the entire flight to Aruba.

"Yes, but I would have been productive. Besides, no one would have seen me. You and Toni were supposed to be away on this cruise, remember. You wouldn't have known how awful I looked. By the time you returned, I would have finished all my work and tidied up the place. I might even have brushed my teeth and hair just to welcome you home," Pat snapped irritably. Every time she thought of the work piled on her desk in the room she called her office, she cringed.

"How disgusting! That's certainly a lovely picture. You, that robe, those slippers, and the clinging stench of you as a member of the great unwashed. You needed rescuing from that plight, and I'm glad I did it," Bea responded without looking up from the pile of clothes on her bunk. It was only a weeklong cruise, but she had packed enough outfits to last a month.

"I wouldn't even be here if Toni hadn't caught the flu. I told her to get a shot. I'd be at home happily dressed in my robe and slippers instead of unpacking these ridiculous outfits you talked me into buying. And to top it off, I'll never wear them again. They aren't even my kind of clothes. I'm more conservative than this. I don't wear these bright colors. I enjoy my browns and blacks," Pat whined again as she hung up bright red slacks, shirts with nautical prints on gleaming white backgrounds, rhinestone encrusted evening bags, glittering satin jackets, and form-fitting burgundy velvet leggings.

"Look, if you don't like them, I'll buy them from you after the cruise. Stop complaining and make the best of it. You're here now, and you'll have a great time if you'll only let yourself. If I had known what you had planned for your holiday, I would have insisted that you join us. You might even meet someone interesting," Bea answered with a tinge of annoyance in her voice.

"We'll see," Pat replied with skepticism in hers.

Looking around the cabin, Pat surveyed the twin beds with their bright red and orange striped spreads, the dressing table and lighted makeup mirror, and the small sitting area with the sofa and two chairs that coordinated with the curtains at the

# NEW YEAR'S EVE

one large window. She could not complain about the accommodations or the itinerary. Their cabin, on one of the upper decks, was spacious and well appointed, and the itinerary promised exciting ports of call. The trip would have been ideal if Pat were not reluctant to become involved with anyone new after a broken relationship. Now all she wanted to do was sit in her kitchen, sipping tea and grading papers.

Suddenly the ship's horn sounded somewhere above them. Its mournful voice chilled Pat's heart. The public address system and the ship's private television station blared the message simultaneously: "All visitors are requested to leave the ship immediately. The *Caribbean Paradise* sets sail in fifteen minutes."

"Oh, Pat! Isn't this exciting? We're setting sail for the most beautiful tropical islands. Over the course of this glorious week, we'll walk on the beaches of Bonaire, Martinique, and Curaçao. We'll swim in the clear Caribbean Sea of the islands of Barbados and Aruba. We'll shop in some of the most fabulous stores in the world. We'll dance away our evenings. It'll be heavenly," Bea gushed as she dragged her friend away from the mountain of clothes that still needed to be put away.

"But the clothes. I haven't finished unpacking. Why are you dragging me on deck? I have things to do down here. This cabin is a mess. How will we sleep tonight if we don't clean up?" Pat objected as she hurriedly grabbed her purse and key. As soon as she joined the throng of people in the corridor, she gave up the struggle. There was no point. The laughing, happy crowd swept her into its embrace and propelled her toward the steps and the upper decks.

"This is ridiculous. The clothes . . ." Pat tried to say as she and Bea took their places along the rails. The sweet, salty smell of the ocean blew its restorative mist into her face. The lively music of the steel drums combined with the twinkling stars in the dark night to cast an almost undeniable spell over everyone. Even Pat felt herself relaxing under the spell of the call of the islands.

"Give it up, Pat. You're on vacation. Everything does not have to be perfect. We're here to have fun and to meet people, maybe even some men. So chill out!'' Bea shouted into her ear over the roar of the mighty smokestacks as the ship slowly pulled away from the pier.

The tugboats looked so small and insignificant as they labored against the weight of the massive seven-story ship. They tooted their horns as they pulled it into the channel from which it would safely travel the warm waters of the Caribbean. Just beyond the fingers of the harbor, the crew waved as the tugboats pulled aside and allowed the ship to sail freely under its own power.

The multicolored lights that festooned the decks twinkled in time to the pulsating drumbeat. Waiters in merrily striped jackets mingled among the guests, carrying overflowing trays of sandwiches and tropical drinks. Travelers, hungry from their flights, filled their plates with the treats and greedily washed them down with mixed drinks bearing the names of the islands and the flavors of luscious fruits. Couples linked arms or kissed unashamedly as they swayed on unsteady legs that had not yet learned the gentle motion of the sea.

"Loosen up, Pat. This is a cruise ship, not a classroom. Get rid of that stuffy teacher demeanor and get down!'' Bea urged as she wiggled her well-proportioned hips to the music and drained yet another glass of the deceptively strong fruity cocktail.

"I'm loose enough for right now. Just give me a little time to get my sea legs. You should be careful with those drinks, Bea. You haven't eaten much today. We've been on the go since early this morning, and you hardly touched the airplane food,'' Pat advised as she watched Bea reach for still another drink. She could not deny that they were refreshing, but, on an empty stomach, they could be lethal. There was no point in starting a trip with a hangover.

"Don't be silly. They're not that strong and, besides, we're going in to dinner in a few minutes. These sandwiches and the meal will absorb anything I drink. I'm going to have a good time while I'm on this trip. I don't want to think about diets and drinking and rules. I'm on vacation and anything goes. I want to find a wealthy man, love him until his eyeballs pop,

# NEW YEAR'S EVE

and marry him as soon as we return home," Bea said as she drained her glass. Her speech was already slurred and thick.

Just then, as Pat was preparing to lecture her on the evils of drinking too much while sailing, the dinner gong sounded, and the voice on the public address system announced the second seating. Seeing that Bea was beginning to reel from too many drinks on an empty stomach, Pat linked her arm through her friend's and directed her across the moving deck and carefully down the stairs.

"Isn't this fun? Oh, look, I'm listing. Oops! I crashed into the wall!" Bea shouted over the sound of the waves splashing against the side of the ship. She was practically bent double from laughter and the difficulty she was having navigating the slippery deck in high heels and under the influence of several strong drinks.

"Hold on to me, Bea," Pat advised, tightening her grip on her friend. "We'll be inside in just a few more steps. Be careful. I don't want you to fall down and break anything on your first day on board."

"Oh, no. That would never do. That would spoil everything. I wouldn't be able to dance if my leg were in a cast. I'll be careful. You'll see," Bea agreed as she wagged her finger at Pat and waved at the couple standing near the door. They laughed as they watched her navigate the ramp in her tipsy condition.

"I told you not to drink so much. You're making a fool of yourself," Pat hissed as she led Bea toward the stairs that led to the dining room.

"I'm not drunk. I simply cannot get my balance. That's all. Stop mothering me, Pat. We're supposed to be having fun. Besides, I don't know any of these people. What do I care about their opinions. I won't see them again after this cruise. I paid my money to have a good time, and I intend to do just that," Bea lisped as she clung to the railing and carefully followed Pat down the three flights to the dining room.

"Good evening, madams. Your table number please," the maitre d' asked as he ushered them into the elegant dining room.

Seeing the lovely white damask tablecloths, the intricately folded napkins, the elaborate floral arrangements and fruit carvings, the sparking crystal, and the gleaming silver, Bea immediately sobered. Her eyes grew wide with childlike enthusiasm and her lips formed the word "Oh!"

Everything seemed to move in slow motion as Pat and Bea followed the red-jacketed headwaiter to their table. The glistening mirrors along the walls reflected their every step as they walked past tables of laughing guests, who, just like themselves, were settling down for a gastronomical experience of a lifetime. The thick carpet underfoot silenced the noise of the scurrying waiters and the occasional dropped silverware.

As they scanned the menu with its almost endless choices, Bea exclaimed, "This is heaven! Look at all this food. I don't know where to begin."

"That's easy for you to say. You're naturally thin. I have to watch my weight. This looks like the beginning of the end of my diet to me," Pat groaned as she read off the delicacies that she knew would be shimmering in butter and covered in thick, rich cream.

"Don't be such a grump. Besides, there are plenty of selections that are low in fat and calories. Stop complaining and enjoy yourself. The staff has thought of everything. You can't possibly have a bad time on this cruise. I see that we're already attracting attention from that table over there. Not bad . . . lots of possibility," Bea confided as she allowed her eyes to travel from the cream-colored menu pages to the table diagonally across the aisle from them.

Following her gaze, Pat looked directly into the eyes of an incredibly handsome man who nodded and lifted his wineglass in greeting. A wicked smile played at the corners of his luscious lips, and a warm glow shone on his healthy brown skin. From the way his chest and shoulders filled out his open-neck shirt, Pat could tell that he was quite trim and muscular.

"Oh, my, how embarrassing. Why didn't you tell me that he was looking at us? We look just terrible in our wrinkled clothes and uncombed hair. Anyway, you forget that I'm not interested in attracting anyone's attention," Pat whined as she fidgeted nervously with her menu.

"Don't be silly. Meeting men is my primary reason for being on this cruise in the first place. Relax. Besides, he started it. This is really going to be a fun vacation. All these handsome men to choose from and seven days in which to get to know them," coaxed Bea as she sipped from her glass while maintaining eye contact.

"Well, you might be on this ship to pick up men, but I'm here to relax. When you asked me to come along, I agreed not because I wanted to go on a hunting expedition but because I wanted to get away and relax. I don't want any men complicating my life right now. I've had enough of relationships for a while," Pat confided in a whisper as she leaned toward Bea.

Dragging her eyes from the handsome stranger, Bea stated firmly, "You enjoy this trip your way, and I'll enjoy it mine. I intend to party, gamble, dance, and flirt until I drop. I could have stayed at home if I had wanted to spend my holidays doing nothing except sit with my feet up and read books. I want to have a good time. It's about time you forgot about Michael. He's in the past. I bet he's not moping about you."

"This has nothing to do with Michael. I'm over him. I just don't want to get involved with anyone right now," Pat replied as she made up her mind to order the swordfish with boiled herbed potatoes and broccoli.

"You don't have to fall in love, just dance and have a good time. I'm not looking for a soul mate on this cruise. I'm here to relax and enjoy myself. You should give it a try. You're too stiff," Bea responded as she allowed her eyes to return to the nearby table. Finding that the men were in deep conversation, she once again studied her menu.

As soon as their waiter hurried away with their order, Bea started her litany of instructions once more. Slathering butter on a fragrant roll, she said, "You need to break loose and shed that conservative exterior. It's not good to be that serious all the time."

"If you don't mind, I'm perfectly happy with myself as I am, thank you. I've done just fine for the last thirty years without your help. I think I can continue without your constructive criticism. Besides, there's nothing conservative about the outfits you talked me into buying. They shout the message that I'm ready for anything," Pat concluded as she pushed aside the bread basket Bea offered her. She had worked too hard on her body to allow the pounds and inches to creep back while on vacation.

"And let's hope they bring you some action. Your life is too dull," Bea retorted as she dove with gusto into her steamship round of beef, baked potato swimming in butter and heaped with sour cream, and green beans with grated pistachio nuts. They ate the remainder of their dinner in silence, with Bea casting the occasional glance toward the other table.

As they sipped their coffee, Bea asked, "What'll we do tonight? Would you like to go to the show or straight to the casino?"

Before Pat could respond, they were joined by the gentlemen from across the aisle. "Good evening," said the man who had saluted them with his wine glass. He smiled. "I'd like to introduce myself. I'm Jeff Bloom and this is my friend, Tom Owen. We're from Texas, if you wondered about the accent."

"Glad to meet both of you," Bea responded as she shook hands with the smiling gentlemen. "I'm Bea Thomas and that's Pat Grimes. We're from Washington, D.C., if you're wondering why we don't have them."

"Ladies, it's my pleasure. Are you going to the show?" Jeff asked as he nodded. He allowed his eyes to sweep appreciatively over their faces. Tom stood by silently with a shy, reserved smile on his face. Although a very attractive man, he was not nearly as striking as Jeff, who loomed a broad-shouldered six feet five with jet black hair and piercing black eyes. Tom's curly brown hair and gray eyes on a barely six-foot frame almost caused him to appear to be Jeff's shadow. His demeanor was certainly much more reserved.

"We were just this minute trying to decide between the show and the casino, but I suppose you've made up our minds for us," Bea chirped happily as she slipped from her seat and linked her arm in Jeff's.

# NEW YEAR'S EVE 233

Rising, Pat joined Tom as they walked behind the other couple through the dining-room door and up the sweeping stairway. Suddenly she felt almost dowdy in her brown silk slacks and cream blouse. Although no one had changed for dinner from their traveling clothes, Pat wished that she had at least washed her face and applied a touch of blush and lipstick. She felt like a little sparrow as she walked behind Bea and Jeff. Tom in his travel-wrinkled black slacks and conservative striped shirt seemed equally self-conscious.

The huge lounge sparkled gaily as the multicolored lights from the stage played across the faces of the appreciative audience. The assembled crowd roared at the jokes, applauded loudly after the dance numbers, and swayed along to the music of the romantic ballads. Already Pat could see that Bea was thoroughly enjoying Jeff's company as she sat with her hand resting lightly in his.

For her part Pat sat stiffly in the center of her seat. She was careful not to allow the gentle rolling of the ship to press her against Tom's shoulder. She did not want him to think that she was coming on to him. She had no intention of being a cruise fling.

Despite what Bea advised about having a good time and relaxing, Pat knew that she was not the type who could throw caution to the wind and become someone she was not simply because she would probably never again see the occupants of the ship. She had no intention of encouraging Tom, or any other man, to think that she had taken the cruise for the purpose of having a quick and easily forgotten holiday affair. Pat had allowed Bea to talk her into replacing the sick Toni at the last minute, but she would not compromise her principles for the sake of a few fun evenings.

As the house lights went up after the entertainment director bade them good night, the two couples strolled to the casino. Already crowds of people stood around the two roulette wheels and the blackjack and banco tables. Every slot machine happily munched nickels, quarters, and dollars as people merrily dropped one coin after the other into their hungry mouths and pulled their waiting arms. The bells and whistles constantly sounded, letting everyone know that someone had won a few coins, although everyone knew that the casino would be triumphant in the end.

Bea was an avid blackjack player and had just discovered that Jeff shared her enthusiasm for the card game. Happily they parked themselves side by side at the green felt table and prepared either to win or lose their fortunes. Pat and Tom were left to their own resources.

"Look, there are two empty slot machines. Shall we try our luck?" Pat asked as she eased toward the empty chair.

"Sure, why not. I'm not much of a gambler, but this looks tame enough even for me," Tom commented as he slid into the seat beside her. His broad shoulders lightly brushed against hers.

Turning toward him, Pat smiled and said, "If you'd rather do something else, don't let me stop you. I don't gamble much myself, but I do like to play the slot machines. I'm quite content here, so you don't have to keep me company."

Although she was warming to his presence, Pat did not want Tom to feel obligated to spend his evening at her side simply because his friend had teamed up with hers. She was perfectly content, sitting alone at the slot machines and then returning early to her cabin to finish the unpacking.

"I'll stick for a while. I might find out that I actually like playing them. This is my first cruise, and I'm open to anything," Tom replied as he slipped four quarters into the slot and pulled the arm. Immediately the bells started ringing, and coins began to tumble into the tray.

Looking down in disbelief, Pat laughed and offered, "For a first timer, I'd say you have pretty good luck. That's at least twenty dollars' worth. Not bad for a one dollar investment."

"Beginner's luck. I bet I'll lose all of it in about a half hour. Somehow the machine sensed that a neophyte had sat down and wanted to ensure that I'd get hooked and return." Tom laughed as he fed more coins into the machine.

Handing him her empty paper cup in which to store his winnings, Pat asked, "What do you usually do for vacations if you don't cruise? This is my third one and I love them.

However, it is the first holiday trip I've ever taken. I wouldn't be here now if my friend hadn't taken ill."

"When I give myself the time off, I enjoy touring the States or Europe. I'm not much for lying in the sun and swimming, although this is enjoyable. Considering the great way this trip has started out, I might give it another try," Tom said as he scooped up the quarters that continued to fall from the machine. Every time he inserted four coins, he received at least ten in exchange.

Forgetting her shyness, Pat commented, "If you keep winning like that, you'll own the ship!"

"It must be the company of a beautiful woman that has given me luck. I've never won anything before tonight," Tom said with a shy, somewhat nervous smile.

"Thanks, but I think lady luck is just smiling on you tonight," Pat replied as she fed the last of her five dollars into the machine. As she pulled the handle, she hoped that a few coins would drop down so that she could continue to sit next to Tom without having to think of small talk. She was not good at keeping a conversation going.

As the dial came to an abrupt stop on one lemon, one cherry, and the number ten, Pat sighed. She knew that she would have to think of something to say quickly or else take a chance on having the evening sour under the weight of a strained silence in a room filled with the sound of people enjoying themselves and each other.

As if sensing her discomfort, Tom asked as he scooped up a handful of coins and deposited them in a cup for Pat, "What's our first port of call?"

"Oh, no, really. I couldn't accept these. These coins are your winnings," Pat said as she tried to return the cup. Her hand lightly brushed against his in the effort.

"Yes, and it would give me a great deal of pleasure to share them with you. Now where are we going tomorrow? I don't remember," Tom replied as he watched more coins fall into his tray.

"Bonaire is our first stop. I think the itinerary said that we'd dock early in the morning. We'll be there until noon. According to the material in our cabins, it's a rather small, arid island . . . quite unlike any you'd expect to see in the tropics of the Caribbean. It's sandy and flat with very little greenery. I understand that there are several preserved slave cabins not far from the salt mines and the world-famous pink flamingoes and a very lovely shopping strip. Otherwise, there isn't too much to see. We'll spend the rest of the afternoon at sea," Pat replied, hoping that she did not sound as if she had devoured the brochure. Worse still, she did not want to give the impression that she was giving a history lesson to a classroom filled with students.

Pat was not interested in winning Tom's affection, but she did not want to send him running from her, either. He was pleasant and attentive and would make an agreeable companion for the trip now that it looked as if Bea had hooked up with Jeff. She did not want to go on the shore excursions alone.

"I'd like to see those slave quarters. I'm an amateur historian, specializing in slavery in the Americas. That's why I booked this trip. Slavery was big business on most of these sugarcane-producing islands," Tom commented as he allowed Pat to pull his attention from the slot machine.

"Really? I'm a history teacher specializing in United States history. If you don't have any other plans, maybe you could share your knowledge of the slave trade with me as we tour the island," Pat suggested as she once again fed the last coins into the machine. She had managed over the course of their conversation to win enough to repay Tom for the coins he had given her and a few extra ones for herself. Now even those had vanished into the belly of the machine.

"I'd be glad to share what little I know. I'm only just beginning to explore the wealth of history this region has to offer. I'd like for us to experience Bonaire together. My idea of touring is to put on a pair of comfortable shoes and hoof it. I hope that's all right with you," Tom answered as he smiled into Pat's upturned face.

"Mine, too. Well, it's getting late. If we're to get an early start in the morning, I'd better call it a night. I haven't finished unpacking yet. The cabin is a wreck. I have to get organized before I go to bed tonight," Pat said as she rose from her seat at the slot machine.

"I haven't unpacked, either. Our bags hadn't even arrived before we went to dinner. I've been in these clothes since six o'clock this morning. Wait a second, and I'll walk you to your cabin. I just need to cash in these coins first," Tom replied as he rushed to the cashier's window.

Returning to her side, Tom lightly touched Pat's elbow and propelled her toward the casino's exit. Looking over her shoulder, she saw that Bea and Jeff had already left the room. They had become quite cozy as they played first blackjack and then the roulette table. She hoped that Bea would not make too much noise when she returned to their cabin later that night.

Although she had work to do before she could retire, Pat did not want the evening to end. She was tired and sleepy, but she was enjoying the gentleness of Tom's company. Almost timidly she suggested, "Shall we take the long way and go for a stroll on deck first?"

"Great idea. We haven't been outside since we sailed. I bet the sky's beautiful in the middle of the ocean," Tom agreed as he held the heavy door. The stiff breeze almost blew Pat into his arms. Quickly he steadied her and slipped her arm through his for extra support.

"Look at all those stars!" Pat exclaimed, "I don't ever see that many from my window at home. And the sea is so calm that it's almost as smooth as glass. I expected a few waves and maybe even some choppiness. I bet we'll sleep like babies tonight."

Standing with both hands on the railing as he looked into the distance away from the ship's lights, Tom replied, "You're certainly right about those stars. I haven't seen anything like this since I left my parents' home in the country. It's certainly a beautiful night. Thank you for sharing it with me, Pat."

"I've enjoyed myself tremendously, Tom. We've had a wonderful start to what promises to be a fabulous cruise. I didn't have any luck in the casino, but maybe tomorrow will be my night," Pat responded with a chuckle. She had agreed to go on the trip very reluctantly, but already she was having a wonderful time.

As the steel band played on the pool deck above them, Pat and Tom breathed deeply of the salty air. The gentle rumble of the ship's powerful engines was very reassuring as the vessel created frothy waves in its wake. As far as they could see, nothing but black open sea and vast emptiness greeted their eyes.

For the first time in her very predictable life, Pat felt as if she were on a great adventure. She had met a strange man and shared an evening with him.

Usually her friends introduced her to dependable men of their long acquaintance in the hopes of helping her to find the right man. That was how she had met Michael, the love of her life for the last five years. They had broken off their relationship six months ago, and she had not started dating again.

When Toni and Bea suggested that she accompany them, Pat had immediately refused. She was not ready to meet anyone and did not want to put herself in the position of having to be gracious to strangers. To her surprise, she discovered that not only had she experienced a lovely evening with someone she had known for only a few hours, but she was looking forward to seeing him again the next day. For a woman who usually preferred the comfort of her apartment and her books to that of the company of unknown men, she had made considerable progress in such a short time.

"I hate to say this, but I really must go to my cabin. If I don't, I won't be able to get up early in the morning. I can barely keep my eyes open now as it is," Pat said as the rocking lulled her into a peaceful sense of tranquility.

Looking at the luminous dial of his watch, Tom exclaimed, "It's almost midnight. You're right. It's time we were asleep. I've already arranged for a seven o'clock wake-up call for every morning that we're in port early. I don't want to miss anything."

Allowing him to steer her toward the door, Pat looked over her shoulder one last time. The deck chairs looked so inviting that she felt that she could spend the night in one of them.

# NEW YEAR'S EVE

With a blanket to ward off the cool night air, she would be quite comfortable.

As they walked through the silent halls to her cabin one deck below, Pat searched through the contents of her small bag for her key. Reaching the door, she knocked. When Bea did not answer, she inserted the key and pushed open the door. Immediately the sight of the clutter reminded her of the work that she had to do before retiring for the night.

Turning to Tom, Pat said as she offered him her hand in a hearty handshake, "Thanks for a great evening. I'll see you on the debarkation deck tomorrow morning."

"Why don't we have breakfast together? We can plan all the things we want to see. I'll bring the map from my cabin. Let's meet at eight o'clock. Okay?" Tom suggested as he held her small hand in his big one.

"Fine. I'll meet you there after my morning run around the deck. I have to get some exercise to burn off the calories from that dinner we ate tonight," Pat agreed as she smiled into his gentle face. Tom might not be as knock-'em-dead handsome as his friend Jeff, but his eyes contained a sincerity that she found very endearing.

"You're a jogger, too? Great. I'll see you on the exercise deck and then we'll meet for breakfast. Good night, Pat. Have a good sleep," Tom answered as he ushered her inside and pulled the door closed. He lingered in the hall until he heard Pat turn the key in the lock, and then he sauntered off toward his cabin on the other side of the vessel.

Pat was busily unpacking when Bea returned to their cabin. Bea looked dreamy-eyed as she flopped down on her bed. Rising on one elbow she gushed, "I hope your evening was as glorious as mine. Jeff is the perfect gentleman. He dances divinely, and he smells so good. He's a stockbroker for one of the large firms in Dallas. I bet he makes a lot of money. We're going to spend the entire morning on the beach together."

"Tom seems quite nice, too. We're planning to tour the island together after breakfast. He's an amateur historian. I don't know what he does for a living," Pat commented as she continued to place neatly folded clothing in the drawers.

"You didn't ask?"

"No, we didn't really talk much. Mostly we fed the slot machines. I lost all of my money and some of what he loaned me, but Tom won about one hundred dollars, I think. Besides, I don't care how he makes his living. He's a cruise companion, not anything else. When we return to Aruba, I won't ever see him again," Pat replied.

"I found out everything about Jeff in the first few minutes after we left the dining room. I didn't want to spend my vacation with a nobody. There are too many available men on this ship to settle for someone boring. Weren't you even slightly curious about Tom's occupation?" Bea asked incredulously.

"No, not really. It's enough for me to know that he has good manners, shares an interest in history, and isn't obnoxious," Pat responded as she disappeared into the bathroom to change into her nightgown and brush her teeth.

Returning she said, "I'm not auditioning him as husband material. There's little chance of a long-term relationship developing from a one-week cruise. I'm happy to take him as he is."

"You never know what'll happen. The last thing you want to do is to fall in love with a loser. You need to be more curious about people. That's what happened with Michael. You didn't ask enough questions and then discovered that he had lied to you," Bea commented as she darted in and out of the tiny bathroom.

"Michael had a relationship with another woman after we had been together for three years. His past was crystal clear. His present was murky," Pat responded as she carefully pulled the sheet over her shoulders and folded back a precise three-inch hem.

"Whatever. You should still learn more about Tom before you spend too much time with him. Why waste the cruise when you can find someone else if you don't wait too long," Bea added as she snapped off her light.

"I don't want anything from him, Bea. I'd be perfectly content to spend the entire cruise alone, and you know it. If he doesn't show up tomorrow for exercise or breakfast, I'll tour the island by myself or join a group. I don't need Tom's company to make me happy. He's simply an extra perk. Good night," Pat retorted as she turned toward the wall.

"Okay, but don't say I didn't warn you if he turns out to be the most boring man on two feet. If you spoil your New Year's, it's not my fault," Bea muttered as she drifted into sleep.

"Don't worry about me," Pat replied as she allowed the ship's gentle rocking to lull her to sleep.

# Chapter Two

The next morning Pat left Bea sleeping soundly in their darkened cabin as she hurried to the pool deck and the first of what would be many sunrise exercise routines. Breathing deeply of the delicious salty air, she joined the others as they stretched and limbered up before beginning the three-mile jog that was an integral part of her day. She had been jogging every day for the past four years and could not imagine missing the opportunity to give her body a good sweat.

Joining the others as they circled the track, Pat was a little disappointed that Tom was not among them. Giving a mental shrug, she allowed the rhythm of her feet and the sun rising in the horizon to block out any further thoughts of him. After all, he was still very much a stranger she had only just met on a vacation cruise in paradise. Tom certainly did not owe her anything.

As the blood began to course more rapidly through her body, Pat found that she could think of nothing other than the sound of her own breathing and the call of the seagulls that circled the ship. They appeared to hover off the stern of the vessel as if awaiting something for which they had become accustomed. Every time Pat returned to the back of the boat as she circled the track, the birds still fluttered just off the surface of the water. They darted and jostled for position as if lining up for a spectacular treat.

Pat was so absorbed with watching the birds and the waves as they lapped at the sides of the ship that she did not feel someone match strides with hers. Slowly pulling her consciousness back from the sea, she turned her head ever so slightly, not wanting to miss seeing the antics of the gulls. Finding herself looking into Tom's gentle gray eyes, she would have stumbled if his strong arm had not grabbed her.

"Sorry, I didn't mean to startle you. I thought you heard me say good morning as you ran past me near the steps. I overslept. The rocking was so soothing that I turned over and went back to sleep after answering the wake-up call," Tom said with a smile as he released her arm.

"I guess I was too busy watching the gulls to hear you. They've been hovering in the same position relative to the ship all morning. I'm glad you joined us. It's a glorious day for a run ... not too humid and with just enough breeze," Pat responded as she regained her equilibrium from more than the misstep. The early morning sun sparkled on Tom's skin and made it glow a healthy reddish hue.

"I guess they're used to having their breakfast served at this hour every day. They're a noisy bunch, aren't they?" Tom commented as they passed the squawking cluster of white feathers and gaping beaks. He had adjusted his long legs so that his stride accompanied Pat's perfectly.

"I was hoping to see them dive for their food, but it's getting late. I have only a few more laps, and then it's to the showers for me. I guess I'll have to wait until tomorrow," Pat said as she wiped her sweaty brow with the small orange towel from her cabin. Her cabin steward had supplied her with the hand towels as soon as she mentioned that she liked to jog every morning. He said that their size would make them more convenient to carry than the larger bath towels.

"I'll need an extra fifteen minutes to try out the weight room, and then I'll join you on deck for breakfast. We can plan our day as we eat," Tom suggested as he slipped on the sunglasses that hung on a cord around his muscular neck.

"Great. Oh, look, Tom, I didn't miss the feeding after all. Look at the way they scoop up the food almost before it touches the water," Pat exclaimed as she pointed toward the soaring, diving seagulls.

"They certainly make enough noise about it," Tom responded, laughing at the show of the acrobatic, aerial clowns as he joined Pat at the railing. Together they watched the birds clean the sea of any sign of fruit peelings.

Standing with her shoulder close to Tom's, Pat felt a peaceful tranquility as it descended on her. She knew that the afterglow of a good workout caused some of it, but she could only explain the rest as the result of having someone with whom to share the little joys of life. She was not her own little island as she had thought.

When she had broken off her long relationship with Michael, Pat had worried that she would never be able to feel close to anyone again. Although their relationship had grown stale almost six months before it ended, she still occasionally missed having him around. She enjoyed having someone with whom to share her thoughts and experiences.

Now she realized that she had not closed the doors of her heart as much as she had originally thought. She was not immune to the need for companionship as she had tried to convince herself. Feeling so comfortable with Tom convinced Pat that she would be open to a partner again someday.

Feeling Tom's eyes on her, Pat tore her attention from the birds as her cheeks colored from the weight of his gaze. Smiling, she said, "We'd better hurry. We'll be docking in Bonaire soon. I'll meet you on the lido deck in thirty minutes."

"Okay, I'll be there and on time," Tom answered with a smile as he watched her rush away. Making one last lap, he vanished down the back stairs that would lead him to the gym.

Back in her cabin Pat found that Bea had already showered and was in the process of applying her makeup. She looked lovely in a turquoise shorts outfit with matching sweater. Her warm brown skin glowed with health.

Looking over her shoulder, Bea exclaimed, "It's about time you returned. I'm hungry. Get dressed quickly so we can grab some breakfast. I'm meeting Jeff in the dining room in about fifteen minutes. You're welcome to join us."

"Thanks, but Tom and I are having breakfast on the lido deck so we can watch the ship dock while we plan our day. I had a lovely run this morning. You should join me sometime," Pat replied as she darted into the tiny bathroom.

"You and Tom have hit it off nicely, haven't you?" Bea shouted through the door.

"What? I can't hear you. I'll be out in a minute," Pat called as she quickly shampooed her medium brown curly hair and washed the perspiration from her body. She felt happy and invigorated from the morning breeze and Tom's company.

Wiping the steam from the mirror, Pat laughed at her own reflection. Her soft brown cheeks were almost ruddy from the heat and the excitement of spending the day with Tom. Her eyes sparkled with anticipation as she toweled her curls dry and sprayed on a touch of conditioner to set them. Reaching for the compact of blush, she almost added a little color to her already healthy complexion but decided against it. She would save the cosmetics for the evening. During the day, she would allow her natural radiance to shine.

As soon as Pat appeared in her bra and panties, Bea repeated with a naughty smile, "You and Tom have certainly become an item. I thought you had planned to hide yourself away for the duration of this cruise. I distinctly remember hearing you say that you didn't need a man's company in order to have fun on New Year's Eve."

"We're not an 'item' as you call it. We simply like exercising in the morning and exploring historical sites. I'm sure I won't see much of him when the islands don't offer as much for amateur historians and history teachers. He'll find someone else for lazing in the sun as soon as he finds out that I'm not a beach person. Besides, New Year's Eve is still two nights away. A lot can happen on a ship of this size in that time," Pat replied nonchalantly as she stepped into her black linen shorts and pulled on the cream linen blouse. Around her waist,

# NEW YEAR'S EVE

she buckled a wide belt that set off the effects of the daily tummy crunches. Her long legs made her look taller than her five feet eight inches.

"What does he do for a living? Has Tom said anything?" Bea asked as she handed Pat the new tube of lipstick that sat on the makeup table.

Returning it unused with a shake of her head, Pat replied, "No, and I haven't asked. All I know is that he's interested in the slave history of this area of the Caribbean. It really doesn't matter how he makes his living, since I'll never see him again after we leave the ship."

"You never know when your paths might cross again. Besides, you could be throwing away the opportunity to meet someone of stature and wealth while you're spending your time with a nobody," Bea replied emphatically as she pressed a stray hair into place and checked her profile in the mirror. She was a beautiful woman who never missed the opportunity to reassure herself that her looks had not faded since she last gazed at herself. Her tall, slender build caused everyone who saw her to wonder if she were a model.

Sighing, Pat replied, "I didn't agree to substitute for Toni in the hopes of finding someone. I'm perfectly happy with whatever companionship Tom can offer while we're on this ship. After that, we'll go our separate ways, and this vacation will become a pleasant memory."

"Well, some of us believe in using every minute to its fullest. I don't see anything wrong with networking," Bea insisted stubbornly as they walked toward the stairs.

"Call it whatever you like, but I don't intend to set a man trap," Pat replied as she reached for the doorknob. She and Bea had been friends for a long time, but they had never agreed on the subject of men and relationships. Bea always looked at a man's net worth before becoming involved with him, and Pat preferred to look at his inner strength. So far, both of them had experienced the same number of hits and misses in love.

Waving good bye, Pat quickly climbed the stairs and rushed out into the sunshine. The ship's speed had slowed almost to a crawl as it crossed the distance from the open sea into the waters of Bonaire. Stopping to admire the scenery, Pat could see in the distance the coastline of the island marked with small clusters of greenery and houses. However, most of the surface appeared barren and a dusty reddish-brown in color.

"I saved us a table. All the choice ones were filling up fast. I also got you some juice, fruit, and oatmeal. I didn't know what else you might want. I didn't want to take the chance on losing that great table by the railing. I didn't want us to lose our chance to sit together. Great view, isn't it?" Tom said as he directed Pat to the table under the shelter of the stairs.

"Everything looks perfect. As a matter of fact, I would have selected the same things. I'm impressed," Pat replied as she smiled warmly at Tom's innate ability to read her thoughts.

"I thought you'd want to carbo load after running. I know I always do. Okay, what should we do first . . . the former slave cabins or the general tour of the island?" Tom asked as he hungrily devoured the cereal and fresh melon slices.

"I think I'd like to see the entire island first. Maybe we could rent bikes and pedal to the main sights. It doesn't appear to be too large. The information channel said that Bonaire is one of the smaller islands we'll visit," Pat commented as she turned her concentration to the heaping bowl of tasty oatmeal that Tom had topped with a generous serving of honey.

"Bikes it is then. As soon as we eat, I'll see what the excursion manager can find for us. If he doesn't have anything, we should be able to find a little shop somewhere on the island," Tom replied as he jotted down a list of the things that he wanted to do on their sightseeing trip.

"It's nice to see that you make lists, too. It's good to know that I'm not the only one who still does that. Bea says that I'm the last person in the world who takes the time to record the fun things that I want to do. She says I should be more spontaneous and less programmed. I'm glad to see that I'm not alone," Pat said with a laugh as she watched a steady stream of items appear on the page of the pocket memo pad.

"Bea's all wrong. How else would I be able to remember to do everything if I didn't write them down? I'm too busy usually to keep everything in my head. Let's see, I wanted to

# NEW YEAR'S EVE

rent bikes, visit the cabins, and buy a gift for my secretary and some shells for me. What was on your list of things to do?" Tom asked as he refused to allow Bea's ideas to stop him from continuing with his careful planning of their morning activities.

"I wanted to look for some fabric as well as see the sights. Bonaire is supposed to sell the best batik of any of the islands. If I find something interesting, I'll probably make a skirt out of it or maybe some pillows for my sofa," Pat responded as she pushed aside her empty plates.

Watching Tom add her item to his list, she was again impressed by the ease with which he fit into her life. Even their need for organization and lists only added to their compatibility. Pat hoped that they would continue to enjoy each other's company. The trip would be so much more satisfying in the company with someone of similar needs and tastes.

Pat had actually worried about substituting for Toni on the trip with Bea. Although she loved her friend dearly, Bea could be a little difficult to live with at times. She never organized anything and preferred to do everything spontaneously and at the last minute.

Although Toni had booked the cruise three months in advance, neither of them had arranged for any shore excursions, thinking that they could make their connections on the ship. Unfortunately the organized passengers had already booked the more exciting and educational trips. They were stuck with only the beach and walking tours as diversions from the ship. Knowing that Bea would walk to nothing, Pat had decided that she would have to go it alone. Now that she and Tom had paired off, she would have a partner for the exploration she wanted to do.

"I see that we've docked right on schedule. Let's get started. By the way, Jeff is the same way about lists as Bea. He's a spontaneous, creative kind of guy. Strange world, isn't it? I thought the old axiom said that opposites attract," Tom commented as he steered Pat toward the main deck and the ramp that would take them onto the island of Bonaire. Pausing briefly, he inquired about the bikes before returning to her side.

"Thank goodness that old adages aren't always correct. I

would have missed out on touring the island if you had been like Bea and Jeff.'' Pat laughed as she slowly followed an older woman down the gangplank.

Immediately Pat was struck not by the beauty of the island but by the warmth of the sun. By the end of December at home, the sun would have felt barely lukewarm, but here it shone with almost the same intensity as it did during the summer. Its glorious rays penetrated her skin and warmed her down to the bone. All thoughts of school, papers to grade, and her former relationship slipped silently from her memory.

Walking through the wrought-iron gate that separated Bonaire's harbor from the tiny town, Pat was immediately transported into a time when life moved at a leisurely pace and no one hurried. The only people she saw walking from the shops were other passengers on the cruise ship. Many of the residents worked in the shops, but they did not seem to frequent them. The few cars on the three-block main street crept along at a sedate pace.

Looking into the window of one of the quaint little shops, Pat spied the material she wanted for a shirt. Leaving Tom to chat with a taxi driver about the best route to take to the cabins, since no bikes were available for hire, she darted inside. The black saleswoman with the lilting island accent mingled with Dutch tinges showed her several lovely designs. Quickly selecting three yards of batik with a black, bold blue, and gold pattern, Pat made her purchase and returned to his side.

In her absence Tom had followed the cabdriver's directions to a little jewelry shop. Opening the box for her approval, he showed her the dainty silver shell earrings he had purchased for his secretary. He looked quite proud of his ability to accomplish the tasks on his list in record time.

"This gentleman says that he'll take us on a tour of the entire island for fifteen dollars. We can stop wherever we'd like for photographs. He'll have us back at the gate by our eleven-thirty boarding time. Okay?" Tom explained as he ushered Pat into the old but well-maintained yellow taxi.

"Fine with me. Let's go," Pat answered as she slipped into

the immaculately clean interior of the cab. With Tom sitting beside her, she felt very secure and safe.

Along the way they stopped as planned to view the small white five-feet-by-five-feet stone structures that had at one time housed four male slaves as they worked in the salt mines. All day they channeled the water from the sea into the reservoirs and drainage ditches and then into the shallow trenches where the sun's rays would dry out the water to leave behind the desired salt. They would then load it onto pallets for further processing inland at the plantation. The men would see their wives only on weekends when they would rest from their labors.

"I know that people were shorter two hundred years ago, but can you imagine living in a house like this? I can almost touch the walls while standing in the middle," Tom exclaimed as he wedged his frame into the tiny house. Its five-foot ceiling made it impossible for him to stand.

"I can't imagine living under slavery, let alone in such deplorable conditions. This structure is incredibly tiny with no windows, and only this one small door facing the ocean to allow in any breeze. Think of how hot and smelly it must have been in here with four men sleeping together. At high tide the water must have flooded the cabin," Pat exclaimed as she stood in the opening and gazed out onto the deep blue of the endless sea.

"It was dreadful," added the taxi driver. "The worse part for the men, however, was being separated from their families. You can live anywhere as long as you have people around who love you. Living away from the wife and kids must have been especially hard on them, physically as well as emotionally. Come away from here. I'll take you to a beautiful sight."

As they returned to the taxi along the walk made of crushed shells and white coral, Pat tripped over a piece of driftwood and lost her balance. Quickly Tom reached out and steadied her. Finding herself in his arms for the second time that day, Pat blushed and muttered as she looked into his smiling eyes, "I guess I don't have my land legs back yet."

"Not to worry, my fair maiden, I'm a sailor from way back.

I'll be here to steady you," Tom replied, feigning a pirate's accent and twisting an imaginary mustache.

Righting herself and reluctantly leaving his arms, Pat quipped, "Thank you, kind sir, but I hope that I will not inflict myself on your generous spirit any further. I am a woman of independent means. This imbalance, I assure you, is only temporary."

Laughing, Pat and Tom linked arms and continued their walk to the vehicle. Thinking that the handsome couple was on their honeymoon, the driver moved discretely away and returned to his taxi. He remembered how it felt to be young and in love and wanted to give the newlyweds plenty of privacy.

From the remains of the slave quarters, they traveled to an area renowned as the nesting site of the pink flamingo. Pat scanned the horizon as thousands of bright pink birds stood in their much photographed one-legged pose. Occasionally one of them would flap its wings as if irritated by their presence. The others would do the same thing before settling down to sleep with their heads under their wings.

"They're beautiful!" Pat cried out. "They look just like cotton candy. All this time I thought that the photographs had been retouched to make their feathers seem so pink. Bea and Jeff are certainly missing a wonderful sight."

"This is definitely one of the benefits of being well organized," Tom bragged with a chuckle as they strolled to the taxi for the short, leisurely drive back to the harbor.

"I doubt that we would have seen those birds if we hadn't planned on sightseeing. I noticed that a number of people returned to the ship when they saw how tiny the island is. They didn't think that there would be much to do here. They certainly missed out on a fabulous treat," Pat added as she settled into the old, soft leather upholstery for the return trip to the pier.

After paying the driver and giving him a generous tip, Tom and Pat climbed the gangplank with only a few minutes to spare. "I think I'll play a little bingo after lunch," Pat commented as she walked down the hall to her cabin. Glancing at Tom, she hoped that he would pick up the hint and join her.

"Great, I'll meet you upstairs in the lounge. I don't often

## NEW YEAR'S EVE

admit this, but I like the game. Most people think it's for older folks on vacation, but I've always enjoyed playing it. I'll see you there if I don't run into you on deck at lunch. Thanks for a great morning," Tom said as he waited for Pat to unlock her stateroom door.

"I really enjoyed myself, too. I'll see you in the lounge," Pat replied as she reluctantly closed the door. She did not want the magic of the morning to end.

Rather than immediately returning to his cabin on the other side of the ship, Tom lingered at her door to reflect on the sweet contours of her face, the gentle swell of her breasts, and the softness of her touch. Shaking his head, Tom whispered, "If I believed in love at first sight, I'd be sunk!" Slowly he walked away with his hands deep in his pockets and his mind occupied with thoughts of Pat.

Throwing herself onto the waiting sofa, Pat slowly took deep breaths to quiet the fluttering of her heart. "This is silly. You hardly know the man. Get a grip on yourself, woman," she scolded herself as she lounged in a helpless pile.

"Talking to yourself now?" Bea asked as she burst into the room.

"Well, you weren't here and I needed to share my thoughts with someone. In a pinch, I'll do," Pat responded, feeling like a child who had just been caught with her hand in the cookie jar. Quickly she walked to the closet and pulled out her suitcase where she stashed the bag of fabric after showing it to Bea.

"I had a wonderful time with Jeff. The water felt fabulous. You should have come with us. What did you and Tom do all morning?" Bea asked as she tossed her wet towel into a corner of the bathroom floor.

"We toured the island in an incredibly old but delightful taxi. The driver has lived in Bonaire all of his life, with the exception of the years he spent in the Netherlands in college. It was great fun. He told us about the island's economy and the fact that young people leave and don't return these days. He took us to historical sights and to see the famed flamingos.

"Tom was the perfect companion. He's so strong and handsome and intelligent. When I tripped, he caught me in the most muscular arms I've ever felt. After lunch we're going to play bingo,'' Pat replied, trying to maintain her composure at the thought of being with Tom again. She still burned from the touch of his hand on her arm.

"It certainly looks as if you two are getting along well. From the sparkle in your eyes, I'd say that you find him appealing. But why would you want to play bingo? Can't you think of something sexier than that to do? Why not try lying out in the sun for a while? The sight of you in that new bikini should warm him up," Bea offered as she darted into the bathroom for a much needed shower.

"Who says I want to start anything that I won't have time to finish? I don't want a shipboard romance. I won't be just another conquest etched into his belt. I'm happy with the way things are progressing. I don't want to change anything," Pat shouted over the running water.

"Have it your way," Bea conceded as she rinsed the last of the sand from her dark brown shoulder-length hair and turned off the water, "But bingo is so . . . old."

"I like it and so does Tom. Hurry up, I'm starved," Pat urged as she paced the cabin floor while she waited for Bea to emerge. She was not in the least bit hungry, but she was anxious to see Tom again.

Bea appeared, dressed in a cream slacks and sweater outfit. "I'll be ready as soon as I add a little color to my cheeks. I think I got a little tan, don't you?" she asked as she touched her cheeks with the mauve blush.

"The tan is very flattering, and you look gorgeous as usual. Now, let's go!" Pat pleaded from the door.

"If I didn't know better, I'd say that you were rushing off to meet someone. But that couldn't be because you're the one who doesn't want to become involved in a shipboard romance. Isn't that right, girlfriend?" Bea teased as she slowly closed the door and joined Pat in the hall.

Casting her a cutting glance, Pat ignored the innuendo and pasted a composed expression on her face. She wanted to look happy to see Tom but not eager. Turning to Bea, she commented, "I don't believe in fleeting affairs, but I do enjoy being

# NEW YEAR'S EVE

with him. There's a big difference between throwing myself at a man for a fling and showing my appreciation for his kindness and consideration during the time that we're together. I am doing the latter."

Puffing from the run up the stairs, Bea replied, "Either way you slice it, you're interested in this guy. I don't blame you. He's attractive and appears to be available. My only advice is for you to check out his credentials. You know my motto . . ."

"Yea, I know . . . 'love 'em rich and leave 'em poor,' " Pat added with a chuckle as Bea stuck out her tongue and pretended to be wounded by the suggestion that her primary interest in a relationship was financial gain.

"There's nothing wrong with having a good time. That's how I got my fur coat, the diamond bracelet, and the car. I can't help it if the men in my life are generous to a fault," Bea replied with feigned wounded feelings.

"Did you ever date anyone who was poor or of modest means?" Pat inquired as she scanned the hungry faces on the sunny deck for Tom's.

"No, and I don't plan to start now. A girl has to have her future in mind at all times. Besides, no poor man would want to spend his time with me. He'd be frightened away by the way I live. I work hard for my money. It's not easy being a black female in the legal profession. I don't care what anyone thinks. I deserve the best. I earned the right to enjoy life from the best address to the most luxurious vacation to the wealthiest significant other. I won't apologize for the way I live," Bea responded.

If anyone else had made comments about her life-style, Bea would have been offended. However, she and Pat had been friends for so long that she knew that Pat was not standing in judgment of her. As a matter of fact, she occasionally thought that Pat might even wish she could change places with her, if only for a day. Being a schoolteacher had its financial drawbacks.

"I'm not criticizing you. You're one of my best friends, and I love you just the way you are. I was just wondering if the thought ever crossed your mind to love a man whose bank account was not as large as yours," Pat said as she arranged a salad on her plate beside the luscious slices of fruit.

"Hi, ladies," Jeff interrupted as he joined them. The sun had added a healthy sheen to his skin, too. His eyes sparkled brightly, and he smiled intimately as he looked at Bea.

Looking past his broad shoulders, Pat greeted him with a sad smile and commented, "Nice to see you this afternoon, Jeff. I guess Tom isn't with you."

"No, I haven't seen him since he left with you this morning. He wasn't in the cabin when I returned from the beach. I thought he was still with you, but I guess not. He'll turn up somewhere. He always does," Jeff responded as he enfolded Bea in his strong arms and buried his nose in her freshly washed hair. From the expression on his face, Pat could tell that their relationship had progressed romantically on the deserted beach.

Taking a seat at a table for four, Pat nibbled at her lunch without much enthusiasm. She was the third wheel as she sat beside the chair that remained empty throughout the meal. She felt out of place as she watched Jeff and Bea feed each other tasty morsels and giggle at an unspoken private joke.

Suddenly she found that she was even less hungry than she had originally thought. Tom's absence had robbed her of her appetite and aroused her latent anxieties and insecurities. Throughout the meal Pat wondered if she had shown too much or too little interest in him. Pat questioned whether she had said just enough or too much. She might have frightened him into another woman's arms. Now she wondered if she would have to endure the rest of the cruise alone while watching him enjoy the company of someone else.

As Bea and Jeff went off to change for an afternoon of basking in the sun together, Pat made her way through the laughing people to the lounge. Paying for her bingo cards, she sat where she would be able to see him when he entered the room. For the first time since she began playing the game as a small girl, Pat did not enjoy punching out the numbers.

"Honey, you have a bingo," the woman sitting next to her said as she nudged Pat with her elbow. "There's a bingo over here!" she shouted, waving her arm wildly.

"Oh, I guess my mind was far away," Pat replied as she slowly handed her card to the crew member who read off each of the numbers that ran diagonally across its face.

Slipping into her seat once more, Pat accepted the applause and the fifty dollars. Looking at the woman to her right, she smiled and thanked her for the help. The woman only nodded and shook her head. She was already pulling out her next card. She was a dedicated bingo player and had little time for this absentminded newcomer.

Finishing her last of three games, Pat quietly left the lounge. She would have liked to have shared her success with Tom, but he still had not arrived. Shrugging her shoulders, she wandered toward the ship's store to see how she could spend her winnings.

Purchasing a little crystal bell as a gift for her mother, Pat returned to her cabin for a quick nap before dressing for dinner. At first when the door would not open, she thought that her key was suddenly defective. However, as she examined it more closely in the silent hall, she heard whispered voices from inside the room. Realizing that Bea and Jeff were probably amorously engaged, she quickly abandoned her hopes of getting a little sleep and retreated to the quiet of the bookshelf-lined, mahogany-paneled reading room two decks up from their cabin.

Pulling a chair in front of the huge picture window that overlooked the expanse of sparkling blue sea, Pat settled down for a restful hour of reading. After scanning the back covers of two romance novels, she selected *It Had to Be You.* It was the story of a young attorney's struggle to find herself within a loving relationship. She decided against reading *Blush,* which was set in a Dallas cosmetics firm and centered around a hostile business takeover and the love that grew out of it, because it seemed too close to home.

Pat had already breezed through the first fifty pages when she felt someone standing at her shoulder. Reluctant to tear herself from the story, she did not look up as the person lingered at her side. Thinking that the visitor was Bea coming to tell her that she could return to their cabin, she spoke without looking up from the novel in her hands.

"So, you've decided to take a break from your afternoon activities," Pat said with a chuckle.

"I'm sorry that I missed our bingo date, but something came up, and I just couldn't get away," a gentle baritone voice replied.

Startled, Pat quickly turned toward the sound, dropping the much-read book on the floor at her feet. Smiling into Tom's handsome face, she replied teasingly without letting on that she had missed him, "I'll forgive you this once, but don't do it again."

Snapping to attention and saluting, Tom replied, "Yes, ma'am. I'll be more careful in the future, ma'am."

Laughing and feeling more relaxed and happy than she had all afternoon, Pat watched as Tom pulled up a chair beside hers. For a while they sat in silence as they watched the whitecaps float on the water. An occasional sea-bird broke the stillness with its graceful hovering over the waves before rising with a wiggling fish in its beak.

Taking Pat's hand in his, Tom said, "I really am sorry about this afternoon. When I returned to my cabin after our morning on the island, I discovered that I had a call from my office. I couldn't ignore it. Unfortunately it took longer than I had anticipated to conduct my business. By the time I finally arrived at the lounge, the bingo games had ended and you had left. I had just about given up on seeing you until dinner. I just happened to look in here on a whim."

"A business call? Is your boss some kind of tyrant? Can't he leave you alone for one short week? After all, you're on vacation," Pat exclaimed with disbelief that anyone would be so insensitive as to hound an employee aboard ship in the middle of the Caribbean.

With a merry chuckle, Tom replied, "He's not a bad guy at all. Something came up that needed my immediate attention. It happens all the time in this business. I promise that I'll do better tonight. After dinner and the show, let's go dancing before we return to the casino. I feel lucky."

Although Pat wanted desperately to know more about the business to which Tom had made such casual reference, she

# NEW YEAR'S EVE

did not ask the question that lingered on the tip of her tongue. If he had wanted her to know the nature of his employment, he certainly had the opportunity to tell her. Obviously he was as private about his life as she was. Considering that the cruise would end in a matter of days and that they were never see each other again, she understood his desire to keep personal information close to his chest. She would divulge only a certain amount about herself to strangers, too.

"Dancing sounds like fun. I'll pencil you into my schedule. I think I can arrange to be available then. Besides, I had a bit of luck this afternoon at bingo. I've spent most of it, but I'd like the opportunity to lose the rest at the slot machines," Pat answered with a laugh. She thoroughly enjoyed the exchange of wits and conversation with Tom.

In the short time that Pat had known Tom, she had already sensed that she would have been able to enjoy a very gratifying friendship with him if time and distance were not working against them. He had a quick sense of humor, loved to laugh, enjoyed many of the same things, appeared intelligent, was definitely hardworking, and was handsome. If she had not known that the reality of their brief acquaintance prevented more than just a pleasant association, Pat would have given him encouragement to continue their relationship as soon as their vacation ended. Knowing that they were from different parts of the country, she was content to enjoy her time with him now while they were together.

"Don't forget that tonight's the captain's cocktail party. We have to dress for dinner," Pat added as they settled into their seats and resumed their gazing into the endless sea.

"Thanks for reminding me," Tom replied with a groan as he cradled her hand in his. "I'd almost forgotten. I'd rather wear slacks and a sweater, but if I have to put on a tux, I will try to muster as much dignity and grace as possible."

Laughing Pat said, "I feel the same way about evening gowns. They're too confining, but it might be nice to go dancing à lá Fred Astaire and Ginger Rogers."

Pat's heart pounded so loudly from the nearness of Tom that she feared he would hear it over the soft classical music that played in the reading room. His hand held hers possessively, as if they had sat this way for years. His palm was neither too large nor too small for hers. She did not feel lost in him, rather a part of him. Pat loved the feeling and wished that it could continue.

Feeling the same way, Tom said with a shy smile, "Now this is the way to take a cruise. There's nothing like gazing out a window with the sea spreading around you while holding the hand of a beautiful woman. I'd count myself a lucky man if this day never ended."

"I was just thinking the same thing. And to think I didn't want to come on this cruise. Look at what I would have missed," Pat replied as she smiled into his open face. Their new feelings for each other were so clearly visible that neither could mistake the interest of the other.

Rising, they slowly walked down the hall toward Pat's cabin. Strolling past the early diners, Pat smiled in appreciation at the lovely gowns and the happy faces as the other vacationers flocked to the lounge where the captain waited to greet them. Soon she and Tom would be among the second-seating cruisers who nibbled canapés at the captain's cocktail party.

Standing in the bustle of hurrying passengers outside her cabin, Tom said with a chuckle from deep inside his muscular frame, "I'll meet you in the lounge in one hour. I'll be the guy in the black tux with the bright red cummerbund. You won't be able to miss me."

Laughing at his joke as yet another man in the same outfit walked past, Pat replied, "And I'll be the woman in the spaghetti-strap black gown with the matching shawl."

Just as Pat reached for the doorknob, the hall grew quiet. Seizing the moment, Tom placed his hands firmly on her shoulders and turned her to face him. Pulling her gently onto her toes, he bent down and placed a gentle kiss on Pat's lips. As his arms enfolded her, she melted against him as all hesitation slipped from her body. Despite her promise to avoid a shipboard romance, Pat knew that she was headed for a fall.

Studying her eyes for any signs of regret and finding none, Tom whispered, "Don't forget to wear your dancing shoes."

# NEW YEAR'S EVE

As Pat backed into her cabin from which the fragrance of perfume mingled with steam rushed into the hall, she hoped that she would be able to regain her equilibrium before seeing Tom again. She did not know if the ship was listing or if it was simply the effect of the closeness of him that had destroyed her balance. Whatever it was that made her feel so giddy, she did not want it to stop.

# Chapter Three

Pat dressed with such care that Bea wondered what had happened to her usually unconcerned friend. Never in all the years that they had been friends had she known Pat to spend more than a few minutes on her appearance. However, that night Pat carefully applied mascara, eye shadow, and blush before outlining and coloring her lips. She primped with her hair until every curl lay carefully in place.

Standing in front of the mirrored closet doors, Pat smoothed her gown over her hips and stomach until all the wrinkles vanished. She stood sideways and noted the flatness of her abdomen, from the countless, torturous tummy crunches, and the perkiness of her breasts from the weights she lifted.

When she reached for the perfume, Bea did a double take. Pat never used any fragrance and had often said that she thought it a waste of money since the aroma lasted for only a few minutes. Tonight she sprayed little puffs of scent on the warm spots behind her ears, in the fold of her arms, and between her breasts.

Chuckling and shaking her head, Bea asked, "Are you ready yet? I've never known you to be so fastidious. What's come over you?"

"Nothing at all. I just want to look my best for our photograph, that's all," Pat replied as she ignored the accusatory tone in her friend's voice. "Is there anything wrong with that?"

Following her down the hall and up the stairs, Bea responded, "No, there's nothing wrong with it except that this is so atypical of you. The entire time that you were with Michael, you dressed up only once. Remember the time we went to the opening night of that dreadful play? You dressed up then, and you haven't done it again since. That was three years ago."

"Well, I guess it's about time I made a change," Pat retorted as she joined the line waiting to greet the captain.

"Humph," Bea shorted, "If you ask me, I'd say that you're falling in love and don't want to admit it. I never thought you really loved Michael anyway. You didn't act swept off your feet. I've seen you show more interest in this one day than you ever did with him. Besides, he wasn't right for you. There was no romance in his soul. He was a pound cake. You need a chocolate torte in your life."

"I'm not falling in love. That would be silly under the circumstances. I simply wanted to look my best tonight. A woman wants to put on a show once in a while, even someone as boring and conservative as you seem to think that I am. There was nothing wrong with Michael—but you're right, he was dependable and not very exciting. I don't know if I'm ready for someone bold," Pat quipped as she and Bea eased their way to an empty table from which they could watch for Jeff and Tom.

"I didn't say you were boring, but you must admit that this isn't the usual you. You certainly do look wonderful. I'm glad I talked you into buying that dress. It shows off your athletic figure perfectly. Don't worry, girlfriend, if Tom's your opportunity for excitement, you'll be ready," Bea said as she took full credit for Pat's transformation.

"Well, for once I'm glad I listened to you. Thanks for insisting that I fill in for Toni, too. This vacation is already off to a great start. You seem to be enjoying yourself, too. I had to spend part of my afternoon in the reading room because our cabin was . . . occupied. I certainly hope you're being careful," Pat commented with a shrewdly raised brow.

"Of course, I am. I want memories of this vacation but not that kind. Jeff and I were getting to know each other better," Bea replied, feigning shyness. "That man is a handful in more ways than one. Speaking of Jeff, I wonder where he is?"

"I don't see Tom, either. We spent a wonderful afternoon gazing at the sea. I didn't mind being locked out of our cabin at all. They're probably further back in that long line. We arrived rather early," Pat said as she accepted a cocktail from the waiter. The depth of his kiss had told Pat that his interest in her was quite genuine. She knew that he would arrive shortly.

"There's Jeff now. Tom should be right behind him," Bea observed as she waved her hand in response to Jeff's frantic search of the crowd for her.

"Good evening, ladies," Jeff purred as he folded his tall frame into the low sofa beside Bea. Leaning toward her, he placed a chaste kiss on her bare shoulder accompanied by a penetrating glance that spoke volumes about his feelings.

"Is Tom with you?" Pat asked as she continued to scan the people in line. Although the crush had diminished, a number of people still waited to meet the captain.

"No, I left him in the cabin on the phone. He said that he'd meet us in the dining room," Jeff responded without taking his eyes from Bea's face. His overt expression of adoration was almost more than Pat could take on an empty stomach.

"Oh, no, not another call to the office!" Pat groaned. "The last one caused him to miss our afternoon of bingo. I probably won't see him at all tonight."

Unable to resist her curiosity, Bea asked, "What does that poor man do for a living? Can't he even get away from the office for a vacation without someone calling him?"

With an uneasy smile Jeff responded, "Tom works for the same brokerage firm that I do. His accounts are just busy right now, that's all. It happens to all of us sometimes despite our best plans."

"Well, I think it's most inconsiderate of his boss to contact him while he's on vacation. Everyone's entitled to a little time off for good or bad behavior," Bea added as she snuggled closer to Jeff.

Although Bea did not seem to notice Jeff's hesitation, Pat did. She wondered what lay behind his reluctance to discuss Tom's job. She and Bea knew nothing about these men except what they had volunteered, which was not much. Since she was not a naturally nosy person, Pat knew only that Tom was a history buff and that his job was demanding. Seeing Jeff's reaction to Bea's simple question, she questioned what she did not know about Tom and wondered if she should get up the courage to learn more. She wondered if these guys might be engaged in shady dealings, were husbands on the run or the love 'em and leave 'em types who would break their hearts and try to ensnare them in some insane investment deal.

When the cocktail party ended, Jeff waited for them as Pat and Bea stopped for the official photograph before continuing to the dining room. Inside, the waiters had decorated the tables with mirrors and gold balls in glass bowls that shimmered in the candlelight. Gold streamers and garland floated along the walls and hung from the rafters. Everything was ready for the first of two elegant evenings on the ship.

Taking their seats, Pat and Bea watched as the other guests entered the room in their finery. All of the women wore sequins on some article of clothing with many of them arriving in gowns that had been skillfully covered in them. They had all applied more makeup than usual, fluffed their hair higher, and painted their nails a deeper shade of red. Their escorts, most of whom were their husbands of thirty or more years, had donned tux and cummerbund for the evening. Everyone looked relaxed from an afternoon at sea and the freely flowing drinks at the captain's cocktail party.

When Tom did not arrive, Bea asked their waiter if Jeff could join them at their table. Happily, the three of them sat amid the flashing camera lights and posed for a photograph together. As they munched their shrimp cocktails or escargot, they were the picture of three buddies enjoying themselves.

Yet Pat could feel the kernel of doubt growing into a nagging question. She resolved as she sliced into the succulent duck that glistened in a wine and honey sauce that she would have to find out more about Tom. Although she had no expectations of permanence from their brief relationship, she did not want to spend her vacation with a man who might be a murderer or a con man—or worse, someone else's unfaithful husband. She also did not want to live each day with the expectation of seeing him only to be disappointed when he did not appear.

The evening with its light, warm breeze was too splendid to spend indoors, so the trio strolled the deck for a while rather than going directly to the show. Stopping at the rail, they looked into the vastness of the black night and the emptiness of the sea. Millions of stars twinkled overhead as the ship gently followed its course toward Barbados.

"I've never seen anything so lovely," Bea cooed as she scanned the horizon for signs of another island or a passing vessel.

Wrapping his arms around her and nuzzling into her neck, Jeff said, "I have."

Looking at him with skepticism and wagging a finger, Pat retorted playfully, "Oh, please, give me a break. Is that all you can think about? We're standing here on this splendid night, and you're tossing around lines like that one. Can't you come up with something more original?"

"Excuse me! I happen to enjoy his banalities. If Tom had said the same thing to you, you wouldn't be complaining right now. You're just feeling sorry for yourself because you're alone," Bea quipped with a chuckle as she turned in Jeff's arms and kissed him lightly.

"Maybe you're right, but I can't imagine that anything he'd say would outdo the spectacle of this evening. Besides, I don't know Tom well enough to miss him. I think it's just being alone that I don't like. However, I came on this cruise to be alone, so I'll just have to become adjusted to going solo again, since it looks as if he'd rather conduct business than spend his time with me," Pat concluded as she enviously watched the lovers.

Quickly Jeff interjected, not wanting Pat to feel sidelined for the evening or stood up, "He'll be here soon. Don't worry.

His business can't last all night. Let's go to the show. By the time it's over, he will have joined us, I'm sure."

"It really doesn't matter. Tom doesn't owe me anything. We've only just met. I'm perfectly content by myself. I guess I misread his intentions and interest, that's all," Pat commented as she followed them into the show. She would have a great time despite the feeling of disappointment that tugged at her heart. She had misread his kiss as promising more than it did.

Watching the dancers perform their lifts and spins on the gently swaying deck, Pat marveled at their ability to move with such agility on a stage that constantly shifted under them. Their hours of practice rendered their execution flawless despite the slight rolling of the ship. She did not remember the ship moving quite so much their first night at sea. Shrugging off the thought and the slight anxiety, she returned her attention to the production.

As the house lights went up again, Pat discretely scanned the room to see if Tom had finally joined them. Mentally checking him off her list, she glided into the casino for an evening at the slot machine while Bea and Jeff took up their positions at the blackjack table. The rhythmic motion of feeding the machine, pulling the handle, and scooping up the coins soon blotted any thought of Tom from her mind.

Suddenly bells began to ring and lights started to flash as the machine Pat was playing went crazy. Everyone gathered around her to watch as coins tumbled in mad profusion from the overflowing tray onto the floor. They applauded wildly with each new surge.

"You've hit the jackpot!" Bea shouted above the clamor as she bent to scoop up the coins with her hands. She ignored her manicure as she dragged her palms along the carpet. The flashing lights on top of the slot machine told her that Pat had won five hundred dollars.

"This is so embarrassing," Pat replied as she joined her in tossing the bounty into a small bucket.

"Well, Pat, I'd say you've had an eventful evening," Jeff added as he joined them in their efforts. His eyes sparkled at the sight of all the coins.

# NEW YEAR'S EVE

"I've never seen so many quarters," Pat commented as she filled yet another cup.

"The sign on the slot machine says that it pays out a maximum of one hundred dollars in coins. Consider all we've gathered, I'd say it's just about finished," Bea shouted.

As the noise from the bells stopped as suddenly as it began, everyone cheered. Leaving Pat, Bea, and Jeff with their hands full of coins, they returned to their games. They hoped that some of Pat's good luck would rub off on them.

"Ma'am, if you'll follow me, I'll cash in those coins for you and give you the rest of your winnings," the casino manager directed with a smile as he took the buckets and cups from Pat's overburdened arms.

As Pat followed him to the cashier's window, the casino returned to normal, and the jovial conversation resumed. Once again, she could hear the happy laughter of the players at the gaming tables and the occasional tinkle of the coins punctuated by the sporadic ringing of the bells. Her embarrassing moments in the spotlight had ended.

"I understand that you caused quite a commotion in here." Tom's voice penetrated her thoughts as Pat watched the cashier count out her winnings in small bills.

Turning quickly to face him, Pat said, "I didn't mean to disturb everyone's peaceful evening, but the machine simply went crazy."

To her surprise, Tom was not alone. On his arm was a stunningly attractive woman of about Pat's age whose sparkling brown eyes were only outshone by the diamonds at her ears and neck. Both of them smiled broadly at Pat's victory over the one-armed bandit.

Pat could feel the muscles in her face freezing into the shape of a smile as she looked from Tom's handsome face into that of the woman who clung to him as if to a life preserver. Her ample bosom pressed invitingly against him as she closed all the spaces that might have existed between them. Her body language made it perfectly clear that she had no intention of sharing Tom with anyone.

"Pat Grimes, this is Crystal Marsh. She boarded the ship in

Bonaire," Tom added without letting his eyes shift from Pat's face. From the intensity of his gaze, he appeared to be trying to read her reaction to the new woman on board.

"I certainly hope you will enjoy the cruise as much as we have so far. The water has been perfect for sailing, and the crew has proven itself to be incredibly helpful and friendly," Pat said as she extended her hand toward Crystal's diamond-encrusted one. She felt suddenly frumpy and out of place in her simple black evening gown and pearls in comparison to Crystal's shimmering satin sheath and sparkling accessories.

"I'm sure I will. My stateroom offers the most delightful view of the sea and the horizon," Crystal cooed as she reclaimed her hold on Tom's arm.

" I don't remember seeing you at dinner. Did you dine early?" Pat asked as she tried to stop her heart from pounding.

"No, Tom and I needed to be alone for a while, so we dined in my stateroom. We watched the sunset from the balcony. It was all so lovely and private," Crystal replied as she wiggled even closer to Tom and oozed sugary sweetness.

"Maybe tomorrow you'll join us on deck for breakfast before we dock at Barbados or perhaps for an early morning jog," Pat offered as she felt her chances of spending any more time alone with Tom slipping from her fingers forever. She had not sailed for the purpose of finding a man, yet she had experienced a brief relationship with Tom that she did not want to end. She had been naive enough to believe from his kiss that he had felt the same attraction for her that she did for him. Obviously from the sight of the brown beauty on his arm, she had been mistaken.

"Oh, no. I never expose my skin to the aging rays of the sun. I might join you on a tour of the island if we happen to be going in the same bus. I prefer to take my meals either in the main dining room or in my cabin but never on the deck," Crystal replied slowly. The downward curve of her red lips showed obvious contempt for the suggestion that she might want to dine among the other vacationers in the sunshine.

"Crystal's a top fashion model, Pat, and has to be very careful about what she eats and about sun exposure. She can't afford to damage her skin or lose her figure," Tom explained with a tone in his voice that was similar to pride. Pat wondered about the nature of their relationship.

"I thought you looked familiar. I've seen your face in many of the high-fashion magazines. It would be lovely if you could accompany us, but I can understand your hesitation. It was very nice meeting you. I'm going for a stroll on deck and then to my cabin. I'm suddenly very tired. I suppose it's the excitement of winning at the slot machine that did it. I've never won anything in my life before tonight. Well, good night," Pat concluded with a rush. She was very anxious to escape the company of this overly sweet woman who clung to the man she had begun to consider her vacation companion.

"If Crystal doesn't keep me up too late, I'll join you on deck in the morning for a jog," Tom remarked as if trying to send Pat a message between the lines of his words.

"Great, I'll see you then," Pat replied as she wove her way through the crush of people who now filled the casino. Whatever he was trying to say, she did not understand the message. Instead Pat only felt abandoned and very disappointed. The kiss that had lingered sweetly on her lips now had a bitter taste.

"Good night, Pat. Pleasant dreams," Crystal called after her.

"Who's that?" Bea asked as soon as Pat joined her. "She's a real beauty. She certainly had her hooks into Tom's arm. He couldn't have broken free if his life depended on it. And that possessive smile of hers almost lit up the room. I was wondering when they'd dim the lights."

"She's a model. Look, I'm really tired. I'm going to bed early," Pat replied without enthusiasm. The casino was too small for both of them.

Bea studied her friend's face for a few moments and then asked, "Are you sure that you're okay? You look more than merely tired."

Knowing that Bea had seen past her charade, Pat responded, "I'll be just fine after a quick stroll around the deck and a good night's sleep. The excitement of the evening was just too much for me, that's all."

Jeff added with a chuckle, "I'd be tired, too, if I had won five hundred dollars at the slot machine."

Trying to put on a happy front, Pat replied with a gaiety that she did not feel, "I guess it's not too shabby for one night. I'll have to do better the next time we're at sea."

Waving, Pat shouldered her way through the crowd and out onto the deck. The stars twinkled brightly as the ship sailed toward Barbados. Looking at the black sea, she noticed that more waves broke in the distance than the previous night. Just as she had in the lounge, Pat felt the ship pitching a bit from the increased currents. Although she could not see any clouds in the sky, she wondered if a storm might be brewing somewhere in the vast ocean. It would be nothing compared to the one that stirred her heart.

"I had hoped that I would find you here," a familiar voice said as it broke the silence of the night.

Turning, Pat looked into Tom's penetrating eyes. He was alone. Crystal did not drape alluringly over his arm or hang on his every word.

"It's a beautiful night, and I needed to take a walk before retiring. Where's Crystal?"

"She's in the ship's store. I have to meet her in the piano bar in fifteen minutes, but I wanted to speak with you alone," Tom replied as he studied Pat's face to see if she still welcomed his company.

"Why? What's there to say between us? If you think you owe me an explanation, you don't. We spent an enjoyable few hours together, that's all. We're in no way obligated to each other," Pat declared as she turned toward the sea and again scanned the churning waves. She took comfort in the fact that the sea appeared to be responding to her emotions.

"Oh, I guess I misunderstood. I apologize for intruding on your evening. I had thought that we had enjoyed each other's company as more than tourists on an unknown island. I'll even go so far as to say that I had hoped that a true relationship might develop between us. I guess I was wrong about that," Tom tried to explain. His voice was tinged with genuine sadness.

Before Pat could answer, a voice rang out above the murmur of the engines and the lapping of the waves on the side of the ship. "There you are, you naughty boy. I've been looking everywhere for you. I told you that I'd be finished in the shop in fifteen minutes. When I turned around, you weren't waiting for me. I'm always true to my word," Crystal exclaimed as she again linked her arms through Tom's and sent a triumphant grin in Pat's direction.

Looking from Crystal's beaming face to Tom's expression of regret, Pat quickly announced, "It's definitely past my bedtime if I'm to exercise in the morning. I'll see you both tomorrow."

As she disappeared through the door, Pat could hear Crystal ask in a sultry, pouting voice, "Whatever made you come out on this windy deck? It's much too chilly. See, I have goose bumps all over my body. Feel."

Alone in her cabin, Pat quickly stripped off the evening gown and pulled on her comfortable old sleep shirt. Stuffing her feet into her slippers, she padded to the bathroom where she angrily scrubbed the makeup from her face. Pat marveled at the change in her spirits as she saw her familiar visage reflected in the mirror.

"To think I plastered this mess on my face so that I would look more alluring to Tom. Now he's in the arms of another woman, and I've clogged my pores with this junk. It just shows that if a man isn't interested in a woman for the person within, he won't be swayed by all the makeup, perfume, and fancy clothes in the world. I feel like such a fool. Well, at least it's over now, and I can still enjoy my vacation alone as planned," Pat muttered to herself as she patted on an astringent and picked up a book. She would read until her body adjusted to the pitch and roll of the ship, and then she would turn out the light and go to sleep.

As she reached the kidnapping scene in *It Had to Be You,* Pat found that she was having trouble concentrating as she struggled to remain in her bed. The ship rocked and pitched with increased fury, almost throwing her onto the floor. The closet doors swung open and shut angrily. The medicine cabinet doors banged shut. Occasionally the lights dimmed, and the water in the pitcher on the dressing table sloshed onto the wood.

Worried voices filled the corridor as people returned to their cabins.

Suddenly Bea entered with a decidedly green tint to her complexion. Immediately she ran for the bathroom. When she returned, she looked no better as she struggled to remove her gown, draw on her nightgown, and crawl between the covers. Weakly she said, "The cruise director ordered all of us to return to our cabins. We'll be sailing through some awfully rough water for a while, he said. You should see the waves. They're pounding against the ship and washing over the decks."

"Are we in any danger?" Pat asked as her book flew off the night table and landed with a thump on the carpet.

"I don't know, but I feel so awful that anything would be all right with me," Bea groaned as the waves tossed the ship high into the air, only for it to return to the water with a heavy thud and a frightening shiver.

"Where did you leave Jeff?"

"The last I of saw of him, he was hurrying toward the nearest empty bathroom. The seasickness hit him even sooner that it got me," Bea responded as she gripped her bed to keep from rolling onto the floor.

Turning out the light, Pat slipped under her covers and tucked them securely around her body. The emergency lights in the hallway flickered off and on. The ship tossed frighteningly, but she felt strangely secure in her faith in the vessel. She listened to the creaking of the ship as Bea moaned softly in her sleep.

As soon as Pat began to doze during a momentary lull in the ship's tossing, the captain's voice broke the silence. In a tone that was at once commanding and unsettling, he announced, "Ladies and gentlemen, this is your captain speaking. We have encountered some unusually severe weather. For the safety of our passengers and crew, and in order to maintain the integrity of this vessel, we will be forced to ride out the storm in an easterly direction that might make docking at Barbados an impossibility. I have been in contact with our home office and the weather bureau, both of which concur with my decision to steer a course out of harm's way. We are trying at this moment to

# NEW YEAR'S EVE

make arrangements to dock at another island once the conditions improve.

"My crew and I would like to apologize to all of you for any discomfort you might be experiencing. However, acts of nature and God are beyond our control. We ask that you remain in your cabins where you will be safe. Try to stay in your beds as much as possible. Do not under any circumstances take it upon yourselves to venture onto the outside decks as the waves are very high and extremely dangerous. For your safety, you should keep your distance from any windows as the winds are strong and the potential for breaking glass is always a possibility in storms of this magnitude.

"I will interrupt your rest as little as possible with updates on our position and on the weather. Try to sleep. Good night."

For a few moments the only sound in the cabin was the water sloshing in the toilet and the waves and wind pounding against the side of the ship. Then, Bea moaned, "I'm so sorry I insisted that you join me on this cruise, Pat. You could be safely sleeping in your own bed if I had kept my big mouth shut. This is awful. I hope we don't sink."

"I don't think we need to worry about that. The captain looked very experienced and capable of handling every situation. We'll be fine as soon as he can steer the ship out of this weather. I'm not at all sorry that I came on this cruise. I've never been in a storm at sea. This is actually kind of exciting. The most unusual thing that's ever happened to me before this cruise was getting stuck in an elevator. This beats that hands down," Pat replied almost cheerfully. Her stomach was only slightly upset by the vigorous pitching and rolling of the ship. In reality, she found this brush with danger very stimulating, considering the quiet life she lived in the classroom.

"If I weren't so sick, I'd throw my pillow at you. But thanks for letting me off the hook. I wouldn't have booked either of us into this cruise if I had known that at the end of December this kind of storm could pop up. I thought there were only hurricanes and gales during the summer. Some Christmas vacation we're having. This was supposed to be the cruise of a lifetime. From the sounds of this moaning ship, tomorrow we'll be tossing on the sea in lifeboats. We'll be too worried about dying to care that it's New Year's Eve." Bea groaned again as she dashed to the bathroom.

As she returned to her bed, the captain's voice again boomed over the public address system. "All available hands to C deck for damage control. All available hands to C deck for damage control. Ladies and gentlemen, I hate to disturb you again, but I felt that I should share this information with you. Although the ship is quite sound, we are being battered by gale force twelve winds. Again, I urge all of you to use considerable caution in moving around the ship. Any step could prove a misstep in waters this rough. Stay in your beds as much as possible. Even going to the bathroom could be dangerous. Thank you."

"Did his voice sound strained to you?" Bea asked in a voice weakened from illness and worry.

"Yes, I could hear some stress in it. I'm still not going to worry. He'll steer us out of this mess before too much longer. Try to get some rest," Pat answered as she adjusted her covers. She did not feel quite as calm as she pretended. The excitement of riding out the storm had faded with the knowledge that the ship was in danger. Something frightening had happened on C deck.

As the night lengthened into dawn, the pitching and bucking slowly calmed to a more manageable yet frightening rolling. The public address system had been silent for the past two hours as the crew scurried through the halls, cleaning up water damage and signs of sickness. From the lack of conversation in the hall, Pat could tell that no passengers ventured out of their cabins, although her watch told her that it was morning.

The breakfast hour came and went without announcement. Pat doubted that anyone had given any thought to preparing food, with all hands busily securing the ship and repairing the storm's damage. Besides, everyone was probably too sick or frightened to eat. Although her stomach had not reacted to the tossing and pitching of the ship, she did not feel any hunger. Fear had scared it out of her.

Lifting a corner of the curtain that covered the window, Pat

# NEW YEAR'S EVE

saw that the sky was still black and the rain continued to fall heavily despite the fact that it was well past eight o'clock. Turning on her personal reading light, she peeked at Bea, who slept soundly with her hand tightly gripping the edge of the bed. Her complexion looked slightly improved now that the ship's motion had stabilized a bit.

Momentarily Pat thought of Tom before she could stop herself. She wondered how he had fared during the frightening night. Pushing him from her mind, she decided that the model who was now his companion would surely have ministered to his every need. From the way Crystal had clung to his arm, Pat doubted that Tom had spent even a night filled with wind and rain alone. She was sure that Crystal had been there to hold his hand and soothe his brow.

Stretching out on her bed again, Pat reflected on her feelings about Tom. She had been too hurt the previous night to give much thought to anything but saving face in front of the other woman who had become her replacement. The perilous night and the fear of sinking in the angry sea had pushed him from her mind. Now, as the ship continued to fight the waves in a more predictable manner, Pat had plenty of time to think about her emotional investment in the fledgling relationship.

Folding her arms under her head, Pat saw Tom's handsome face and winning smile. She heard the sound of his voice and smelled the fragrance of his cologne in her memory. She felt the warmth and strength of his hand as he guided her over rocky terrain in their exploration of Bonaire. And she experienced the sweetness of their first and only kiss.

"Are you awake?" asked a small voice.

"Yes, I'm just lying here thinking. How are you feeling?" Pat replied.

"Much better. Now that the ship is behaving nicely again, I'm in much better shape. What were you thinking about . . . Tom?" Bea asked, sensing that Pat might want to talk out her feelings.

"Of course. But Bea, you know I'm too practical to have fallen for him so soon. Our relationship was too new to be more than a hint of something better yet to come. I don't know why I'm carrying on like this. I don't even know anything about him other than he works at a brokerage firm, which could mean that he holds any position from janitor to president. Considering the amount of time Tom spends on the telephone, I assume that he must occupy a position with some degree of authority. However, he might have been cleaning up messes with furnace contractors rather than conducting investment business.

"I didn't see a ring on his left hand or the telltale sign that he had recently removed one. However, I do know that not all men wear wedding bands. He might be one of those married men who considers a ring to be a brand of ownership, which he will not wear. Our relationship hasn't lasted long enough for me to ask him.

"Yet having Tom ever so briefly in my life has given me a little something extra to anticipate each day. I looked forward to seeing him at meals, to dancing through the night in his arms, to exploring the islands and coves under his guidance, and to spending quiet time alone with him on the deck. Now all of those plans have vanished with the appearance of this mysterious late-arriving woman named Crystal. She certainly swooped down and took over the man with whom I had planned to spend my vacation."

"Well, what are you going to do about it? Are you going to stand by and do nothing to stop her?" Bea demanded, feeling better now that she had a cause to fight.

"What can I do? I don't know enough about him to justify making a move on Tom, demanding my time with him, or threatening to throw this intruder overboard. I certainly don't want to make a fool of myself without good cause. Besides, this relationship might be completely one-sided. I could have blown it up into something that doesn't really exist. After all, he's not chained up. He could have walked away from Crystal or told her that he was already with someone on the ship. He didn't seem to me to be resisting very hard," Pat concluded as she headed for the shower. She left Bea to figure out her next move.

When she returned, Bea was sitting up in bed. Although she

looked a bit pale, the greenish tinge to her skin from the previous night had completely vanished. Her eyes sparkled happily as she said, "I'll ask Jeff to tell me everything he knows about Tom. I'm sure that since they work for the same firm, he has all kinds of insider information."

"No, don't do that! What if he tells Tom that I've been inquiring about him? Tom will think that I'm interested in him. If he's married to someone he left at home or if he's involved with Crystal, I'll look pathetic. No, I'll figure out a way to get the information I need. I can always call his office in Texas. As a matter of fact, I think I'll do just that. I'll pretend to be a potential client and ask for information about the firm and about him. If that doesn't work, I have an old college friend who lives in Dallas. She'll be able to get the information for me," Pat confided with a huge smile on her face.

"I knew you'd think of some way to fight back. It's not like you to give up without trying," Bea replied as she gathered her things for her turn in the shower.

"Hurry up. I'm starved. Maybe we can find something to eat in the dining room. Someone must have fixed lunch by now. By the way, don't tell Jeff anything. I'll be able to find out about Tom's personal and professional business, but I still won't know how he feels about me until I confront him. I don't want anyone to know what I'm doing," Pat confided as she shooed Bea into the bathroom.

"Don't worry. My lips are sealed," her friend replied as she hastily closed the door.

As Pat waited for Bea to shower and dress, she pulled her credit card from her purse. Turning it over in her hand, she decided to place a call ship-to-shore immediately rather than to wait until the ship finally docked. She might miss the opportunity to strike before Crystal made any further inroads if she waited.

After giving the ship-to-shore operator her charge card number, Pat waited for the connection. Shortly a voice sang out, "Binder, Laser, and Dell. May I help you?"

"Yes, I'm interested in investing and would like to retain the services of a well-established company. Might I speak with either the president or the owner of your firm?" Pat asked in a voice that shook with the nervousness that tightened her stomach into a hard knot.

"I'm sorry, but Mr. Thomas Owens, the president and owner, isn't in the office this week. He's on vacation in the Caribbean. However, his assistant, Gwen Wilson is handling all of his calls. I'm sure she would be more than happy to speak with you," the voice offered expectantly.

"Is Jeff Bloom available? A mutual friend told me that he worked for the firm also. He might be able to help me," Pat asked in a softer voice. She did not want Bea to know that she was also checking on the identity of her friend.

"Mr. Bloom? He's not a broker, ma'am. He's in our public relations department. At the moment, he's also on vacation. If you require investment assistance, the best person with whom to speak is Ms. Wilson," the voice insisted.

"Thank you for your assistance, but I think I'll wait until Mr. Owens returns. I'd prefer to conduct my information gathering with him. He would know the most about the firm's plans and direction," Pat replied as she slowly hung up the telephone.

"Very well, ma'am," the voice responded as the line went dead.

"Tom's the president of the firm," Pat muttered in a barely audible voice. "I wouldn't have guessed. He's so self-effacing. He can't be much older than thirty-six. He must be a real whiz to have reached that level so fast."

As the sound of Bea's singing penetrated the fog in Pat's mind, she quickly decided that she would not tell her of the call. She had not figured out how she would tell Bea that Jeff was not a broker and therefore probably did not have all the ready cash he pretended to have. Also, Pat still needed the answer to one last question about Tom. She would keep all of her new knowledge to herself for a while.

At that moment a much restored Bea reappeared. "I'm ready, and I'm hungry, too. Did you make your call, or are you planning to wait until the ship docks?" Bea asked as she added a touch of blush to her cheeks. For the first time since Pat had known her, Bea actually needed the extra color to brighten her complexion.

Feeling a bit guilty about the half truth she was about to tell her dear friend, Pat carefully formed her response. "I couldn't connect with the right person to get the information I needed. I'll try again later."

"Oh, that's too bad," Bea replied as she studied her reflection in the mirror. Satisfied that the night of sickness had not too terribly diminished her cherished beauty, she waved Pat toward the door.

Pushing aside the lingering thoughts of Tom, Pat followed Bea out of their cabin. The second phone call would have to wait until later. Their need for food took precedence.

# Chapter Four

The dining room was filled with hungry people in various shades of pale. They had survived the night of fear and endured the seasickness, now they were sufficiently recovered to feel the pangs of hunger gnawing at their empty stomachs. They arrived in couples and alone. Several explained that their companions were still under the influence of medication for their discomfort and were too ill to join them.

Now that the ship only rolled, they were ready to put the past evening behind them and look forward to that night's fun and festivities. After all, it was New Year's Eve. Nothing, not even a gale, could prevent them from having a good time.

"Didn't the captain say that we'd arrive in Martinique later today?" Bea asked as she slathered butter on a steaming hot roll.

"We should be there around two o'clock, I think. Why?" Pat replied as she sipped a tall glass of iced tea.

"Nothing really. I was just wondering about tonight. We were supposed to party in Barbados, but I guess Martinique can show us an equally good time," Pat commented, munching contentedly. Her vibrant coloring seemed to return with the first bite of the bread.

"I would imagine that after last night's storm and being unable to visit our next port of call, the captain has arranged for a wonderful show on Martinique. I'm sure that people with close ties to France in their past know how to throw a party. We'll have to wait and see. It certainly is good to see you looking better," Pat said as she succumbed to the temptation of the hot rolls.

With a laugh, Bea replied, "I'm feeling great. I can't wait to reach the island, do some sightseeing, visit the shops, and party tonight. I wonder why Jeff and Tom haven't appeared. Do you think they're still sick?"

"The only way to find out is to call them when we return to our cabin. Tom is probably spending all of his time with Miss Crystal Marsh. If I don't do something quickly, I doubt that I'll see much of him for the rest of the cruise," Pat remarked almost sorrowfully. Pat would have liked to have told Bea about her discovery concerning both of the men, but she wanted to wait until she had all the pieces in place. Besides, if Tom was married, her problem would solve itself. Bea was having such a good time with Jeff that she did not want to be the one who spoiled it.

After eating their lunch in silence, Pat and Bea returned to their cabin to collect their things for the afternoon in Martinique. They were both looking forward to standing on solid ground again. After calling Jeff and arranging to meet him on the observation deck, Bea scurried away, leaving Pat alone to make her phone call.

Dialing the number she knew from memory, Pat waited until a familiar voice on the other end answered. Overflowing with excitement, she quickly told her friend, Margie, all about Tom and explained the nature of her call. Immediately they agreed that Margie would contact a few friends and find out about Tom's marital status. She promised to leave a message on Pat's home answering machine by six o'clock that evening. Margie was confident that by placing a few discrete calls, she would have the information that Pat desired.

Hardly able to contain her excitement, Pat grabbed up her camera, keys, and bag. She hurried on deck to watch the ship

# NEW YEAR'S EVE

dock in Martinique and to join Bea and Jeff on their excursions. In the recesses of her mind, she hoped that Margie's news would be good. However, being practical, she was prepared for the possibility that a man of Tom's connections and financial success would probably be either married or in a serious relationship. There was always the possibility that Crystal was his significant other.

As they walked down the gangplank into the sunshine, Jeff exclaimed, "It certainly is great seeing the sun again after last night. I was a bit worried that we might not survive that storm. I've been around ships all my life, but I've never felt anything like that."

"How did Tom make out?" Pat asked in a conversational tone as she tried to appear concerned but not too involved in the subject of his health.

"I don't know. He didn't return to our cabin last night. I haven't seen him since he stopped by the casino. I guess Crystal demanded his attention during the storm," Jeff replied as he purchased a red hibiscus bloom from a flower girl and handed it to Bea. Giggling at the attention, Bea carefully inserted the blossom behind her ear.

"Oh," Pat responded, "who is Crystal anyway? She joined the cruise late. Is she someone he knew from the States?"

Before he could answer, Tom and Crystal appeared at their side. "Hi, everyone. It's great to see that we are all in one piece after last night. Shall we hail a cab for a quick tour of the island, or would you rather walk?" Tom asked as Crystal clung hungrily to his arm.

Without hesitation, Jeff replied, "Let's walk. I'd like to get some shots of the local flora and fauna that I'd miss from a cab window."

Now that there were five members of their little group, Pat felt even more conspicuous. She was almost sorry that she had not signed up for one of the planned excursions rather than going along with Bea and Jeff. She hated feeling like the fifth wheel that she was now that Tom and Crystal had joined them.

Eagerly the group set out to explore the lush green of the mountainous island of Martinique. After seeing Bonaire, Martinique was more in keeping with the way they had expected a tropical island to look. Streams and rivers flowed down the hillsides, thick wide-leafed vegetation grew along the roadsides, and flowers bloomed in mad profusion everywhere. Even the people seemed more plentiful on this paradise island. They ran up to greet the group and offered sweets and trinkets for them to purchase.

While the others were preoccupied with the sights, Tom managed to break free of Crystal's grip. He carefully eased closer to Pat and confided in a soft voice meant for her ears only, "I'd like to have a chance to explain a few things to you. I don't want you to think poorly of me. Do you think we could meet before dinner? Would six o'clock in the reading room work for you? I'd like to get this all cleared up between us before the New Year's festivities begin. I don't want to start the new year with bad vibes between us. Things were going so well at first."

"I'm expecting a call from home at six. I could meet you before dinner. Let's say around seven-thirty?" Pat replied quickly, not wanting to attract the attention of the others. She knew that, depending on Margie's findings, she might have to cancel the rendezvous.

As he slipped away under Crystal's watchful eye, Tom agreed saying, "Fine. I'll see you there."

Mingling with the beautiful, brown-skinned residents of Martinique, Pat soon discovered that her fractured college French made a valuable contribution to their afternoon. Although everyone spoke English, it was not the first language of many of the locals who sold their wares along the roadside and at the little cafe at which they stopped for sodas and bottled water. It was helpful to be able to at least order drinks in French.

After ordering bottles of the refreshments for everyone, Pat and the others sat looking out the open windows at the splendor that was the majestic island home of the very hospitable people. She had never seen such a display of colors and textures anywhere except in Hawaii, and even that had been spoiled by overdevelopment. Martinique was still relatively untouched and pure.

# NEW YEAR'S EVE

"Wouldn't you just love to wake up every morning in a place like this?" Pat asked dreamily as she gazed into the distance at the display of flowers.

"I could handle this life for a while, but I wouldn't want to live here year round," Crystal offered.

"Why not? It's paradise," Bea asked sharply. She did not want this interloper to contradict her friend's enthusiastic appreciation for the island.

"Too many bugs. I've already killed two tiny mosquitoes on my arm. Also, life here is too isolated from the world. There are no theaters, no shopping malls, and no places of high fashion. I couldn't bear to abandon all of civilization to live here permanently," Crystal replied as she swatted another insect.

"It certainly would make a perfect honeymoon location," Bea added as she batted her eyes and smiled sweetly at Jeff.

Jeff immediately started plucking the petals from a flower and said, "She loves me. She loves me not. She loves me." When only the stem remained, he repeated his efforts until he stopped on the desired negative response.

The group roared with laughter. Even Bea could not help but join in their lighthearted moment at her expense. After the fright of the previous night, they were all happy to be together again and safely on dry land.

Despite Crystal's presence, Pat managed to enjoy their wanderings around the island. Perhaps it was the sheer beauty of the place or maybe it was knowing that tension between herself and Tom would soon end that made the afternoon so perfect. Whatever the reason, Pat was pleasantly surprised to find that she could enjoy herself so completely despite Crystal's constant clinging to Tom's arms.

The afternoon grew late as they explored the entire island and visited with the people who inhabited it. They saw the areas of extreme wealth and those of equally desperate poverty. Regardless of where they traveled, the islanders welcomed them warmly and even showed them the spot where the sweetest water flowed freely from the rocks.

Returning to the ship with bags of goodies they had purchased along their walk, the group disbanded until dinner and the New

Year's celebration that would follow. Rushing to their room, Pat anxiously deposited her purchases on her bed and dialed her home telephone number. Bea studied her face as Pat listened carefully to the messages.

"Well? What did you find out?" Bea asked as soon as Pat hung up the telephone.

"Nothing yet," Pat replied dejectedly. "Margie hasn't called. She still has a little time left. I was just hoping that she had gotten back to me sooner than planned. This waiting is nerve-wracking."

"While we wait, let's shower and dress for dinner. I can hardly wait to see which costume the crew sent up for me to wear tonight," Bea suggested as she opened the large box that lay in the center of her bed.

"An evening in costumes is a great idea," Pat agreed as she shook out her costume. "It goes so well with the French's passion for costume balls."

"I haven't been to a costume party since I was a little girl. This is so exciting. After last night I'm glad that the captain planned something pleasant for us to do tonight. Just think of it ... New Year's Eve on a ship in the Caribbean. It's just too romantic," Bea gushed as she held her costume to her body and gazed at her reflection in the mirror.

"This should definitely be an evening to remember," Pat agreed as she slipped out of her slacks and shirt and into her robe. She wanted to complete her shower in plenty of time to check her messages before meeting Tom in the reading room. The complexity of her costume would require extra time for her to dress. She did not want to keep him waiting.

After helping Bea adjust her body suit and long flowing dark brown wig, Pat stepped into the voluminous skirts of her costume. As she slipped the brocade over her shoulders, she watched herself transform from a thoroughly modern American woman into a leader of French society. Fastening the foot-tall pompadour with yet another strategically placed hairpin, she surveyed her image with satisfaction. As a history teacher, the Marie Antoinette costume fit her interests perfectly.

"Wow!" Bea exclaimed as they stood together in front of

their mirrors. "Don't we make an unusual-looking pair? You with all that fabric covering your body and me with almost nothing on at all."

"I wonder what Jeff will be wearing? Do you think that his costume will coordinate with yours?" Pat asked as she carefully turned to view the back of her gown.

"I don't know, but I hope if he's my Adam that his fig leaf covers more than mine does. I can feel a draft in this outfit." Bea laughed as she adjusted the strategically placed leaves that covered her buttocks and crotch and adjusted the hair to hide her breasts.

"Don't forget about Crystal. I wonder which one of us will be more suited to Tom's costume?" Pat mused as she checked her watch. Margie should have left her message by now.

"Well, I can't wait to see them. I'm going to the lounge now. Come up as soon as you can. Don't forget that the captain wanted everyone to assemble a half hour before dinner for photographs," Bea said as she searched her costume for someplace to hide her key. Finding nothing, she looked helplessly at Pat.

Laughing, Pat replied, "I'll be there. Nothing could keep me away from the spectacle of all these costumed people gathering in one place. By the way, you might want to store the key in your slipper. It won't be comfortable, but it's just about the only place you have. You might look a little funny carrying a purse while wearing so little."

"Very funny," Bea said with a snide grin as she eased the key under her foot and gracefully slipped from the room. "Wait until you try entering doors with those wide hips and that mad beehive. I'll have the last laugh then."

Waving her friend on her way as the door closed behind her, Pat picked up the telephone. Her hands shook as she dialed the numbers of her home telephone. Her heart pounded as she waited for the four rings and then entered the code that would bypass the recorded announcement. Pat's mouth went dry as Margie's voice carefully relayed the information for which she had anxiously waited.

Sinking into the cushions of her bed, Pat slowly hung up

the telephone. She did not know whether she should feel relief or worry. Rising and carefully adjusting her skirt, Pat slipped her key into the bodice of her gown. Satisfied with her reflection, she clicked off the light and left the room. It was already after seven o'clock, and she had to navigate the narrow corridors carefully in her unfamiliar attire.

Everyone was in the halls and lobbies as Pat tried to climb the two flights of wide stairs to the reading room. The passengers laughed and talked in large groups, making passage with her massive hips almost impossible. Pat constantly had to stop and ask someone to move. Naturally she was then obliged to pass a moment in conversation so that she would not appear rude. They took turns guessing each other's identity, since everyone she met had dressed as a well-known character from either history or literature.

When Pat finally arrived at the reading room, winded and sweating from the exertion, it was empty. "Darn!" she muttered as she leaned against the nearest chair. Breathing deeply and slowly, she encouraged her heartbeat to return to its normal pace before looking around the room for any sign that Tom had been there and had waited for her.

Scanning the tables and chairs, Pat finally saw a note discretely protruding from a book on the table. Picking up the copy of *The Three Musketeers*, Pat extracted the carefully folded paper. In very crisp, formal handwriting, Tom had written: *P—I waited until seven-thirty for you to arrive. When you did not, I decided that you either did not wish to hear my explanation or that you were unavoidably detained. Hoping that your absence was caused by the latter, I will again wait for you here after the first part of the evening's festivities concludes. If you wish to speak with me, please join me at eleven-thirty. Yours, T—"*

Stuffing the note into the snug bodice of her gown, Pat muttered, "You'll bet I'll be here. Nothing could keep me away."

Entering the lounge filled with costumed vacationers, Pat found Bea the center of attention from several admiring men. Jeff stood off to the side and nursed his wounded feelings as she smiled and flirted with her new entourage. As Pat approached, he smiled and bowed.

"You make a great Marie Antoinette, but it must be difficult navigating these halls with those killer hips." Jeff laughed.

"I'd say from the looks of things that you should have more on your mind than my hips, although you really do look cute in your knickers," Pat retorted as she gazed toward her friend. Bea seemed to be oblivious to Jeff's misery as he stood fiddling with the tie of his David Copperfield costume.

"She's mad at me. I couldn't continue the deception any longer. I wasn't exactly honest with either of you about what I do for a living. I led you to believe that I was a wealthy stockbroker, and I'm not. I work for a brokerage firm all right, but I'm the vice president for public relations. I make a good living but not as much as I'd let you believe.

"Bea's making me suffer for my sins. She's doing a good job of it, too. I'm miserable without her. I hate it that all those guys are staring at her like that. I didn't plan on falling for someone on this cruise. It was only supposed to be a vacation trip, but Bea's special. I really care for her. Watching her with those other men is making me crazy," Jeff lamented in the manner of the screen stars of the golden age of movies. He wrinkled his brow, pursed his lips, pouted, sighed, and looked totally miserable.

"Well, I'm sure she'll come to her senses after dinner. She does look fabulous in that costume. I guess she wanted to flaunt it a bit. Too bad that you're not her Adam," Pat commented as she watched Bea glow from the attention.

"No, that chubby guy over there is Adam. His wife is the angry Little Bo Peep who hasn't stopped tapping her foot since he joined Bea's adoring fan club. If possible, she's more upset than I am," Jeff conceded with a dry chuckle. Pat could tell that he was feeling less neglected now that she was comforting him.

Satisfied that Jeff would weather this lover's tiff, Pat asked, "Have you seen Tom lately?"

"No, he rushed out of the cabin around six forty-five, and I haven't seen him since. Crystal isn't here, either. Maybe they're together again," Jeff commented, oblivious to the expression of pain that fleetingly crossed Pat's face.

"Who is she? She's very demanding of his attention," Pat asked as she watched Bea's little charade. Pat knew that she was partly to blame for Tom's tardiness.

"She's one of the firm's largest customers, and she's hot for Tom. When she found out that he was taking this cruise, she arranged to meet the ship at Bonaire just so she could be with him. He has told her that he's interested in someone else, but she won't let him go. He doesn't want to alienate her, but he's not sure how much longer he can allow her to interfere in his life. He's hoping that she'll meet someone on the ship tonight at the ball," Jeff concluded without taking his eyes from Bea.

"Would you happen to know who Tom's love interest might be? Is she someone back home in Texas?" Pat queried subtly. She did not want to appear too interested, although she really wanted the information.

"What? I'm sorry, I wasn't listening. Damn that woman! She's driving me mad," Jeff fumed as Bea threw her head back and laughed appreciatively at yet another joke.

Before she could restate her question, Tom and Crystal entered the lounge. Tom made a smashing D'Artagnan with his feathered hat perching jauntily on his wig-adorned head and his sword clanging against his thigh. Crystal created quite a stir as the voluptuous Cleopatra, queen of the Nile, wrapped in diaphanous fabric that barely concealed her figure. Her bejeweled hands clung to Tom's arm as usual.

Remembering the note hidden in her bodice, Pat decided to resist the urge to approach Tom. Instead she would wait until the designated time and meet him in the reading room. They needed a private place to talk. The noisy lounge amid happy revelers gearing up for the New Year's Eve celebration was not the appropriate setting.

Bea saw Tom and Crystal enter the room, too, and freed herself from her admiring entourage. Standing beside Jeff, who beamed happily at her return to his side, she waited to see if Pat needed her assistance in either confronting Crystal with her

# NEW YEAR'S EVE

intrusion or in maintaining her composure under duress. The two women looked like avenging angels waiting to right the wrongs heaped on their fellow man or woman.

Lightly touching Pat's hand, Bea asked in a whisper, "Are you okay? Should I distract Crystal so you can have a few minutes with Tom?"

"No, I'm fine. Thanks. I missed our earlier meeting because of the interest this costume caused among the other guests. When I arrived, he had already left. He has suggested that we meet later tonight after everything settles down a bit and before the big New Year's blast of horns. I'm okay with that," Pat answered as she smiled lovingly at her dearest friend.

"Did Margie find the information you needed?" Bea inquired as she glanced toward Tom and Crystal. They were engaged in conversation with a curvaceous female devil and Daniel Webster.

"Oh, yes, she was very helpful," Pat responded with a raised eyebrow and a knowing smile.

"Well, then, what are you waiting for? Go get him, girl! You don't want to leave him for even another minute with Crystal. He might already be having second thoughts about this budding relationship since you didn't keep your appointment. He might fall under her spell if you don't hurry," Bea urged as she gave Pat little pushes in Tom's direction.

"I guess I could—" Pat began.

At that moment the dinner announcement sounded over the public address system. Taking the microphone from the band conductor, the captain thanked everyone for remaining so calm during the storm and wished all of them a pleasant dinner and a Happy New Year. Promising to join them at their festivities later in the evening, he sent them off to the waiting feast.

Shaking her head and giving Pat a look of frustration, Bea and Jeff led the way to the dining room. When they arrived, they realized that there was not enough space at their table for a party of five, so Tom and Jeff returned to their original table with Crystal merrily in attendance. She flashed a large, victorious smile at Pat as she walked past.

Bea kept up a constant stream of chatter throughout their

meal in an effort to keep Pat's mind off Tom and Crystal. "Don't keep me waiting any longer. What did Margie tell you?" Bea demanded as she handed the waiter the menu.

"She said that Tom is neither married nor engaged. He lives alone, too, which means that he has no serious significant other. However, according to Jeff, Crystal has her heart set on that position," Pat replied softly.

"Well, that means that you have to do something quickly. You don't want her to succeed," Bea encouraged as she looked longingly at the appetizers that had just arrived.

"I still don't know how he feels about me. Until I find out that last piece of the puzzle, I'm going to move cautiously. The last thing I want to do is make a spectacle of myself by admitting to a man who is not in the least interested in me that I find him appealing. This ship isn't large enough for me to avoid seeing him and the look of pity on his face if he can't return the affection," Pat confided as she dove into the overflowing shrimp cocktail.

"If I eat too much, everyone will see that I've pigged out. This costume doesn't give me anyplace to hide even a crumb," Bea groaned as she nibbled daintily of the caviar, pate, and crackers.

"Don't worry. Everyone is drinking so much that they'll all be too plastered to notice that your tummy is protruding a bit," Pat advised as she tried to find a comfortable position. Her hip pads stuck out into the aisle unless she sat awkwardly to her right where she had to be careful not to bump the woman at the next table.

"That's easy for you to say. Those hips of yours could conceal a myriad of courses including several desserts, but this body suit leaves nothing to the imagination," Bea complained as she hungrily devoured the last of the beef Wellington, buttery roll, duchess potatoes, and salad.

"You seem to be doing all right," Pat observed with a chuckle.

"I paid to enjoy every morsel of food, every note of music,

# NEW YEAR'S EVE

and every grain of sand on the beach. I'm not leaving here hungry. I'll just have to hold my stomach in harder," Bea concluded as she signaled the waiter that she was ready for the menu. With a chuckle of glee, she ordered a slice of chocolate cake to accompany the baked Alaska that was the special treat of the evening.

While the lights dimmed and the waiters carried the flaming treats to the tables, Pat glanced in Tom's direction. She was not surprised to find that Crystal sat at his side literally feeding on his every syllable. She had barely touched her plate in her effort to entertain him. Jeff looked understandably bored since he was not the center of anyone's attention and longed to be with Bea. As Pat smiled at him, Jeff bravely nodded his head and rolled his eyes.

As soon as the meal ended, Jeff escorted Pat and Bea to the lounge to watch the floor show. They selected seats on the end of the row so that Pat would have plenty of space for her hip bolsters. Watching the others arrive, they saw that Tom and Crystal had occupied seats on the other side of the room.

"Why do you suppose he decided to sit all the way over there? There are plenty of seats next to us," Bea whispered as she leaned closer to Pat.

"I don't know that he had much choice. I saw Crystal point toward that row. She appears to be in control of things," Pat replied without taking her eyes from the sight of Crystal leaning against Tom in a most provocative manner.

"She certainly is demanding for a client. Jeff must be right about her interest in Tom. She doesn't seem to realize what a spectacle she's making of herself. You should go over there and let her know that you were the first to stake claim to Tom," Bea sneered with her disdain for Crystal showing in every word.

"And make myself as obvious as she is? I don't think so! I'll have my time soon enough and without her being there," Pat responded as she turned her attention to the show.

The performers worked harder than the previous night to put on a memorable show. They wore costumes that were even more elaborate than those of the guests as they danced before a backdrop containing a collage of photographs from well-known musicals. The small band that supplemented the accompaniment tape played with great gusto. The singing and dancing were spirited and energetic. Nothing was too much for this special night. New Year's Eve came only once a year.

The audience applauded enthusiastically and gave two standing ovations to the beaming cast. Once completed, the master of ceremonies bowed deeply and reminded them of the midnight buffet and New Year's Eve celebration in the dining room. Then he wished them a good evening as the house lights came up. Joining the stream of happy people, Pat, Bea, and Jeff eased their way out of the lounge.

"I'll meet you in the dining room later," Pat said as Bea and Jeff headed toward the upper decks to watch the New Year's fireworks display on the island.

"Okay. Good luck. Should we plan on going ashore after the party downstairs?" Bea asked.

"That sounds like great fun. If all goes well, I won't be alone. And, if I am, I'll still have a good time. I'm not all dolled-up for nothing," Pat confided with a wink as she picked her way through the crowd and up the one flight of stairs to the anxiously awaited rendezvous.

Arriving at the empty reading room five minutes early, Pat checked to be sure that Tom had not left another message for her. Finding none, she carefully checked her appearance in the mirror that hung over the credenza. She wanted to make sure that her wig had not shifted and that her ample hips were still straight. Then Pat positioned herself at the big window from which she could watch Martinique's fireworks as they soared high over the harbor.

Becoming engrossed in the pyrotechnics, Pat did not hear the gentle swish of the door as Tom entered the room. Seeing someone's reflection in the glass, she turned to find him standing behind her. Smiling she said, "Looks like we both made it this time. Where's Crystal? How did you ever get away from her?"

"I told her that I had an important call to make. She wasn't happy about being left on deck alone, but she'll survive. If she were not one of the firm's best clients, I would have shaken her off as soon as she boarded the ship," Tom responded as he stepped closer and looked out at the fireworks bursting in the sparkling sky.

"She's one of *your* firm's clients, you mean," Pat corrected with a smile.

"Oh, so you know about me. I try to keep that part of my life under wraps when I first meet people. All too often they want to cozy up to my money rather than get to know me. I've been burned a few times and have learned my lesson the hard way," Tom stated without any sign of sorrow or pain in his voice.

"I only just found out. I wanted to make sure that you weren't some sort of wolf in amateur historian's clothing. I was involved with someone until about six months ago. The end was painful. I don't want to get hurt again by letting an unknown man into my life," Pat confided with as much candor as she could offer without exposing all of her vulnerability.

"I guess that seeing me with Crystal gave you plenty of room to doubt my intentions. I'm sorry that she followed me. There's nothing between us, but it's dangerous to alienate a major client. I had tried to tell her of my inclinations toward someone on this cruise, but she wasn't receptive to the message. After you appeared to lose interest in me, I stopped working so hard to convince her. I didn't especially want to spend my vacation alone now that Jeff seems to have found his soul mate in Bea. At any rate, my feelings were a little hurt and I wanted to get back at you. Pretty childish, wasn't it?" Tom concluded with a look of helplessness on his handsome face.

"I suppose we were a bit like Shakespeare's star-crossed lovers. We were at cross purposes but with the best of intentions," Pat added with a shy smile.

"I guess you're right. I came on this cruise to get away from people and relax. I was perfectly happy to spend my time sightseeing with Jeff until I met you. You made me see Bonaire through two pairs of eyes, and I liked what I saw. Now I don't want to go solo. I managed to convince myself that Crystal, with all her clinging, is better than having no one," Tom commented as he looked deeply into Pat's eyes for any sign of her true feelings about him.

"Bea talked me into joining her on this cruise after a mutual friend of ours couldn't make the trip. I had planned to stay home this holiday and grade the stack of papers waiting for me. I'm glad now that I decided to come," Pat replied softly as she returned his steady gaze.

"Do you think we could start over?" Tom pleaded as he gently cradled Pat's hands in his.

"I don't see why not. The cruise is still young," Pat replied as she returned his squeeze.

"All right then. Here goes. Good evening, Your Majesty. I'm D'Artagnan, also known as Tom Owens of Dallas, Texas. I'm a stockbroker and owner of a firm that does business out of that city. I'm on this cruise to have a good time, meet people, explore historical sights, and unwind from a very demanding life. Although I'm a whiz at managing a company, I'm not too astute in love. I've met a wonderful woman with whom I have much in common and would like to plan a future. However, because of my stupid bungling, I almost let her and our chance for happiness get away." Tom introduced himself with a deep bow and a sweep of his plumed hat.

"I'm Marie Antoinette, formerly Pat Grimes of Washington, D.C. I'm a history teacher. I'm having a ball playing hooky from the papers stacked on my desk. I met a fantastic man and almost lost him in the storm. Somehow we were passengers on different lifeboats sailing in opposite directions," Pat responded with a slight inclination of her head. She was afraid to do more for fear the carefully pinned wig would tumble to the floor.

"I think I can remedy that with a little careful maneuvering. It's easy to change course when you realize that your dreams lie in another direction," Tom remarked. He searched her face for the signs of reconciliation that he so desperately wanted to find there.

## NEW YEAR'S EVE

"I would like to think that's possible. I would certainly like to give it a try," Pat replied as she smiled into his eyes.

"May I intrude upon your solitude, Ms. Grimes, for the purpose of enjoying the fireworks and perhaps celebrating the advent of the new year with you?" Tom asked as he placed a chaste kiss on Pat's outstretched hand.

"My dear Mr. Owens, I would certainly enjoy your company tonight," Pat responded as a glow of color swept over her face.

Reading her emotions and taking courage in what he saw, Tom asked, "Only tonight, Pat? I had something more permanent in mind. When you find the person who is right for you, you think in terms of a lifetime. Must I spend the rest of the cruise and my life without you? Won't you let me share all the other days of this new year and every year with you?"

"I don't know what to say, Tom. What about Crystal?" Pat asked as she allowed the warm feelings to flow through her body.

"Crystal is merely a client. She means nothing more to me than that. Now that I know that there's a chance for us, I'll explain the situation to her. I'm sure she'll understand. If she doesn't, she'll leave the ship at the next port," Tom replied in a very matter-of-fact tone.

"But your firm? What about the impact on the bottom line?" Pat queried as her heart fluttered from the warmth of his hand on hers.

"I can always find other clients, but the opportunity to find someone to fill my life so perfectly doesn't present itself every day. I won't let anything interfere in our happiness," Tom responded as he gently enfolded Pat in his strong arms.

"But, Tom," Pat objected softly and practically as the fireworks blazed and the ship's orchestra blared, "we live miles apart. This will never work."

"Yes, it will, if we want it badly enough. Usually I come to Washington at least once a month for business. Now I'll fly up every week, or we could take turns traveling between cities. We'll see just as much of each other as most people do while living in the same town. When the school year is over, we'll get married and make a home in Dallas. You will marry me, won't you, Pat?" Tom asked as he traced little tantalizing kisses along the corners of her lips, the tip of her nose, and the dimple in her cheeks.

Feeling her knees grow weak, Pat sighed and replied as she looked into his soft eyes, "I guess you've thought of everything. I can't imagine spending next year and the one after that without you, either. Yes, Tom, I will marry you."

At that moment the door to the reading room burst open, and Bea and Jeff entered carrying a magnum of champagne, trays of sandwiches and cookies, and fluted glasses. "When you lovebirds didn't join us, we thought we'd come to you. It's almost New Year's. Quick, turn on the television. Maybe we can get one of the New York celebrations. It wouldn't be a party without watching that ball descend and light up the new year!" Bea laughed as she hastily poured some of the intoxicating liquid for all of them.

Almost immediately the noise of Times Square filled the staid reading room. The voices of thousands of people mingled with the shouts of joy from the cruise passengers who watched the fireworks from their own private parties on the deck. Everyone waited anxiously for that magic moment when they would ring out the old year and ring in the new.

As the countdown began, the four friends stood together with the fireworks of Martinique illuminating the night sky behind them. "Four, three, two, one ... Happy New Year!!" they cried in unison as they joined their voices to those of the other revelers.

Clicking their glasses, they toasted the new year as Martinique's cannons roared, the ship's horn blasted, and the halls and decks filled with shouts of glee. Immediately Bea and Jeff fell into each other's arms, spilling champagne in their haste. Almost shyly, Pat and Tom turned and gazed lovingly at each other as Tom carefully placed their glasses on the table. They wanted their first kiss of the new year to be special and a harbinger of the joy that they would share forever.

Slowly Tom pulled Pat into his arms. His hands gently caressed her waist and shoulders. Then his fingers memorized

# NEW YEAR'S EVE

every line and curve of her upturned face. Gently he pressed his lips against hers.

As the warmth swept through their bodies, they forgot their newness and relished the pleasure of each other. Without looking for it, they had found love on a ship in the Caribbean in the shadow of the mountains of Martinique. It would be a happy new year indeed.

## COMING IN JANUARY ...

BEYOND DESIRE (0-7860-0607-2, $4.99/$6.50)
by Gwynne Forster
Amanda Ross is pregnant and single. Certainly not a role model for junior high school students, the board of education may deny her promotion to principal if they learn the truth. What she needs is a husband and music engineer Marcus Hickson agrees to it. His daughter needs surgery and Amanda will pay the huge medical bill. But love creeps in and soon theirs is an affair of the heart.

LOVE SO TRUE (0-7860-0608-0, $4.99/$6.50)
by Loure Bussey
Janelle Sims defied her attraction to wealthy businessman Aaron Deverreau because he reminded Janelle of her womanizing father. Yet he is the perfect person to back her new fashion boutique and she seeks him out. Now they are partners, friends ... and lovers. But a cunning woman's lies separate them and Janelle must go to him to confirm their love.

ALL THAT GLITTERS (0-7860-0609-9, $4.99/$6.50)
by Viveca Carlysle
After her sister's death, Leigh Barrington inherited a huge share of Cassiopeia Salons, a chain of exclusive beauty parlors. The business was Leigh's idea in the first place and now she wants to run it her way. To retain control, Leigh marries board member Caesar Montgomery, who is instantly smitten with her. When she may be the next target of her sister's killer, Leigh learns to trust in Caesar's love.

AT LONG LAST LOVE (0-7860-0610-2, $4.99/$6.50)
by Bettye Griffin
Owner of restaurant chain Soul Food To Go, Kendall Lucas has finally found love with her new neighbor, Spencer Barnes. Until she discovers he owns the new restaurant that is threatening her business. They compromise, but Spencer learns Kendall has launched a secret advertising campaign. Embittered by her own lies, Kendall loses hope in their love. But she underestimates Spencer's devotion and his vow to make her his partner for life.

*Available wherever paperbacks are sold, or order direct from the Publisher. Send cover price plus 50¢ per copy for mailing and handling to Kensington Publishing Corp., Consumer Orders, or call (toll free) 888-345-BOOK, to place your order using Mastercard or Visa. Residents of New York and Tennessee must include sales tax. DO NOT SEND CASH.*

# WARMHEARTED AFRICAN-AMERICAN ROMANCES BY *FRANCIS RAY*

FOREVER YOURS (0-7860-0483-5, $4.99/$6.50)
Victoria Chandler must find a husband or her grandparents will call in loans that support her chain of lingerie boutiques. She fixes a mock marriage to ranch owner Kane Taggert. The marriage will only last one year, and her business will be secure. The only problem is that Kane has other plans for Victoria. He'll cast a spell that will make her his forever.

HEART OF THE FALCON (0-7860-0483-5, $4.99/$6.50)
A passionate night with millionaire Daniel Falcon, leaves Madelyn Taggert enamored . . . and heartbroken. She never accepted that the long-time family friend would fulfill her dreams, only to see him walk away without regrets. After his parent's bitter marriage, the last thing Daniel expected was to be consumed by the need to have her for a lifetime.

INCOGNITO (0-7860-0364-2, $4.99/$6.50)
Owner of an advertising firm, Erin Cortland witnessed an awful crime and lived to tell about it. Frightened, she runs into the arms of Jake Hunter, the man sent to protect her. He doesn't want the job. He left the police force after a similar assignment ended in tragedy. But when he learns not only one man is after her and that he is falling in love, he will risk anything to protect her.

ONLY HERS (07860-0255-7, $4.99/$6.50)
St. Louis R.N. Shannon Johnson recently inherited a parcel of Texas land. She sought it as refuge until landowner Matt Taggart challenged her to prove she's got what it takes to work a sprawling ranch. She, on the other hand, soon challenges him to dare to love again.

SILKEN BETRAYAL (0-7860-0426-6, $4.99/$6.50)
The only man executive secretary Lauren Bennett needed was her five-year-old son Joshua. Her only intent was to keep Joshua away from powerful in-laws. Then Jordan Hamilton entered her life. He sought her because of a personal vendetta against her father-in-law. When Jordan develops strong feelings for Lauren and Joshua, he must choose revenge or love.

UNDENIABLE (07860-0125-9, $4.99/$6.50)
Wealthy Texas heiress Rachel Malone defied her powerful father and eloped with Logan Williams. But a trump-up assault charge set the whole town and Rachel against him and he fled Stanton with a heart full of pain. Eight years later, he's back and he wants revenge . . . and Rachel.

*Available wherever paperbacks are sold, or order direct from the Publisher. Send cover price plus 50¢ per copy for mailing and handling to Kensington Publishing Corp., Consumer Orders, or call (toll free) 888-345-BOOK, to place your order using Mastercard or Visa. Residents of New York and Tennessee must include sales tax. DO NOT SEND CASH.*